The Ancient Lie

The Unwritten Words II

ALSO BY CHRISTOPHER G. NUTTALL

The Mind's Eye

Bookworm series
Bookworm
Bookworm II: The Very Ugly Duckling
Bookworm III: The Best Laid Plans
Bookworm IV: Full Circle

Unwritten Words series
I: The Promised Lie

DIZZY SPELLS SERIES
A LIFE LESS ORDINARY

Royal Sorceress series
The Royal Sorceress
The Great Game
Necropolis
Sons of Liberty

INVERSE SHADOWS UNIVERSE
SUFFICIENTLY ADVANCED TECHNOLOGY

The Ancient Lie

The Unwritten Words II

Christopher G. Nuttall

Elsewhen Press

The Ancient Lie
First published in Great Britain by Elsewhen Press, 2020
An imprint of Alnpete Limited

Copyright © Christopher G. Nuttall, 2020. All rights reserved
The right of Christopher G. Nuttall to be identified as the author of this work has been asserted in accordance with sections 77 and 78 of the Copyright, Designs and Patents Act 1988. No part of this publication may be reproduced, stored in a retrieval system or transmitted in any form, or by any means (electronic, mechanical, telepathic, magical, or otherwise) without the prior written permission of the copyright owner.

Elsewhen Press, PO Box 757, Dartford, Kent DA2 7TQ
www.elsewhen.press

British Library Cataloguing in Publication Data.
A catalogue record for this book is available from the British Library.

ISBN 978-1-911409-29-8 Print edition
ISBN 978-1-911409-39-7 eBook edition

Designed and formatted by Elsewhen Press

Dear Readers

As you may have noticed, this book was quite significantly delayed … but, as I think you'll agree, I have a very good excuse.

I wrote the first draft of *The Promised Lie* with the intention of writing the following two books in a fairly tight stream. In 2018, however, my persistent health problems – dating from November 2017 – were finally identified as lymphoma. Chemotherapy was prescribed. This may just have been in time to save my life. I collapsed when I went for the first set of treatments, allowing the doctors to realise that I *also* had a nasty chest infection. I ended up spending three weeks in the hospital, having antibiotics fed into my system and my lung drained of fluid. This was not a pleasant experience.

I'm sorry for the delay and I'll try to write the third book in a much more reasonable timeframe.

Christopher G. Nuttall
Edinburgh, 2019

The Summer Isle
Cold Harbour
Northern Realm
The Narrows
Georgetown
Galsmyd Lands
Hereford Lands
Wild Mountains
Temple of Dusk
Allenstown
Racal's Bay
Racal River
Summer Bay
Wildlands
Oxley Lands
Andalusia
Havelock

Prologue I

It was bitterly – bitterly – cold.

Alden Majuro, Patriarch of House Majuro, pulled his fur-lined coat tightly around him as he started the ascent to Ida. Five years ago, the trip would have taken only a few hours – a day at most – and would have been accomplished in relative comfort. His wealth, power and magic would have ensured a private coach on an iron dragon. But now, it had taken nearly two *weeks* to make the trip, travelling over shattered roads and passing through burned-out villages, towns and cities fighting desperately to keep their independence from warring kings and princes. It felt as if the Empire had never existed at all. It felt …

Wrong, he thought. *It feels wrong.*

It had been an interesting trip, for all the wrong reasons. He hadn't seen anything himself, but there had been stories … always stories. Tales of miracles, of things beyond the limits of any known magic; tales of ghosts and resurrections and hundreds of other deeds he would have sworn blind were impossible. The stories were spreading, radiating out from the forbidden zones. It wouldn't be long before they were everywhere. He wondered, morbidly, if they'd already reached Ida.

Dark clouds, forebodingly pregnant with snow, hovered around the peaks as he made his way up the slippery road. Ida had always been isolated, even though it had been part of the Empire. The population had kept itself apart, relying on their mountains to protect them from their larger and more powerful neighbours. Now … the weather was growing even worse, freezing bandit gangs and invading armies with a dispassion Alden could only admire. It was possible to believe, as he reached the top and walked towards the gates, that Ida would remain civilised even as the rest of the world plunged into chaos. The mountain folk knew better than to throw away everything they'd built, at the behest of a king or rogue sorcerer.

The guards eyed him narrowly, then nodded. "Her Majesty has sent for you," the leader said, stiffly. "Come with me."

Alden nodded and followed the guard through winding streets, towards a palace that looked to have been hewn out of the mountain rock itself. Snow started to fall, covering the dark buildings in a wintery haze. The handful of people on the streets hurriedly sought shelter, suggesting there was worse to come. Alden didn't relax until they were inside the palace, where it was mercifully warm. He stripped off his coat and changed into dry clothes with a sense of relief. His outfit was so sodden that the washerwomen would have to use powerful spells to dry it.

He stepped into the next room and frowned. A young woman was standing by the window, studying him. She was ... small, almost mousy. Her dress was practically colourless. She was the sort of woman he would have ignored, back at the Peerless School. And yet ... his eyes narrowed as he realised who she was. Elaine, Her Lineage Unknown; Elaine, the Last Empress of the Golden Empire; Elaine ...

Alden swallowed, suddenly unsure of himself. He'd sent a message before he'd left, naturally, but there had been no time to wait for a reply. Who knew *how* the Empress would react, when she laid eyes on him? She'd refused to stay in the Golden City and rule, even though it was her birthright. And they told strange tales about her ... Alden knew, if she chose to be displeased at his intrusion, it might be the end of his lifeline. She was the Empress! If she wanted to kill him, she could.

He bowed, stiffly. "Your Majesty."

"I gave up the title." Elaine's voice was soft, but there was a quiet strength in her tone that warned him not to underestimate her. "It's just *Elaine*, if you please."

"As you please," Alden said. "I ... I need to consult with you."

"I read your letter." Elaine gave no hint of her feelings. "You left out the specifics."

Alden nodded. Reaching into his pouch, he produced the letters from Isabella. "We received these tidings from the

Summer Isle," he said. It occurred to him, too late, that Elaine and Isabella – his estranged sister – were practically contemporaries. "There are strange … *things* on the island. Or there were."

Elaine took the letters and read them, quickly. "Gods. Entities."

"Yes." Alden met her eyes. "Very *strange* entities."

"Yes." Elaine read the letters twice, skimming over the text to reread the important points. "And clearly not part of the former canon."

Alden's eyes narrowed. "They say you know *everything*," he said. "Do you know *them*?"

Elaine looked back at him, evenly. "Do you know what happened to *me*?"

Alden shook his head. There had been rumours, of course, but none of them had ever been substantiated. And then the families had had worse problems to worry about. Elaine … had been allowed to slip into obscurity. If Alden were honest, at least with himself, he would have to concede that the families hadn't *wanted* her to stick around. The last thing they wanted was a ruler who had the power and will to make them behave.

Not that it matters, he thought, with a hint of the old bitterness. *Once, our word was law from one side of the continent to the other. Now … we barely command one city.*

"I absorbed all the knowledge in the Great Library," Elaine said, slowly. "Everything, from the mundane to the forbidden. It's all in here."

She tapped the side of her head. Alden stared, torn between astonishment and fear. The Great Library had been sealed for the past five years, the wards denying entry to each and every person who tried to visit. And the woman in front of him knew everything in the library? Elaine was formidable, perhaps more formidable than she knew. There was more than just books of *magic* in the library. There were history books that had been banned and removed from circulation long ago.

"There are … *hints* … of something, right from the Dark Ages before the first Grand Sorcerer," Elaine said. "Stories of … *things*. Of entities with striking power. Of … the Empire, as it was in those days, practically devising a religion.   Of cutting and pasting elements into a single consistent theology ..."

"Blasphemy," Alden said.

"Is it?" Elaine shrugged. "It's hard to tell these days, isn't it?"

"Yes." Alden conceded the point without rancour. He'd studied history in school. There was very little on the era before the Empire, very little that could be substantiated. His tutors had liked to pretend the Empire had *always* existed. "And they're seemingly linked to the forbidden zones."

He sighed. "What else can you tell me?"

"Very little." Elaine turned to peer out the window. Snow brushed against the glass, dropping down to the streets below. "Whatever truths there were, in the old texts, were removed long ago. There were ... just a list of warnings and instructions of what *not* to do."

Alden stepped up beside her, watching the clouds growing darker. "And you think those instructions were connected to the ... *gods*?"

"Call them *entities*," Elaine said, sharply. "Once you start accepting them as *gods*, you will start worshipping them."

"We *do* worship the gods," Alden said. "Don't we?"

Elaine shrugged. "How many of those gods were actually *real*?"

Her voice hardened. "How many people liked the idea of an Emperor or an Empress until one actually turned up?"

"Touché." Alden shook his head. "If these ... *entities* ... are real ..."

"Then we may have a problem," Elaine said. "And there may not be much I can do to help you."

Alden glanced at her, surprised.   "But you know *everything*!"

"I know the words written," Elaine said. "But the words *unwritten*? Those, I don't know."

She shrugged. "You may have had a wasted journey," she cautioned. "But stay a while. Her Majesty wishes to speak with you. And we may find something you can use, given time."

"I hope you're right." Alden looked back out the window. He'd hoped Elaine would have answers for him. Instead ... she seemed to be as ignorant as himself. "And if you're not …?"

"Then we may find ourselves in the grip of greater powers," Elaine said. "And that never works out well for *anyone*."

Prologue II

"I can't help him, Goodwoman," the Hedge Witch said. "He's dying."

Goodwoman Charlotte barely heard his words as her son started to cough, again. She had no idea what was wrong with him, but ... he'd been coughing and vomiting for weeks, steadily growing weaker and weaker until he was on the verge of death. Golan was *five*, the age where he should be starting in the fields with his father or learning a trade with his uncles. Instead ... she glared at the Hedge Witch, cursing the bastard under her breath. He'd taken every last coin she'd been able to scrape up, from her extended family, but what had he done? Nothing, damn him. Her son was dying ...

Golan coughed, harder this time. There were flecks of blood on his lips. Charlotte reached for him, drawing him into her arms as the coughing intensified. Golan was dying ... he'd only been hers for five years and he was dying. Charlotte was a farmwife, from a farming community. She knew death came early and often, to young babes only a few weeks and months old, but ... she'd thought Golan had survived the most dangerous part of his childhood. She'd dared to love him. She'd told herself he was the most handsome boy in the world, a boy who would grow into a man who'd make her proud. Instead ...

The Hedge Witch was talking, but Charlotte barely heard him as her son coughed his life away. Golan felt cold, too cold ... she shuddered, helplessly, as he coughed one final time and fell still. She didn't need the Hedge Witch's worthless spells and poultices to know her son was dead. The man was babbling away about something, probably something to do with his payment ... Charlotte barely cared. Her son was dead. Her son was dead ... she knew she should send to the fields, to summon her husband for the funeral rites, but ... it was hard, so hard, to care. She wanted to die herself, if it meant her son came back to life.

Strong arms touched her, held her. Others took the body from her arms, taking him to be washed before he was placed on the pyre. Charlotte knew she should be the one to wash him – she'd brought Golan into the world, it was her duty to see him out – but she couldn't bring herself to insist on her rights. It would have been an admission, to herself if no one else, that it was hopeless, that her son was dead. Golan had been so *alive*, his face practically glowing with life. Everyone had loved him. How could he be dead?

She was barely aware of anything until she stood in front of the funeral pyre, staring at what remained of her son. Golan had been stripped, washed and dressed in a simple white shift, then placed on top of the wood. Her husband stood next to her, holding her gently. She wondered if his family had already started asking him to cast Charlotte aside, to find another wife … someone who might be more fertile, who might bear a healthy child. There was no room for sentiment on the farm, no room for anything … she cursed them all, glaring past the pyre to the tiny shrine beyond. Golan had been a good boy. What good *were* the gods, if they couldn't save one child?

The priest started to talk, his words blurring together into a meaningless babble. Golan was gone, yet … Charlotte refused to believe. Her son couldn't be dead. She wanted to attack the priest, to tear him limb from limb for daring to suggest there might be something *good* in her son's death. How *dare* he? The smiling, warmly dressed man … the man who collected tithes that went … where? What good did he do? Hatred washed through her breast, demanding release. She wanted to strangle him with her bare hands.

"Hold."

She looked up, astonished. No one would interrupt a funeral, yet … someone had. A tall man, wrapped in a ragged grey cloak that brushed against the ground. Charlotte swallowed, hard. A wandering preacher … they went from village, seeking alms and converts. She'd been warned not to have anything to do with them, ever. The priest had made it clear that the wanderers were not *true* preachers, yet … there was something about the man in front of her that drew her to him. He felt more … *real*, as though he were larger than life.

She could *feel* his presence even when she kept her eyes decently lowered.

His voice throbbed with power. It seemed to be for her and her alone. "He is not dead. His story is not yet told. He can come back, if you believe."

Charlotte stared at him, heedless of the gathered crowd. "Bring him back!"

The priest took a step forward, raising his cane. "Begone!"

"No." The preacher's voice grew darker. No, the *world* was getting darker. "*You* begone."

Lightning stabbed down, from a darkening sky. The priest's body lit up, then disintegrated in a flash of tearing white light. Charlotte was rooted to the spot, unable to move. The rest of the crowd scattered, strong men and women running in all directions, as if they were scared out of their minds. They were brave, faced with something they understood, but this ... Charlotte didn't blame them for running. The unknown was always terrifying.

"I can bring him back, if you embrace my lord," the preacher said. "Do you vow to devote yourself to him?"

"Yes." Charlotte didn't have to think about it. "Yes, yes, yes!"

The preacher placed his hand on Golan's chest. Charlotte watched, feeling something *new* blossom to life within her heart and soul. She had never truly believed in the gods, not when they seemed to turn their backs on their people. But now ... hope became faith, became belief ... she felt *something* surrounding her, blessing her. Golan's body twitched, his eyes opening ...

"Mama?"

Charlotte reached for him, yanking him off the pyre. He was alive! Her son was alive!

"Embrace my lord," the preacher said. "And serve him for the rest of your days."

"I will," Charlotte promised. Tears streamed down her face. No price was too high, for the return of her son. The villagers were already returning, drawn by the miracle in her arms. "I will."

And she knew, whatever happened, that she would keep her promise.

Chapter One

The tiny hut was empty, save for a single fire in the exact centre of the room. It burned with an eerie flame, as if it were more magic than mundane. Shadows flickered around the chamber, growing and lengthening as the flames threatened to die down. It was easy to believe that *something* lurked within the shadows, that they were gateways to realms that existed beyond the reach of human perception. There was a sense that anyone who walked into the shadows wouldn't come out again.

Isabella, formerly of House Majuro, knelt on one side of the fire, staring into the flickering light. She'd spent the last few months studying the old magics – if indeed they *were* magics – and yet they kept scaring her, as if they were something greater than she could comprehend. She was a trained sorceress, yet ... there was something about the old magics that worried her more than she dared admit. Magic, *her* magic, was *hers*. The old magics were something from before the dawn of recorded time, something ... something *borrowed*. She couldn't escape the feeling that, one day, she'd have to pay a terrible price for what she'd learnt.

And my family may condemn me to death, if they find out, Isabella thought. It was impossible to deny, even to herself, that she was studying forbidden rites. She'd been taught what to watch for, back when she'd graduated from school. *They'll say I've crossed a line.*

She sighed, inwardly. She wasn't the person she'd been, for sure. The powerful sorceress who'd deliberately broken the rules, ensuring she'd be kicked out of training and be disowned by her family, was gone. So was the mercenary, who'd fought for Prince Reginald in his bid to lay claim to the Summer Isle. It was hard to be sure, but ... was she the sole survivor of Lord Robin's Free Company? So many were dead or missing, their fates unknown ... it was possible. And

… she wondered, sometimes, if she'd recognise herself in the mirror. If she looked. She'd never been particularly vain – mercenaries couldn't afford it – but she knew she was growing older. Her dark hair was already tinged with white.

A wisp of wind crossed her face. She looked up. Mother Lembu knelt on the far side of the fire … she hadn't been there a second ago. Isabella was no longer surprised by such things, but … she shook her head. Mother Lembu, Patron of Women, was something very inhuman, whatever aspect she wore. The rules didn't apply to her. Isabella was still trying to work out what rules *did*.

She forced herself to look the entity in the face. Mother Lembu was wearing her motherly aspect, a warm friendly appearance that reminded Isabella of her *real* mother. And yet, there was something about her appearance that was impossible to pin down. It wasn't that it was constantly shifting, although it never seemed to be quite constant. It was that … she shook her head, slowly. She rather suspected that, if someone *else* saw the entity, she would look like *their* mother, as if the entity was trying – deliberately or not – to manipulate their perceptions and feelings. It made her wonder what lay behind the entity's smile.

"Daughter." Mother Lembu's *voice* was motherly too, *just* like Isabella's mother. It grated on Isabella's very soul. "You have studied well."

"Thank you." Isabella knew it was true, even though there was something curiously slapdash about the rites and rituals she'd been taught. The potions and poultices she'd made, at Mother Lembu's direction, had nothing in common with the art she'd been taught at the Peerless School. "You're a good teacher."

Mother Lembu looked charmed, as if she accepted it as her due. Isabella wondered if she'd noticed the sarcasm and chosen to ignore it or, perhaps, missed it altogether. It was hard to tell. Mother Lembu didn't seem to have the emotional range of a human, let alone the tutors who'd drilled brewing into her head. *They* would have noticed the flattery instantly and given her detention. Mother Lembu … wasn't human. Isabella reminded herself, again, that her tutor had little in common with her.

And she isn't teaching me out of the goodness of her heart, she thought. *She'll want something in return, sooner or later.*

She settled back on her haunches, calming herself. They were effectively trapped on the Summer Isle, at least until spring came. Isabella had seen the towering waves, pounding the coastline and destroying any boat foolish enough to set sail. Havant and the Red Monks had done *something*, something that ensured the storms were stronger and nastier than any in recorded history. The cynical part of her mind noted they hadn't had to work very hard. The Summer Isle had always been isolated from the mainland. Crossing safely was never easy, even during the summer months.

"There is symbolism in all things," Mother Lembu said, once again. "You must be aware of it at all times."

Isabella nodded. She'd heard it before, time and time again. And yet, it was hard to believe. She'd been taught rational magic, magic that worked the same way for everyone. It was hard to wrap her head around spells that called on entities and petitioned them to do the work ... and that the spells might not work, if the entity in question was having a bad day. She knew spells – rituals, really – that could only be carried out under a full moon, or after a week of careful purification, or ... she tried, hard, to keep her face under tight control. She'd been warned about spells that required such odd precision. They were almost always dangerous beyond belief.

And not without reason, she told herself. The more she knew, the more she worried about what was happening on the mainland. She wasn't even sure her letter to Alden had reached its destination. *The effects are either very small, and thus hard to detect and counter, or terrifyingly big.*

She listened, silently. She'd commit everything to paper, once the lecture was over. Mother Lembu hadn't raised any objections to Isabella writing everything down, even though she *had* to know the notebooks would get Isabella into *real* trouble if the Inquisition – or what was left of it – ever found them. Isabella suspected Mother Lembu expected the notebooks to go wandering, sooner or later, and fall into the hands of someone who'd try the rites without any real awareness of the dangers. And if they did ... there were times when Isabella seriously considered destroying the notebooks herself. The spells *she'd* been taught took years to master. The rites and rituals could be carried out by *anyone*.

Which is why they're regarded with such horror, she thought, cynically. *The Grand Sorcerers didn't want* everyone *practising magic.*

Mother Lembu caught her eye. For a moment, she seemed to have three shadows.

"Are we paying attention?"

Isabella nodded, quickly. Mother Lembu had three aspects: a maiden, a mother and a crone. Isabella had never *seen* the crone, but … she'd heard stories. She knew she never *wanted* to come face-to-face with the crone. If the stories were true …

"You were explaining how certain rites call on different entities," she said. Thankfully, she'd long since mastered the art of mentally recording everything she was told for later consideration, even if she wasn't paying precise attention. It had come in handy at school … and, also, when her father had started yet another lecture on The Proper Duties to One's Family. "And how they must all be bribed for the ritual to go ahead."

"*Placated*, dear," Mother Lembu said. She gave Isabella a warm smile. "The gods are not *bribed*."

If you say so, Isabella thought. They *were* bribed, as far as she could tell. Some entities wanted specific offerings, others seemed to be happy with whatever they were given. And they bestowed their blessings in response. *Who is actually in charge?*

She considered the question as Mother Lembu resumed her lecture, outlining the precise gifts that must be offered to certain entities and the meaning behind them. Who had the power? The shopkeeper, who had the food someone wanted to buy, or the customer, who had the money the shopkeeper wanted? Or was it a mutually beneficial relationship? She understood why someone might want to curry favour with the gods … *entities*, she corrected herself sharply. But what did the entities get out of it? How did they benefit? Or were they just slaves to the handful who knew how to call on them?

"So," Mother Lembu said. She clapped her hands, as if she knew Isabella's conscious mind hadn't been paying attention.

"Have we studied enough?"

"Yes, Mother," Isabella said. She hastily reviewed what she'd been told, in case Mother Lembu wanted to quiz her. "I think that's enough for the day."

"You need some rest," Mother Lembu agreed. Her voice dropped. She gave Isabella a sly wink. "And your young man in your bed."

Isabella blushed, furiously. Reginald – Crown Prince Reginald of Andalusia – had asked her to marry him, after the final battle with Havant and the entity behind him. She wasn't sure how she felt about it. She liked him – she loved him, in some ways – but she didn't think she wanted to live the life of a queen. Queen Carline, Reginald's mother, had died giving birth; Queen Emetine, wife and murderer of King Edwin of the Summer Isle, had gone mad. The entities probably hadn't helped, Isabella was sure. She'd heard enough of the queen's ranting to know she'd been sold a bill of goods.

"He's gone to Racal's Bay," she said, stiffly. She didn't want to have *that* conversation, not with an entity who reminded her so strongly of *her* mother. Her mother ... these days, her mother would probably approve of Reginald as a prospective husband. It wasn't as if there were many sorcerers left. "And we haven't decided yet ..."

"Remember what I taught you," Mother Lembu said. "You can use him to perform rites."

"I know." Isabella felt her blush deepen. "But I won't ask him to do it."

"You should." Mother Lembu shrugged. "You'll need it."

Isabella looked up, into the entity's eyes. "Is that true?"

"Yes," Mother Lembu said.

"Oh." Isabella wasn't sure what to make of it. Predicting the future was yet another sign of forbidden arts ... although, her tutors had admitted dryly, most people ran into trouble because they predicted the future *unsuccessfully*. And yet ... nothing she'd been taught, in the Peerless School, had offered any real hope of predicting the future. Sure, she could say that someone would be hexed in the very near future – and then hex him herself – but it wasn't *real*. "How do you know?"

Mother Lembu gave her an enigmatic smile. "There are

layers you have yet to reach, my dear."

I'm sure there are, Isabella thought. Her lessons had been detailed, but … she was starting to think that she was gaining a generalist education. There were tricks that were well beyond her, hints of rituals that Mother Lembu had never taught her to perform. *And just what are you keeping from me?*

"I look forward to reaching them," she said, out loud. She wasn't sure that was true. "Can you teach me how to predict the future?"

"Maybe." Mother Lembu's smile deepened, until it became the expression one might expect to see on a prowling tiger. It was hard to look into her face without feeling cold. "When you're ready."

"Ready to learn?" Isabella asked. "Or ready to pay the price?"

Mother Lembu merely smiled. "You don't have to leave now. Why don't you ask for something from me?"

Isabella frowned, aware that – once again – the rules had changed. Mother Lembu wanted something, but what? Permission to do something? Or … just a test, to see what Isabella would do? What she'd ask for, given the chance? Or … or what? Isabella gritted her teeth in frustration. She knew how to play the game, back home. She knew the rules and the price for breaking them. Here … she wasn't so sure. The slightest mistake could condemn her to an eternity of suffering.

She looked back into the fire. The flames seemed to reach towards her. "What should I ask for?"

"What *should* you ask for?" Mother Lembu seemed amused. "Nothing may be known until it is spoken."

Isabella lifted her eyes. "You keep saying that."

"And it's always true," Mother Lembu said.

For you, Isabella thought. *But for me?*

She took a breath. "Answer me a question," she said, with scant hope the question *would* be answered. "Where do you come from? All of you."

Mother Lembu looked displeased. It was … it was a very *motherly* kind of displeasure, the kind of displeasure that suggested one had disappointed one's parents beyond all hope of redemption. Isabella felt a pang – a sense of dismay, an urge to throw herself on her knees and beg forgiveness – that nearly overwhelmed her. If she hadn't been so familiar with parental disappointment, if she hadn't been so used to coping with her father's anger and her mother's tears, it *would* have overwhelmed her. Even so, it was a near-run thing.

"I would ask you to ask a different question," Mother Lembu said. Her voice was so even that Isabella *knew* she was angry. "But I know you will not."

Because you've seen the future, Isabella asked herself, *or because you know me?*

She frowned, reminding herself – once again – that overestimating someone's powers and abilities could be as dangerous as underestimating them. It was easy to work oneself into a paralysis born of self-doubt, of fear that one's opponent was simply too powerful and too capable to stop. She'd learnt the hard way that – sometimes – those who were too impressed with their own abilities had feet of clay, that they could be brought down through a careful use of magic and skill. And that others, boastful braggarts who got on her nerves, had a great deal to boast *about*.

"We were born in the light, children of the Great Old Ones and Sons and Daughters of Mankind," Mother Lembu said. "They were the raging storm. We were the passion and the glory and the *everything*. We were born of their desire to be something more, shaped by their determination to remain unchanged for an endless eternity. And we came to take their place. We caged them, imprisoned them, and ruled for eternity.

"And then eternity came to an end."

"Eternity doesn't end, by definition," Isabella said, tartly. She suspected Mother Lembu had to tell the truth, but ... there was nothing stopping her from telling the truth in a manner that made it impossible to understand. Or simply mislead her. "What happened?"

Mother Lembu waved her hand. The fire died. The chamber was plunged into darkness. Isabella sensed ... *things*, crawling closer and closer until they were practically breathing down the back of her neck. She clenched her fists, ready to lash out. The sense of something *behind* her, not quite *touching* her, was overwhelming. The only thing that kept her from throwing a punch was the grim certainty that it might be the last thing she ever did.

"The Great Old Ones were *big*." Mother Lembu's voice echoed in the darkness. "This world is a fragile structure. It was never meant to bear their presence. Mankind was never designed to see them. Madness always followed in their wake. And then we were born, children of the Great Old Ones and Mankind alike. We fought the Great Old Ones. We caged them. We banished them. And then we were banished too."

Her voice rose. "We were betrayed."

Thunder cracked. The air seemed to grow very hot, just for a second. Isabella felt *something* all around her, pressing down on her. She heard a creaking sound, then ... the air cleared. She opened her eyes, without ever being quite sure when she'd closed them. The door was open. Light was streaming through. And Mother Lembu was gone.

She sat there for a long moment, gathering herself. She'd been in hundreds of fights, physical and magical, but ... this was different. She had never felt so vulnerable, not even when she'd picked a fight with an older student at school. There, at least, there had been limits. She could lose, but she couldn't die. Here ... she knew she was confronting powers that were older than her entire family, powers that played by rules she didn't even begin to understand. Her training insisted that there would be an underlying logic, somewhere. She just had to find it. But everything she'd seen in the last few months suggested there was *no* underlying logic.

Perhaps the lack of logic is, in itself, a form of logic, she thought, as she staggered to her feet and brushed down her trousers. *The system is logically illogical.*

She snorted at the thought, then took one last look around the chamber and walked out of the door. The building was a tiny stone shack, a short distance outside the city's walls. Mother Lembu had insisted on holding their lessons there, even though she would have been welcome in Allenstown itself. Isabella had no idea why, but she suspected it was something to do with territory. She and Reginald had killed the entity who'd nearly destroyed the city, yet ... Isabella shrugged. She had a feeling she should be relieved. Mother Lembu was not human. Better to keep her at a distance.

But that might not be possible, she mused. The cold air brushed against her skin as she headed back to the gates. *The world isn't what it was. And the entities may be here to stay.*

Chapter Two

The waves were towering over the land.

Crown Prince Reginald of Andalusia, Lord of the Summer Isle, stood on the shore and watched the waves roaring in the distance. Racal's Bay itself was relatively smooth – he could see a handful of fishermen braving the waters to catch the fish that had taken shelter from the storm – but beyond the bay there was nothing but darkness and thunder. Gloomy clouds hung low over the sea, towering waves reaching up to kiss them before falling back to the waters below. It seemed impossible that anything could survive on the open sea.

Reginald shivered, despite the warm winter clothes he'd donned before leaving the tower and heading down to the shoreline. Cold droplets of water hung in the air, splashing against his face, soaking his clothes ... it was meant to be spring, but he'd seen precious little sign of it since he'd left Allenstown. The snow had melted as he'd travelled east, the primitive roads steadily turning to muddy nightmares as the water swelled out of the ditches, but ... it still felt cold. And yet, it wasn't the cold that made him shiver. It was the sheer titanic power of the waves breaking against the distant cliffs, mocking him. He knew, with a certainty that could not be denied, that Racal's Bay and all the other works of humanity would be destroyed in a heartbeat, if the waves came crashing into the bay.

The cold seemed to grow worse as the wind picked up, great gusts of watery air brushing against his bare skin. Reginald knew, without false modesty, that he was a brave man. He'd been raised to be a warrior, even though – back then – everyone had thought he'd find himself restricted to the training ground and jousting field. On land, he *was* a brave man. He knew that beyond a shadow of a doubt. But on the waters, he was a coward. He would never admit it, not when leadership often depended on making a show of bravery, but … the waters scared him. You couldn't fight a storm. You could merely endure and hope it chose to let you live.

He lifted his gaze until he was staring directly at the gloomy clouds, pulsing with anger. It was still possible to see hints of *faces* within the clouds, as if there were something behind them … he knew there *was* something behind them, directing them. Reginald had seen the entity which Lord Havant the Usurper had summoned, watched in horror as it blossomed into the world and nearly destroyed Allenstown before it was stopped. Magic he understood, but this was different. The rules were different. The entities … he shivered, again. It was hard to believe that such creatures were *not* gods. If he hadn't seen men and women working miracles, back when the Grand Sorcerers had ruled the world, he might have believed in their divinity himself.

It was not a reassuring thought. He'd never really taken religion seriously, even though – as the Crown Prince – he would one day become the country's religious leader. His father had agreed, pointing out – in the lessons he'd given his heir and no others – that it didn't matter *what* the commoners chose to believe, as long as they were loyal and obedient. The gods might or might not exist, but they had no influence over human affairs. And they could hardly be bought by donations from needy humans. Why would they be?

But he'd seen things, on the Summer Isle, that had shaken him to the core.

Reginald took a long breath, calming himself. He wasn't used to sitting around doing nothing, even though there was no choice. The Summer Isle practically shut down for the winter as travel became difficult, if not impossible. Reginald had had to work hard merely to get from Allenstown to Racal's Bay, even though it was a relatively short journey. Riding up to the narrows, and the kingdom beyond, was unthinkable. He hadn't wasted the winter – if nothing else, he'd been able to recruit new armsmen as the core of a local military garrison – but it felt as if he could have done more. And the lack of word from his homeland bothered him. There had been no reply to his messages. His father hadn't even written a note of congratulations before the seas became impassable.

He shook his head, slowly. He knew, better than most, just how badly communications had fallen apart in the last few years. His father's messenger could be sitting on the other side of the channel, waiting impatiently for the storms to clear, or he could have drowned in a desperate attempt to cross the waters. Reginald gritted his teeth at the thought, reminding himself – sharply – that there was nothing to be gained by penalising someone for being unable to do the impossible. His father had drilled that lesson into him, time and time again. A prince could not afford to seem unjust, for fear of his supporters growing to fear him and – eventually – turning on him. And yet ... he wanted to know what was happening on the other side of the waters. He'd been gone for months. Anything could have happened.

Father will handle it, he thought. His father was an old man, but he wasn't *that* old. He'd given the nobles enough drubbings over the last few years to keep them from doing anything stupid, even if the Crown Prince was on the other side of the channel. *And when I get back ...*

He frowned, feeling ... he wasn't sure *how* he felt. He'd wanted more power and responsibility, even though he'd *known* there were limits to what his father could reasonably give him. It had hurt to know that many of his former classmates were wielding real power now, while *he* remained under his father's tutelage. Reginald was proud enough to find that maddening despite the awareness that, one day, he would have it all. He'd pushed for the invasion, at least in part, because it would give him lands of his own. It would hurt to give it up and go back to being the Crown Prince again.

Something cleared their throat, behind him.

Reginald turned, slowly. A messenger stood there, eyes flickering from side to side as he took in the mounted armsmen. Reginald wondered, idly, if the messenger had expected him to be alone. The bodyguards were part of the background, but they were always there. It only took one lone madman to cause chaos, by killing – or threatening to kill – the heir to the throne. The man hesitated, then went down on his knees. A merchant, then. No one else would have hesitated before dropping in submission.

"Rise," Reginald said. "What news do you have for me?"

"A ship has been sighted from the tower, Your Highness," the messenger said. He stumbled over the honorific. Technically, Reginald was *both* a king – by right of conquest – and a prince. The locals seemed to find the duality a little confusing. "It's coming into the bay."

Reginald blinked, turning to look back over the waters. The waves hadn't abated. If anything, they were growing stronger. The fishermen were hauling in their nets and hurrying back to the docks, hoping to get through the mouse hole and find safety before it was too late. It was so overcast that it felt as if night were falling, even though it was early afternoon. There was no sign of a ship coming into the bay. And yet, he didn't doubt the man. No one would tell a lie like that and expect it to be believed.

"I see." Reginald whistled. His bodyguard came forward, escorting his horse. "We'll go back to the tower."

The horse whinnied uncomfortably as Reginald mounted it, slipping into the saddle with the ease of long practice. Reginald stroked its hair, silently grateful that he'd had the foresight to bring dozens of the beasts with him when he'd led his fleet across the waters. The locals didn't train their horses properly, not by *his* standards. He supposed he should be grateful. If they'd deployed better cavalry, Lord Havant the Usurper might have won the war and taken control of the island. *And* killed or captured Reginald. The thought was unthinkable.

Reginald moved the horse into a trot, ignoring the merchant as he scurried alongside. The commoners weren't allowed to ride horses, not on the Summer Isle. Only aristocrats were allowed to own horses, let alone ride them. Few merchants could have *afforded* to buy horses ... he sighed, inwardly. Things were different on the mainland. But not *that* different.

He settled back in the saddle as Racal's Bay came into view. It was the second-largest city on the Summer Isle, but – by Reginald's standards – it was really nothing more than a large town. A cluster of stone buildings, carefully designed to withstand the worst of the winter storms ... it was drab, almost colourless, and yet ... there was a certain charm around it. He wasn't sure what it was. The streets were practically empty, only a handful of men – and no women –

within eyesight. Reginald felt a pang of regret. The locals still didn't trust him to guarantee their safety, even after he'd hanged a dozen men for rape. He supposed he couldn't really blame them. They didn't *know* him.

The wind shifted, blowing the stench of rotting fish into his nostrils. Reginald almost smiled. It wasn't pleasant, not by any reasonable standard, but it beat a battlefield. Besides, it was a sign that the locals were starting to accept his rule. They wouldn't be cutting up the fish in the open if they feared his men would march down and help themselves. Reginald had issued strong orders against looting, with floggings for the first offence and hanging for repeat offenders, but he'd been a campaigner long enough to know that orders meant nothing when the men were on the verge of starvation. The nobles in his company might bitch and moan about having fish for breakfast, lunch and dinner, but the enlisted men knew better. They preferred eating a monotonous diet to starving.

Although I would kill for fresh meat, he thought, dryly. The stockpiles of salted beef, pork and venison were starting to run dry. The Summer Isle had never supported vast herds of farm animals, let alone wild animals. It wasn't really surprising. The aristocracy had made it impossible for the commoners to raise herds and then professed themselves bemused by the constant series of famines. *Idiots*.

He kept his face impassive as he reached the tower and dismounted, passing the horse to one of his horsemen. The Summer Isle had *potential*, if it wound up with a good lord and an aristocracy with the common sense of the average squirrel. Reginald was determined to *be* that lord, even if he had to accidentally-on-purpose provoke a handful of aristocrats into rebelling so he could kill them, exile their extended families and distribute their lands to his supporters. There was nothing wrong with the land, not really. Just letting peasant farmers keep half their crops would do wonders for production. The fact that it would also make him popular was just the icing on the cake.

The tower warden bowed as he approached. "Your Highness. We have sighted a ship ..."

"So I've been told," Reginald said. "Show me."

He followed the warden up the cramped stairs, cursing the

tower's designer under his breath. He'd never liked confined spaces, even though he understood the military logic. And yet ... it was clear the designer had never been in a *real* battle. If the attacking force got into the tower, the defenders were screwed. Reginald had proved that himself, when *he'd* attacked the building. He could still see signs of the brief, but savage engagement everywhere he looked.

It was colder, somehow, at the top of the tower. It was the highest building in the city, even though it wasn't *that* high compared to some of the castles and palaces in Andalusia. The wind blew against him, forcing him to grab hold of the railing to keep from being pushed towards and over the battlements. It was hard to escape the impression that, one day, the entire tower would simply be blown over. Reginald took the offered beltline, snapped it onto his belt and inched forward until he was peering over the city, the bay and the churning waves beyond. The wind blew so hard that his eyes started to fill with tears.

He wiped them away, impatiently, as he peered into the distance. Mist hung over the water, bringing back memories of the enchanted haze they'd encountered during the march to Allenstown. He shivered, protecting his eyes with one hand as the warden pointed into the waves. It was hard to be sure, but there was *something* there. A rock? The waters surrounding the bay were dangerous, even in summertime. He'd seen the charts. The Summer Isle had been, technically, part of the Empire, but it had never been fully integrated into the continental system. It was simply too difficult to travel routinely between the island and the mainland. He supposed it might have worked in the islanders' favour. The Empire had collapsed and they'd barely noticed.

A frisson of excitement shot down his spine as he saw the boat. No, a *ship*. It was a midsized two-master, a warship ... it had to have come from Andalusia. Where *else* could it come from? Now, of all times, there would be no contact between the Summer Isle and any of Andalusia's mainland rivals. The Summer Isle was surprisingly insular. There had never been any hint, even the slightest rumour, of Havant or his followers trying to find allies on the mainland. It wouldn't have made any difference, Reginald was sure, but they hadn't even *tried*.

His eyes narrowed as the ship glided into the bay. He was no sailor, but … there was something *wrong*. The ship seemed to be travelling *too* smoothly, as if the wind and the waves weren't quite touching it. Magic? It seemed unlikely. The great magicians were either dead or hundreds of miles to the east. Isabella – he felt a pang as he remembered her – was the most powerful magician on the island. There weren't many more back on Andalusia.

"She's heading for the mouse hole," the warden said. "Should we try to warn her off?"

Reginald frowned. No sailor worthy of the name would wish to drop anchor in the bay when he could pass through the mouse hole and enter the docks. The bay was untrustworthy. The *locals* didn't trust the bay and they lived right next to it. But … his instincts were sounding the alarm. Something wasn't right. He peered at the boat, gliding forward like something out of a supernatural fantasy. The flag at the top of the mast was his father's pennant …

"No." He couldn't refuse his father's messenger, whatever else he did. "And send two detachments of troops to meet her. *No one* is to get off that boat until I say so."

"Yes, Your Highness."

Reginald turned and hurried down the stairs, resisting the urge to return to his quarters and have a hot bath … or, at least, change into something warm and dry. Technically, protocol stated that his father's messenger should come to him, but … his instincts insisted that letting the man run free was a very bad idea. Reginald was the Crown Prince, yet his aristocratic followers owed allegiance – first and foremost – to his father, the king. A messenger could cause a great deal of trouble for him, as long as he enjoyed the support of his patron. It was no surprise that a number of royal messengers tended to end up dead. But if Reginald killed his father's messenger …

He checked his sword, then walked into the courtyard and mounted a fresh horse. His bodyguard fell in around him as he cantered out of the gates and down the cobbled road to the docks. The ship was already docking, sailors tossing lines to the shore to ensure the ship was pulled into the right place. Up close, the ship appeared almost … normal. Reginald wondered, sourly, if he was making a fool of himself. And yet, something prickled at the back of his mind. He touched his sword, reminding himself that he'd made sure to issue iron blades to his men. If they were about to confront another entity, they would be prepared.

The gangplank fell into place. Reginald stayed on his horse, watching as a pair of heralds appeared at the top of the gangplank and made their way onto dry land. The messenger was either a low-ranking aristocrat or a common-born social climber. No one born to high rank needed heralds to signal their importance. His lips twitched in disdain as an overweight man appeared, inching down the gangplank. Reginald recognised him, instantly. Sir Handel had been his father's messenger since time out of mind, a jumped-up commoner who could be discarded instantly if he became a liability. And would be, when Reginald took the throne.

Sir Handel bowed deeply as he saw Reginald. "Your Highness. I bring word from your father, the King."

Reginald frowned. He detested Sir Handel, but ... there was something wrong. He wasn't sure what, yet ... it was there. He could practically *smell* it. His skin crawled. He knew he wouldn't be turning his back on the older man in a hurry.

"You are ordered to return to Andalusia at once," Sir Handel continued, stiffly. *That* was a surprise. Protocol dictated that the message was to be given in private, not in front of a growing audience of guardsmen, sailors and commoners. Sir Handel wouldn't break protocol, not unless something was *very* wrong. "Immediately."

Chapter Three

Isabella checked the clock, then sat down at the wooden table and went to work.

It had taken her weeks to gather the ingredients, even though all of them were – alarmingly – common. The recipe hadn't called for dragon's blood, phoenix feathers or basilisk eyes, nothing that required a brave man with a death wish to venture into a monster's cave to collect ingredients that even her family, at the height of its power, had found cripplingly expensive. The herbs in front of her had all been plucked from the ground, from flower gardens and hedgerows ... half of them had a multitude of uses that had nothing to do with magic. Isabella found it alarming, even though she knew there weren't many people who understood how the herbs could be used for ritual magic. Anyone could do it if they knew the recipe.

She frowned, her old training insisting – once again – that she was making a mistake, that she was opening a box that was best left closed. Half the *really* dangerous spells and potions on the banned list weren't unknown, merely impossible to actually *do* without rare and dangerous ingredients that the average dark sorcerer wouldn't be able to find. Anyone with the wealth and power needed to obtain them wouldn't *want* them. They'd certainly be able to accomplish their aims without dark sorcery. But the recipe in front of her was different. A skilled housewife could brew the potion without difficulty.

Her eyes narrowed as she started to place the herbs and spices in the pot, allowing her instincts to guide her as much as possible. It wasn't easy. She'd grown up in a world where precision was important, where an extra milligram of *something* could be the difference between a successful potion and a colossal explosion. Her tutors had rapped her knuckles for making mistakes, cautioning her that the consequences would have been far worse if they'd allowed her to go ahead. But now … Mother Lembu had taught her to let her *feelings* guide her. There could be no worse sin, at the Peerless School. Everyone knew that feelings led straight to dark sorcery.

Or ritual magic, she thought, as she ground the herbs into a squashy mess. *What were they trying to keep from us?*

She lit the fire in the stove, then poured water into the pot and placed it on top of the heat. Mother Lembu had advised her to make *everything* herself, right down to the cooking pot and stove, but Isabella simply hadn't had the time. Besides, she was no blacksmith. She supposed it explained why so many covens had operated in the countryside, with open fires and rituals. They'd needed to do everything themselves, even if they hadn't understood why. Isabella thought *she* knew why. The ritual didn't begin when the potion was ready. It began when the brewer started to work. It was as much about preparing the brewer as it was about preparing the brew.

Which makes one wonder if you can't make potions for anyone but yourself, she mused, thoughtfully. Much of the herblore she'd learnt in the last few months seemed to have little *real* magic, as far as she could tell, but she'd also learnt not to take anything for granted. *If I asked someone else to drink, what would he see?*

The mixture began to bubble. A faint smell of herbs – and something else, something that made her head swim – hung in the air. Isabella reached for the wooden spoon – it struck her, suddenly, that Mother Lembu had cautioned her to stay away from iron without ever quite saying it openly – and stirred, resisting the urge to count the strokes. She didn't have to, she thought. There was no need to be precise, not with ritual magic. She just had to stir until the potion *felt* ready.

She let out a heavy sigh as the mixture thickened. It was ready, she thought. She lifted the pot off the stove and poured a healthy dollop of the brew into a pewter mug, giving it a moment to cool. She'd been cautioned never to use pewter in brewing, but – as with so much else – her tutors had never bothered to explain *why*. Mother Lembu, on the other hand, had expected her merely to avoid iron. Isabella shrugged, putting the rest of the mixture to one side. If it worked, she would need it again. She just wondered how long it would be before the mixture lost its potency.

Pacing over to the door, she checked the lock. It was firmly shut. She'd told the guards – and Reginald's administrators – that the door was heavily warded, with any intruders certain to meet a horrible fate, but that was a lie. Mother Lembu had warned her not to use magic anywhere near the shack. Reginald knew, but she hadn't risked telling anyone else. Who knew what they'd do if they thought she was defenceless? She was the sole sorcerer in the garrison. Anyone who wanted to kill Reginald would have to go through her first.

And if they realise what I'm training to do, she thought morbidly, *they might try to kill me anyway.*

Isabella undressed quickly, removing her leathers, trousers and underclothes until she was completely naked. The cold air bit at her skin, a mocking reminder that – if she went outside – she'd freeze to death in seconds. It was supposed to be spring, but there were still snow on the ground. She would have preferred to be dressed for the ritual, yet ... Mother Lembu had insisted Isabella had to be naked. It made Isabella feel defenceless. She had a nasty feeling that was the point. Naked, vulnerable ... who knew what might come crawling into her mind?

She picked up the mug and sat down, arranging herself as comfortably as possible. The cold faded from her awareness as she clasped the mug in her hands, bracing herself to drink. It smelt funny, both attractive and repulsive at the same time. She gritted her teeth, remembering the healing potions that had been forced down her throat when she'd caught something *really* nasty as a child. Then, she'd been allowed to swallow them bit by bit until she drained the mug. Now, she had to drink the whole brew in one gulp. She couldn't stop.

Funny, she thought. *It shouldn't make any difference. But it does.*

She lifted the mug to her lips and drank. The potion tasted awful, in a manner she *knew* she couldn't put into words. She had to fight to keep from spitting, to keep her gorge from rising and vomiting the entire mess over the earthen floor. It settled uncomfortably in her stomach, a dead weight that seemed to bind her to the ground … she wondered, just for a second, if she'd made a terrible mistake. There was nothing poisonous in the ingredients, but … if they worked together, could they kill her? Her skin prickled, as if she was no longer alone …

… And then the world seemed to open up around her.

She was dimly aware, on some level, that she was still tethered to her body, but it was difficult to *believe*. The world was growing larger, as if her perceptions had been limited … as if she'd opened her eyes after a lifetime of being blind. Shadowy *things* surrounded her, giant veins twitching in the air … she felt as if she was exploring a body, a giant pulsing mass of life, from the start. The world was so much *bigger* than she'd realised.

Her awareness kept expanding, reaching out to the world beyond the walls. She could sense the two guardsmen waiting for her, their thoughts calm and placid despite the cold. One of them was thinking of the girl he'd left back home, waiting for him; the other was contemplating the prostitutes he'd fucked the previous night. The contrast between them was so striking that she couldn't understand why she hadn't seen it at once, why she hadn't realised they were so different. She supposed it didn't really matter. Her friends were dead, her family a lost cause. She'd fallen out of the habit of allowing herself to grow closer to people. Reginald was the only person she'd allowed to get close to her since they'd come to the Summer Isle …

Her thoughts slid through the outer world. A young girl was lying in bed, her thoughts of her approaching marriage caught between anticipation of finally becoming a woman and fear of what bedding a man would actually be like. Beyond her, a young boy was driven by anger and bitterness and a strange kind of *surliness* that felt utterly alien to Isabella. He wanted and resented not having … she shuddered, looking away. Another woman loomed up in her mind, a merchant's wife plotting marriages for her children. She was the sort of person Isabella would have detested, as a young girl, but now … now she saw the woman from the inside out. She was desperate to arrange good matches because they were the only hope for the family's future.

Who knew? She might have been right.

A wave of ... *something* ... caught her mental presence, tossing her up and away as if she were a leaf caught in a storm. Her mind swam, the tether back to her body weakening just enough to make her panic. Isabella reached out desperately and felt ... *Reginald*, back at Racal's Bay. She had the oddest sense he'd *seen* her, just for a second. And yet ... he was overshadowed by something worse, something *darker*. Her vision started to blur. She struggled to hang on to the last traces of insight before it faded away. Something bad had come to the Summer Isle ...

The thought drove her upwards, up so high she could see the circumference of the entire world. It *was* a globe, a sphere hanging in the inky blackness of space. It was ... her mind reached out to Andalusia and recoiled in horror. A shadow was clearly visible on the land. The country was falling into darkness. She felt her entire body shudder, twitching in disbelief. She'd seen ... *things* in Andalusia, back when they'd been harassing villagers into paying their taxes. It looked as if things had gotten worse.

And then something looked back at her.

Isabella froze, horrified. She couldn't move. She knew, with utter certainty, that the *thing* hadn't brought its full awareness to bear on her. She knew, somehow, that the moment it did, she would evaporate under its gaze. Her thoughts started to come apart, fracturing as the *thing* turned towards her. *Death* turned towards her. Sheer terror gibbered at the back of her mind, a terror that was almost completely overwhelming. It shocked her out of her paralysis. She grabbed for the tether, yanking herself back to her own mind ... something brushed against her, a slight touch that made her scream and ...

... She fell back into her body, the force of the impact almost a physical blow. She convulsed, throwing up so violently that she felt as if she was throwing up food she'd eaten weeks or months ago. Her chest hurt, badly. For a moment, she was convinced she was surrounded by men intent on beating her into a bloody mass. It took her long minutes to remember that she was alone, that the door was shut and locked. She swallowed hard, tasting the remnants of the potion in her mouth. The world felt fragile. She was a woman of iron in a world of fragile glass. The slightest mistake could break everything.

"… Crap." Isabella's voice sounded funny, even to her. "What happened?"

She stumbled to her feet, ignoring the mess. She'd been in worse places. She stumbled over to the table and grabbed for a pencil, hastily scribbling down everything she'd seen. It wasn't easy to put her feelings into words. Something was deeply *wrong* in Andalusia, something so wrong that … she couldn't quite remember what she'd seen, as if the memory was deliberately hiding itself from her, but something was wrong. She felt queasy every time she tried to think about it, as if pushing too hard would make her retch. The remaining potion sat on the table, mocking her. The mere thought of picking it up and drinking it was unthinkable.

Reginald will have to be warned, she thought, although she was grimly certain Reginald was already in trouble. She hoped he could get out of it. He was no sorcerer, but he *was* a decent warrior and a brilliant leader. And yet … she could stop him in his tracks with a single spell. She dared not assume that she was the *only* magic-user on the island. The gods alone knew how many other ritual magicians might be out there. The thought made her smile, humourlessly. *The gods do indeed know*.

She picked up the cauldron of water and placed it over the flame, then started to clean herself up. There was no way she was going outside looking like she'd been kicked out of a tavern, not when it wouldn't take much to get rumours started. Everyone knew Reginald had asked her to marry him, damn them. The local aristocracy had not been happy, even though common sense should have told them to be relieved. If one of their daughters had married the Crown Prince of Andalusia, it would have *really* upset the local balance of power. And landed Reginald with in-laws he might not be able to control.

The water started to bubble. She washed herself, dried herself and hastily scrambled back into her clothes. The cold was starting to bite, now the ritual was over. She took a swig of local rotgut from her flask – it tasted vile, but at least it was warming – and glanced back over her notes. They were imprecise – her tutors would have given her a week's detention if she'd handed them in – but they conveyed the gist of what she'd seen. She had to contact Reginald as quickly as possible.

Which won't be that quick, she thought. The last report had suggested the eastern road had become even *more* impassable over the last week or two. *Even if I go myself, it will still take days to reach the city.*

She pulled her cloak over her clothes, then unlocked the door and ventured out of the shack. It was early afternoon, but the skies were so dark it was easy to convince herself that it was near midnight. Wisps of snow drifted from the heavens, mocking the humans who dared think it was spring. Isabella understood, suddenly, why the Summer Isles had never really been united until now. No one, not even the titular king, could put together an army and conquer the entire island in a single campaigning season. The poor roads and bad terrain were only the half of it. The king might crush one foe, only to have the rest of his enemies unite against him. Reginald was the first man in hundreds of years to wield power all over the island and it wouldn't last. Isabella was morbidly sure of it.

Her two guards straightened up as they saw her, snapping to attention. Isabella nodded curtly to them, wondering which one had a girl back home and which one liked the prostitutes a little too much. She wasn't sure why it bothered her. Camp followers had been a part of war – and jousting – since time out of mind. The poor women on the streets had the choice of selling themselves or starving to death … she scowled. It *did* bother her, for all sorts of reasons. The fact that women appeared to be better at ritual magic was just the icing on the cake.

She glanced at one of the guards, keeping her expression under tight control. "Have we heard anything from the prince?"

"No, My Lady." The guard sounded, like so many others, as if he didn't know what to make of her. She was a sorceress who was also an aristocrat who might be marrying his liege lord … it was a mess. She simply didn't fit into a single category. "We haven't had any messengers from Racal's Bay or up north."

Where anything could be happening, Isabella thought.

Earls Goldenrod and Hereford were dead, but the mischief they'd wrought remained. *Reginald's men may not have been able to keep themselves in power.*

"Have a rider prepared as soon as we reach the castle," she ordered, stiffly. "I want him to take a message to the prince."

"Yes, My Lady." Isabella had spent enough time around servants to know the guard thought she was making a mistake, even though he wasn't fool enough to say it out loud. "I'll see to it at once."

Isabella nodded, stiffly. It wasn't much, but ... she couldn't do *nothing*. She was tempted to set out herself, perhaps with a couple of guards, even though Reginald had told her to remain in the city. He didn't own her, damn it. But ... she knew the occupation force could easily lose control if its leadership pulled out. She might not be the administrator – she'd told Reginald she had to concentrate on her studies, not rule the city – but she was the face of the occupation. She couldn't leave unless someone took her place.

And that someone will have to be someone very high-ranking indeed, she thought, as they walked through the icy streets. *Anyone lesser will have real problems taking control.*

A shaft of sunlight broke through the dark clouds. She frowned, sensing that the storm was coming to an end. Only a few snowflakes hung in the air ...

It should have reassured her. But she felt, deep inside, that the worst was yet to come.

Chapter Four

The sense of *wrongness* grew stronger as Sir Handel was escorted through the streets to the tower, Reginald lingering behind to collect the reports from the men who'd searched Sir Handel's ship. They hadn't found anything, they'd said, but ... the sailors had been *odd*. Brave men, who'd taken their ship through the worst storm on record, yet ... jumping and starting at shadows. Reginald had seen men who'd been through hell – and their first taste of combat, their first awareness that they might actually *die* – who'd come out of it better. It was definitely odd.

"Get them something to drink, then see what they say," he ordered. Normally, he frowned on drunkenness – his father had beaten him for drinking games when he'd been younger, pointing out the dangers of losing control – but he would make an exception. "And record everything for me."

He ordered Sir Handel to the throne room, then took a moment to order extra guards before entering the room himself and taking the throne. Sir Handel wouldn't have *dared* challenge him, not openly, but he should have shown *some* reaction to Reginald aping his father's prerogatives. No one sat on a throne, save for the king himself. And Reginald was not – yet – king.

"Your Highness," Sir Handel began. "Lord of the Summer Isle, Prince of the Marches ..."

Reginald waved his hand, impatiently. "I know my titles. What's the message?"

Sir Handel still showed no real reaction. He merely smiled lazily, as if he wasn't quite used to smiling. Reginald leaned forward, one hand dropping to his sword. The man looked insolent, as if he was practically *begging* for a lesson in respect, yet ... somehow, Reginald was sure he was looking at something far darker. Sir Handel moved as if the force behind him wasn't quite sure how to control his body. And pass for human … the thought jumped out of the back of Reginald's mind, but once it was there, it refused to go away. He was tempted to stab Sir Handel with an iron blade. It would be interesting to see what happened.

"Most beloved son," Sir Handel recited. "Child of my …"

"The message," Reginald snapped, allowing his voice to harden. He didn't have time for flowery language, not now. "What is the message?"

"He wants you back home. Now." Sir Handel's smile didn't change. "You are to take ship with me and return home."

"I see." Reginald kept his voice carefully flat. "And is there any *reason*?"

For the first time, Sir Handel looked unsure of himself. "Those are your orders, My Prince," he said. "I was not given any reason."

Reginald thought, fast. Logically, his father wouldn't have recalled him unless the situation was truly urgent. His father had been a king long enough to understand that an occupation needed *time* to turn into a permanent conquest. Nothing short of a major rising, or foreign invasion, or … his father on the verge of death would have sufficed. And yet, if any of those things had happened, Sir Handel would have told him. There was nothing to be gained by keeping him in the dark. Sir Handel wasn't that stupid.

"No reason," Reginald said. "And what was happening when you left?"

Sir Handel looked, just for a second, utterly perplexed, as if he couldn't believe Reginald was asking. Reginald couldn't believe that anyone could be surprised by the question. What did he expect to hear? Even if Reginald braved the seas and set out at once, it would take at least a week to reach Andalusia. And that was being optimistic, perhaps foolishly optimistic. He'd heard stories of sailors being driven back to land, their ships dashed against rocks or forced to take shelter in harbour until the storms finally abated. He wasn't remotely keen on crossing the waters until the weather improved.

"I ask again," Reginald said. "What was happening when you left?"

"I was told to give you the message," Sir Handel said.

"And I did."

I could put you to the question, you limp-wristed asshole, Reginald thought, with a vindictiveness that surprised him. He'd never liked Sir Handel, but he'd always known the jumped-up commoner was his father's mouthpiece. *And yet, I have the feeling you wouldn't be able to tell us anything no matter how badly we tortured you.*

He summoned his guards. "Escort Sir Handel to the ironhold cell," he ordered. "He is not to leave without permission from me specifically. His meals are to be delivered under armed guard. You have full authority to use whatever measures are necessary to keep him under control, up to and including the use of lethal force. Take him away."

The guards saluted. "Yes, sir!"

Sir Handel still showed no reaction, clear proof – if any were needed – that he was no longer the man he'd been. No one clung to power and position like someone who had climbed out of the gutter, someone who *had* to cling desperately to what little they had for fear of losing it. Sir Handel should have been protesting, loudly, at the mere *thought* of being locked away, or manhandled by lowborn guards. They rarely had a chance to push their social superiors around and tended to make the most of it, when they had an opportunity. And even if Sir Handel hadn't objected to how *he* was treated, he should have objected to the insult delivered to the king's messenger. Instead, he'd just taken it.

"Odd," Reginald mused. He wondered, grimly, if something was merely wearing Sir Handel's face. "What *are* you?"

He stood and headed to the door. His personal guard fell in around him as he made his way down the corridor to his quarters, to the rooms prepared for the island's former king on the rare occasions he visited the tower. The warden hadn't dared move into them … Reginald snorted at the conceit, although he knew it made a certain kind of sense. It was better to have a set of rooms for the king rather than displacing everyone when the king made one of his infrequent visits. He nodded to his bodyguards, telling them to remain outside and stepped into the room itself. It was oddly bare, for a kingly suite. The king probably hadn't spent more than a few days in the tower, if at all. Reginald didn't care. He'd been on campaign. The tower was practically luxury itself, compared to a camp bed or sleeping under the stars.

The windows were reinforced glass, hundreds of tiny panes secured by iron framework and – beyond them – iron bars. Reginald stood by the window and peered out, his gaze drifting over the drab city and the towering waves beyond. Sir Handel shouldn't have been able to get to them, not in *that* sort of weather … surely. Had he had a little help? And, if so, what was happening in Andalusia? He felt a shiver that had nothing to do with the cold. He'd sent reports home, but … it was possible they hadn't been taken seriously.

Or they arrived too late, he thought. There hadn't been any sign of the Red Monks over the past few months. He'd liked to think the entire group had been wiped out, but he didn't believe it. *The infection might already have reached Havelock.*

He forced himself to think. Sir Handel – damn the man, damn whatever was wearing his face – had given the gist of his message in public. He'd tried to keep it quiet, which meant the entire island would know in a few days. And then … he'd chosen his supporters for loyalty to him, rather than the king, but … they'd think they had to obey the king anyway. They could hardly be blamed for *that*, whatever happened. Going against the king meant risking everything, for what?

I should have asked Isabella to come with me, he thought. *Isabella never swore an oath to the king.*

It was maddening, all the more so because he didn't know what to do. If he went back, as ordered, he suspected he'd regret it. And if he didn't go back … he might face a mutiny. Or worse. And yet … if something was wrong in Andalusia, it was his duty to do something about it. Lord Havant had been able to do a hell of a lot of damage in the Summer Isle. He dreaded to think how much damage someone else, someone like him, would be able to do in Andalusia. The fact they'd already subverted a king's messenger boded ill for the future.

There was a sharp knock at the door. Reginald tensed, one hand dropping to his sword. He'd given strict orders that he was not to be disturbed, in his quarters, for anything other than a full-scale emergency. He had so little time to himself that he valued what free moments he could snatch from a busy schedule. And privacy ... he'd rarely been alone, even as a teenager. He'd always been surrounded by friends, servants and his father's mouthpieces, by prying eyes and listening ears ... Isabella had offered, once, to give him a permanent privacy ward. He'd been very tempted to take her up on it.

"Come," he barked.

The door opened, revealing a pale young girl in a drab black dress who looked utterly terrified. Reginald blinked, then guessed she'd probably been sent as a messenger. It didn't bode well. Normally, a girl so lowly wouldn't be allowed to so much as meet his eyes. Whoever had sent her feared his reaction, then. Better to put the girl in harm's way than put himself in danger. Reginald scowled as the girl stumbled through a curtsy, nearly tripping over herself and winding up on the floor. The stone would hurt, but the embarrassment would be far worse.

"Your Majesty," the girl stammered. "I ..."

"Take a deep breath," Reginald advised. Kindness cost nothing. Besides, his father had pointed out, more than once, that loyalty was worth any price. A king who was kind to his servants could expect loyalty in return. "And then give me your message."

The girl glanced up, remembered herself and looked down, hastily. Reginald concealed his amusement with an effort. If the poor girl, barely into her teens, thought he was laughing at her ...

"Your Majesty, another ship is approaching," the girl said. "She made it into the bay and headed to the dock."

Reginald turned and peered back out the window. There *was* another ship in the bay, but this one ... his heart clenched as he took in the sight before him. The ship had been battered savagely. The sails were a tattered mess, the mainmast shattered beyond repair ... it had been sheer luck, he guessed, that the foremast had lasted long enough for the ship to get into the bay. Even so ... the sailors were tiny, from the tower, but it still looked as though they'd been through hell.

"Have her crew held, for the moment," he ordered. The girl wouldn't do it herself, of course. She'd take his orders to her superior. "And if there's another messenger onboard, have him brought here under guard."

"Yes, Your Majesty." The girl bowed so low her head practically touched the floor. "I'll see to it at once, Your Majesty."

She turned and scurried out of the room. Reginald sighed, then headed to the door himself. He'd have to meet the newcomer, whoever it was, in the throne room … his life really wasn't his own. He wondered, as his bodyguard fell in around him, what would have happened if the Empire hadn't fallen. Would he have been happy, playacting at being a king while the real power rested with the Court Wizard? Or would he have deserted his post and headed somewhere uncivilised? He would have been very tempted.

And I'll have to find out who sent that poor girl to me, he thought. *The man needs a lesson in manners. And to be reassured that I don't kill messengers.*

He took his seat and waited, calming himself as best he could. Messengers popped in and out, keeping him updated. Reginald listened, without comment. The newcomer was being escorted to the tower … it was a breach of protocol to have him searched without good reason, but he was being searched anyway. That didn't sound good. Reginald kept one hand on his sword as the newcomer was finally shown into the chamber. He was a *very* familiar face.

Reginald leaned forward. "Lord Greely?"

Greely had been a young, dapper man when they'd first met. He'd been one of the noblemen who'd been raised with Reginald, both so the future king would know his future aristocracy *and* to serve as hostage for his father's good behaviour. He'd never been one of Reginald's closest friends, but they'd known each other. It was lucky, in a way. The idiot had made advances to Princess Sofia, Reginald's sister, and only his family's importance had kept him from being executed. Reginald had no idea what he would have done if one of his *closest* friends had made advances.

And even if Sofia had been happy, he thought, *she doesn't get to choose who she marries.*

"Your Highness." Lord Greely giggled, as if he'd just

survived utter hell itself. Reginald clearly held no terrors for him. "You're alive. They said you were dead."

He giggled, again. Reginald frowned, unable to reconcile the playboy of his memories with the half-mad person in front of him. Greely looked as if he'd forgotten how to wash himself, let alone how to dress. His swashbuckler's outfit had been fashionable, once upon a time, but now … it looked as if he'd been wearing it for days, if not weeks. And he stank of piss and shit and fear, naked fear. Reginald felt a flicker of sympathy. Greely had crossed the waves during a terrifying storm. He deserved a certain amount of respect.

"Who said I was dead?" Reginald met Greely's eyes. "What happened?"

"I should have gone with you." Greely chuckled. It was a deeply disturbing sound. "I was too much of a coward."

And I might not have been allowed to take you, Reginald added, silently. *Father would have sent you into exile, or to the block, if you hadn't had such a powerful family.*

"I should have gone further," Greely said. "Your father's gone mad."

Reginald straightened up. "What happened?"

"I don't know where to start," Greely said. "I …"

"Start at the beginning." Reginald remembered precisely *why* Greely and he had never been particularly close. The man had never been practical. And cowardly, too. He'd been useless on the battlefield. "And go on to the end, and stop."

"You set sail," Greely said. "I suppose I was the lucky one, at first. I wasn't welcome in court, so I bummed around the estate. Did a lot of drinking, as you can imagine. Deflowered a lot of lassies. You know how it is."

"Get to the point," Reginald growled. He didn't care *what* Greely had been doing during his exile. "Or I'll have you put to the question."

The threat made Greely giggle. "A couple of months after you left, something happened. I'm not sure what. My old man was at court when … it happened. He never came back. I … I heard your father had gone mad, that Princess Sofia had assumed the regency. And … and that you were dead. They said you'd died on this shithole of an island."

"Really," Reginald said. It was easy to come up with a short list of people who gained from spreading rumours the

Crown Prince was dead. Without Reginald … he wasn't sure *who* would have the best claim to the throne. It wasn't as if he had a little brother. "*Do* continue."

"The princess moved quickly," Greely continued. "A bunch of lords got killed, really – like *really* – quickly. Their ladies were taken hostage. A boatload of other ladies were taken hostage too, even though … ah, ladies are less useful as hostages. And then she put a bunch of troops on the streets. They marched up and down, smashing old temples and building new ones. She even sent troops to my estate. I thought she hated me."

"She does," Reginald confirmed, absently.

"And so I fled to the docks," Greely said. "I couldn't believe you were dead. And I …"

Reginald lifted an eyebrow, a mannerism he'd copied from his father. "And …?"

Greely paled. "I thought … I thought that enough of your army might have survived to give us a chance to retake the kingdom, even if you were dead. And I thought …"

"I'm surprised you thought at all," Reginald said, dryly. Greely had just confessed to *de jure* treason. "Or were you planning to liberate my father from captivity?"

"Yes, Your Highness." Greely snatched at the lifeline with a desperation born of fear he might just have crossed a line. "He is the monarch. We are sworn to him …"

"Well, *quite*," Reginald said. He knew from bitter experience that sworn oaths could be violated easily, unless they were reinforced by magic. The aristocracy were past masters at evading the spirit, if not the letter, of their oaths. "Who else is coming?"

"There were nine ships," Greely said. "And … am I the only one?"

"So far," Reginald said. He had a feeling that Sir Handel wasn't involved with Greely and his … conspiracy. "The others may not have made it."

"You have to go back," Greely said. His voice became pleading. "I don't know what's happened to your father, Your Highness, but your sister … she can't stay on the throne."

Not given that I'm the heir, Reginald thought, coldly. *And if she's holding Father prisoner …*

He didn't want to think about it. But there was no choice.

Chapter Five

"I'm sure there was supposed to be a *road* under here, Your Highness," Sergeant Ruthven said. He'd taken over command of Reginald's personal guard. "It appears to have vanished."

Reginald had to smile. "Either that or we're dreadfully lost," he said. "Did you get promoted to lieutenant when I wasn't looking?"

"I failed the exam to become an officer," Sergeant Ruthven said. "I managed to read a map properly."

"A terrible failure," Reginald agreed, dryly. He'd seen enough poorly-drawn maps, in the years since the entire world had fallen apart, to know that map-reading wasn't always a useful skill. "I think the road is buried under the mud."

He sighed as he surveyed the countryside. He'd already started laying down plans for a better road network – he'd need them, when the time came to move troops around the island – but nothing had been done when winter rolled in and put a stop to almost everything. The primitive road was lost beneath a sea of mud and water, the latter filling the ditches and flooding what remained of the fields. He didn't want to *think* about how much damage it was doing to the local farms, even though the locals were presumably used to it. A proper drainage system was also a must, clearly. He made a mental note to see to it as soon as possible.

The horse picked up speed as they headed west, the bodyguards fanning out around him in fear they might be attacked at any moment. Reginald thought they were worried over nothing, but he knew better than to reject their protection. There was no shortage of people on the Summer Isle who wanted to kill him, either because they wanted power for themselves or simple revenge for his invasion. They didn't recognise his kingdom's rightful claim to the

Summer Isle. The local aristocracy, those who'd survived, had pledged their loyalty, but Reginald didn't trust them any further than he could throw them. The island had been a snake pit for centuries. It had even claimed the life of both of its former monarchs.

They cantered past a thicket of trees, looking weak and pathetic in the sea of mud. It looked as if someone had been harvesting them for firewood, but the wood was so stained by water that he doubted the branches would burn well unless they were dried thoroughly first. He peered around, but saw no sign of any locals. They were probably hiding in the hills and forests to the north or south, keeping their distance from strange men on horseback. Reginald didn't really blame them. The locals had good reason to fear. His army was merely one of an endless series of invaders who killed men, raped women and devastated the surrounding fields. It would be different this time, Reginald was sure, but the locals wouldn't believe it. Not at first. Perhaps not ever.

"Your Highness!" Lord Greely sounded as if he was having the worst time of his life. "I thought you said this island had *potential*."

"It does," Reginald growled. He'd spent two days trying to drag more out of Lord Greely, only to discover that the idiot hadn't been paying attention to courtly politics until it was much too late to learn anything *useful*. His mother or grandmother would have been *far* more informative. Reginald had hated the elder women around court, but he couldn't deny their skill at keeping abreast of what was actually going on. "Just you wait until we have time to do some *proper* work."

A lump of ice formed in his chest as he contemplated the future. He'd assumed he'd have at least five years on the Summer Isle, long enough to teach the aristocracy the perils of defying him and convince the peasants that he had their best interests in mind. It wouldn't be that difficult. Cutting taxes and tithes in half alone would do wonders for public opinion, insofar as it mattered. But now ... he gritted his teeth as the wind picked up, blowing cold droplets of water into his face. He was going to have to leave someone behind to rule the island, someone who wouldn't have the prestige of being Crown Prince. That person wasn't going to have an easy time of it even if he didn't try to build a power base of his own.

He felt his head start to pound in frustration. No *wonder* his father had always looked like an angry bear with a toothache, even when he *wasn't* responding to Reginald's childish misdeeds. It wouldn't be *easy* to pick someone to serve as *de facto* regent, let alone entrust them with the power to keep the aristocracy in line. Anyone with the rank and title to do it would have ambitions of his own. It was human nature to want power. And to look down on someone who tried to wield power without rank and title.

The sergeant would make an excellent regent, he thought, sourly. *But everyone would be too busy defying him to actually do as they were told.*

The landscape changed slowly as they continued their ride west. The giant lakes of slushy water and mud gave way to sodden fields, half-covered in snow and ice. Winter might be losing its grip on the countryside, but it wasn't going without a fight. The hell of it was that he might have preferred to travel in the dead of winter, despite the cold. Muddy fields, impassable roads and invisible ditches, lying in wait for a careless rider, would pose all sorts of problems if he had to move the army east. He didn't dare ride too fast for fear of being thrown from the horse.

"So, what are you going to do?" Lord Greely rode up next to him, as if they were friends. "Your father ..."

"I know," Reginald growled. Perhaps he should have left Lord Greely behind. But there was no way he could be trusted, not in Racal's Bay. He would have been, technically, the senior nobleman. He could have caused all sorts of problems if he'd tried to assume command of the garrison. Reginald would have broken his nose, if not his neck, but by then the damage would have been done. "I'm still thinking about it."

He turned his gaze to the horizon, his eyes passing over a handful of burned-out shacks and barns. It looked as if they'd been destroyed during the invasion, although it was hard to tell. The local commoners built well – he'd give them that much – even though most of their farmhouses looked as if one gust of wind would blow them over. They probably didn't want to look too prosperous. A show of wealth attracted parasites – taxmen – like shit attracted flies. He hoped the owners were safe, wherever they were. Too many people had fled to the forest during the invasion and insurgency. It wouldn't be long before they took to banditry.

Not that there's much to steal, he thought, as they passed through the remains of what might have been a farm. It was hard to tell. The hints of seed corn – dead now – amongst the mud weren't enough to make him *sure*. *There's nothing worth taking for miles around.*

The weather grew worse as they kept moving, the wind growing colder despite his heavy clothing. He rubbed the horse's hair, hoping the beast would hold out until they reached the inn. The skies were growing darker, the gloomy clouds pregnant with snow. It was hard to believe, deep inside, that winter was truly gone. He wondered, as Sergeant Ruthven took them off the road, if they were going to die in the countryside. The cold was bleeding into his body and soul. It was hard to feel concerned about the prospect of freezing to death.

"There's a farm over there, Your Highness," Sergeant Ruthven said. "I think we'll have to stop there for the night."

"Yeah." Reginald ignored Lord Greely's snort of protest. Snow was already starting to fall lightly, drifting down from high above. It would get worse very quickly. "Take us there."

The farm looked surprisingly prosperous, he noted, as they cantered up to the small cluster of buildings. A single large farmhouse, surrounded by banked earth; a handful of barns, half-hidden within a thicket of trees. The fields themselves were covered by snow, but he could make out the boundary markers easily. He was surprised the farm had survived the warring armies of the last few years. They weren't *that* far from the road. Maybe they'd just been lucky.

Sure, his thoughts mocked him. *Or maybe there's something else at work.*

A man emerged from the farmhouse, wrapped in so many layers of clothes that – for a moment – Reginald honestly couldn't tell if he was male or female. It wasn't until he saw the beard that he was *sure*. He looked like most peasants, his face pockmarked by disease and deprivation. He blanched, then bowed low as he spotted the horsemen. Reginald was *sure* he wanted to tell the womenfolk to run and hide, if they hadn't set off already. The poor bastard had no way to know – and no reason to believe – that they came in peace.

"We beg shelter for the night," Sergeant Ruthven said. "A barn would …"

"A barn?" Lord Greely sounded astonished. "A barn? We're …"

"Be quiet," Reginald snapped.

Sergeant Ruthven talked briefly to the farmer, who – reluctantly – pointed the small party to the nearest barn. A handful of pigs sat inside, sleeping on straw or wallowing in mud. The stench made Reginald recoil – behind him, he heard Lord Greely choking – but he knew damn well they should be grateful for any shelter. Besides, he didn't want to force their way into the farmhouse itself. They were alone, miles from any support. The gods alone knew what might happen if they pressed the locals too far.

The gods alone, his thoughts mocked him. *That means something different now, doesn't it?*

"Tell them not to worry about feeding us," Reginald ordered, as he dismounted and marched the horse into the barn. "We have food with us for a few days."

"Yes, Your Highness," Sergeant Ruthven said.

"We could kill one of the pigs," Lord Greely said. "I fancy roast pork …"

"No," Reginald said. "And I mean it."

He told himself, again, that he'd slept in worse places as he found a comfortable position on the straw. There was no point in being prideful, not now. The barn was reassuringly solid, but he could hear the howling gale outside as they lit a fire to warm themselves. He wondered, again, just how the farm had managed to survive for so long. It didn't *look* like something that had been put together in a few months of backbreaking labour. It looked and felt like a farm that had been in the family for generations.

The door opened, slowly. A young girl entered, carrying a large bucket of water. She couldn't have been more than fourteen, wearing a headscarf and a dress so old and shapeless that it had probably been passed down from her grandmother. Her face was absolutely terrified. It struck Reginald that she might be the sacrifice, sent to the soldiers to serve them in the hopes they'd leave her younger siblings and cousins alone. He felt his stomach heave in disgust. He wanted to throw up. No one should have to do *that*, not even when law and order had broken down. Things would be different, when he was firmly in control. A naked virgin with a bag of corn in one hand and a bag of gold in the other would be able to walk from one end of the island to the other without being molested.

"Leave the water, then return to your father," he ordered, shortly. "You have nothing to fear."

The girl didn't look as though she believed him. She didn't look as though she *recognised* him either. Reginald knew he had an ego, but ... why would a random girl from the Summer Isle recognise her rightful prince? She'd probably never seen a picture of King Edwin or King Rufus, let alone Reginald himself. It struck him she'd probably never seen a picture of *anyone*. Her entire world was the farm and the surrounding fields. She'd probably never even been to the nearest town.

He frowned as the girl left, feeling an odd little prickle running down her spine. Something wasn't quite right. He rested a hand on the pommel of his sword as he looked around, trying to spot ... he wasn't sure *what* he was looking for. There didn't seem to be *anything* out of place, as far as he could tell. And yet ... the wind howled louder, gusts striking the wooden barn and shaking the building to its foundations. It felt as if someone was smashing the walls with a hammer. He glanced at Sergeant Ruthven, who looked as spooked as Reginald himself. There was no visible danger, but it was impossible to relax.

"Stay here," Reginald muttered.

He crossed to the door and peered outside. The blizzard was stronger, yet ... his eyes narrowed as he realised he could see all the way to the farmhouse and, beyond, the edge of the forest. Night was falling rapidly. In the semi-darkness, the forest looked alien, something utterly inhuman. The branches seemed to be moving of their own accord. He tensed, remembering what he'd seen during the war. Was the entire forest alive? Or was it being animated by one of the entities?

A flicker of movement caught his eye. The girl – he

thought it was the girl – was standing by the edge of the trees, her back to him. She was kneeling, holding up her arms in supplication. The trees seemed to bend towards her, the branches brushing the top of her head. She'd lost her headscarf somewhere, her hair blowing loosely in the wind. It crossed his mind that that was odd, amongst the peasants. A woman with uncovered hair was a noblewoman or a whore. But the girl seemed unbothered by something her male relatives would probably have regarded as nakedness. The sight chilled Reginald to the bone.

Lord Greely appeared beside him. "What's she doing?"

"I don't know," Reginald lied. He had a feeling he *did* know. The farm was under the protection of something far greater than a noble lord. He could see hints of *things* within the growing darkness. "But I think we should leave as soon as possible."

The girl rose, turning to look towards him. Reginald froze, torn between the desire to run and the urge to fight. An entity couldn't be good news, not here. But ... the girl merely nodded to him, as if they were equals, as she made her slow way back to the farmhouse. It wasn't just *her*, Reginald realised, numbly. The entire family paid homage to the entities. Or at least *one* entity. He glanced back at the forest, grimly aware they were being watched. It wasn't remotely safe. And yet ... he shook his head as he led the way back into the barn and closed the door. They were probably safe, as long as they left the family alone.

"I want two men on watch at all times, with cold iron in their hands," he ordered, shortly. It was hard to hide his nerves from experienced men. He had the feeling they saw right through his poise. "And everyone is to stay in the barn until we actually leave. No going out and chasing the local girls."

"Yes, Your Highness," Sergeant Ruthven said.

Reginald lay on the straw, trying to ignore the smell. He was going to stink tomorrow, but ... he was used to that. No one would notice, not while they were on the road. And ... he felt his thoughts start to wander as he closed his eyes. The entity outside seemed ... maybe not friendly, not towards him, but not particularly hostile either. He wasn't sure what made him feel that way. The entity itself, perhaps. And ...

He jumped as Lord Greely nudged him. "What are we going to do?"

"Get some sleep," Reginald snapped. It wasn't the answer his former friend wanted, but it would have to do. He wasn't going to pick a fight with an entity of unknown power if it could be avoided. Live and let live was the order of the day. It was simple prudence, driven by fear of the unknown. "We have a long ride tomorrow morning."

He frowned, inwardly. Who really ruled the island? Him? Or the entities? If the farmers were trading worship for protection ... who really ruled? Would the entity protect the farm when the taxmen came calling? It probably *had* protected the farm, since well before King Edwin's death. The farm shouldn't have survived, not so close to the road. *Something* had definitely protected it from taxmen and other parasites. The poor farmers should never have survived the wars.

And if they are protected by the entity, he asked himself, *who's really in charge?*

It wasn't a pleasant thought. Peasants – and serfs – weren't allowed to leave their farms. They did, of course. They wanted to serve masters who actually let them keep something for themselves, masters who treated them with a little dollop of human kindness ... Reginald shivered, remembering just how vile most of the island's lords had been. They'd treated runaways worse than murderers and rapists, because runaways struck at the very heart of their economy. No wonder the serfs were turning to the entities. Who knew what might be brewing under his feet, now Lord Havant and his followers were gone?

And who, he asked himself, *could blame them?*

He closed his eyes, but it was a long time before he got any sleep.

Chapter Six

"The prince," someone called, as the small cluster of horsemen came into view. "The prince!"

Isabella stood on the battlements and watched the horsemen canter towards the city, one of them unfurling a large banner to show that it was indeed Prince Reginald, Lord of the Summer Isle, returning to his city. The handful of people on the streets cheered loudly, although she rather suspected that most of the population had remained indoors. There were more guards and soldiers on the streets than civilians. She smiled to herself, then headed down to the courtyard as Reginald galloped through the streets and led his men through the castle gates. She owed it to him to be there when he arrived.

Particularly as few others will come onto the streets to greet him, she thought, making her way down the stairs. *The locals aren't convinced he'll stay in power.*

It wasn't a groundless concern, she knew. She'd spent some time over the last few months studying the island's history. The Summer Isle had had *hundreds* of kings, including a number who'd only reigned for a handful of days or weeks before being overthrown and replaced by successors who hadn't lasted much longer. Allenstown itself had changed hands so many times that the newcomers hadn't even managed to stamp their personalities on the city before being booted out by their replacements. Isabella knew Reginald was different, that he had a loyal army and a shortage of significant enemies, but still … she didn't blame the locals for being wary. Anyone who cheered too loudly might find himself bisected when the *next* monarch took power. It was a minor miracle that *anyone* was left alive in Allenstown.

Reginald had already cantered into the courtyard when she reached the bottom of the stairs, sliding off his horse and dropping to the ground. Isabella surprised herself by giving him a hug, despite the watching crowd. Reginald smelt terrible, but that was common. A man who'd spent three days on horseback could hardly be expected to smell *sweet*. She would have been surprised if he *didn't* stink.

"It's good to see you again," she said, feeling her heart sink. "We have to talk."

"We all have to talk," Reginald said. He glanced at Captain-General Gars. "We're having a meeting in two hours. Tell everyone."

"Yes, Your Highness." Captain-General Gars slammed a fist into his chest in salute. "It will be done."

Reginald looked ... *awkward*. "Lady Sorceress, this is Lord Greely, a ... *friend* of mine from home."

Isabella glanced at Lord Greely, decided she didn't like him on sight, then looked at Reginald. "From *home*?"

"I sailed the channel to bring you word," Lord Greely said. "All is not well ..."

"You can tell your story at the meeting," Reginald said, cutting him off. "Until then, my people will show you to your suite. Have a wash and wait."

Lord Greely looked as if he wanted to object, but didn't quite dare in front of a growing audience. Reginald didn't give him time to muster his courage. He took Isabella's hand and led her back up the stairs, back to his quarters. Isabella was torn between amusement and irritation. She could look after herself, and she had no intention of becoming a pretty bauble on his arm, but part of her enjoyed the attention. She knew it wasn't going to last. The looming shadow she'd seen over Andalusia boded ill.

A maid met them at the door. "Your Highness," she said, dropping a deep curtsy. "Do you wish a bath ...?"

"I do," Reginald said, gravely. "Just fill the tub with cold water."

Isabella felt a flicker of pity, mingled with grim amusement at the island's backwardness. Hot and cold running water was common on the mainland, but here ... the poor maid and her comrades would have to carry the water from the well to the prince's quarters. They were lucky they didn't have to heat the water first. She'd see to that, with a simple spell. She watched the maid scurry away, then followed Reginald into his chambers. The rooms were smaller than he might have expected, but she'd never heard him complain. There were worse places to be.

And he was nearly killed here, she reminded herself. *He knows better than to be completely alone.*

"There have been developments," she said, perching on the bed and trying not to watch as he undressed. His tunic was so thoroughly stained with mud that she doubted it could be cleaned magically, let alone washed without magic. "I saw a shadow hanging over Andalusia."

She outlined what had happened, as carefully as possible. Reginald listened, asking a handful of questions when she'd finished. He was good at teasing out information, at making her realise she knew more than she'd thought. Her memories had faded, but ... she allowed herself a moment of relief that she'd written everything down as quickly as possible. She didn't want to forget what she'd seen.

"And two ships made it through the storms," Reginald mused, when she'd finished. "One ship, with a messenger summoning me home; another ship, with an old acquaintance who warned me about trouble back home. And both of them want me to *go* home."

"I imagine one of them wants you to bring an army," Isabella said. A line of maids started coming in and out of the rooms, carrying buckets of cold water. "What do you intend to do?"

"If my father is in danger ..." Reginald swallowed, hard. "I can't *leave* him in danger."

Isabella kept her face carefully blank. *Her* father had been a nightmare, an abusive monster who'd seen his children – male and female alike – as nothing more than tools. He'd tried to steer her life, with everything from threats and beatings when she refused to obey, to the point where she'd had to cause a major scandal just to escape his plans for her life. She found it hard to understand Reginald's obvious love for his father ... she felt a twinge of guilt at wondering, deep inside, if part of him might be relieved if his father passed away. Reginald had spent his entire life training for a job, but it was a job he couldn't hold as long as his father remained alive.

And his father wasn't a monster, she reminded herself,

sharply. *Just because your father was a bastard doesn't mean that* all *fathers are bastards.*

"And Sofia too," Reginald added. "I can't leave her in danger."

Isabella stood and paced into the bathroom as the last of the maids departed. The bath looked silly – a wrought-iron tub, rather than the china baths she remembered from home – but it was large enough for two. She dipped her fingers in the icy water, muttering a spell she'd mastered when she was a little girl. The water grew warmer, steadily growing hotter and hotter until she yanked her fingers out. She was tempted, very tempted, to join him in the bath, but common decency forbade it. Someone would notice, damn it. Someone would notice and talk and it would cause problems …

"The water's warm," she said, sitting down just outside the bathroom. "If your sister is the regent …"

"She shouldn't be the regent." Reginald paced past her and clambered into the bathtub. She heard water splashing to the floor as he settled in the tub. "She's a girl."

Isabella scowled. "What does *that* have to do with it?"

"She can't wield power, not as regent or queen," Reginald said. "Her husband – when she gets married – will wield power in her name."

"Really, now." Isabella wasn't impressed. Maybe Reginald's father was a bastard after all. *Her* father had been a bastard to his sons, as well as his daughters. The thought there might be worse bastards out there was horrific. "I'm sure she's smart enough to run a kingdom."

"Not if people refuse to listen to her," Reginald said. "And a weakling on the throne is asking for civil war."

"Maybe she got married," Isabella said. "And her husband is the regent."

"I don't think so," Reginald said. She could hear splashing as he spoke. "Her husband would automatically become the third man in the kingdom – the second, after I became king. Father always said that I would have a say in who my sister married, as he would be either a close ally or a deadly threat. She wouldn't have been married without my consent."

Isabella rolled her eyes. "Because the gods forbid she might have opinions of her own."

Reginald said nothing for a long moment. "What she

wants doesn't matter. What *I* want doesn't matter. We both have to get married for the good of the realm, not for personal feelings."

"And there I was, thinking you were in love with me," Isabella said, more tartly than she'd intended. "Or were we lucky enough to have both a love match *and* a … good of the realm match?"

"Yes." Reginald sounded confident. "You have many advantages as well as my heart."

Isabella snorted, then changed the subject. "The entities have reached Andalusia."

"It looks that way," Reginald said. "Some things are different, but … it sounds very much like what happened here. Temples being smashed, newer ones being built … people ordered to worship … Isabella, Sofia was a religious fanatic *before*. What is she like now?"

Isabella remembered Queen Emetine and shuddered. "It certainly *sounds* as though your sister had cause to be resentful," she said. Queen Emetine had resented her position too, from what she'd said when she'd been a prisoner. She'd been easy prey for the entities when they'd manifested on the Summer Isle. "And now she has power."

"At a price," Reginald said. "She could tear the kingdom apart."

"Or unite it under her banner." Isabella smiled as she heard him squawk in protest. "I'm just pointing it out."

"Hah." Reginald didn't sound pleased. "You know as well as I do that she's not *just* a fanatic, not if the entities are involved. She's a fanatic with real power."

"And one with a cause," Isabella reminded him. "And she'll have no trouble finding supporters."

"I doubt it," Reginald said. "Half the lords in the kingdom will be pissed she didn't marry one of them. The rest will be plotting rebellion because they won't think she has the fire to keep them in line."

Isabella lifted her eyebrows, although she knew he couldn't see her. "They couldn't *all* marry her."

"No, but each and every one of them thought they *could* marry the king's daughter," Reginald said, sourly. "As long as Sofia remained unmarried, there was always a prospect the king might toss her to one of his lords in exchange for …

something. It's hard to think of *anything* that might be worth the reward, but … I'm sure *they* could think of something. And now … whoever marries her will be regent."

Isabella frowned. Reginald, like most men, seemed to underestimate women. It had never been a problem in the Golden City, where sorcerers and sorceresses had ruled their families with rods of iron, but outside … she'd had to fight, literally, to earn respect when she'd become a mercenary. Reginald, on the other hand, had grown up in a world where princesses were nothing more than bargaining chips, every important decision in their lives made for them by their male relatives. And lower-ranking women? Who cared what *they* thought, about anything? She was sure it was something that would come back to bite him, hard, if it hadn't already. It certainly *had* bitten King Edwin. His wife had effectively murdered him.

"If she has an entity behind her, she's going to be more than any mere lord could handle," Isabella thought. They'd learnt enough to make life difficult for the entities, but they were still awesomely dangerous. The aristocrats on the mainland would be fighting blind. "And even without an entity, she might be able to take control of the king's armies."

"How?" Reginald clambered out the tub. "She can't give orders to the men."

"She can find someone else to give orders in her name," Isabella said. Sir Robin, her former commander, had planned to marry a wealthy heiress, once upon a time. He would have commanded her guards and protected her … she shook her head. The world had been much simpler before the entities had started manifesting. "A mercenary, perhaps. Someone who would be loyal to her, if only because he'd have nothing else."

"She wouldn't lower herself," Reginald said. "She wouldn't marry anyone less than a …"

"Maybe she wants someone who will do as he's told," Isabella said, dryly. "Or someone who has to stay with her, because without her he's nothing."

Reginald stalked back into the chamber, a towel wrapped around his waist. Isabella looked, despite herself. Reginald was fit and healthy, as far as she could tell, but his back was covered in scars. She felt a sudden urge to stand and trace them with her fingers, to enjoy the proof that he was more than just a glorified pretty boy. No one could deny that Reginald had nerve, not when he constantly put himself in the midst of battle. She'd met plenty of noblemen who were cowards. Reginald wasn't one of them.

"I have to do everything in my power to save my sister," Reginald said. He dropped the towel on the floor and hastily donned a set of underclothes, followed by trousers and a shirt. "And if that means heading back home with an army ..."

"If you go without an army, you'll be killed in a heartbeat." Isabella had no doubt of it. If the legitimate heir returned home, the usurper would have to kill him or risk civil war. The hell of it was that the nobility might *prefer* Sofia as their ruler, if they saw her as weak and foolish. A strong king was one who could keep the nobility in line. "I'm sure your father will understand."

Reginald shot her a sidelong glance. "What if he's dead?"

"You have to hope for the best," Isabella said. She felt her heart clench. Ritual magic was all about symbolism. If someone could craft wonders, or nightmares, with virgin's blood ... what could one do with a *king's* blood? "As long as the king is alive, or believed to be alive, the nobility won't be sure what to do. They certainly won't be sure who's in charge."

"I suppose." Reginald didn't sound convinced. "Sofia will need time to build a power base ..."

His voice trailed off. Isabella understood. Reginald didn't really believe that his sister *could* have taken power, not in her own right. And he might be right, if the entities were involved. Sofia might be a puppet, her strings pulled by something lurking in the godly realm. And yet ... it was going to cripple him, if he couldn't wrap his head around the fact his sister might be his enemy. He'd hesitate, when the time came to strike the killing blow. Isabella felt a flicker of pity, mingled with the grim awareness that hesitation might be fatal. The entities were just too powerful to be taken lightly.

And they can do things no sorcerer can do, she mused. Sofia wasn't a sorceress, but ... the entities could have given her power. *A few thunderbolts and the new regime will be accepted without resistance.*

She gritted her teeth. "What were you planning to tell them about me?"

Reginald blinked, taken aback by the sudden change in subject. "What do you mean?"

"When you told the aristocracy you were going to marry me," Isabella said. "What were you going to tell them?"

"The truth," Reginald said. "That you're highly qualified to be queen. That you have strong blood ties to the Golden City. That you *don't* have blood ties to the aristocracy *here*, which means that no one has been spited ... well, that they've *all* been spited, but spited equally. None of *them* would become my father-in-law, so ..."

"I get the point," Isabella said. "It won't change the balance of power."

"Not really." Reginald shrugged as he buckled his sword to his belt. "I wish things were different ..."

Isabella snorted. "You wish you were a commoner, rather than a prince?"

Reginald had the grace to look embarrassed. "Father told me that being king was like being in prison, only with better food. I thought he was talking nonsense. But ... if you're king and you want to actually stay on the throne ... yes, you *are* a prisoner. And the only person who can make you do your chores" – he smiled, rather wanly – "is yourself. You don't get the prison guards unless you get booted off the throne and straight to the executioner's block."

"True, I suppose." Isabella stood, brushing down her trousers. "How do you intend to cross the channel?"

"I don't know," Reginald said. "That's something we're going to have to discuss."

And hope we can come up with an answer, Isabella said.

There was a knock on the door. "Your Highness?"

Reginald opened the door. "Yes?"

"Your officers are waiting for you," a messenger said. "I ..."

"Good." Reginald cut him off, effortlessly. "I'm on my way."

He glanced at Isabella. "Are you coming?"

"I wouldn't miss it for the world," Isabella said. She held out her arm. "Shall we go?"

Reginald gave her a quick kiss. Isabella felt her body respond, reminding her that it had been too long. The cold days and colder nights had made her want someone in her bed … she kissed him back, just long enough to promise the world when they had time and privacy. He met her eyes, returning the promise. His hands twitched towards her, then stopped. He didn't have time for anything, save for his duty. And he *was* a dutiful man.

His voice was thick, as if he didn't believe what he was saying. "Yes. I think we should."

Chapter Seven

Reginald had rebelled against protocol as a young man, although – as he'd grown older – he'd come to appreciate protocol's role in keeping everyone in their place. His father had made it clear that he was the second man in the kingdom – and he would be the first, when he took the throne. There was no one, not even his wife, who would *ever* be his equal ... and he would only ever have one superior, as long as his father was alive. He understood the value of protocol and yet ... he also understood its limits. The socially inferior would hesitate to question their superiors even when their superiors were clearly in the wrong.

He stepped into the room, Isabella on his arm. The meeting room wasn't *much* – a long wooden table, a cluster of wooden chairs, a roaring fire in the grate – but it was usable, big enough to accommodate his closest friends, supporters and allies without being *dauntingly* large. Or, for that matter, large enough to force him to invite others who might not be as supportive as he wished. His father had warned him, more than once, that he would spend most of his life surrounded by people who wanted to use him, from social climbers to fairweather friends and knock-kneed allies who'd turn their coat at the merest hint of weakness. Here, at least, he knew most of his allies intimately. Earl Oxley and Isabella herself were the only ones he hadn't known for years.

"Be seated," he ordered, as they rose. "We have much to cover."

He showed Isabella to her seat, then took the throne-line chair at the end of the table. He'd never met anyone quite like her before, someone he could trust to tell him the truth – as she saw it – rather than a flattering lie. And she had good connections as well as a ... he pushed the thought aside, sharply. He didn't dare show weakness, not here. Earl

Oxley was a potential enemy, if he thought he saw weakness. The man had to have realised, by now, that he would never enjoy the freedoms he'd had under King Edwin unless *something* happened to Reginald. Reginald would be surprised if the man *wasn't* plotting. He was the kind of person to whom plots came as easily as breathing.

"I received two messengers from home four days ago," he said, once everyone had returned to their seats. He ran through a brief outline of what had happened. "Things are not well in Andalusia."

And Sir Handel was clearly touched by the entities, he added, silently. *The entire kingdom is in serious danger.*

"My father is apparently being held prisoner," he continued. "And the entities appear to be ... *influencing* ... my sister."

He nodded to Lord Greely. "If you would tell them what you told me ...?"

"Yes, Your Highness," Lord Greely said. "I was in my estate, minding my own business, when ..."

Reginald listened with half an ear, preferring to watch his followers and assess their reactions to Lord Greely's story. They'd all *seen* the entities and their twisted servants, directly or indirectly; they'd all watched, helplessly, as men had been killed by forces beyond their comprehension. A story that would have been fantastical only a year ago was now all too easy to believe. Andalusia was falling into darkness. They believed him. The only question was what they should – or could – do about it.

"And so we tried to come here, to you," Lord Greely finished. "I appear to have been the only one who made it."

"That's not surprising." Admiral Tanoan looked grim. "The channel isn't an easy crossing at the best of times. Crossing in the midst of a storm ..."

Reginald nodded, feeling a twinge of disquiet. "We count ourselves lucky that you reached us," he said, sincerely. Lord Greely was an ass, but he might have saved Reginald's life. "If the others should happen to make it, we will – of course – welcome them too."

Lord Greely bowed. "Of course, Your Highness."

"But you have orders to return home," Academic Milhous said. "Should you not obey?"

Reginald allowed himself a moment of relief. *Someone* had been practically *certain* to ask that question … and, thankfully, it had been a man with little support and no real power base. It would have been a great deal harder to circumvent objections from the Captain-Generals or the Admiral. The question was a reasonable one – he admitted that, at least to himself – and a harder one to answer than he would have wished …

"Sir Handel is not in his right mind," Reginald said, simply. "And I have grave reasons to doubt that my father sent the message. Amongst other things" – he shot Academic Milhous a look that killed a renewed objection before it could be born – "the text lacked certain codewords we use to confirm both the sender and the validity of the message. I am certain" – he allowed his voice to harden – "that my father did not send the message."

He paused. "Should I be in error, the mistake will be mine and mine alone."

There was a long pause. No one spoke.

Reginald relaxed, slightly. He'd feared more objections. Going back with an army at their back could easily be defined as treason, particularly if they *lost*. King Romulus would not be happy, even if they discovered the whole thing had been a ghastly mistake and disbanded the army as soon as they arrived. And there were limits to how much punishment the king could pour on his only son. Reginald wasn't a child any longer. Humiliating him would only make it harder for him to take the throne without a fight.

And so my followers would serve as my whipping boys, he thought, grimly. *And if that happens …*

He dismissed the thought and leaned forward. "Captain-General Gars. How many men can we muster in a hurry?"

Captain-General Gars didn't need to think before answering. "We can muster upwards of six thousand men within a week, Your Highness, if we muster them at Allenstown. There's another five hundred at Racal's Bay. The remainder were parcelled out to garrison various points of interest – gathering them will take around three weeks to a month."

"And then we'll be leaving large parts of the island without a garrison," Isabella said, quietly.

"The islanders are loyal," Earl Oxley insisted. "They welcomed their rightful king."

Kindly remove your tongue from my ass, Reginald thought, coldly. He was pretty sure Earl Oxley was flattering him, presumably hoping that Reginald would leave him as regent or pull out the entire army. *And if I leave you at my back, you'll stick a knife in me.*

"We came with a much larger army," Admiral Tanoan protested. "Where did they go?"

"Some are dead," Gars countered. "Some claimed their packets of land as they left the army. And some just chose to desert."

"We *are* training new recruits," Captain-General Stuart said. The Master of Horse looked cross. He hadn't really wanted the job. "If we speed up their training, Your Highness, we might be able to muster another two to three thousand men."

"All of whom will be chopped to ribbons by the Royal Army," Gars objected. "They're nowhere near ready to depart."

"And not all of them will *want* to leave the island," Earl Oxley said. "King Edwin had the greatest difficulty in convincing his soldiers to serve outside their homelands, let alone the island itself."

Reginald nodded, slowly. King Edwin had been a weak king, lacking the stomach to bang heads together until his noblemen accepted his rule, but ... he hadn't had the resources Reginald and his father took for granted. An army that wouldn't leave its barracks was useless, in the long run; a king who couldn't overawe his nobility was a king who had no power, outside his city. And perhaps none inside it too. An army was a double-edged sword. A king who lost control could easily lose his head.

"Gars, assemble five thousand men," he said. It would pose a logistics challenge, but – thankfully – their supplies should hold out till spring. "Stuart, ask for volunteers amongst the new recruits. Offer extra bounties and suchlike to men who cross the channel with us. The remainder of the force will be folded into the island garrison. They can hold the line here while we're gone."

"Yes, Your Highness," Gars said.

"I can raise additional troops," Earl Oxley offered. "And reinforce the garrisons ..."

"Perhaps you could," Reginald said. It was hard to hide his irritation. On the surface, the offer looked *very* reasonable. But it would put too much power into the earl's hands. "You will, of course, remain here. My regent will need your advice."

A flash of anger, quickly hidden, crossed Earl Oxley's face. He couldn't refuse, not when Reginald had made a *very* reasonable request ... a request he *knew* came with a sting in the tail. The earl couldn't cause trouble if he was right under the regent's nose, a hostage for his family's good behaviour ... Reginald made a mental note to ensure his commanders had clear orders detailing what they were to do when – if – the earl rebelled. Devastating his lands from one end to the other would be harsh, but it would keep him from causing trouble in the long run.

He turned his gaze to Admiral Tanoan. "How many ships can you put to sea?"

Admiral Tanoan looked deeply worried. "Your Highness ... we have around four hundred ships in various protected anchorages," he said. "The remainder of the fleet was sent home once we had a secure lodgement. However, getting them concentrated at one point will be difficult and ... and I cannot guarantee crossing the channel safely. We might lose the entire fleet to the storm."

Reginald gritted his teeth. The admiral was right. There was no way he *could* guarantee a safe crossing. Hell, there was no way he could guarantee that Reginald himself would survive the crossing. And if he died ...

We could lose everything on a single throw of the dice, he thought, sourly. *And there would be a mutiny if I tried to force soldiers onto the ships and sailors to sea.*

"We *could* wait for spring," Lord Greely suggested.

"It *is* spring," Gars growled.

"Crossing the channel has never been *safe*," Stuart pointed out. "We can do it. We did it once already ..."

"Yes, during summer," Admiral Tanoan insisted. "Realistically, we should wait at least two months for the storm to die down."

Which it might not, Reginald thought. He'd seen the faces

in the storm. There was nothing *natural* about it. Lord Havant had done something – Reginald dreaded to think *what* – and the effects had lingered, even after the man's death. *And if we wait two months, what will happen to the kingdom?*

He kept his face under tight control. It was hard to believe that Sofia had *really* taken the regency. His little sister was … well, his little *sister*. It was far more likely that something else had happened, from her being married without his consent to Lord Greely simply being mistaken. And yet, he knew his sister had been deeply religious. What would she have done if she'd encountered the entities? And …

Reginald looked down at his hands. He'd been a prisoner of his rank and station for his entire life, but … he'd been free, compared to his sisters. They'd been prisoners too, without the rewards he'd enjoyed. Their lives had been so tightly constrained that … he felt his heart twist at the thought. He'd never really realised that they might have resented their treatment, that … they might have sought a way to rebel. And the entities had provided it.

I'm sorry, he thought. *Things will be better …*

He looked up. "Prepare your plans, Admiral," he ordered. "We'll cross the channel when we come to it."

"Yes, Your Highness." Admiral Tanoan *really* didn't sound pleased. "I'd suggest that we refrain from concentrating the ships at Racal's Bay. It will limit the time they spend on the open waters."

"I trust your judgement," Reginald said.

"Magic," Gars said, suddenly. He looked at Isabella. "Can you cast a spell to get us across the waters?"

"No," Isabella said. "Not in the sense you mean, at least. The waves are just too strong."

And in what sense do you *mean*? Reginald wanted to ask, but he knew it would have to wait until they were alone. *Do you have something up your sleeve?*

He looked around the table, silently assessing his followers. It wasn't easy to choose a regent. Isabella, Gars and Stuart needed to accompany him … Sergeant Ruthven would have been ideal, but without a title he would be easily outshone by the aristocrats. Earl Oxley would have been perfect if Reginald dared trust him. It was almost a shame he couldn't leave Isabella behind. Her magic would have made her the equal of any aristocrat.

"Captain-General Jones, you will serve as my regent," Reginald said. The Master of Foot was probably the best choice, although he wasn't the best soldier. Given a skilled subordinate, he could keep the aristocracy in line until Reginald returned. "We'll discuss specific orders later, but your priority will be keeping the island under control, building better roads and generally relaxing the laws on land ownership."

He could practically *feel* Earl Oxley's displeasure, but ignored it. "In the long run, I hope to return and resume developing the island into a modern nation. The Summer Isle has great potential. We can and we will work to develop it."

And if we slaughter the aristocrats, he added in the privacy of his own mind, *it will be a very good start.*

Captain-General Jones looked astonished. "Your Highness ..."

"It isn't a job for a soldier," Reginald assured him. "It requires an expert in logistics."

"Thank you, Your Highness." Captain-General Jones managed to bow, even though he was sitting down. "I won't fail you."

Reginald nodded. Jones was clever enough to avoid the obvious mistakes, high-ranking enough to keep his subordinates from objecting to serving under him and calculating enough to refrain from starting a war if he felt insulted. Not perfect, but ... there was no such thing as a perfect choice for *anything*. Reginald would have preferred to remain himself, learning the ropes for the day he succeeded his father. But that was no longer an option.

"Earl Oxley will advise you," Reginald said. "I'll assign the rest of your subordinates later."

"Yes, Your Highness," Jones said.

Reginald allowed himself a tight smile, then looked around the table. "We all saw the entities," he said. "We know just how dangerous they can be. And we know they're still out there, waiting. We don't know what they want, but ... we know they want it.

"And now they've infested our homeland."

He paused, allowing his words to sink in. "I would like to believe that this is all nothing, a case of hysterical overreaction. I would like to believe that our messenger" – he nodded to Lord Greely – "was mistaken. But I cannot. Our homeland is facing the gravest challenge since the Empire collapsed, a few short years ago. And here we are, stuck on the far side of the channel, the most dangerous body of water for hundreds of miles around. They think there's nothing we can do.

"But they're wrong. We may be the only people who *can* save our homeland.

"We're going to do it. We're going to find a way to cross the channel. We're going to get our army back home and we're going to drive out those monsters, free my father and reset the world. This is our test. We're going to do it. I expect each and every one of you – and each and every one of your subordinates – to do everything in your power to make it work. Our kingdom is at risk. Our parents, our wives, our children … if we fail, they will become nothing more than pawns in the hands of horrific monsters. We must not fail.

"We will not fail."

He lowered his voice. "You have your orders. Dismissed."

The room emptied rapidly, men heading for the doors as quickly as they could without running. Reginald allowed himself a tight smile, grimly aware that they were driven more by his plans for the regency than his inspirational speechmaking. He'd never been *that* good at speaking to a crowd, even though he was the Crown Prince. His father had ordered him to have his speeches written by professional writers …

"Your Highness." Lord Greely had remained seated. So had Isabella. "I would like to request permission to remain behind."

"Oh, you would, would you?" Reginald's voice was almost a snarl. "And you think I'd *let* you remain behind?"

He calmed himself with an effort. He really *didn't* want Lord Greely remaining behind. The man was foolish enough to try to subvert Captain-General Jones, which meant he'd either take the regency for himself or start a minor civil war. And then Earl Oxley would swoop in and pick up the pieces … Oxley was probably planning it already. Greely wore his weaknesses on his sleeve. A man like Oxley would have no trouble taking advantage of him.

"I crossed the waters once already," Lord Greely protested. "I …"

"But I need you," Reginald said. It wasn't – quite – a lie. Greely presumably had contacts on the mainland, people who'd been preparing to resist the coup. "And without you, the invasion might fail."

He clapped Lord Greely on his shoulder. "You did it once already," he said. "I'm sure it holds no terrors for you."

And that, he knew, was a flat-out lie.

Chapter Eight

Isabella had been told, back when her father had been trying to convince some poor family to arrange a match between her and their son, who had no idea what he was getting into, that it was a bad idea to contradict one's partner in public. It was important to show a united front to the world, rather than suggesting weakness by disagreeing openly. And yet, she'd never really bought into it until she'd become a mercenary. It was terrifyingly easy for an enemy to exploit weaknesses, even if expressing disagreement openly *didn't* lead to someone being summarily fired. It grated on her, but she knew she couldn't disagree with Reginald in public. She had to wait until they returned to the prince's quarters to discuss her concerns with him.

"It isn't going to be *easy* to get across the waters," she said, once they were alone. Someone would probably talk, but … she found it hard to care. She had more important concerns right now. "If we set sail now …"

"I know." Reginald took off his sword and placed it beside the bed. "But we can't give the entities time to get settled. If they take over the entire kingdom, there might be no stopping them."

Isabella nodded, stiffly. The Empire was gone. There was no one *else* who could challenge the entities, not now. The neighbouring kingdoms might not realise that something had gone badly wrong in Andalusia, something far worse than a simple coup or transfer of power, until it was far too late. She'd sent a message to her brother, in the Golden City, but she had no way to know if he'd received it. And even if he had, what could he do? The days when the Golden City commanded and everyone else obeyed were long gone.

Reginald sat down on the bed, his eyes hard. "The Admiral was fairly clear on the dangers," he said, dryly. "Is there anything *you* can do about it?"

"There are limits to the number of protective wards I can cast," Isabella said. In the old days, there had been a handful of charmed ships that had sailed in all weathers. Now … she had no idea what had happened to the ships or their crews. "And even if I did, they wouldn't last …"

"I didn't mean with your magic … your *normal* magic," Reginald said. "I meant with the rituals you're learning."

Isabella felt cold, her stomach turning to ice. She should have expected it. Reginald was a practical man – and he *wasn't* a magician. He had no true concept of how dangerous *normal* magic could be, not in any real sense. Sure, a man could be turned into a slug and squashed beneath her heel … but that was the least of it. There were dangers that no one outside the senior magicians realised, let alone comprehended. And ritual magic – godly magic – might well be worse. The more she studied it, the more she feared she would never truly understand it.

"I don't know," she temporised. It was possible, perhaps. And, once she'd had the thought, she found it impossible to let it go. "I'd have to consult with *her*."

She remembered the shadow she'd seen looming over Andalusia and shivered. She had never been an Inquisitor – she'd managed to escape before taking her final oaths – but she knew her duty. In truth, she'd never objected to the *duty*. If something was rotten in the kingdom, it had to be rooted out before it could spread. Havant had caused a *lot* of damage to the Summer Isle. She dreaded to think what another entity could do in Andalusia. The mainland kingdom was far wealthier than the Summer Isle.

"Do it." Reginald spoke like a man who expected to be obeyed. "Whatever the risk, we will bear it."

"Really?" Isabella met his gaze, evenly. "Do you have *any* awareness of the risk?"

A chain of odd emotions crossed his face, coming and going too quickly for her to recognise them. She hid her amusement with an effort. She was no courtly lady, willing to bend the knee to her husband in exchange for rank and title, she was no slattern willing to sleep with him in exchange for a handful of coins. If they were going to have a genuine marriage, he was going to have to get used to her arguing with him. He wasn't a fool. He should be smart enough to realise that having *someone* willing to give him unvarnished opinions would work out well for him, in the long run. But some men were prideful asses.

Reginald smiled, grimly. "Do *you* have any awareness of the dangers of leaving the entities unmolested?"

Isabella conceded the point with a nod. "You're worried about your sister?"

"And everyone else," Reginald said. "My father ... if he's truly being held prisoner, he could be killed at any moment. And then ... I'm not sure what will happen then."

"Things have changed," Isabella agreed. "What do you *think* will happen?"

Reginald looked down at his hands, scarred from years of hard fighting. "I don't know. Legally, I would become king the moment my father died. But if everyone thinks I'm dead, that the entire army was wiped out ... I don't know. Sofia and my younger sisters weren't in the line of succession. I've got a couple of cousins, male cousins, who have equal claims to the throne. Ten years ago, the Golden City would have ruled on just who took the throne. Now ... they'd probably try to settle the issue through civil war. Or try to marry one of my sisters through force."

He shook his head. "But if the entities are in power instead, I don't know what will happen. Sofia has no legal grounds to power, no legitimate claim to the throne, but if she has an army and the entities are backing her ..."

"Then she can do whatever she likes." Isabella felt a twinge of pity for the princess, as pampered as she would probably have been before the entities arrived. "As long as she keeps them happy ..."

"Perhaps." Reginald shivered. "I never *liked* Sir Handel. He was one of my father's gobshites, one of the wretched little lickspittles I intended to banish from court when I took the throne. And yet ... whatever they did to him, he isn't completely *himself* any longer. I think something was wearing his face."

Isabella tensed. "What did you *do* with him?"

"I put him in the ironhold," Reginald said. "It should constrain him ..."

Isabella nodded. One thing they'd learnt about the entities was that they had an aversion to cold iron. It seemed to impede them. It was pretty much the only thing that could *kill* them – and the creatures they'd brought in their wake. She didn't know why – Mother Lembu had refused to discuss it – but she'd made sure everyone knew how to use it. She'd even gone to the trouble of charming a dozen blades in the hopes of sneaking one close enough to the entities to use it.

"I'll have a look at him, when we get to Racal's Bay." Isabella took a breath. "If you want me to call her, and ask her, I will."

"I can ask her too, as king and prince," Reginald said. "I just …"

He looked up at her, his eyes pleading. "If they keep my father alive, everyone outside their circle won't know what's *really* going on. They'll be reluctant to commit themselves for fear of striking against their lawful monarch. But … sooner or later, they'll have to remove him anyway. They can't take the risk of him slipping out of their control."

"And raising an army to take back his kingdom," Isabella finished. She had no doubt of it. If one struck at a king, one must make certain to *kill* him. And yet … she sighed. These days, what *was* legitimate authority? It was hard to say. "We'll get there in time."

She frowned as a thought struck her. Mother Lembu had taught her, time and time again, that symbolism *mattered* to ritual magic. And if that was true, what could one do with the blood of a king? A *real* king? She wasn't sure she wanted to know. She'd certainly never been taught anything about it when she'd been at school, when blood-based potions had been discussed. Hell, they'd been discouraged from studying such potions unless they intended to become druids.

"I can ask her too," Reginald repeated. "Do you think she'd listen to me?"

"Let me ask first," Isabella said. She knew enough to be cautious. "I'm neither king nor prince. I can't bind you or anyone else to anything."

Reginald lifted his eyebrows. "And you think I can?"

"You're the prince, and you will be king," Isabella pointed out. "Are you not allowed to make deals on behalf of your kingdom?"

"True." Reginald looked pensive. "What do you think she might want? From me?"

"It would probably not be a good idea to ask," Isabella said. If Reginald bargained with the entities, would they hold his whole kingdom to account? It seemed impossible, but they'd already done far too many impossible things. "You could accidentally give them *everything*."

She sat down facing him, remembering the stories she'd heard from her tutors. Most of them had focused around foolish wizards who'd tried to use magic to solve all their problems, casting spells that would grant their every wish. She'd always thought the tales were nothing more than stories – they talked about magics that simply didn't exist – but now, in hindsight, she wondered if there was a grain of truth behind the lies. A wizard foolish enough to cast such spells might get what he wanted, yet … it might not make him happy. The dangers were simply too great.

"We have to be careful," she said, warningly. "And we dare not make mistakes."

"No." Reginald rubbed his hands together. "We don't even know the rules. Not here."

"The rules have been in flux ever since the Golden City fell." Isabella felt an odd little pang. She hadn't liked the Golden City, and she'd been happy to leave, but … it had been her home, once upon a time. Would it have been different, she asked herself, if she'd been there? If she'd added her weight to the defenders? Or would she have simply added another name to the casualty lists? "Things aren't what they used to be."

"Better or worse?" Reginald smiled, humourlessly. "I wouldn't have met *you* if the Golden City hadn't fallen."

Isabella chuckled. "You never know."

"I know," Reginald said. "I wouldn't have been able to raise an army five years ago. Now … I am more than just a figurehead on a gold-coloured throne."

"Yeah." Isabella affected a manner she *knew* would infuriate her father. "And, in the meantime, millions upon millions of people are suffering."

Reginald didn't look infuriated. "We can make things better for them …"

"Hah." Isabella felt a wave of despondency, mixed with bitter helplessness. "There's no way to repair the damage to society."

She looked down at her hands, feeling guilty. Five years ago, she'd been a wandering mercenary and *he'd* been a figurehead prince, biding his time until he could succeed his father as figurehead king. He would have had no real authority, no power to do *anything* with his life but look good on the throne ... instead, the Golden City had fallen and chaos had broken loose everywhere. Reginald's father had established himself as a local monarch, wielding real power for the first time in his life, but it had come at a price. The continent had been devastated. Millions of people had been killed, or raped, or enslaved, or ... everything they'd known, everything they'd taken for granted, had been shattered overnight. She remembered riding through burned-out villages and shuddered. It didn't matter who'd killed the villagers and burned their homes: invading armies, retreating armies, tax farmers, bandits ... or whatever. All that mattered was that they'd been killed.

And the people who killed them probably didn't even know their names, Isabella thought, grimly. She'd been on campaign. She'd seen hundreds of civilians caught in the gears and ground to bloody dust. *They were just in the way.*

Reginald reached out and rested a hand on her shoulder. "We may not be able to rebuild the empire," he said. "But we can build something new in its place."

Isabella nodded, shortly. "Yeah ..."

She found it hard to maintain any sense of optimism. The world had changed. Reginald and his father meant well, but ... their people had already paid a high price for their empire-building. It would get worse, as the successor states shook themselves down and launched wars in hopes of reuniting the empire under their rule. Or when the aristocrats started fighting amongst themselves, battling to bring down the monarchs or secure their positions against the peasants. She'd never really understood how much the Golden City had done to keep the peace until it was gone. Now ...

"We'll get over the channel and save the day," Reginald said. He shot her a boyish smile that made him look a decade younger. "And then we can unite the Summer Isle with Andalusia."

Isabella cleared her throat, putting her doubts aside. "Is it wise to leave Oxley here?"

Reginald didn't scold her for not saying the earl's title. Instead, he looked pensive. She knew him well enough to know that meant he had doubts of his own. Earl Oxley couldn't be trusted, if Reginald turned his back. He wasn't loyal to Reginald personally. And, now the other two earls and the king himself were gone, he was the most powerful aristocrat on the Summer Isle. Sure, there were others. But none of them enjoyed his power or prestige.

"It's a calculated risk," Reginald said. There was little real conviction in his tone. "I need someone here who knows the island, someone who can guide Jones through the snake pit … someone who is dependent on me for power."

"That's not Oxley," Isabella pointed out. "His power comes from his lands and lords, not you."

"Unfortunately true." Reginald smiled, humourlessly. "And there aren't many women I can trust to advise Jones."

Isabella shot him a sharp look, but she took his point. Queen Emetine, King Edwin's murderous wife, was missing. Isabella was sure she wasn't *dead*. Earl Oxley's daughters – the bastard had tried to offer one or both of them to Reginald – couldn't be trusted. The other high-ranking women on the island were either too young, married already or simply untrustworthy. Reginald might have planned to give his followers heiresses who'd bring lands and power with their names, but … he had a shortage of candidates. There simply weren't any who could be safely married to Jones.

"You *could* look at Oxley's daughters," she mused. "If *I* rebelled against my father …"

"You had magic," Reginald pointed out. "And who would trust a daughter who rebelled against her father?"

Isabella bit off the obvious rejoinder. "You know what I mean," she said. "One or both of his daughters might prefer to give her loyalty to a half-decent husband than a bastard father."

"Perhaps," Reginald said. If he spotted the irony, he didn't show it. "But can I take the chance?"

"Probably not," Isabella conceded. "Have you thought of looking amongst the merchant class?"

Reginald snorted. "Do you think *Jones* would be happy?"

Isabella shook her head, reluctantly. Aristocrats only married *other* aristocrats. It was stupid – everyone knew that mixing bloodlines produced stronger magicians – but they did it anyway. Jones wanted – needed – a wife who was, at the very least, his social equal. There wasn't enough money on the Summer Isle to make up for a wife whose family had crawled out of the gutter only a generation or two ago. It was stupid – Isabella knew up and coming merchants were often smarter than aristocrats – but it was the way of things. Jones would be offended beyond words if Reginald insulted him with anything less than a high-born lady.

And then he'd start plotting trouble too, Isabella thought. *And that's the last thing we need.*

"I think we should take Oxley with us, perhaps as titular commander of the islander contingent," she said. It was something she definitely couldn't have said in public. "He can't cause trouble on the mainland."

"I admire your optimism," Reginald said. There was no real heat in his voice. "I'm sure he can make things *really* difficult for me."

"He'll be a long way from his power base," Isabella countered. It was easy to tell that he wasn't pleased with his decision either. "And whoever rules his lands won't be able to cause trouble *here*."

"I *really* admire your optimism." Reginald grinned. "We'll take him with us. You want to give him the bad news?"

"No." Isabella stood. "I have to start figuring out how to approach *her*."

Reginald lifted an eyebrow. "You don't want to stay the night?"

"Not yet." Isabella felt her cheeks heat. She was tempted, but ... "People will talk."

She sighed, inwardly. Double standards. Double standards, everywhere. Five years ago, she could have taken whoever she liked to her bed and ... she shook her head. She'd spent most of her adult life choosing partners she *knew* would horrify her father, even though the bastard had died long before the Golden City. Now ... now she had to be a little more careful. It wasn't just *her* at stake any longer.

The whole kingdom is at stake, she thought, as she headed for the door. *No, the whole world is at stake. And a single mistake could tear everything down.*

Chapter Nine

Well, Isabella thought. *Here goes nothing.*

She stood in the centre of the shack, trying not to feel as if she were about to humiliate herself. She hadn't felt so … ashamed of herself since she'd been forced to beg her father for a simple favour, a simple favour he refused to grant until she shaped up and became, at least for a few moments, his ideal daughter. It had felt, back then, as though he'd forced her to grovel in the mud. She felt the same way now.

Isabella took a long breath, then closed her eyes and centred her thoughts as best she could. Mother Lembu's face drifted in front of her mind's eye. It was hard to keep focused on the entity's appearance as she opened her eyes, walked four paces to the table and poured two mugs of fresh water, but somehow she managed it. Turning, she walked back to the door and held it open for ten heartbeats. There was no sense of anything, as far as she could tell, but when she turned around Mother Lembu was standing behind her. Isabella nearly jumped out of her skin. The entity was just … *there*.

She was the maiden this time, a young lady permanently poised between girlhood and womanhood. Isabella felt a surge of protectiveness, mingled with a hint of jealousy. She wasn't sure where that had come from, but it was there. The maiden was innocent, so innocent that it was hard to see her as anything *other* than a carefree young girl. She had nothing to fear, nothing to suggest that her life might be marred by the slightest trouble. And yet, the more Isabella looked, the stranger the maiden appeared. There was something about her appearance that was impossible to pin down. Her hair, her clothes … even her *face* were indistinct.

"I bid thee welcome," Isabella managed. "Eat and drink, in my house."

"I thank you." The maiden giggled. "It has been a long

time since you summoned me."

"I was expecting the mother," Isabella said. She walked to the table, picked up one of the mugs and sipped. The water tasted pure, rather than flat. "You …"

The maiden giggled again. "Would you have preferred the crone?"

"No." Isabella sat down, carefully. "Why did *you* come?"

"You called. I came." The maiden sat down, smoothing her translucent dress. "What can I do for you?"

Isabella lifted her eyes. "Don't you already know?"

The maiden smiled. "Nothing may be known …"

"Until it is spoken," Isabella finished. "I need to cross the channel to the mainland and …"

"Oh!" The maiden threw up her hands in mock shock. "I know what you could do. You could walk through the Godly Realm."

Isabella blinked. "I thought that isn't safe."

"Oh, it isn't." The maiden winked at her. It was oddly disconcerting. "But we're hoping to please a man, aren't we? Nothing impresses men like stupid risk-taking."

"Really." Isabella was *certain* she was being mocked. "What happened to the Red Monks when *they* passed through the Godly Realm?"

"That *has* been spoken," the maiden said. "And you already know the answer."

They made themselves vulnerable to the entities, Isabella thought. *They walked in as regular humans and they walked out monsters.*

"Yeah." Isabella let out a long breath. "Are there any other options?"

"Oh sure, sure," the maiden said. "But I should teach you how to enter the Godly Realm."

Isabella frowned. The maiden was *too* enthusiastic for her peace of mind. "Can you teach me how to cross it safely?"

"Of course." The maiden clapped her hands. "Shall we begin?"

"Not yet." Isabella felt guilty for even saying it. The maiden looked like a kicked puppy. Isabella *knew* the entity was manipulating her emotions, that the maiden was trying to push Isabella in a certain direction … that it was, in some sense, a reflection of what the entities truly *were*. It didn't make her disappointment any easier to handle. "Are there other ways to cross the waters?"

The maiden frowned. "Do you understand what Havant *did*?"

Isabella remembered the faces within the storm and shuddered. "He summoned one of you and asked him to raise a storm?"

"Quite." The maiden looked displeased. It wasn't directed at her, but Isabella still felt an overwhelming urge to cringe. "The elementals are still there, within the storm. You will need to placate them if you wish to travel safely."

Lord Greely passed safely, Isabella thought, curtly. Sir Handel had also passed safely, she supposed, but he wasn't human any longer. *Why did the elementals let him go?*

"I see," she said. She supposed it made a certain kind of sense, once one accepted the existence of elemental entities. "How do I placate them?"

The maiden smiled, as if they were two girlfriends whispering secrets. "You offer them a bribe."

Isabella resisted the urge to snap at the young-seeming entity. The guilt would have crushed her. "And what sort of bribe do I offer them?"

"Something of value to you," the maiden said. "Something that has meaning to you, something you're prepared to give up. Something …"

"I understand," Isabella said. She forced herself to think. She didn't *have* much with her, not really. She'd learnt the value of travelling light when she'd fled the Golden City. "I'll think about it."

"Something *meaningful*," the maiden said. "You don't want to anger them."

"Because they'll kill me?" Isabella felt her stomach clench. Sailing was fun, sometimes, but being caught in a storm was utterly terrifying. "Or worse?"

"They can't kill you," the maiden said. "They can just make things bad for you."

Isabella gritted her teeth. It made sense, she supposed. The elementals couldn't kill someone directly, but they *could* do things that would cost someone their life. She recalled a murderer she'd met, once, who'd claimed it wasn't *his* fault that he'd frightened someone into falling off a cliff. Perhaps the elementals believed it was the waves that killed people, conveniently ignoring the fact that they were *causing* the waves. She'd met quite a few humans, come to think of it, who blithely condemned their fellows without ever bothering to consider their own role in affairs.

Perhaps Greely survived because he's too stupid to be scared, she thought. *And the sailors died because they were smart enough to realise the danger ...*

It sounded contradictory. But so did the entities themselves.

The maiden smiled, warmly. "Does that answer your question?"

"I think so." Isabella knew she had other questions, but she didn't want to ask them until she had a chance to *think*. "I thank you."

"Thank me by listening." The maiden met her eyes. Isabella shivered, suddenly very aware – again – that the maiden was far from human. She felt tears pricking at the corner of her eyes as she looked away. "I'm going to teach you how to enter the Godly Realm."

She jumped up and knelt down on the earthen floor. "Sit. Listen."

Isabella knelt, facing her. "I'm ready."

The maiden smiled, challengingly. "We shall see."

"I'm listening." Isabella tried to keep the irritation out of her voice. "Carry on."

"The Godly Realm is everywhere and nowhere," the maiden said. She sounded like a young girl trying to sound portentous and failing. "It is infinitesimally small and infinitely big. And it is everything and nothing."

"Clear as mud," Isabella said, dryly.

"It is our place of power," the maiden said. "But it can also be yours. When you perform a ritual, you call upon the Godly Realm and its inhabitants."

So it isn't really my power, Isabella thought. She knew her magic intimately. She knew its strengths and weaknesses. It was *hers*. But the Godly Realm was something else altogether. How could one rely on *anything* that depended on something else – *someone* else – to work? *And why are you telling me this?*

"You can take a shortcut through the Godly Realm, if you

are prepared, protected and willing to pay the price," the maiden said. "And you can take others with you, if they are properly prepared."

And if they're not properly prepared – and protected – they open themselves up to the entities, Isabella thought. *And that's what happened to the Red Monks.*

She resisted the urge to reach for her notebook as the maiden discussed the various ways to enter the Godly Realm. Some of them were surprisingly simple, although ... she wasn't sure she wanted to risk them. Others ... were a great deal more complex, relying on her to gather the supplies – the bribes – and deploy them at the right moments. And there were rules ... stay on the road, be polite to everyone you meet, don't eat or drink or take anything you might happen to encounter and, above all, don't look back.

"Stay on the road," the maiden repeated. "If you wander off the path, you will never get back."

Isabella nodded, slowly. The maiden seemed to believe that one could take an entire army through the Godly Realm, travelling from Allenstown to Havelock in the blink of an eye. She found it astonishing ... and terrifying. The idea of jumping a whole army from the Summer Isle to Andalusia, without having to cross the channel ... she knew kings and generals who'd leap at the chance to strike their enemies without having to cross the border and fight their way to the enemy's capital. And they would, given the chance. They wouldn't care about the dangers as long as someone else paid the price.

And when they make a mistake, Isabella thought coldly, *who knows what will emerge at the far end.*

She frowned, knowing it wasn't an option. Not for them, not now. They couldn't take cold iron into the Godly Realm, which meant they would be defenceless when they reached Andalusia. Reginald *might* be able to source iron weapons, but ... she shook her head. Most swords weren't *iron*. She rather suspected the *real* rulers of Andalusia had banned iron swords by now. The Red Monks certainly had, where they'd ruled. They'd understood the dangers. Their enemies had not until it was too late.

"You're a good student," the maiden said. "Do you want to *try*? You could come to *my* home."

"No, thank you," Isabella said. "I have to go soon."

"We could spend a lifetime there and return in the blink of an eye," the maiden said. "It will broaden your mind."

"No, thank you," Isabella repeated. The sense of kicking a helpless puppy grew stronger, gnawing at her resolution. "I don't have time."

She looked down at her hands. The maiden had spoken in riddles, seemingly dancing around the truth, but *some* things were clear. The Godly Realm operated on different rules. If she ate something, it could cost her ... even if she had *permission* to eat it. And if she spent a lifetime in the Godly Realm, she might crumble to dust the moment she emerged. She wondered, sourly, what Reginald would think if she didn't come home. Would he break his word and go to the shack? What would he think when he saw the pile of dust? Would he realise it had once been *her*?

"Sad," the maiden said. "You're thinking about *him*."

Isabella looked up, sharply. "Stay out of my head!"

"I'm not *in* your head." The maiden smiled, warmly. It would have been more reassuring if there hadn't been a toothy *edge* to her smile. "You're just emoting openly. You've become a lot more open since you started studying with me."

"Thank you," Isabella said. She didn't mistake the kind words for a compliment. "It's been very interesting indeed."

"Quite." The maiden stood, brushing down her dress. "And now we have to talk about something more serious."

Isabella felt ice trickling down her back. "We do?"

"Yes." The maiden looked down at her. "We do."

Isabella rose. She'd never liked people peering down at her. "What do we have to talk about?"

The maiden said nothing for a long moment. When she spoke, her voice was very calm. "I have been giving you lessons for the last while," she said. "And I have not demanded a price."

"No," Isabella said, carefully. Five months of lessons ... Mother Lembu, whatever aspect she wore, had never mentioned a price. Isabella was damned, probably literally, if she allowed the entity to retroactively set a price. "You never mentioned a price."

"Indeed?" The maiden smiled. "Did I not?"

"Nothing may be known until it is spoken," Isabella recited. "As you well know."

The maiden's good humour vanished. Isabella felt her temper lashing out, brushing against Isabella with almost physical force. Her legs buckled. It was all she could do to keep from dropping to her knees. The maiden's face was so angry ... Isabella blinked. The maiden was no longer angry. She looked ... calm, placid. Isabella felt her head spin. It made no sense, none at all. The entity just wasn't human.

"Quite." The maiden's voice was flat. "Today, you called on me. I did not choose to come."

Isabella said nothing, although she thought fast. She'd assumed Mother Lembu would decide, when she heard the call, if she would come. But ... if she hadn't *chosen* to come, did that mean Isabella had summoned her against her will? And did that mean ... for a second, she was sure she was on the brink of a great insight into the entities. Who was *really* in charge? The entities themselves ... or the humans they patronised?

"There will be a price for your next set of lessons," the maiden said. "And you will have no choice but to pay it."

"What if I don't *want* the lessons?" Isabella forced herself to look into the heartbreakingly beautiful face. Heartbreakingly beautiful ... and yet, more a mask than anything *real*. The more she looked, the less real it seemed. "I could decide to end it now."

"You won't." The maiden spoke with total confidence. "When the time comes, you will call on me. And then you will pay the price."

"Really." Isabella looked away as the maiden's smile grew brighter. "And ..."

She looked back. The maiden was gone. She felt a wisp of cold air brushing against her back and turned, just in time to see the door swinging on its hinges. A shiver ran down her spine as she stepped forward and closed the door. Who knew who – human or otherwise – would take the open door as an invitation? And who knew who might be watching her from the Godly Realm?

"Damn it," she muttered. The mug of water she'd poured for the entity was empty, although Isabella hadn't seen the maiden drink. "What will you want from me?"

She tensed, half-expecting to hear an answer echoing on the air, but there was nothing. She picked up her mug and drained it dry, trying to focus her mind. Her emotions were spinning out of control, leaving her convinced she was on the verge of tears – or a tantrum. She had to bite her lip to keep from breaking down and sobbing like a little girl. The maiden had affected her at a level so deep she didn't want to admit it existed. She wasn't even sure why.

Perhaps because she represented something I could never have, Isabella thought. It had been a long time since she'd been a maiden in any real sense of the word. And longer still, she conceded, since she'd been *innocent*. She'd known from a revoltingly early age that she could either accept her place in the family or rebel constantly, to the point where she did something that would get her exiled for life. *A concept of innocence rather than reality.*

She sat down and ruthlessly centred herself. The maiden had been right about one thing, at least. She'd become a great deal more emotional lately. The Peerless School had taught her to control her emotions, pointing out the dangers of spellcasting when she was in a vile mood or bent on revenge rather than punishment, but ... ritual magic seemed to require a degree of emotional commitment. She could – she should – let her emotions and feelings guide her, even though it felt fundamentally wrong. She could wish for anything – perhaps literally – but that wouldn't make it real. Or would it? These days, it was hard to tell.

There was a knock at the door. Isabella stood, brushing down her trousers. "Come."

The door opened. A messenger stood there. "My Lady, His Highness commands me to inform you that he will be departing to Racal's Bay this afternoon. He wishes to know if you will attend on him first."

If I will attend on him first, Isabella thought, crossly. It was the formal phrasing, but it had never ceased to grate. *We'll see.*

She gathered herself. The messenger looked terrified, as if he expected to be turned into a frog or struck by lightning or ... simply whipped to within an inch of his life. Isabella felt a flicker of pity. Reginald had told her that messengers were irritating, even when they brought good news, but that was hardly their fault. There was nothing to be gained by flogging the messenger. Even her *father* had known that.

"Inform His Highness that I will be with him in an hour," she said, curtly. It should be long enough for her to clean the shack, pick up her supplies and walk to the castle. "And then I'll accompany him to Racal's Bay."

The messenger bowed. "Yes, My Lady."

Isabella sighed, inwardly, as the man turned and hurried away. She had the sense she shouldn't stay behind, not this time. She wasn't sure where it had come from, but it was there. And if the maiden had been right, they might be able to cross the channel fairly quickly. They could get an army across before Sofia – and whatever lurked behind her – could reasonably expect it to arrive.

Sure, her own thoughts mocked her, as she started to pack up. *And what are you going to use as a bribe?*

Chapter Ten

"Your Highness." Captain-General Gars bowed as Reginald rode up to him. "Your army awaits."

Reginald nodded, looking down over the sodden field. Hundreds of men were within eyeshot, their sergeants and lieutenants barking orders as they marched up and down, shaking off the effects of garrison life and – slowly – becoming soldiers again. Reginald allowed his gaze to drift over the nearest men, wondering how many resented him for summoning them back to Racal's Bay. He would have been surprised if they hadn't found sweethearts – or wives – on the island. They'd done their best to help the communities they'd garrisoned, endearing both themselves and their master to their unwilling hosts. He liked to think it was a step towards a unified culture.

He smiled, grimly, as he looked from man to man. They looked ready for action, although it would be a week or two before they could be marched onto the boats. Desertion was going to be a problem. The men might have been commoners, often criminals who'd been given a choice between enlisting or execution, but they weren't stupid. Anyone could climb one of the nearby hills and peer over the bay, to the raging seas beyond. And ... he didn't want to think about how many men might prefer to go back to their new sweethearts. They wouldn't want to return to the mainland to fight for him ...

The horse whinnied, uncomfortably, as a gust of cold wind lashed across the land. Reginald felt flecks of ice brushing against his bare face. He sighed, inwardly, as he dismounted the horse, trying not to land in a muddy puddle. The weather had been improving over the last few days, apparently. Reginald found it hard to believe. It was still cold, it was still wet and the mud was *everywhere*. His men looked as if they'd been rolling in the mud.

"The tents didn't survive the first night," Captain-General Gars said, as they walked around the campsite. "The winds blew them down, no matter how strongly they were anchored. I ended up parcelling out the troops to homes within the city and the surrounding villages. It was a mess, but ..."

His voice trailed off. Reginald nodded in understanding. "As long as the troops behave themselves," he said. No one would *like* being forced to billet troops on their property, but it would be a great deal worse if the troops *really* didn't behave themselves. "And don't loot the city."

"I had two men flogged for looting," Gars assured him. "After that, there was no trouble."

"That will change," Reginald said. He glanced towards the city – and the bay beyond. "How's morale?"

"They're about ready to kill someone, so we'd better make sure they're pointed in the right direction," Gars told him. "Really, I don't expect serious trouble for at least a couple of weeks. We're working them hard on the training field, then giving them only a few short hours of rest before we start working them hard again. They got a bit soft over the winter, so it's good for them. And I have their lieutenants working with them too."

"Good," Reginald said. He had no patience for men who bought their commissions and seemed to think that excused them from their duties. They could work or get out, as far as he was concerned. His father had backed him up, the one and only time someone had dared complain. "How are *they* doing?"

"They still can't read maps to save their lives, but ... otherwise, they're not doing that badly," Gars said. He smirked, unpleasantly. "The really dumb ones got killed during the earlier fighting, so ... the remainder at least know to go before they don armour."

Reginald laughed at a joke that had been old when his grandfather had been a child. "And they're leading the men?"

"They know the ropes," Gars said. "I've been sure to pair weak officers with good sergeants, men who'll keep them on the straight and narrow. It helps there's nowhere to go here."

"I suppose," Reginald said. Racal's Bay was barren,

compared to Havelock. There were only a handful of bars, all closed and bolted while the army was in town. The aristocrats had nowhere to socialise outside camp, save perhaps for the castle. "As long as they're focusing on their duties …"

He let out a long breath as he spotted a sergeant urging a tired-looking soldier to finish the run. It was never easy to tell which aristocrats would become good officers and bad ones sometimes remained undetected until they found themselves plunged into battle. And even the good ones sometimes lacked any awareness of their men as more than pieces on their personal chess boards. He would have preferred to promote sergeants to officer ranks, but … it wasn't allowed. That would have to change, he told himself. He'd see to it when he became king. A bad officer in the worst possible place could do a great deal of damage before he was forcibly removed from power.

Or gets himself and everyone else killed, he thought, grimly. *The sooner we put a stop to it, the better.*

He listened, carefully, as Gars led him through the muddy camp. The ground was practically churning underneath him, churned up time and time again by soldiers as they marched up and down the field. Dozens of archers stood in another field, practising drawing and firing their bows at scarecrows. They weren't very accurate, Reginald recalled, but it didn't matter. Their role was to put as many arrows in the air as possible. It didn't matter which arrow hit the target as long as one of them did. He'd seen cavalry charges disintegrated by archers, the horses and riders sent tumbling to the ground. It wasn't a sight to gladden the aristocratic heart. Reginald had a private theory that the kingdom would have banned the longbow altogether if it hadn't meant they'd be at a severe disadvantage if – when – they went to war against their neighbours.

"We should be ready to depart, as planned," Gars finished. "The only problem is getting across the channel."

"We have it in hand," Reginald said. He'd listened, very carefully, to Isabella's report. "The real question is … where do we land?"

Gars frowned. "The closer we land to Havelock, the quicker *they* will respond."

Reginald nodded. He'd considered all the possibilities, but

none of them were very good. If they landed further away, they'd be able to disembark without interference … at the price of giving whoever was in charge of Havelock ample time to prepare their defences. And, perhaps, making themselves pawns in an ongoing power struggle. But if they landed too close, they might be caught on the beaches and torn to ribbons. It wasn't going to be easy to choose a landing site.

The weather might make the choice for us, he mused. The winds were always nasty, with or without the elementals. Going north would be tricky, particularly with an entire fleet. Going south would be easier, but they'd run the risk of being blown far off course. *We might have to place our faith in the gods*.

The irony gnawed at his mind as he walked away from the camp, towards the other training ground. His bodyguards fell in around him, watching suspiciously as the camp came into view. Earl Oxley – or, more accurately, the commanding officers under Oxley's nominal command – had taken over a small hamlet, driving the locals out and installing their own people. Reginald saw a handful of tents, flaps twisting and buckling in the winds. It looked as if Oxley had no concern for his own people, even his personal armsmen. Gars *must* have told him that the tents wouldn't last a day.

Earl Oxley looked supremely displeased when he saw Reginald. He certainly didn't *want* to stand and salute. Reginald wished, just for a moment, that he'd thought to bring Isabella with him. Her magic might have been enough of a deterrent to keep the earl from trying to kill him – or having him assassinated. Gars would have killed the bastard, naturally, and laid waste to the Oxley Lands … but there was no way he could prevent a civil war. And the entities, on the other side of the channel, would eventually take the entire world.

Chin up, Reginald told himself. Oxley wasn't stupid. Reginald had nothing to fear as long as he didn't *show* fear. *And remember for next time*.

"Your Highness," Earl Oxley said. "The men are ready to go to war."

Reginald looked past him, studying the islander troops as they marched up and down. They looked tough, but utterly unprepared for war. Their sergeants shouted and raged, bullying and striking men who threatened to fall out of line. Their uniforms were tattered, their weapons rusty … he hated to think what they might be eating. They looked beaten down, ready to turn and run – or turn on their masters – at the slightest provocation. He rather suspected they would be worse than useless on the battlefield.

"Your men need more training," he said, stiffly. Sergeants were harsh – that was the way of things – but they weren't meant to be bullies. Bullying for the sake of bullying led to hatred, hatred led to violence … he wouldn't have cared to turn his back on an armed man who had every reason to bury a knife in him. "And they need better food."

Earl Oxley sniffed. "They're commoners."

"Yes. And they're under your command," Reginald told him. He'd been on campaigns where men had begged for food from neighbouring units, after their commanders either sold off the food or simply didn't bother to buy it in the first place. "And that makes you responsible for them."

The earl didn't look pleased. No doubt he'd been anticipating the chance to make a bid for power, when Reginald returned to the mainland. And he couldn't get his relatives to make a bid for power without running the risk of one or more of them sticking a knife in *his* back at the same time. The Summer Isle really *was* a snake pit, Reginald thought. There were times when he wondered if it would be better to simply execute all the nobles and promote his followers into their places.

"Yes, Your Highness," Earl Oxley grunted, finally. "I'll see to it personally."

"See that you do," Reginald said. He was tempted to apply the stick, but he knew it would be better to offer the carrot. This time. "These men will win you an estate on the mainland, if you treat them right."

The earl looked up. "An estate on the *mainland*?"

"Yes." Reginald had no illusions and he suspected Earl Oxley didn't either. An estate on the mainland wouldn't be worth *that* much, in terms of power, but it would give him influence that he might be able to translate into something useful. "Once the war is over, you will have your pick of estates."

And a number of others will be booted off their lands to make way for my supporters, he thought, grimly. He had a little list of noblemen who wouldn't be missed, men who'd tried to pressure his father or sent their sons to pressure *him*. Attainting them for treason, on the grounds they'd done nothing to save their monarch, would avoid any pesky questions about the legality of depriving them of their lands. *And once I get rid of them, I can start thinking about a little further expansion.*

He watched the soldiers for a minute longer, then remounted his horse and rode back towards the city. Racal's Bay seemed more lively than ever, now the streets were clear of water and ice. There were still few women on the streets – and those he saw were either prostitutes or escorted by grim-faced men – but the shops were largely open and the merchants were doing a roaring trade. He'd even heard from a handful of merchants who wanted to expand over the channel, although he'd had to turn them down for the moment. There was no way to know what would happen when they reached the mainland.

His mood soured as he looked over the bay and saw the raging storms beyond. The faces in the clouds were more visible now, although he wasn't sure if they were coming closer or if he was simply more aware of their presence. He hoped Isabella was right, when she said the elementals could be bribed into allowing their passage. If she was wrong … it was hard to believe the elementals couldn't kill them directly. It was easy to see how even experienced sailors might make fatal mistakes, mistakes that killed them. Or maybe the elementals, like humans, were good at lying to themselves. They might not want to believe they'd committed murder.

Admiral Tanoan had taken over a suite of rooms to serve as an office, his staffers coming and going at all hours of the day. He jumped to his feet and saluted, the moment he saw Reginald. Reginald waved him back to his chair, then sat down himself. It wasn't quite protocol – and his father would have said sharp things about it, once upon a time – but Reginald couldn't bring himself to care. He wanted to be *doing* something, not sitting around waiting and worrying. And if his father were truly dead …

He shivered. The throne was a prison as much as anything

else. His father was, to all intents and purposes, draped with so many chains he could barely walk. He was certainly not allowed to lead his troops on the battlefield, not any longer. Reginald knew that *he* wouldn't be on the battlefield, not once *he* was king. He needed to sire an heir, a young boy who would need at least fourteen years to grow into a man. And then … if something happened to his son, Reginald would be back at square one.

"Your Highness." Admiral Tanoan sounded calm, thankfully. "Two-thirds of the fleet are ready to depart, when the storms abate. The remainder is in no condition to sail."

"I wish I was surprised," Reginald said. The ships hadn't been built for local winters. They might sink if someone took them onto a calm sea, let alone the raging storms outside. "When can we start loading?"

"I'd prefer to wait until everything else was in place," Admiral Tanoan told him. "Once the stores are ready, we can board the army in a couple of days and set sail."

Reginald nodded, feeling a flicker of nausea. Two days in the dark, dank holds would *not* please the soldiers … and that would be *before* they set sail. There'd be at least five days on the water, assuming they survived the trip. The channel had never been easy to sail … he shook his head, trying not to think about it. There would be time enough for seasickness once they got underway.

"We should be ready to leave as planned, then," he said. "Have you considered possible landing sites?"

Admiral Tanoan gave him a sharp look. He'd served Reginald long enough to know that it wasn't a casual question. Reginald had considered his options, but … he wanted the admiral's uninfluenced opinion. Once Reginald gave *his* opinion, even the freest of free thinkers would hesitate to contradict him.

"I'd suggest aiming for Humber, rather than Havelock," Admiral Tanoan said. He pointed to the table. Someone had placed a map there and weighed it down with a collection of beer mugs. "We have to disembark the men and horses as quickly as possible. Humber has docks and … everything else we need. There's even walls, just in case they respond quicker than we expect."

Reginald nodded, slowly. He'd served his father on the

battlefield long enough to know it *always* took a long time to mobilise troops and dispatch them to their targets. Normally, he'd expect his father to need at least two to three weeks to get reinforcements to Humber. But now … if the country was on the verge of civil war, the forces in Havelock might be ready to march at once. The more he thought about it, the more he feared it might be so. And if he was caught on the beaches, he was in deep shit.

"It'll take them some time to notify Havelock that we've landed," he said, although he wasn't sure that was true. The old sorcerous communications network was gone, but it was quite possible that the entities and their servants could use the Godly Realm to communicate. If they could travel hundreds of miles in the blink of an eye, surely they could send messages too. "Even if they set out at once, and march like the wind, it will still take them hours to reach us."

Unless they use the Godly Realm, he reminded himself. *Or unless they have some other tricks up their sleeves.*

He scowled as he studied the map. He knew, without false modesty, that he was a brave man. He had no qualms about risking his life on the battlefield, even if his death meant utter disaster. But he was scared of the unknown. He understood Isabella's magic, even though he couldn't use it. Ritual magic, on the other hand, was disturbingly unpredictable. There seemed to be no rhyme or reason to its workings. Someone could be using it against him, right now, and he wouldn't have the slightest idea …

His eyes traced out Andalusia on the map. The country had always been large, even before his father had bumped off a pair of neighbouring kings and claimed their lands for his own. Reginald had resolved that he would leave *his* son an even bigger kingdom. But now … the sheer size of his homeland worked against him. It was already taking far too long to get home.

And what, he asked himself, *will I find when I get there?*

Chapter Eleven

Her room was starting to feel like a prison.

Princess Silverdale stood in front of the door and pressed her ear against the wood, trying to determine if there was a guard outside. She'd been allowed to roam the upper levels of the palace freely, when she'd been younger, but now …she'd been warned to stay in her rooms unless she was specifically summoned by her oldest sister. Silverdale had never really *liked* her sister – Sofia was four years older than her, a gulf that no amount of family feeling could surmount – but she'd never hated her. Now …

She listened as carefully as she could, hearing nothing. Was there a guard outside? She couldn't tell. There shouldn't have been, not here. The rules governing royal princesses were strict. Men who weren't related to them were *not* to be close to them, unless they were heavily chaperoned or … she wasn't quite sure of the details, but apparently there was a shortage of volunteers for a procedure that made them safe. There really shouldn't have been a guard outside.

The knob turned in her hand, but the door refused to open. Silverdale gasped, honestly shocked. The door was … *locked*? There was no keyhole. Had someone put a bolt on the far side of the door? Or … or what? She was locked in her room? By whose authority? She threw discretion to the winds and banged on the door, trying to open it by force, but the wood refused to give way. The handful of spells at her disposal, the magic she'd been told never to use, failed to budge the door.

She stumbled backwards, reeling in shock. She was locked in. Locked up, like a common prisoner. She was … she opened her mouth to throw a tantrum, then thought better of it. She was a big girl now. She couldn't shout and scream, particularly when there wasn't an audience. Her governess was nowhere to be seen. Silverdale told herself, firmly, that she should be relieved. The wretched woman was full of proper ideas of how a little princess should behave and her father supported her completely.

Silverdale turned slowly, surveying her room. It was, as befitted her rank as the king's youngest daughter, smaller than her older sister's room ... but it was still large, crammed with luxuries – she'd been told – beyond compare. She often thought her father still considered her a little girl, given how much of the room was crammed with toys and games she'd outgrown long ago. The golden rocking horse had been fun, when she was five. Now, she couldn't even sit on it without her feet touching the floor. She sighed as she paced towards the window and peered outside. The guards were patrolling the battlements, as always. There seemed to be more of them and they looked jumpy. *Very* jumpy.

She glanced at the portrait hanging from the wall and sighed, again. She'd never really known her mother. Queen Carline had died giving birth to her, according to her older siblings. Her father rarely talked about her. He'd certainly never taken another wife. And yet ... Silverdale couldn't help thinking that she and her mother had, once upon a time, looked very alike. Her dark hair and pale face, pretty rather than beautiful, looked *just* like a younger version of her mother. The queen had been beautiful. Everyone said so.

"I wish you were here," Silverdale said. She'd fallen into the habit of talking to the portrait a long time ago, although the portrait had never replied. "Or Reginald was here. I don't know what to do."

She sat back on the bed, wondering if she should go back to sleep. Her brother had gone six months ago, leaving her behind. Silverdale had pleaded with him to be allowed to go, even though she was a child. She'd wanted to see *something* of the world besides the castle and the royal estates, before she grew up and entered the marriage market. Her father had never tried to hide it from her. Instead, he'd made it clear that it was her duty to marry for the sake of the family. Silverdale wasn't clear on all the details – her governess had slapped her when she'd asked too many questions – but she understood duty. She just wished she had a chance to *live* a little first.

And things had changed. Silverdale didn't know what – no one had talked to her – but it was clear that *something* had changed. Her father was ill, her sister – of all people – seemed to be in charge and ... and what? It was hard to escape the feeling, sometimes, that she was being watched, even though there was no one there. The shadows in the corners seemed to move when she wasn't looking, as if there was a whole other world lurking in the darkness. She'd insisted on keeping the lanterns lit, even in the middle of the day. She just hadn't been able to sleep without them.

The door rattled. Silverdale glanced up, hearing the unmistakable sound of a bolt being drawn back. Someone was outside ... she tensed, wondering if she should try to hide. But there was nowhere *to* hide. There was no other way out of the room, unless she tried to open and climb out of the window. And she had a nasty feeling she'd plunge to her death if she tried. She stood as the door opened, reminding herself that she was the trueborn daughter of a king. Whatever was coming, she'd face it with dignity.

"Your Highness." Her governess – a sour-faced woman who looked as if she were permanently sucking on a lemon – stepped into the room. "You are summoned to court."

Silverdale blinked. She was too *young* to be summoned to court. It wasn't fair – Reginald had been attending court since he'd been old enough to string two words together – but it was the way of things. Her father rarely permitted her to attend court – or do *anything*, beyond the occasional presentation to foreign guests. She was simply too young. Sofia had taken over a number of their mother's duties, now she was a grown woman, but Silverdale? She had no role at court.

"I'm coming," Silverdale said. The governess might treat her with respect, but she had the power and she'd never let her young charge forget it. "Let me get dressed first ..."

"Come as you are," her governess said. "Now."

Silverdale looked down at herself – her green dress was decent, but it was hardly courtly wear – then shrugged. The governess would be the one in trouble, if the king – or his regent – objected to Silverdale's dress. It would do the older woman good to be on the receiving end of the king's temper for once. Or Sofia's, if she was really in charge. Maybe *that* was why the governess was so cranky. She'd been Sofia's governess, once upon a time. Now ... her former charge could take revenge for everything the governess had done.

She picked up her tiara, a present from her brother, and placed it firmly on her head. The governess would normally be fussing around her, trying to remove non-existent dust from her clothes and pin her hair into whatever style was fashionable these days, but now ... she just stood there, as if she was distracted by a far weightier matter. Silverdale found it a little worrying, if she were honest. The governess was acting out of character. *Very* out of character.

"This way," the governess snapped. "Now."

Maybe not that *out of character*, Silverdale thought, as she followed the older woman out of the door. There were no guards outside, but someone had fixed a bolt to the door. She wondered, morbidly, what she was supposed to do if there were a fire. Jump out of the window? Try to break down the door? *What does she want me to do?*

Her forebodings grew stronger as they made their way down the royal family's private staircase. The castle felt *wrong*, as if it wasn't truly *her* castle any longer. Perhaps it wasn't even her *home*. She thought she saw things out of the corner of her eye, glimpses of things her mind refused to grasp, but when she turned to look there was nothing there. There were hints of corridors and passageways that led in directions she couldn't comprehend ... she rubbed her eyes and they were gone, reality snapping back into place effortlessly. Her entire body felt drained, as she reached the bottom of the stairs. And yet, she knew she'd eaten a good breakfast. The governess had stood over her as she'd eaten it.

Silverdale shivered as they approached the audience chamber, even though the air was decently warm. She was tempted to turn and run, to rely on her speed to outrun the governess ... the old hag would catch up with her eventually, she knew from experience, but she would have a few glorious hours of freedom. And she had the feeling that, whatever was behind that door, she didn't want to see it. Once, she would have liked to attend court. It would have been a sign of her father's trust. Now ...

The governess placed a bony arm on her shoulder, holding

her firmly in place as she opened the door. Silverdale glanced up resentfully and froze as she met the governess's eyes. The older woman was *scared*. Silverdale couldn't believe it. The governess had snapped and snarled at noblemen who'd got in her way, even though they outranked her socially. She'd even whipped the *princesses* when they'd disobeyed her. And yet, she was scared? Utterly terrified? Silverdale couldn't imagine anything scaring the governess. But she was scared, too scared to disobey.

She braced herself as she was half-pushed into the courtroom. It had changed, since her father had fallen unwell. The portraits on the walls, paintings of kings who had ruled in name only since time out of mind, were gone. Instead, there were strange signs and sigils on the walls. Silverdale looked at them, then looked away as her head started to spin. The governess pointed her towards the dais, where her sisters were waiting for her. Sofia sat on her father's throne, looking every bit the ice princess; Ruby stood next to her, her face schooled into a mask that suggested she was as terrified as Silverdale herself. And, on the other side ...

Silverdale stopped, dead. No one, but royalty, was allowed to stand on the dais. It elevated them above the crowd. But now, there was a tall thin woman standing next to Sofia. She shouldn't have been there. Silverdale felt her mouth drop open with outrage. Who *was* this woman? Why was Sofia treating her as a near-equal ...?

She met her sister's eyes and swallowed the protest before it was fully formed. Sofia had always been cold and calculating, but now ... she looked as though she had been carved from a block of ice. Sofia wore a long white dress, as if she were attending her own wedding, but there was nothing *vulnerable* about her. Not now. Her blue eyes glinted with a power – and a malice – that chilled her younger sister to the bone. Silverdale had no doubt that Sofia would squash her like a bug, if she disobeyed. She felt her legs wobble as she took her place on the dais, too close to her elder sister for comfort. Something tickled the back of her neck – it felt as if someone was standing right behind her – but when she looked no one was there.

Sofia made a sign to the guards, who opened the far doors.

A crowd of courtiers – mostly men – poured into the room. The lords and ladies led the way, decked out in their finery; they were followed by minor nobility, a handful of magicians and, right at the back, a tiny number of merchants and traders who'd earned a place at court. Their faces were stony masks, but it was easy to tell they were displeased. Hardly *anyone* seemed pleased, she thought. Some of them were just better at hiding it than others.

The crowd seemed to waver as it realised that Sofia was on the throne, then bent the knee as one. Silverdale hesitated, then went down too. Sofia was standing ... Silverdale blinked, unsure when her elder sister had *stood*. Her presence was almost overpowering. Silverdale's father had had presence, when he'd sat on the throne, but his daughter outshone him. And yet ... Silverdale felt another chill. Something was wrong. She could barely force herself to *look* at her sister. It was like staring into a cold sun.

Sofia sat, with no discernable motion. "We greet you," she said. Her voice was cold and hard, effortlessly echoing through the chamber. "We welcome you to our court. You may rise."

Silverdale stood, brushing down her dress. The lords and ladies looked relieved as they stumbled to their feet. They weren't accustomed to bending the knee to anyone, save for their royal master. Silverdale wondered, idly, how long it would take for one or more of them to question Sofia's right to the regency. She'd had the laws drilled into her almost as soon as she'd learnt to read. A woman couldn't be regent. The position normally went to the king's brothers or cousins.

"My royal father is unwell." Sofia's voice grew stronger, carrying so much conviction that it was hard to doubt her. "He was struck down for failure, for failure to carry out the will of the gods. It nearly killed him."

Silverdale gasped. She wasn't alone. Sofia had always been deeply religious, perhaps the most religious person in the family, but ... hardly *anyone* spoke of the gods like that. No one *really* believed, did they? She glanced from face to face, wondering who would be the first to challenge the regent. Sofia's mere *presence* made it hard to formulate a response. Silverdale had to look away just to keep herself from accepting her sister's words without question. Her thoughts threatened to break up every time her sister spoke.

"He will recover, in time." Sofia's voice echoed around the chamber. "Or do you doubt it?"

There was a long chilling pause. And then someone stepped forward. Silverdale's eyes narrowed. The man was a junior lord, so junior she honestly couldn't remember his name ... if she'd ever known it in the first place. They probably hadn't been introduced. He was way too junior to be a prospective husband for either of her sisters. Silverdale was surprised he hadn't gone with the army. Reginald would have found a use for him.

Sure, her thoughts whispered. *Arrow fodder.*

The nobleman went to his knees, dramatically. "Your Highness," he said. "There is deep concern over your programme ..."

Silverdale felt a flash of contempt, mingled with a fear she didn't quite understand. The nobleman was ... *weak*, she thought. He spoke as if the slightest disagreement would be enough to shut his mouth. And yet ... it wasn't *right*. She couldn't put her finger on it, but it was there. He ... was behaving strangely. He ...

Sofia spoke with icy calm. "Do you dare to defy the will of the gods?"

The nobleman seemed to cringe, then – as the rest of the crowd backed away – rallied. "Your Highness, you are destroying temples that have stood since time out of mind. You are killing priests who refuse your commands. You are forcing people to pray in manners they don't understand. You are ..."

"I am obeying the will of the gods." Sofia didn't sound angry. *That* was scarier, somehow, than anything else. Silverdale would almost have preferred a fit of rage. Her father was always at his worst when he was coldly angry, rather than shouting loudly. "And are you doubting their will?"

"Your Highness." The nobleman started to stammer. Tears glittered in his eyes. "I ..."

He stumbled, then fell to the floor. Silverdale started, watching in horror as blood flowed from his mouth. She'd never seen anything like it. She ... she turned and glanced at her sister, then looked away hastily. Sofia seemed so much *bigger* than …

"You will have your chance to recant," Sofia said. She clicked her fingers. A pair of guards picked up the nobleman and carried him off. "And I trust there will be no one else who will question the will of the gods."

She stood, again. "The kingdom will be put on the right path," she said. "Whatever it takes, I will put the kingdom on the right path. And those who stand in our way will not stand for long."

Silverdale gritted her teeth. Something was wrong. Something was very wrong. She glanced past Sofia, at the woman standing next to her, and shuddered. The woman hadn't said a word, but … there was something about her that put Silverdale's teeth on edge. It was hard to put into words. Her body looked … *odd*, as if it wasn't quite right. As if … she simply *couldn't* put it into words. Her instincts told her to run.

She met her other sister's eyes. Ruby looked as scared as Silverdale herself, her hands clasped tightly behind her back to keep them from shaking. Silverdale wondered just what had happened to *Ruby*, over the last few days. Had she been locked in her room too? Or … Ruby was two years older. Surely, she would have been allowed to assist her older sister …

"Come," Sofia said. Her voice was tinged with confidence, as if there wasn't the slightest doubt in her mind that she was in charge. "Let us pray."

And the crowd offered no resistance at all.

Chapter Twelve

"I shouldn't be talking to you, Your Highness," Greta said, the following morning. "I …"

"I will take the blame, if blame there is," Silverdale said. She had been pleasantly surprised when Greta, rather than her governess, had brought her breakfast, but that wouldn't stop her taking advantage of it. "If anyone asks, blame it on me."

She tried not to feel sorry for Greta, even though she knew she'd placed the poor girl in a terrible position. She was only two years older than Silverdale herself. If she were dismissed from the kitchen staff, she'd have no hope of finding another position. And yet, Greta could hardly refuse orders from her princess. What was she supposed to do? Ignore them?

"Yes, Your Highness," Greta said. She didn't sound pleased. She might not be dismissed – she would hardly dare *lie* about following orders from her princess – but she might get a whipping, if her superiors found out. "I … I have to be back soon or they'll notice I'm gone."

"Blame it on me." Silverdale tried not to feel guilty. She was royal blood. She was protected. Greta had no such protections. "What's *happening* out there?"

Greta's face tightened. "Things have changed, Your Highness. I …"

"In what way?" Silverdale tried to sound reassuring. "You can tell me anything."

"Things have changed," Greta repeated. "The temples are being pulled down. People are being forced to pray in public. And … there are guards on the streets, harassing people who don't pray. No one is happy, but what can they do?"

Silverdale frowned. There were laws against praying in public, weren't there? They'd come out of the Golden City itself. Her governess had made her study the laws, even though most of them no longer applied. The laws were so pointless, on the face of it, that they *had* to be important. There *had* to be some kind of reasoning behind them. And yet, what was it? And what would happen if the laws were defied?

"And the High Priestess is creepy," Greta added. She jumped, as if she expected a hand to fall on her shoulder. "She's just … creepy."

The woman who stood next to Sofia, Silverdale thought. Priestesses were rare. They tended to be seen as disorderly, although she didn't know why. *Who is she and what is she doing here?*

"And we're expected to pray here too," Greta said. "The handful of porters who refused to pray were taken away. And I … I couldn't lose this job."

She glanced at the door, clearly hoping to be dismissed. Silverdale tried to ignore the wrenching sense of guilt in her heart. No matter what she did, Greta would be in some trouble. Unless … an idea crossed her mind. It wasn't a very good idea – it was the kind of idea her governess would have hated, if Silverdale had dared tell her – but that alone recommended it. In fact, it was the kind of idea her older brother would have loved.

The thought cost her another pang. "Has there been any word from my brother?"

"Not as far as I know," Greta said. "But I don't think they'd tell me."

"Probably not," Silverdale agreed. Greta was a kitchen maid, only two or three steps from the absolute bottom. She wouldn't be told any state secrets, although … who knew what she might have picked up just by keeping her ears open? "And my father?"

"He's in his chambers, I think," Greta said. "I'm not the one who takes his meals to his rooms."

"I see," Silverdale said. The idea was growing stronger. She wanted to put it into action before she thought better of it. "Let's go, shall we?"

Greta started to splutter – and then she remembered herself – as Silverdale led her towards the door. A guard stood outside, a fresh-faced young man who gaped at her before crashing his gauntlet against his chest in salute. Silverdale reminded herself, sharply, that she was a royal princess and command was in her blood. The key to giving orders was confidence, she'd been told. She could not allow herself to reveal the slightest *hint* of fear that her orders might not be obeyed.

"Your Highness," the guard stammered. "I ..."

Silverdale cut him off. "Take Greta down to the kitchens. Inform her superior that I detained her and that she is *not* to face any punishment for obeying my orders. If they have a problem with it, they can complain to the regent."

"Yes, Your Highness," the guard said. "I ..."

"Go. Now." Silverdale pressed her advantage, hoping she could avoid having the door shut and bolted. If she were lucky ... "Go ..."

Greta shot her a grateful look as the guard beckoned for her to follow him down the corridor. Silverdale allowed herself a smile. The kitchen staff would be insane to disobey her, particularly with the entire castle seemingly on the brink of insanity. They *might* complain to Sofia, or to the governess, but it was much more likely they'd simply grin and bear it. Silverdale knew how her father would have reacted to a spurious complaint about his daughter's behaviour. Sofia might not be any better.

She smirked as she pushed the door closed. Hopefully, when – if – the guard came back he would assume she'd gone back into her room. He wouldn't be foolish enough to open the door to *check*. Silverdale felt her smile grow wider as she hurried down the corridor, keeping her ears open for approaching servants. The royal chambers were supposed to be restricted, but that meant – in reality – that only a few dozen people were allowed entry. If she ran into a maid ...

I'll have to tell her to keep her mouth shut, she thought, although she knew it wasn't likely to work. She might be a princess, but she was the lowest-ranking princess in the castle. *And most of them bow the knee to the governess anyway.*

She slowed as she reached Ruby's corridor, carefully peering around the corner to make sure there were no guards outside her sister's chamber. There were none, but there was another bolt – firmly closed – on the door. Silverdale hurried forward, then pulled back the bolt and opened the door. Her older sister was sitting in a wooden rocking chair, doing needlework. Silverdale couldn't help feeling sorry for her. *She'd* jabbed her finger so often when her governess had tried to teach her needlework that the wretched woman had given up.

"Silverdale!" Ruby jumped to her feet, throwing the needlework to one side. "What happened?"

"I got out." Silverdale smirked. Ruby might be two years older, but *she* hadn't managed to get out of her room. "I think we have to find father."

Ruby hurried through the door. Silverdale closed and bolted it. No one would be coming to check on Ruby until lunchtime, four or so hours away. She didn't have any duties, not any longer. And she was too old for the governess to push around ... Silverdale envied her, even though she was sure there were a few disadvantages. It wouldn't be long before Ruby was married off to someone she barely knew.

"There's a secret passage through here," Ruby said, as she led the way into a smaller chamber. The room was empty, save for a large rug covering the rear wall. "We won't be seen ..."

She pulled back the rug and pressed her fingers against a stone. A faint rumbling echoed through the chamber as a hidden door opened, revealing a dark passageway leading downwards. Ruby took a lantern from the wall and passed it to Silverdale, then took a second one for herself. Silverdale frowned, then followed her into the passageway. Behind her, the door rumbled closed.

"I never knew," she said, torn between envy and alarm. "How did you ...?"

"Reginald told me, back when ... well, he thought I should know." Ruby's voice sounded odd in the semi-darkness. "I think he planned to tell you when you were older."

Silverdale took a breath, tasting dust on the air. "Who *built* these passageways?"

"I have no idea." Ruby's voice was very flat. "One of our distant ancestors, I imagine."

The passageway grew wider as they walked slowly onwards. There were faint hints that *someone* had used the secret passageways, once upon a time, but it was hard to tell. The dust lay everywhere, so thick it barely moved when they walked on it. She cringed at the thought of explaining a dusty dress to her governess. There was no way she could explain it, unless … maybe she could change, as soon as she got back to her room, and hide the dusty dress somewhere else. Maybe Greta would get rid of it for her. The maid could hardly refuse a direct order.

She looked around, interested, as they passed a crossroads and began to climb upwards again. The other passageways seemed to head further down into the bowels of the castle … she wondered, suddenly, if there was a secret way *out* of the castle. It was quite likely, although … she wondered if her *father* knew. She kicked herself a moment later. Of *course* her father knew. His father had probably told Reginald personally. The real question was if *Sofia* knew.

"One of the passageways opens in the servant quarters," Ruby commented. "The other seems to open near the barracks."

Silverdale frowned at her sister's back. "How long have you spent exploring?"

"Long enough," Ruby said. "But I haven't been *everywhere*."

Silverdale clamped down on a surge of jealousy as the passageway levelled out again. It wasn't Ruby's fault she hadn't told Silverdale the passages existed. She'd probably been told to keep them to herself. Reginald would have warned her not to tell anyone … Silverdale scowled, promising her brother an angry lecture when he came home. If he'd told her too … it might have given her faith that she could escape, if things went very badly wrong. Instead …

I would probably have hidden from the governess in here, she thought, dryly. *And father would not have been pleased.*

She put the thought aside as they reached the end of the line. Ruby stood on tiptoes and peered through a peephole, muttering a word neither of them were supposed to know at what she saw. She dropped down a moment later and pressed her fingers against a stone. The wall opened slowly, revealing … nothing. Silverdale scowled at herself as Ruby pushed the tapestry aside and stepped into the antechamber. She should have expected it. And … she frowned as she realised that the antechamber was empty. A faint smell – cloying and slightly unpleasant – hung in the air.

A shiver ran down her back. Her father shouldn't be *alone*. She'd anticipated having to push her way past a druid or a butcher-doctor, not ... not stepping into an empty room. She looked around with interest as Ruby pushed open the door to her father's bedchamber and peered inside. Neither of them had been allowed to visit very often, even as babies. Private chambers were meant to be *private*. And yet ... she gritted her teeth, deeply worried. Her father was alone.

"Father?" Ruby was practically whispering. "Father?"

Silverdale pushed past her. King Romulus XIII of Andalusia was lying on his bed, dead to the world. He looked as if he were sleeping, but his face was pale and his beard was turning gray. His sheets were covered with hairs ... it took her a moment to realise that his hair was literally falling out. She wondered, in horror, if the man before her truly *was* her father. It was so hard to believe that the pallid man was even alive. She tried to force herself to touch his skin, but some instinct warned her it would be dangerous. What had happened to him?

"I think he's been drugged," Ruby said. She glanced around the room, her eyes alighting on a bottle of liquid. "I wonder ..."

She picked up the liquid and took a sniff, then recoiled, choking and coughing. Silverdale pounded Ruby's back as her older sister coughed loudly, her knees buckling and nearly sending her to the floor. She took the bottle and hastily put it back, unwilling to take the risk of sniffing it herself. Whatever it was, she doubted it was doing her father any good. If he was being drugged, by whom? Sofia? Or her mysterious High Priestess? Or ...

"Quiet," Ruby snapped. Outside, a door opened into the antechamber. "Find a place to hide!"

Silverdale looked around, then threw herself into a corner. She was used to playing hide and seek with the governess. There were enough tables and chairs around to hide her as long as she didn't move. Nothing drew the eye like motion. It was astonishing what people missed as long as it stood very still. She got into a position to watch and willed herself to freeze, to remain as still as possible. Ruby was ducking under the bed ...

The High Priestess, looking stranger than ever before,

strode into the room. Silverdale felt her heart starting to pound, the sound thudding in her ears so loudly she was *sure* the strange woman could hear it. Ruby froze, horribly. The High Priestess peered down at her. For a moment, from her vantage point, Silverdale believed the High Priestess couldn't *see* Ruby, as if she couldn't wrap her head around the girl's presence. But the moment quickly passed.

"On your feet," she ordered. Her voice dripped honey and power. Silverdale had to bite her lip to keep from obeying and she wasn't even the target. "Why are you here?"

"I wanted to see my father," Ruby stammered. "I ... I ..."

Don't say anything about me, Silverdale thought, desperately. It was fear, now, that kept her rooted to the spot. *Don't tell her I'm here.*

"You've seen your father." The High Priestess sounded ... unconcerned, as if Ruby was too unimportant to bother with. "You may go."

"I will *not* go." Ruby stood straight, as if the insult to her standing as a princess overrode her fear. "What have you done to him?"

The room seemed to *shift*, just slightly. Silverdale felt her head start to spin. The room was bigger, somehow. She was sure the three of them weren't alone. The High Priestess seemed to shift too ...it struck Silverdale, suddenly, that she was a glove worn by someone – or something – who didn't quite know how to be human. The thought was strange, but – once she'd had it – the thought refused to go away. She thought the room was growing darker ...

"I'm going to go to Sofia," Ruby said. Her bravado seemed to drive back the shadows, just for a moment. "She has to know ..."

"No." The High Priestess ... *changed.* Silverdale had to look away, squeezing her eyes closed. "You won't say a word. To anyone."

The world seemed to *snap* around them. Silverdale whimpered, heedless of who might be listening. She thought she heard Ruby cry out, she thought she heard someone laughing ... she covered her ears, but the sound echoed in her mind. The pressure against her thoughts grew stronger and stronger, bringing her to the brink of collapse before it snapped out of existence. She rocked backwards, catching herself a second too late. Thankfully, the High Priestess was nowhere to be seen.

She looked around, frowning. Ruby was gone. Her father was still lying on his bed, breathing steadily, but Ruby was gone. Silverdale inched forward, slipping back into the antechamber. Ruby stood there, leaning against the stone wall. Her face was slick with sweat. There was no sign of the High Priestess.

"Ruby?" Silverdale found it hard to speak. Her dress was drenched with sweat too. Her stomach growled, reminding her that she'd barely eaten. "What happened? Are you alright?"

Ruby opened her mouth. Nothing came out, but piggish noises. Silverdale stared at her in shock, all too certain that her sister wasn't playing a joke. Ruby snapped her mouth closed, her eyes going wide in horror. She couldn't believe what had happened. She ...

"Silverdale," Ruby managed. "I ..."

She broke down into more piggish noises. Silverdale recoiled, trying to understand what had happened. Was her sister cursed? Or ... or what? What had the High Priestess *done* to her?

"Ruby," Silverdale said. She had an idea. Maybe they could work their way around the curse, whatever it was. "Talk about something else."

"My new dress is quite comfortable," Ruby said. She sounded normal, but ... Silverdale could *hear* the frustration. "I can't ..."

Silverdale swallowed a word that would *really* have gotten her in trouble if she said it in front of the governess. Whatever the High Priestess had done, it was powerful. Ruby could talk about anything, she figured, apart from their father's condition. She might not be able to talk to anyone about it ... no, she probably *couldn't* talk to anyone about it. There was no way Ruby could raise the alarm. People would think she was playing a joke, if she hadn't gone mad. They rarely paid attention to the princesses, Silverdale knew all too well. And if they heard Ruby oinking like a pig ...

They'll definitely refuse to pay attention to her, she thought, sourly. *And they won't realise she's under a spell.*

"We have to get back to our rooms," she said, trying not to

notice the tears in her sister's eyes. They'd have to find a way to break the curse – or subvert it – before it was too late. And then … and then *what*? Silverdale didn't know. "We'll find a way, somehow."

But she knew, all too well, that she didn't have the slightest idea where to begin.

Chapter Thirteen

The curse, whatever it was, proved to be remarkably resilient.

They slipped back to Ruby's room, changed their dresses and spent nearly an hour trying to subvert the curse. But nothing seemed to work. Ruby couldn't talk about her father, or what the High Priestess had done to her, or anything that touched upon the subject. She tried to write it down, but her hand refused to do more than draw offensive doodles. Silverdale made sure to toss them in the fire before someone saw them. It would merely have gotten them both in trouble.

"We'll get out of this somehow," she told her sister, although she wasn't sure how. She didn't have the slightest idea if the secret passages led out of the castle, let alone what she could do once she was outside. Her father had warned her, more than once, that people outside would seek to use her, if she fell into their hands. "We'll think of something."

She kissed her sister goodbye, then hurried back to her chamber. The guard hadn't returned – she *hoped* that was a good sign – and she entered without incident. The tray of food was right where she'd left it, cold and congealed. She ate it anyway as she tried to think. Perhaps there'd be something in the library. There weren't *many* books of magic outside the Golden City, but … there might be *something*. Her father might have a book on countering or resisting magic. He'd certainly had good reason to fear hostile magicians over the past few decades.

It will be a start, she told herself. She wondered if she could get a message to Reginald. Maybe Greta could take a message on a ship and sail to the Summer Isle … it sounded practical, if the maid was willing. *And if he comes back …*

She glanced up, sharply, as she heard a knock on the door. If someone had realised she'd been missing … she composed herself with an effort, then shouted for them to come in. She frowned as a messenger appeared, wearing her father's livery. It was odd to see them so far inside the castle, at least outside her father's audience chambers. They were normally restricted to the lower floors.

"Your Highness," the messenger said. "The Regent requests the pleasure of your company for lunch."

"Oh," Silverdale said. She wondered if she should refuse. The High Priestess might have told Sofia something ... she wasn't sure *what* she'd have told her patron. Surely, Sofia would never have tolerated someone cursing her sister. And ... Silverdale told herself, firmly, that the High Priestess didn't know she'd been in her father's room. She would have cursed Silverdale too if she had. "I'm coming."

She stood, pulling her dress around her. There was no point in changing into anything fancy, not now. Besides, she wanted something she could hitch up and run in, if there was no other choice. Half the fancy – and expensive – dresses in her wardrobes were tailored to make it difficult to run. Ruby had joked, back when the world had made sense, that that was the point. The girls weren't *meant* to run.

The messenger led her out of the room and up the stairs to Sofia's quarters. She'd moved into the queen's former rooms, Silverdale noted. She wasn't sure how she felt about *that,* but she was *very* sure her father would be furious. He'd left the rooms completely alone, leaving everything as it had been when their owner died. He was going to *kill* Sofia when he found out, perhaps literally. Silverdale shivered. It was the clearest sign yet that Sofia and the High Priestess knew that the king would never recover.

"Silverdale," Sofia said, as Silverdale was shown into her private dining room. "It's good to see you again."

"Likewise," Silverdale managed. The High Priestess was sitting next to Sofia, even though it was a *private* dining room. She shouldn't have been allowed to enter the chambers, let alone join the royal family for lunch. "I'm glad we can meet *alone*."

She stressed the final word, but Sofia didn't seem to notice. "It's been too long since we've had a chance to *really* talk," she said, motioning for Silverdale to take a seat. "Our father rarely let us have the chance to be *sisters*."

Silverdale opened her mouth to snap something she'd probably regret, but the door opened again before she could say a word. Ruby stepped into the room, looking thunderous. A flicker of fear crossed her face when she saw the High Priestess, but she said nothing. Silverdale didn't really blame her. Three royal princesses at the table and … the one who had the power wasn't even an *aristocrat*. It didn't seem right.

She allowed anger to guide her. "And who is your guest, *sister*?"

Sofia indicated the High Priestess. "This is Queen Emetine, formerly of the Summer Isle, High Priestess of Ethane," she said. "And my loyal servant."

Ruby opened her mouth and tried to speak. But, again, nothing came out apart from piggish noises. Sofia's face darkened in irritation, her hand lifting as if she intended to slap her younger sister. Silverdale braced herself as Ruby shrank back, the full import of Sofia's words slowly sinking into her mind. Queen of the Summer Isle? *Reginald* had gone to the Summer Isle.

"I've never met a queen from foreign places," she said, hoping to distract Sofia from Ruby. "What are the Summer Isles *like*?"

Emetine smiled. Silverdale saw something *old* and utterly inhuman behind her smile.

"Cold," she said. "I was driven away by unbelievers. But I shall return."

That was my brother, Silverdale thought, coldly. Ice prickled down her spine. What had *happened* on the Summer Isle? Emetine … was she really the Queen? Or … or what? She wanted to ask about Reginald, but she didn't dare. The sense that Emetine wasn't human, if she'd ever *been* human, was growing stronger. The more Silverdale looked at her, the less human she seemed. And yet, there was nothing she could point to and say …

Sofia broke into her thoughts. "Father has left me with an immense problem," she said, as the maids brought the first course. "You two will assist me in clearing it up."

"Well, of *course*," Ruby said, sarcastically. "We are at your command."

"Quite," Sofia said, as if she'd missed the sarcasm completely. "I am the Regent. You will obey."

Silverdale and Ruby exchanged glances. Their older sister had always been humourless, but now … she was almost a mocking parody of her former self. Strict, yes, yet ... she'd always been decent enough to her younger sisters. Now, she was a fanatic. Silverdale glanced at Emetine, wondering just what the High Priestess had said to Sofia. It was clear she was more than just a travelling preacher, moving from place to place and spreading the word. She'd tapped into a source of *real* power.

Or perhaps it tapped into her, Silverdale thought. Her instincts were telling her to run. *What is she?*

Silverdale looked down at the plate the maid put in front of her. Chicken, she thought, but it smelt odd. There was something about it that bothered her. Perhaps it was a dish from the Summer Isle ... everyone said that islander food was bland and boring, but everyone said a lot of things. Her instincts were screaming at her, insisting she shouldn't touch it. She pretended to nibble as Sofia tucked in, eating with surprising gusto for a royal princess. She'd had table manners drilled into her for the last eighteen years.

"You wish us to assist you," Ruby said, in a tone she would never have dared use in front of their father. "How do you wish us to assist you?"

"I will let you know, when I decide." Sofia gave them a droll smile. "There is much work to be done."

Sofia finished her food and put the plate to one side. Silverdale allowed herself a moment of relief as the maids swooped in, collecting *all* the plates. Protocol stated that a course was finished when the host was finished, but normally she found it annoying. She could lose half a plate of food because the maids had snatched it away. Now, however ... Sofia might not have noticed that Silverdale had barely touched her food.

"I'm sure there is," Ruby said. "How many more temples do you intend to pull down?"

Sofia's smile sharpened. "*All* of them."

"They will have no place in our new world," Emetine agreed. The High Priestess seemed unaware she was talking to three princesses, one of them a regent. "Everyone will worship the Lord of Might."

"Really?" Ruby opened her eyes wide in mock astonishment. "And you are ..."

She started oinking again, helplessly. Silverdale felt her

heart sink. She looked at Emetine and saw her smirk, clearly enjoying her work. She clasped the knife in her hand, wondering what would happen if she buried it in Emetine's chest. Only a grim awareness that she didn't know where to bury it kept her from trying. She had no idea where Emetine's heart was, or even if she *had* a heart. Whatever she was, she wasn't human.

Sofia's voice hardened. "Ruby, if you do that again, I will have a guard beat you bloody with his belt."

Ruby glared at her sister. "Do your own dirty work."

Sofia half-rose. Silverdale, suddenly convinced that Sofia *would* beat her younger sister into a pulp, hastily asked a question. "What's happening outside the walls?"

"The northern barons have risen against me," Sofia said. She sat back, seemingly forgetting her anger. "They have united their armies and started a march to the south."

Silverdale blanched. The northern barons had never been part of the kingdom, not until their *former* kingdom had collapsed shortly after the Golden City itself. Their former ruler hadn't been able to hold his lands together. The barons had rapidly been brought to heel by King Romulus, but … they'd never quite grown used to being under a strong king. Silverdale had heard enough whispers, even in her chamber, to know they were just biding their time before they rebelled. And now, with the king in a coma, they were making their bid for freedom.

"They will, of course, be crushed," Sofia continued. "I have the Lord of Might on my side."

A year ago, Silverdale would have scoffed. Ruby would have scoffed too. The gods didn't intervene, not openly. She'd prayed, more than once, for things the gods had never seen fit to grant her, things that would have made her life a little more bearable. But now … she looked at Emetine, and her strange appearance, and *knew* there was something real behind the fanaticism. Something dark and dangerous and utterly terrifying.

"You've never led troops in battle," Ruby said, quietly. "None of us have. Reginald was the only one who …"

"It doesn't matter." Sofia cut her off. "My troops will be guided by the Lord of Might and aided by his servants. He will take them there and destroy our enemies. My troops will not lose."

Silverdale found herself exchanging another glance with Ruby. Sofia had gone mad, except ... was it really madness, if there was something behind the fanaticism? If she had power the barons didn't know to expect ... what would happen, when the armies met? Silverdale shivered, helplessly. She wondered if she'd ever know. Greta was the only person who might tell her what was happening outside the walls and *she* might not know the answers either. Who knew what *would* happen, when the armies met?

She looked at Emetine and knew the answer. The High Priestess's face was utterly confident, utterly certain of victory. And there was something in her eyes that told her that she had *reason* to be confident. Silverdale peered closer, heedless of the risk. The High Priestess was something far greater than human, something ...

Ruby kicked her. "Sofia's talking to you."

Silverdale looked up. Sofia was scowling at her. "Sorry. I was miles away."

"I could tell," Sofia said, tartly. "You two will assist me, later. You will be taught how to call upon the gods and ... *request* their assistance. You will devote yourself to your lessons or you will regret it."

"If that is your command," Ruby said, "I most certainly will *try*."

"You will do more than *try*," Sofia said. "You will succeed."

Silverdale looked at Emetine. "I've never heard of Ethane," she said. "Not even stories. Who is he?"

She tensed, half-expecting a blow or ... or something worse, a curse perhaps. She didn't pretend to have heard of *all* the gods – some gods had dozens of different names – but she was sure she had heard of all the major gods. The Summer Isle wasn't *that* far away. Legend claimed the island had been *settled* from Andalusia, so long ago that recorded history was more guesswork than anything else. Surely, she would have heard of Ethane.

Emetine merely smiled. "Ethane is one of the Forgotten Gods, the gods who were banished long ago. And now they have returned. And they will create a new world. And they will reward their followers and punish those who turn their heads from truth. And you must worship them, or be cast into utter darkness."

"That isn't an answer," Silverdale said. "What *is* he?"

"He is the Lord of Might," Emetine said. She seemed to swell, her presence suddenly far – far – stronger. "And he will make you great, if you believe in him, if you take him into your heart. I will serve him for the rest of my days."

"And I will serve him too," Sofia said. She sounded … different. She sounded … as if she was grateful. It made her seem younger, much younger. "He freed me from my torment. He freed me from my suffering. He gave me a world of my own. And I will be forever grateful to him."

"You had torment?" Ruby's voice was sardonic. "You suffered?"

Sofia's eyes flashed angrily. "I would be married by now, if Ethane hadn't sent his messenger to me. Father was going to give me to a pompous ducal windbag with bad breath and worse. I could have ruled, but the law did not allow it. I could have … and now I will! I will rule and I will serve him and …"

"You wouldn't have ruled," Ruby said, quietly. "Reginald is the first in line."

"And Reginald is trapped on the Summer Isle," Sofia hissed. Her anger was almost palatable, pulsing on the air like a living thing. "Do you think he's suitable? Do you think he can rule a country when his first move as an adult is to invade a worthless island that will never be of any consequence? He's on the far side of impassable storms and he will *never* come home!"

Emetine came from the Summer Isle, Silverdale thought. *And you really think the island is worthless?*

"I will rule." Sofia's voice grew louder. "And you will accept it. Or I will …"

Ruby oinked, helplessly. Sofia leaned forward and slapped her sister, hard enough to *really* hurt. Silverdale jumped up and stumbled backwards, staring at Ruby's face in horror. A nasty red mark had appeared on her pale skin, mocking her. It looked … wrong, somehow. It looked … she'd been slapped often enough to know the bruise should have been lighter …

Sofia looked at her. "Go back to your room and wait. Your lessons will begin shortly."

Silverdale found herself pleading. "Don't hurt Ruby," she said. She didn't want to see her sister beaten to death. "I …"

"She can go back to her room too." Sofia seemed to sag, as if what animated her had suddenly pulled back, leaving her powerless. "And she will start lessons too."

Silverdale caught Ruby's hand and practically pulled her out of the room. The door slammed shut behind them, although no one had been in place to close it. Silverdale barely heeded it as she yanked Ruby down the stairs, feeling as if they were being chased by invisible monsters. Her sister had gone mad, her father was in a coma, her brother was lost on the other side of the channel … and her other sister had been cursed. Silverdale didn't know what to do. She couldn't think of anything.

"We'll get out of this somehow," she told Ruby. It was hard to remain optimistic, but … whatever they were dealing with wasn't all-powerful. The tales of the gods had always made it clear that they weren't omnipotent. Quite a few stories talked about humans who'd outwitted the gods. "Take care of yourself."

Ruby touched her cheek, lightly. Her hands were suddenly stained with blood. "What did she *do* to me?"

Silverdale winced. The bruise wasn't bleeding, but … "I don't know," she said. She touched the wound gingerly. It felt dry, but when she pulled her fingers away they were covered with blood. "I think you'd better be careful."

Ruby glared. "Really? You *think*?"

"Yeah." Silverdale gave her sister a hug. "And we'd better think hard."

Silverdale tried to fit action to words. What could they do? If they slipped out of the castle … what then? Go north? She rather suspected that would be disastrous. The northern barons would be truly delighted to see them, if they got that far. Ruby was old enough to marry, if she fell into their hands. She wouldn't have much of a choice in the matter. And whoever married her would have a claim to the throne.

"We have to get word to Reginald," she said, finally. Their brother was their only hope. He was the rightful ruler, if their father was dead or otherwise unable to rule. Everyone else would try to take advantage of the sisters. "I just don't know how."

Chapter Fourteen

Isabella felt cold as she approached the ironhold, despite the pair of warming spells she'd cast on her clothes. The sense of ... *something* ... at the edge of her awareness wore away at her composure, even though it wasn't the first time she'd encountered someone who'd been overshadowed by the entities. The servants and guards had kept their distance – they'd reported seeing all sorts of things, things they hadn't been able to put into words – but they were sure Sir Handel was still in his cell. Isabella didn't disagree. She could feel the entity's presence from quite some distance.

The ironhold had been cunningly devised, even though it wouldn't have held a mundane prisoner any longer than it took the captive to parse out the cell's weaknesses, step over the lines and escape. Isabella had designed it personally, reasoning that a symbolic captivity would be enough to hold an entity prisoner until it was released or it found a chink in the cell's armour. It had taken days of arguing to convince the blacksmiths to build it – they'd been certain that it was a waste of time – but thankfully she'd had it ready by the time Sir Handel made his appearance. She allowed herself a slight smile as she reached the first door and carefully opened it, bracing herself. They wouldn't be complaining any longer.

She opened the door with a heavy iron key, rolling her eyes at just how easy it would be to pick the lock if one could manipulate cold iron. *She* would have no trouble at all breaking out, assuming there weren't any guards on the far side. The entity had to be getting frustrated, although it hadn't made any attempt to trick the guards into letting it go. She wondered, sourly, if it had *wanted* to be taken prisoner. Or, perhaps, if the entity behind Sir Handel didn't really care *what* happened to him. The ironhold might have blocked its way home too.

Nothing sprang out at her as she stepped through the door,

closing and locking it behind her. The sense of *presence* didn't seem to grow any stronger. Isabella took a long breath, centring herself, then walked to the second door. The feeder tray was closed, reminding her that Sir Handel had been fed only an hour ago. It wasn't clear if he was actually *eating*. The guards hadn't wanted to go inside the cell itself. Isabella didn't blame them. The sense of imminent doom was almost overpowering. *She* would sooner have walked into a knife-fight without magic or knife than step through the door. But there was no choice.

The presence flared around her as she opened the inner door and peered into the cell. She could feel a giant heartbeat shaking the air, hear the flutter of enormous wings ... she shivered, reminding herself that the entity couldn't touch her unless she let it. Sir Handel lay on the floor, unmoving. Isabella frowned and drew an iron bar from her belt, holding it at the ready as she advanced towards him. It was a crude weapon, far cruder than anything she'd used as a mercenary, but it should suffice. She'd seen the entities – and their servants – shrug off blows from more elegant weapons.

Her eyes narrowed as Sir Handel came into view. His face looked ... *parched*, as if it had steadily been drained of life and hope. She poked the body gingerly with the bar and swore out loud as it crumbled into dust. The entity must have drained its host completely, she reasoned as she probed Sir Handel's clothes. No one had dared search him, but ... it looked as if they hadn't needed to bother. Sir Handel hadn't been carrying anything a man of his station should have carried as a matter of course. No weapons, no seals, no money ... he didn't even have a copy of his credentials. It made her wonder how the entities had ever thought Reginald would listen to the overshadowed man.

Poor bastard, she thought. Reginald had been cutting, when he'd talked about Sir Handel, but she didn't think he'd deserved such a horrific death. *Rest in peace, wherever you are.*

Something brushed against the back of her neck. She tensed, resisting the impulse to spin around and lash out wildly with the iron bar. There was no point. The entity that had been puppeting Sir Handel was insubstantial, without a host. It shouldn't have been able to remain on the mundane plane. But it was trapped, just like Sir Handel had been. It couldn't leave as long as it remained inside the ironhold.

Isabella gritted her teeth as she felt the entity pressing against her mind. It wanted in, but … it couldn't force her to do anything. She smiled, coldly, as she stood. The entity seemed to move with her, as if it were *part* of her. She clamped down on *that* thought hard, before the entity could use it as a gateway to her mind, and headed for the door. The entity shadowed her as she rested her hand on the iron doorknob. She could almost *taste* its frustration.

"You may not leave, without my leave." Isabella focused her mind, concentrating on the sheer *truth* of her words. "And you only have leave to go if you return to the Godly Realm."

She opened the door. This time, she was careful to leave it open. The entity's presence grew stronger as she walked through the antechamber and threw open the second door. Reality itself seemed to *twist* around her – she heard someone screaming, a very long way away – as the entity rushed past her, the stone corridors beyond warping in directions no human mind could comprehend. She bit her lip, tasting blood. The entity had only a few seconds left if it wanted to snatch her mind or try to drag her into the Godly Realm … she held up the iron bar, silently daring the entity to take it with her. It didn't accept the challenge. There was a final flash of … *something*, a glimpse of a being so *different* that her mind practically shut down rather than look at it … and then it was gone.

Isabella sagged against the iron door, suddenly feeling very tired. It was cold, too cold, but she could feel sweat running down her back and trickling down her legs. She took another moment to centre herself, then looked back at Sir Handel's body. It was nothing more than a pile of dust. The sense of something *alien* was gone. The ironhold was empty.

"And what happened to you?" She checked the clothes again, just to be sure. "And what's happening on the mainland?"

She turned and walked out of the ironhold. A pair of scared-looking maids stood outside, one of them clutching an improvised weapon in one hand. She dropped it as soon as she saw Isabella, trying to look as if she'd never so much *thought* of picking up a stick and using it in anger. Isabella snorted, inwardly. Commoners on the Summer Isle weren't supposed to bear weapons. It wouldn't do to have them attacking their social superiors, would it? But she didn't blame the maid. The poor girl would have spent the last two weeks far too close to the entity.

"Clean the ironhold, then return to your duties," she ordered, tartly. The maids were safer in the castle than on the streets, although they probably didn't appreciate it. "The entity is gone."

The maids curtseyed, then hurried past her and into the ironhold. Isabella heard one of them exclaim in disgust when she saw Sir Handel's remains. She was probably new. She'd see worse things, if she stayed in the castle. Isabella's lips quirked at the thought. If the maid ever saw a quarter of what *Isabella* had seen ... she put the thought out of her head as she hurried towards the stairs. The maid was lucky, if she'd managed to retain some of her innocence. Isabella had lost *hers* long ago.

She reached out with her senses as she climbed the stairs, silently noting how much *better* the castle felt without the entity. The building still struck her as unsafe – it was a strange combination of too large and too small – but at least it was *stable*. She nodded to a pair of servants as she passed, both of whom seemed shocked to be acknowledged by her ... shocked and terrified. Isabella rolled her eyes. They couldn't pigeonhole her as ... well, *anything*. She was a woman who wielded power in her own right, not because of an accident of birth or a good marriage ... she shook her head in annoyance. They would just have to grow used to it. She would always be more than *just* Reginald's Queen.

Two guards stood outside the Royal Suite, holding their weapons at the ready even though they were inside the castle. Isabella knew they were more for show than anything else – she'd carefully warded the suite, ensuring that only a handful of people could get in without special permission – but she was careful not to make an issue of it. A visible show of force could sometimes nip trouble in the bud before it became a real problem. Her wards were simply invisible to non-sorcerers until they walked right *into* them.

She nodded to the guards and stepped into the suite. It was

smaller than she'd expected, even though it was quite well laid out by local standards. A large fire burned merrily in the fireplace, a window looked out over the city and the unruly seas beyond ... she frowned as she walked to the window and peered into the distance. Reginald's fleet was assembling in the bay, the ships rising and falling as waves washed against their hulls. She felt her stomach twist, even though she was a confident sailor. If it looked bad now, when the ships were in a sheltered bay, what would it be like when they were on the open sea?

Terrible, she thought. They'd been lucky to cross during the summer, when they'd come to the island. *And we might not survive.*

She shuddered, helplessly, as she saw the faces within the raging storm. The elementals were hard to spot, at first, but once she saw them she couldn't look away. They were *always* there, driving the storm ... she shuddered, again, as her stomach turned to ice. It wasn't easy to manipulate the weather and most sorcerers knew better than to try. The power requirements were so great that it took at least a dozen magicians working in unison to make it work ... and, even then, the effects were dangerously unpredictable. But now ... the elementals did it casually, with as little effort as she cast a fireball. The sheer power was almost unimaginable. She thought she understood, now, how Emetine had been seduced. She'd known hundreds of sorcerers who would have sold their souls – perhaps literally – for that kind of power.

The castle shivered, very slightly, as a gust of wind crashed against the stone walls. Isabella sucked in her breath as she turned away. The castle, whatever its deficiencies, was very strongly built. The locals knew what to expect from their weather. The winds outside had to be very strong if they were shaking the castle. She looked at the ships and saw the crews scurrying over the wooden hulls, trying desperately to keep them safe. She had a nasty feeling that some of the ships weren't going to last long enough to set out to sea.

She turned and walked through the door into her suite. The queen was apparently entitled to a bed of her own, away from her husband. It had surprised Isabella when she'd first seen it, even though she'd heard that kings and queens were not allowed to share beds like normal people. She wasn't going to do that herself … she snorted at the thought as she picked up her bag and dropped it on the bed. She'd learnt to travel light over the last few years. Most of her possessions had been left in the Golden City … most of them, she suspected, had probably been given away. Her father hadn't wanted any reminder of his rebel daughter. He'd probably been reluctant to let Isabella's siblings keep anything that had once been hers.

Bastard, she thought, as she opened her bag. *I bet he didn't leave anything of mine in the house.*

Isabella poked through the bag, pulling out a handful of clothes, a small collection of rare herbs and spices and, below them, the medal she'd earned when she'd left the Peerless School. No one disputed that she'd earned it, if only because the selection committee was impossible to influence. Her father had been one of the richest men in the city, but even *he* couldn't have bought the award for his daughter. Magic – a minor protective charm – sparkled over the golden disc as she held it in her fingers, remembering the day they'd presented it to her. Everyone had cheered. They'd known she'd worked hard and won fairly.

And that didn't stop my father from using it himself, she mused. *Did it?*

She glanced up as she heard someone step into the suite. Reginald. It had to be Reginald. Anyone else would have set off an alarm. Isabella knew her wards might not stand up to someone who had been overshadowed by the entities, but she was certain the wards would alert her to his presence. She turned, holding the medal in one hand, as Reginald peered into her bedroom. He made no move to come in, even though the door was open. Proof, she supposed, that he *hadn't* been overshadowed. The entities seemed to regard an open door as an invitation.

"Come in," she said, quietly. "What do you make of this?"

Reginald took the medal and studied it. "I can't read the writing," he said. "What is it?"

"An award." Isabella took it back and pocketed it. It was hard to keep the bitterness out of her voice. "I earned it for mastering a hundred advanced spells and *using* them, modifying them to suit my … circumstances. They don't give out medals like that for looking pretty or having lots of money or ..."

Reginald frowned. "And you intend to give it to *them*?"

"I have to sacrifice *something*," Isabella said, "and the sacrifice has to be something *meaningful*."

She indicated her bag with a wave of her hand. There was nothing in the bag that meant anything to her, from the cheap clothes to the potions ingredients. The latter might be expensive, but they could be replaced with enough money and time. She certainly had never had the time, since she'd been disowned, to develop any expensive tastes. And ... she shook her head. The medal was the only thing she had that could be sacrificed. The entities wouldn't be impressed with anything less.

And they might not be impressed with the medal either, she thought. It meant a lot to her, but ... would it mean anything to the *entities*? Mother Lembu had impressed upon her that it didn't matter – that what mattered was what *she* made of it – yet she found it hard to believe. *If they don't accept it, we'll be sailing to our doom.*

She closed the bag and returned it to her drawers. "How are things down there?"

"Oxley is bitching up a storm, whenever he thinks I'm not listening," Reginald said. "Gars is keeping me informed, naturally."

Isabella had to smile. Reginald had one great advantage over the late unlamented King Edwin. He could actually *trust* his subordinates. His Captain-Generals had fought with him in a dozen campaigns before they'd followed him to the Summer Isle. There might be a great deal of jockeying for position amongst them – they'd be more than human if there wasn't – but they weren't going to betray their prince. Oxley didn't realise that they played by different rules. He wasn't going to subvert them simply by complaining about the prince. And they weren't going to let him put together a conspiracy to put a knife in Reginald's back.

"It might be better if Oxley never returned to the Summer Isle," she said, slowly. She didn't care for Oxley and she suspected the feeling was mutual. The earl might have overlooked her sex, and her sorcery, but he'd never forgive her for stealing Reginald's heart. Or at least the royal marriage bed. "He'll just keep causing trouble for you."

"He may fall in battle, if he doesn't train his men properly," Reginald said. "Or one of them might put a knife in his back."

"He might try to put a knife in yours," Isabella warned. "And don't forget, the entities work through such people. Emetine's resentments were the gateway to her heart …"

Reginald looked uncomfortable. Isabella understood. A prince – and one who would be a king – found it hard to accept that a queen might plot against her king. Emetine was supposed to accept her lot in life, not conspire with her brothers against her husband. And yet … Isabella knew *she* would have simply walked away, if she'd been married off to a man she didn't love. It might have happened, if things had been different. Her father wouldn't have let her marry for love.

She felt her magic shiver and scowled. Emetine hadn't had magic, not at first. And then the entities had worked *their* magic. They'd made her powerful, at a price. She'd come far too close to killing Reginald. And now …

And now, if she's lucky, she's dead, Isabella thought. They'd never found a body. *And if she isn't dead, she might wish – deep inside – that she was.*

Chapter Fifteen

"Well," Captain-General Gars said. "Shall we board?"

Reginald nodded, then led the way onto the ship. *King Romulus* looked reassuringly solid, from the shoreline, but the boat seemed to shift underneath him as soon as he stepped off the gangplank. And she was still within the harbour, within the bay itself. He felt a flicker of guilt for the men he'd loaded onto the other ships, the ones waiting in the bay. They'd been riding up and down for days now, emptying their guts as they waited for the remaining ships to board. He should have been with them, even though he had too much to do on shore. It was good politics for a leader to share the sufferings of his men.

He heard the ship's captain start to bark orders once the remainder of the party came onboard. A handful of servants – and Isabella – headed for the rear cabin, where Reginald and Isabella would be sleeping for the duration of the voyage; the remainder stayed on deck, perhaps half-hoping they'd have a chance to escape if the vessel capsized. Reginald rather suspected they were deluding themselves. Quite apart from the danger of being thrown into the water and lost without trace, they'd probably be pulled down when the ship itself sank. And even if they managed to remain afloat, where would they go? They'd have scant hope of swimming to land before their bodies gave out.

The ship shuddered underneath him as the captain shouted more orders, orders that meant very little to his prince. Reginald forced himself to watch, gritting his teeth as the quivering grew stronger. His stomach started to churn, reminding him that he really shouldn't have eaten such a big breakfast before boarding the ship. Perhaps it would have been better to eat something dry, something that wouldn't threaten to burst out of his stomach and embarrass him in front of the crew. The soldiers wouldn't mind – they'd be amused to discover their prince was human – but the sailors would laugh. They knew Reginald had never bothered to learn how to sail.

And if I had a brother, Reginald thought as he found a seat, *he would have become Lord High Admiral.*

He watched, grimly, as the sailors unfurled the sails. *King Romulus* picked up speed, weaving her way through the mouse hole and onto the bay. Reginald felt waves beating against the ship's hull, each one making him feel more and more uneasy. He looked up and saw the faces in the gloomy clouds, laughing at him. A gust of cold wind, pregnant with drops of water, slapped him in the face. Isabella had sworn that the elementals couldn't hurt them directly, but Reginald wasn't so sure. The monstrous creatures were doing their level best to cause harm, if not death. It was impossible to believe that they were chained.

Gars stepped up to him. "The men will be sick as dogs, Your Highness, by the time we reach Humber."

"And so will we." Reginald felt his stomach twist as another wave slammed into the hull. It was hard to believe it could get worse. And yet, they hadn't even cleared the bay. "We'd better hope the City Fathers are unaware of our coming."

"We could land further to the north, or the south," Gars pointed out. "We …"

Reginald shook his head. His army was strong and experienced, but his father's army was stronger. The king's legions had been drilling the next season of recruits when he'd sailed for the Summer Isle. Now … he shook his head. Whoever was in charge on the mainland would have more soldiers than they knew what to do with, if they had the time to prepare their forces. The more he thought about it, the more he disliked the odds. The only hope for victory was to land at Humber and strike for Havelock as quickly as possible. They didn't dare give the entities more time than they'd already had.

And if they have the king under their control, he thought, *they could call upon hundreds of commanders who know what they're doing.*

He scowled. Sofia had never seen a battlefield. It was rare beyond words for a woman to serve in the army, let alone take command. Isabella was the only woman he'd known who'd served *openly*. And yet ... Sofia wasn't stupid. She could find an experienced commanding officer and put him in charge, if she couldn't lead the troops in person. Or ... he wondered, bitterly, just what was going on in Havelock. Sofia might have other ways to tip the balance in her favour ...

It felt wrong, somehow, to be planning war against his sister. He'd been taught to love, honour and respect his sister, even though he'd *also* been taught that she was a pawn who had to be deployed to best advantage. It was hard to accept that she could have taken control of the kingdom ... it would have been impossible to believe, if he hadn't met Emetine. The Summer Isle's Queen had been a monster, warped and twisted by the entities. And she'd wielded power. If Sofia had the same power, now ...

"No," he said, quietly.

Gars looked at him. "Your Highness?"

"Never mind," Reginald said. There was no one he could confide in, save for Isabella. And she was busy. If the ritual failed, they probably wouldn't last a day. "We just have to move fast."

But he knew, as he forced himself to relax, that wasn't going to be easy.

***

Isabella dismissed the maids as soon as she entered the cabin, then closed the door and cleaned the compartment from top to bottom with her bare hands. It wasn't something she would have done normally, even when she'd lived alone, but ... it helped prepare her for the ritual. Mother Lembu had made it clear, after all, that she had to prepare herself as much as everything else. She sat up as soon as she'd finished, carefully closing and locking both the door to the outside world *and* the door to the washroom. There was no way for a *human* to use the toilet as a way to break into the cabin, but the entities played by different rules. She needed them to come through the windows.

She closed her eyes for a long moment, then looked around the cabin, carefully fixing everything in her mind. It was smaller than she'd expected, although it was still the largest cabin on the ship. Two beds, each a little *too* small for both Reginald and herself; a wooden table, an empty bookshelf, a chest that had been emptied well before Reginald's servants had arrived to prepare the cabin for his presence ... she smiled, rather tiredly. The ship's crew had been reshuffled over the last few days, probably causing no end of confusion. She hoped the captain could deal with it. It wouldn't be an easy job.

Particularly as they had to give up a lower cabin for the maids, she thought, as she felt the boat begin to rock beneath her. *And the sailors will be trying to sneak into their room.*

She drew out a set of lines on the deck with chalk and placed the medal in the centre, then opened the cabin window. A gust of cold air brushed against her skin, like a kiss from a former lover. Isabella shivered, even though it wasn't *that* cold. There was a sudden *tension* in the air, as if the elementals were already aware of her. She supposed it made sense. The creatures pervaded the air itself. They were everywhere and nowhere. They probably knew everything that happened within their domain. She hadn't understood what Mother Lembu had tried to tell her, but now ... she thought she understood. Now ...

Isabella braced herself, then undressed slowly. The air seemed to get colder as she removed the last of her clothes and stood naked in front of the diagram. Her skin prickled, the sense she was being watched suddenly overpowering. She gritted her teeth, reminding herself that she was used to a complete lack of privacy. She'd been to the Peerless School. She'd had more privacy as a mercenary than as a schoolgirl. But then, she'd been allowed to kill mercenaries who'd tried to peek at her. No one would have batted an eyelid.

"I beg thee, come to me," she said. The words felt odd, in her throat. She tried to shape them in her mind, to *believe* in them. It went against everything she'd been taught, but ... she forced herself to focus. She could worry about how ritual magic related to *her* magic later. "I wish to bargain with thee."

The temperature *plunged*. Isabella felt her skin tingle uncomfortably, as if it was on the verge of turning to ice. She thought she felt her limbs start to freeze. Water droplets materialised out of nowhere, flying through the air. Isabella shivered again. This time, it was nothing to do with the cold. Conjuring water out of thin air was very difficult, almost impossible. And yet, the elementals were doing it *casually*. She kept her emotions under tight control, refusing to admit to fear. Losing control now, with the ship heading out to sea, would be disastrous.

She felt droplets splashing against her bare skin and looked up. A watery form was taking shape, in the centre of the cabin. It looked human, but … up close, it was composed of hundreds upon hundreds of water drops. She couldn't see a face, yet she knew it was looking at her. The pressure of its regard scared her more than she cared to admit. She was a powerful sorceress, from a line of powerful sorcerers, but …. she was nothing in the face of its power. She had the urge to throw herself down in prostration. It was all she could do to keep herself upright.

"I wish to bargain for a safe passage, for this ship and the rest of the fleet," she said. Her lips felt numb, as if they were already half-frozen. "And in exchange, I offer this medal."

She picked it up with trembling hands and held it out, concentrating on just how much the medal meant to her. She wanted to keep it. She wanted to offer something else, even though there was little else she *could* offer. Nothing that meant anything to *her*, at least. Reginald had offered a handful of his possessions, but … she shook her head, trying to ignore the tears prickling at the corner of her eyes. The Golden City was effectively gone. The Peerless School had been badly weakened. There was little hope of being given another medal …

Water splashed over her hands, then brushed against her eyes. She squeezed them shut as she felt the medal being yanked out of her hand, then opened them in time to see a giant watery face looking back at her. It was real and yet … her mind recoiled as she sensed vast strata of power all around her. Water exploded, splashing in all directions. For a terrible moment, she thought the boat had sunk like a stone. And then the elemental was gone. The force that had animated the water was gone too. Her mind seemed to skip a beat, her eyes closing of their own accord. When she opened them, she found herself kneeling naked in a puddle of water.

She didn't move for a long moment as she felt the boat

shifting underneath her. The medal was gone. The elementals had accepted the sacrifice ... Mother Lembu hadn't been very clear, but she'd hinted that the elementals would simply refuse to take a sacrifice that didn't suit them. And that they might be angry if they didn't like what they were offered ... Isabella realised that her hand was still outstretched and pulled it back. Her pale skin was marred with faint scratches, as if she'd been cut a week or two ago. She frowned as she picked herself up, feeling water dripping out of her hair and running down her back. The elementals must have left their calling card.

Her clothes were a sodden mess on the deck. The mattresses and blankets weren't any better. Isabella closed her eyes and risked a simple drying spell, followed by a warming chant that should have made her feel a great deal better. Her magic felt squinty, as it wasn't working quite right. That wasn't uncommon – she'd discovered that the entities interfered with magic during the invasion – but now ... she put the thought aside as the cabin steadily warmed, her clothes drying as she hung them from the ceiling. Outside, the ship was passing the jagged rocks by the entrance to the bay. They were on the way to the mainland.

We'll see, she thought, as she closed the window and started to dress. She couldn't stay naked, not when Reginald would want his cabin sooner or later. *And then we'll know.*

She thought she heard, just for a second, a titter echoing through the air. It was a remarkably childish sound, but it came from an adult throat. It was deeply – deeply – disturbing. And yet ... she listened carefully, but it didn't come again. She tried to tell herself that it didn't matter, that whatever had made the sound couldn't hurt her ...

... But she knew, deep inside, that that wasn't true.

***

"The weather is behaving oddly, Your Highness," Captain Morrow said. He was a tall heavyset man, with years of experience under his belt. He'd been going to sea since he was a child. "Look at the waves."

Reginald followed his gaze, despite an overwhelming urge to go inside and try to sleep until they reached the mainland. The waves were churning wildly, climbing up higher than the mainmast before falling back into the waters, but … they weren't crashing into the ship. The voyage felt smooth, impossibly smooth. Mighty winds howled in the distance, great flashes of lightning tore through the sky, yet … none of them came close to the fleet. A gentle breeze pushed them along, directing the ships towards the mainland. The currents he knew to be endemic around the island didn't seem to be anywhere in evidence.

He shuddered as he saw a wave reach up so high it was practically touching the sky before it splashed back down again. He was a strong man – he had no doubt of it – but the sheer power in front of him left him feeling weak and helpless. The strongest man in the world could not have swum back to the island, let alone made it to the mainland. Faces moved within the waves, flittering about as the waters rose and subsidised. He knew, beyond a shadow of a doubt, that they were controlling the storm. They were keeping it back from the ships.

"We're making good time." Morrow sounded as if he didn't quite believe himself. "We should be at Humber within three days, perhaps less."

"Perhaps," Reginald echoed. It wasn't *that* far from Racal's Bay to Humber, as the dragon flew, but the waves and currents made it difficult to sail even during the summer. "If we get there without puking our guts out …"

He glanced at Gars, who shrugged. He'd been at some pains to point out that most of the army would not be combat-effective until they reached dry land. Reginald hadn't been able to disagree. Ideally, he would have preferred to give the men a day or two to recover before launching the offensive. But he didn't have much of a choice. They *had* to take Humber before Sofia – and the forces behind her – realised they were there. If they had time to react, the invasion would become impossible.

And they may already know we're coming, Reginald thought. He'd listened, carefully, to Isabella's reports. She'd made it clear that the Godly Realm could be used to spy on the human world. And if so … there were limits to what they could do with cold iron. He'd had most of the planning done in ironholds, but … he simply didn't know. *If they have an army in the city when we arrive, we'll have to back off and land elsewhere.*

"We'll see how things go," he said, as another towering wave rose and fell in the distance. The elementals were *definitely* keeping their side of the bargain. "And if they're ready for us, we'll deal with it."

He felt a stab of guilt. Isabella had made light of it, but Reginald could tell that giving up the medal had hurt her badly. It had been special to her, special in a way that nothing else could be ... Reginald had offered a whole string of *his* possessions, but they hadn't been good enough. How could they be? They weren't *hers*.

I should have given her a ring, he thought. His mother's engagement ring was in the castle, waiting for him to bring home his future bride. It would have sufficed, he was sure, if it had belonged to Isabella. *But if she'd given that away, what would have happened to us?*

"Keep us on course," he ordered, putting the thought out of his head. He'd make it up to Isabella somehow, whatever it took. Maybe he could find her a replacement. The Peerless School *had* to know she'd earned it. He could write to them and ask for a new medal. "And have the men ready to move when we enter the river's mouth."

"Yes, sir." Gars gave him a sharp look. "Have you thought about sailing up the river?"

"Too risky," Reginald said. "We know what they can do. We'd be far too vulnerable."

"Yes, Your Highness," Gars said. "But it's also the quickest way to Havelock."

"Too risky," Reginald repeated. He tapped his lips. "And remember, you never know who might be listening."

Chapter Sixteen

Isabella dreamed.

She knew she was dreaming, although she wasn't sure how she knew. The world seemed to be twisting around her, as if she was walking while, at the same time, utterly unable to move. Her feet felt as if they were trapped in treacle, as if she couldn't get her legs to move no matter how hard she tried. And strange images billowed around her, each one so indistinct that she simply couldn't make them out. She tried to open her mouth, but … no matter how loudly she screamed, she heard nothing. She was enveloped by silence.

The Godly Realm, she thought. Or she dreamed she thought. *I'm in the Godly Realm.*

The images sharpened, as if her mind had been waiting for her to understand what was happening before it allowed her to see … to see what she was seeing. There was no structure, as far as she could tell. There was no cause and effect, no logic … she saw an endless series of images and impressions, flashes of emotion so powerful that she found herself torn between gibbering fear, blinding rage and an arousal so overwhelming that she thought she felt a man thrusting inside her. Her hips spasmed helplessly as her mind rose through the Godly Realm, her awareness spinning until she was looking down at the Summer Isle. Its inhabitants moved around her feet, utterly unaware of her presence …

"Isabella," a voice said.

Isabella jumped. Mother Lembu was standing beside her, facing away. Her body was weighed down with chains, so heavily chained that the sheer weight alone should have sent her to the floor. It felt wrong, yet – in the dream – it felt almost *right*. Isabella shuddered, reminding herself that she was looking at a metaphor. The entities tried to show themselves to humans in a manner humans could grasp. But it wasn't *all* they were.

"Mother," Isabella managed. It was a dream, but it felt *real*. "What ... what happened?"

"I cannot accompany you to Andalusia," Mother Lembu said. The wave of despondency in her voice was so strong that it almost brought Isabella to tears. "You are moving out of my territory."

"I'm sorry," Isabella said. She *was* sorry. She just didn't know why. "I ..."

"You must call me, when you are there," Mother Lembu said. Her appearance flickered, as if she was shifting between her three aspects. "I will come, if you are prepared to pay the price."

Isabella tensed. "What price?"

Mother Lembu said nothing. Instead ... Isabella felt something *tear* deep inside her, as if someone had torn her heart in two. She felt odd, as if she were in pain and yet not in pain. It was a dream ... she felt the Godly Realm spinning around her, countless alien faces flickering in and out of existence. *Things* moved at the edge of her awareness, great swarms of entities flooding their way into the human world ... she looked up, sharply. Mother Lembu was gone.

Her absence was almost a gaping wound in Isabella's soul. She wanted to reach out to the entity, even though she knew it could be dangerous ... even though part of her suspected she should be relieved. She wanted ... The world spun around her again, the dimension warping and twisting as she fell ... fell right into her body. The feeling of living flesh hit her like a physical blow. Her eyes snapped open. Someone was looming over her ...

She hit out, throwing the hardest punch she could. Her fist slammed into flesh and bone. She felt a nose shatter under the force of the blow. The feeling snapped her back to full awareness. She was in her cabin, the cabin she shared with Reginald ... she swore as she sat upright, hastily casting an illumination spell. Reginald was glaring at her, one hand holding his nose. Blood dripped through his fingers and splashed on the deck.

"You were screaming," Reginald said. He sounded more irritated than hurt. "What happened?"

"I'm not sure." Isabella felt a pang of guilt. It had been a dream ... except, on some level, she was sure it had been anything *but*. "I just woke up ..."

She swung her legs over the side of the bed and stood. She was still fully dressed. There was no suggestion that she'd ever been undressed, let alone ...she shook her head, banishing the sense that – on some level – everything she'd felt in the Godly Realm had been real. It might not have been a dream, but ... it hadn't been entirely *real* either. She motioned for him to come closer and carefully cast a healing spell. The effort took more out of her than she expected, but the damage healed itself. Reginald looked relieved as he sat on the bunk.

"Sorry," she said, embarrassed. "I just saw ..."

"Don't worry about it." Reginald shrugged. "What did you see?"

Isabella hesitated, then stumbled through an explanation. It was hard to put her feelings into words. Mother Lembu had told her that she couldn't accompany Isabella ... but she hadn't been accompanying Isabella anyway. Or had she? They were linked on some level, Isabella was sure. Did she take the entity with her, wherever she went? Even inside an ironhold? Or ... she shook her head. There was no way to know.

"I thought you could go anywhere through the Godly Realm," Reginald said, when she'd finished. She'd forced herself to tell him everything, even the bits she would have preferred not to mention. "Why can't she come to Andalusia?"

"I don't know," Isabella said. "Perhaps she isn't welcome in Andalusia. Or ... maybe the king didn't give her permission to visit."

Reginald smiled. "Wouldn't it be nice if that was true? Perhaps all we have to do is tell them that they're not welcome."

"I think you'd have to be king first," Isabella said. Symbolically, it made sense. A king was the ruler of his land and people, in name if not in fact. And yet, she doubted it would be that easy. There would always be *someone* willing to dicker with the entities, trading power in exchange for ... for what? What did the entities get out of it? Worship? Or what? "Or we could ask your father, once we rescue him."

"We could," Reginald agreed. He shifted as she sat down

next to him, then put an arm around her shoulder. "You have any plans for the morning?"

Isabella snorted. They'd been in transit for just over a day. She didn't have any plans, beyond ... it struck her, suddenly, that they'd just crossed the outer edge of the Summer Isle's waters. Hardly anyone had paid attention to them, even before the Empire had collapsed, but ... they'd just left the Summer Isle's formal territory. The fishermen might treat the borders as a joke, and they'd hardly kept Reginald from mounting an invasion, yet ... the entities might take them seriously. If Mother Lembu was bound, in some way, to the Summer Isle, they might just have crossed the limits of her influence.

"I have some thinking to do," she said. She leaned into his arm for a long moment, even though she knew he could offer no comfort. He held her tightly, his lips brushing against her forehead. "And you?"

"Hardtack and lime juice, the breakfast of kings," Reginald said. His voice was oddly amused. He was a seasoned campaigner. He didn't *need* fancy food to be happy. "Lord Greely isn't happy."

"You forgot to bring the aristocratic food," Isabella said, dryly. She turned, allowing her lips to meet his. "How *terrible*."

"Quite." Reginald let go of her and stood. "I'll see you on deck, when you're ready."

Isabella watched him go, then lay back on her bunk and tried to think. The Godly Realm was everywhere and nowhere ... she scowled, silently cursing Mother Lembu for talking in riddles. Was there a *rule* that she could never be direct? And yet, there was something about it that made a certain kind of sense. Illogical sense, but sense nonetheless. Isabella smiled, wondering what her father would have made of that argument. He would have been angry at her for talking nonsense. And yet ... she studied her scarred hands for a long moment. If the Godly Realm was a whole different world, with whole different rules ...

She frowned. She'd grown up in the Golden City, which had had one set of rules. And then she'd joined a mercenary band, which had a *different* set of rules. And *then* she'd joined Prince Reginald, with the promise of moving to a *third* set of rules. She wondered, sourly, just how hard it would be to change again. It hadn't been easy the first time, when she'd left the Golden City. The culture shock alone had come far too close to killing her.

If the rules are different, you can do different things, she thought. She'd learnt to use aspects from *both* of her cultures, over the years. It had made her a more effective mercenary, once she'd overcome the first hurdles. *What can I do with the Godly Realm?*

She closed her eyes, carefully reviewing everything she'd learnt since the first fateful encounter with a creature from the Godly Realm. And it *had* to have come from the Godly Realm. It simply hadn't behaved as if it were bound by human limits. It made a certain kind of sense, she supposed. If she, a sorceress, hadn't had to behave by mercenary rules, why should it? And yet, she had accepted some of the rules …

Her mind slowly drifted towards the Godly Realm. She could *feel* it now, at the back of her mind. It was there, as if she was aware of it when she thought of it and … she frowned. It felt like breathing, almost. She wasn't aware of her breathing except when she thought of it. She leaned forward mentally, trying to peer into the Godly Realm without actually entering it. If one could use the Godly Realm to look down at the human world, why couldn't you do the same in reverse?

The world seemed to spin around her, as if she couldn't quite grasp what she was seeing. The Godly Realm was a sphere. A huge sphere. No, a *tiny* sphere. It was impossibly big and, at the same time, impossibly small. She understood, just for a second, how one *could* use the Godly Realm to move vast distances in a heartbeat. Distance simply didn't exist in the Godly Realm. She hung in the space between worlds, watching as … *things* … scratched at the edge of realities. She thought she finally saw a logic to the realm …

She fell back into her body, her head spinning in pain. Her mind twitched, as if she'd blacked out and recovered so quickly that she wasn't sure if anything had happened at all. She thought something had been there, once upon a time. And yet, what …? She reached for her magic, wondering if she could use *her* powers within the Godly Realm. Logically, if Mother Lembu and her fellows could work miracles in the human realm, she could do the same.

Her head swam again, the moment she tried to touch the Godly Realm. She felt her chest heave, as if she wanted to be sick. Her entire body felt heavy, so heavy she could barely move. For a horrible moment, she thought she'd been transfigured ... but the feeling was all wrong. She felt so drained she couldn't even call for help. Her body was useless, a great heavy lump that held her down ... it tied her down. Her arms and feet were worse than useless.

She understood, in a flash of insight. She was *bound* to the human realm. She was tied down by her own flesh and blood. And ... the reverse was *also* true. The entities were bound to the Godly Realm. There were limits to what they could do in the human realm, even if those limits were poorly understood and ...

And dependent on the Godly Realm, she mused. Havant had tried to bring the Godly Realm into direct contact with the human realm, changing the laws of reality itself to allow his master to manifest. *Are they trying to blur the two realms together?*

She wanted to shudder, but her body wouldn't even let her do *that*. She lay in the bunk helplessly, wondering what would happen when Reginald came back. Or if someone *else* entered the cabin. She hadn't been able to ward it, not when the sailors might have to break in at a moment's notice. What would they do if they thought she was defenceless? She felt a flicker of panic, howling at the back of her mind. What if ... she called on her magic, directing it at the bunk underneath her. An invisible force hurled her out of bed. She landed on the deck, the impact knocking the wind out of her. But it also shocked her out of her stupor.

It drained me, she thought, as she staggered to her feet. She felt tired, yet unwilling to lie down and go back to sleep. In truth, she was scared *to* sleep. She didn't want to go back to sleep until Reginald was with her. And yet, what could he do if she ran into trouble in her dreams? *He couldn't even wake me up.*

She rubbed her forehead as she splashed water on her face. Her father, damn the man, had always commented that the danger of keeping an open mind was that something might crawl inside. Isabella had dismissed it at the time – it had always struck her as an excuse for refusing to consider that he might be wrong – but now, she was starting to wonder if he'd had a point. The more she touched the Godly Realm, the more she reached into it, the more the inhabitants of the realm could touch her back. And yet … they couldn't touch her without her permission.

Which I give them, when I open my mind to their realm, she thought, sourly. She couldn't see any way to avoid it, worse luck. *And then they can play their games with me.*

She opened her logbook and wrote down everything that had happened, as quickly and concisely as possible, then walked out on deck. The air was colder than she remembered, but not cold enough to cause problems. A chill ran down her spine as she saw the towering waves in the distance, pressing against an invisible bubble surrounding the fleet. There was nothing there, as far as she could tell, but … she swallowed, hard. The sheer power was terrifying. Being able to turn someone into a frog wasn't as impressive as she'd thought.

But the power isn't very precise, she mused. It was odd, very different from anything she'd seen at the Peerless School. It was a reminder that there were rules she had yet to fathom. *They can do very small things, or very large things, but they can't do anything in between.*

She watched the waves for a moment, ignoring the incomprehensible shouts as the sailors went about their business. They seemed aware of the waves, but not *awed* by them. The soldiers and noblemen, on the other hand, kept glancing at the waves, as if they expected their immunity to pop like a soap bubble. Isabella allowed herself a tight smile as she passed an ashen-faced Earl Oxley, who shot her a nasty look. She wondered, idly, which one of his many reasons for disliking her was foremost in his mind. There were so *many* of them.

Reginald was sitting in the dining room, studying a map while drinking something that almost – but not quite – passed for coffee. He smiled at her as she took a seat and poured herself a mug, a servant materialising with a plate of hardtack and jam. Isabella took it, feeling a flicker of guilt. The sailors would be eating the same thing, minus the jam. It might make the voyage a little more bearable.

"We are making very good time," Reginald said. He sounded pleased with himself. "We should reach our destination sooner than we thought."

"That's good," Isabella said. She chewed the hardtack thoughtfully. The jam didn't do *that* much for it. She knew hardtack was good for sailors, but it was too dry and hard to be pleasant. "Or should we be worried?"

"They may know we're coming," Reginald said. He peered down at the map, his fingers tracing the roads between Havelock and Humber. They hadn't been badly damaged by the civil wars. "Do they?"

Isabella shrugged. "I don't know," she said. "They may have a way to watch us from the Godly Realm. Or they may be able to predict the future, as impossible as that seems."

Or is it? She frowned. *She* was tied to the human realm, but the entities weren't. It was possible they could see ahead or behind of the omnipresent *now*. And yet, if the future was impossible to change, would having advance warning do them any good? *They might see us coming and yet find themselves unable to do anything about it.*

She rubbed her forehead. "I don't know," she repeated. "We can't cover everything in cold iron."

"No." Reginald took a sip of his drink. "And we don't have the slightest idea what to expect when we get to Humber."

Isabella changed the subject. "I was thinking we could try a few experiments," she said, slowly. She had a couple of ideas, but they relied upon having someone willing to help ... someone who trusted her. There weren't many people who fitted the bill. "Do you want to help?"

"If you'll have me." Reginald smiled, tightly. "Just don't punch my nose this time."

Isabella flushed. "I'll do my best."

Chapter Seventeen

"You will understand, of course, that the world is primarily dominated by the *masculine* essence," Emetine said. She spoke with an utter certainty that everyone would not only listen to her, but agree with her. "It overlooks the *feminine* essence."

Silverdale tried to listen as Emetine went on and on and on. The lecture was tedious beyond words – and *she'd* had to endure her tutors reciting a family tree that dated back hundreds of years, with sharp warnings and severe punishments for any name she left off the list. The High Priestess was madly in love with the sound of her own voice, Silverdale decided. It was a common problem at court, but Emetine took it further than anyone else. Silverdale had caught her repeating herself at least twice before she'd stopped paying attention.

"I trust that you'll reflect well on your lesson," Emetine finished. She stood, the shadows seeming to glide around her without actually *touching* her. "You are young enough to be truly invested in our world."

"Thanks," Silverdale said, sourly. She lifted her voice, adopting the sweet tone that infuriated her governess. "Can I go riding on horseback now?"

Emetine's face flickered. "You can stay in your room and contemplate your lesson," she said, stiffly. "And tomorrow we will continue the lesson."

Silverdale opened her mouth to protest, then thought better of it. Emetine had done *something* to Ruby and … Silverdale didn't want to give the High Priestess, whatever she really was, any excuse to curse her too. She had the feeling that Emetine was just *waiting* for an excuse to do something nasty. She'd had tutors who'd found her such a difficult pupil that they'd gone out of their way to find reasons to punish her. Emetine might not need to go too far out of her way at all.

She felt tears prickling at the corner of her eyes and closed them, wiping away the liquid with the back of her hand. Princesses didn't cry, she'd been told. She'd been reprimanded for crying from the day she'd learnt to string a coherent sentence together, rebuked for every tear she'd allowed to fall from her eyes. And yet ... the more she thought about it, the more she wanted to cry. Her days were filled with lessons that made no sense and her nights were filled with terrors. She hadn't seen either of her sisters for the past two days. She had no idea what had happened to them.

Emetine must be tutoring Ruby too, she thought, slowly. *And Sofia ...*

Silverdale opened her eyes. Emetine was gone. The door was open, but ... Silverdale hadn't heard her go. She scowled. Technically, Emetine should have begged her leave to depart. She might have been a queen, once upon a time, but Silverdale was her social superior. And yet ... Silverdale was too relieved to care. She winced as the door banged closed, the bolt snapping into place. Emetine must have slipped out so quietly that she hadn't made a sound.

"And what," Silverdale asked herself, "do I do now?"

She stood and paced over to the window. The courtyard below was deserted, save for a pair of noblemen making their way out of the castle. The battlements were lined with soldiers, weapons at the ready. Silverdale shivered, helplessly. Sofia presumably expected trouble, even though the northern barons were a very long way away. And, beyond them, the streets were almost empty. She could only spot a couple of people, both keeping their distance from the castle. Silverdale had the oddest feeling that they weren't even willing to *look* at the castle.

The door rattled as the bolt was drawn back, then opened. Silverdale turned, just in time to see Greta step into the room. The maid was carrying a heavy tray, balancing it neatly on one hand while she held the door open with the other. Silverdale smiled, relieved to see a friendly face. Greta had been bringing her meals for the last few days, ever since Silverdale had shown her favour. Silverdale wondered, absently, if Greta was being rewarded or punished. Either one could be true, below stairs.

"Your Highness," Greta said. She placed the tray on the table and curtsied, awkwardly. Her fingers twitched, as if they'd been struck with a ruler. And yet, there were no visible marks. "The kitchen staff ..."

Silverdale cut her off "What happened to your hand?"

Greta didn't look embarrassed. She looked ... puzzled. "I'm not sure," she admitted, holding up her hand. "I brushed against one of the new lords and ... my fingers went cold. Very cold. They still *feel* cold."

"Cold?" Silverdale frowned, coming forward. "You weren't *hit*?"

"No." Greta didn't sound as though she was lying. "He was coming down the corridor and ... I brushed against him. And my hand turned cold."

Silverdale frowned as she touched Greta's hand gingerly. It was cold, so cold she thought it had turned to ice. A maid who touched a nobleman without permission would be lucky if she was merely dismissed without a reference, but ... Silverdale had no idea what to make of it. Magic? Or ... or something to do with Emetine?

"Who did it to you?" Silverdale looked up, into the maid's brown eyes. "Who did this ...?"

"I don't know his name," Greta said. "He's one of the new lords. And he ..."

"New lords?" Silverdale repeated. "Which new lords?"

Greta looked uncomfortable. "I believe your sister ennobled them, Your Highness. I don't" – her voice wavered, just for a second – "I don't recall what he looked like. His face just went out of my mind."

Silverdale's eyes narrowed. Greta had every reason to draw a veil over which lord had assaulted her. There was little Silverdale could do, if the newcomer enjoyed Sofia's favour. And yet, Greta didn't sound as if she was hiding something. It sounded as though she honestly couldn't remember *anything* about the new lord. New lords? Silverdale didn't like the sound of it. Technically, the only person who could ennoble *anyone* was the king himself. And King Romulus was in a coma. He wasn't doing anything.

"I'm sure it will get better, with time," Silverdale said. What had happened? Really? She didn't know. "Stay out of his way."

"I will." Greta clasped her hands together. "The kitchen staff were hoping you'd like the food."

Silverdale took the hint and sat down, removing the lid to reveal a simple stew. It smelt odd, as if the cooks were experimenting with new herbs. They'd never been encouraged to do *that* before. Silverdale frowned, wondering if Sofia had had a word with whoever was in charge of the kitchens. King Romulus had been a heavy eater, but he hadn't been a particularly adventurous one. He had a selection of dishes he'd eat and woe betide the cooks if they dared serve anything else. Now ...

She picked up a spoon and took a bite, feeling a twinge of embarrassment at eating in front of Greta. It had never bothered her before, but ... before, the servants had just been part of the furniture. They walked in the shadows, picking up dropped clothes, cleaning rooms and generally keeping themselves busy while the royal family ruled the kingdom. Now, Greta was the closest thing to a true friend she had and it was pathetic. How could they ever be *really* close? The gap between them was so wide that no power could ever bring them together.

The stew tasted odd too, the herbs a little stronger than she'd have preferred. She ate it anyway, reminding herself that she had no idea when the next meal would be served. Sofia had bragged of fasting, in the past. She might decide that her sisters should fast too, if they refused to eat what they were served. And yet, there would be something else ... she put the thought aside as she ate a piece of meat. She wasn't sure what it actually was. The taste was masked by the herby sauce.

"So," she said. "What's happening outside?"

Greta winced. "I haven't been able to leave the castle, Your Highness. Half the staff have been dismissed and the remainder have been told to stay inside, on pain of death. I haven't been able to get back to my family."

Silverdale blinked. Greta had a family? She kicked herself a second later. Of *course* Greta had a family. She couldn't have come out of nowhere, could she? She'd have parents and siblings and probably a whole host of relatives who *weren't* trying to do her down. Silverdale felt a stab of envy. Her siblings weren't bad – she missed her brother dreadfully

– but her more distant relatives were backstabbing schemers who hated her family with a passion. Or so she'd been told. She had never been allowed to spend time with any of them, even the ones who were close to her age.

"And we've been kept busy, feeding all the newcomers," Greta continued. "The Regent has been calling noblemen from all over the country, bringing them here and accepting their fealty. The High Priestess has been tutoring us in her religion and" – her face twisted – "she's really creepy, isn't she?"

"Yes," Silverdale agreed. She knew she should have rebuked Greta for daring to comment on her social superior – maids weren't supposed to have opinions – but she found it hard to care. Greta was entirely correct. "Where's she staying?"

"I'm not sure." Greta frowned as she started to clear up the tray. "I think she's actually sharing your sister's suite."

Silverdale blinked. Her sister's old suite – and her mother's suite – had a guest bedroom, although she couldn't recall it actually being *used*. Sofia had been so isolated, through choice and convention, that she'd had few friends ... none of whom had volunteered to spend the night in the castle. And now Emetine was sharing the suite ... Silverdale shuddered. It was a sign of great favour. It was also a sign that Emetine really *did* have her hooks in Sofia.

"I see," she said, stunned. "Could you find out for me?"

"I could try." Greta looked uncomfortable. She would have no business anywhere near Sofia's suite and, if she were caught there, she'd have a number of very unpleasant questions to answer. She couldn't rely on her fellows to cover for her, either. Sofia's staff would suspect that she was muscling in on their territory and report her to the guard. "If I ask the kitchen porters ..."

"Please." Silverdale wasn't sure what she'd do with the information, but she was sure she'd think of something. Her father had taught her that information was power, although she didn't believe it. It didn't matter *how* much she knew. She'd still be the third princess, barred from the succession. And, perhaps, from the best matches, when the time came to get married. "If you can find out, let me know."

"I will." Greta picked up the tray. "Is there anything else I can get for you, Your Highness?"

Silverdale started to answer, but found herself yawning helplessly. Her vision seemed to blur, just for a moment. It was late, but it wasn't *that* late. And yet, she felt woozy.

"I don't think so," she managed. Her legs felt weak. It was all she could do to stand. "I'll see you later."

Greta half-bowed and hurried out the door. Silverdale barely noticed. She found herself staggering to the bedroom instead. Her legs buckled before she reached the door. She hit the floor with no clear memory of how she'd gotten there. Her body felt heavy, as if she'd eaten solid lead. A flash of alarm ran through her mind as it dawned on her she might have been poisoned, that the herbs had been used to hide the taste of the poison ... she opened her mouth to scream, but it was too late. The world seemed to come apart around her ...

... She found herself drifting upwards, passing through the ceiling as if it wasn't there. Her vision splintered, flashes of light and sound assailing her from all sides. A maid walked up to her, without ducking away or dropping to her knees. She walked right *through* Silverdale. There was a sense of *presence*, of thoughts and feelings that weren't hers ... and then it was gone, as if it had never been. Silverdale knew she should be outraged – the maid had no *permission* to walk through her – but she was too dazed to care. She'd been poisoned or ... or what?

The world seemed to grow translucent around her, as if everything had turned to water. It was blurred, so blurry that she couldn't see anything clearly. She could make out a blinding light in the distance, so bright it hurt to look at it. It struck her that she was looking at Sofia's suite ... was she looking at Emetine? Or ... or what? The thought of her sister seemed to send her drifting through translucent walls, gliding soundlessly towards the throne room. She saw flashes of others on the way: noblemen, merchants, servants ... she tasted their incomprehensible thoughts as she passed through them, unable to understand what she was seeing. They were so ... different. Or maybe her mind was refusing to work properly.

She found herself in the throne room, staring at Sofia. Her sister had always been beautiful, but now ... she was cold, captivating and completely invulnerable. There was something about her – now – that made it impossible to defy her. Sofia was glowing with light, a light that pulsed around her ... and went away, travelling in a direction Silverdale couldn't follow. Other threads of light pulsed towards her, from her court and beyond. Silverdale shuddered as she saw the darkening threads, suddenly convinced they were dangerous. They looked almost like puppet strings.

Silverdale looked away ... and saw Ruby. Her older sister was standing on the dais, looking helpless. Her hands and feet were tied. A metal gag covered her mouth. It was unbelievable. No one would put a tied-up princess on display, yet ... Silverdale found herself drifting forward. The gag wasn't real, but ... it was real. It struck her, as she touched the gag with her ghostly fingers, that she was looking at the curse. A faint sound echoed in her ears as she tugged at it, finding it impossible to remove. Emetine had tied it firmly in place.

I should be able to untie it, Silverdale thought. The curse had a presence in the ghostly world ... she wasn't sure what she was touching, but she was touching *something*. She could see a knot, tying the gag in place. Her fingers brushed against it. *And if I can ...*

Sofia looked up. Silverdale froze, suddenly convinced her sister could *see* her. Sofia smiled, so coldly that Silverdale felt her entire soul turn to ice. She couldn't *move*! And yet ... she could still feel a thread leading back to her body. She yanked on the thread, trying desperately to convince her frozen limbs to move. She wasn't even sure if she *had* limbs any longer. And then she was falling backwards, spinning helplessly as she crashed through floor after floor until she was back in her rooms. Her body lay below her, utterly unmoving. She wasn't sure how to get back inside. Her body felt as insubstantial as the rest of the world.

And then it hit her. She was *already* inside. She just had to pull herself back properly and open her eyes. She closed them, somehow, and opened them ...

The sensation of being *alive* crashed into her mind. She convulsed, retching violently. She struggled to stand, but found it impossible. Her entire body seemed to be immovable. She was tempted to throw herself back into the ghostly world, but she wasn't sure how. She choked, rolling over in a desperate attempt to keep from throwing up. The wall hit her – she was so dazed she thought the wall had actually hit her – the pain helping her to focus. She bit her lip, forcing herself to think. The experience had been real. She had no doubt of it.

She struggled, slowly, to her feet. Her body was coming back to life, but … she felt as if she'd been beaten to within an inch of her life. And yet, there were no bruises. Her arms ached, but – when she drew back her sleeve – she saw nothing. It felt wrong. The aches and pains seemed as insubstantial as her ghostly form. She gritted her teeth, remembering everything she'd seen. Ruby had been cursed and Sofia … Silverdale wasn't sure what had happened to Sofia. She had people on strings, but she was on strings herself.

And who, Silverdale asked herself, *is pulling her strings?*

She sat on the bed, breathing deeply as she struggled to calm herself. Her emotions felt stronger than ever before, tearing away at the poise she'd been taught to maintain since almost as soon as she could walk. Tears dripped from her eyes freely … she swallowed hard to keep from crying. She wasn't sure what she'd eaten – it was clear, now, that the kitchen staff had given her *something* – but the effects had been stunning. And … she recalled her fingers brushing against Ruby's curse. If she did it again, with a better idea of what to expect …

It would be dangerous, she was sure. She had no idea what they'd given her. She had no idea if *Greta* knew what they'd given her. And she didn't know if she should ask … she swallowed, again. She'd have to find out, quickly. She had a feeling that time was not on her side.

And if Sofia really did see me, she thought, *what is she going to do about it?*

Chapter Eighteen

"Take us right into the harbour," Reginald ordered. The sun was coming up, shedding light over the city. "And bring the rest of the lead ships with us."

Captain Morrow barked orders as the lead squadron moved into the bay. Humber was a mid-sized city, dominated by the giant harbour and the pair of fortresses on each side of the mouse hole. Reginald's gaze swept the bay, wondering if anyone would dare resist his forces when they landed. The remainder of the fleet would be holding back, waiting until he secured the docks, but ... he needed to take the docks intact, if he wanted to unload his ships without undue delay. And, ideally, he needed to take the city too.

He gritted his teeth as they moved further into the bay, a handful of fishing boats scattering in all directions. There had been no time to announce himself, no time to demand surrender ... the hell of it, he knew, was that a great many innocent men and women were about to die because he didn't dare wait and see if the city fathers would welcome him. They should, as their Crown Prince, but Sofia might have put her own people in charge. Or one or more of them might have been overshadowed ... his eyes narrowed as he saw a pile of debris by the water's edge. The temple to the God of the Seas, the one whose name must never be spoken, had been destroyed. Clear proof, if any were needed, that the entities were in control.

"Order the troops to proceed," he snapped, as the ship crashed into the dock. Wood screamed, protesting in outrage. He didn't care. Either they won quickly or they died, leaving the entities poised to overrun the entire world. "Now!"

He watched, grimly, as the first assault forces jumped off the ship and hurried into the dockyard. The harbour master had to be captured before he could coordinate resistance, the fortresses seized before the gates could be barred and archers hurried to the walls to snipe at his men. He heard an arrow hissing through the air and cursed, although he had no idea who was shooting at whom. Someone had loosed an arrow and all hell was about to break loose. He lifted his hand, signalling to two more ships. They turned to advance on the fortresses, their archers snapping off arrows at anyone unwary enough to stick their heads above the battlements. The death toll was already starting to mount rapidly.

A low shudder ran through the ship as the remainder of his men rushed forward, hurrying down the gangplanks and running into the dockyard houses. Hopefully, most civilians would have the sense to keep their heads down and wait for order to be restored. Storming a city was always costly, all the more so if the locals were foolish enough to resist beyond the point of reason. Maddened troops would loot, rape and burn as they saw fit, no matter what their commanders said. He cursed under his breath, feeling a spasm of guilt. Humber was no enemy town, no wretched hive of rebels. It was a friendly city, a city in his homeland … a city he would rule, if he lived long enough to take the crown. He hated the thought of unleashing his men, knowing that there would be atrocities, but … he had no choice. He didn't dare let the city fathers have time to defend themselves.

He turned and walked to the gangplank as the lead elements started reporting back, informing him that they'd seized the docks without serious resistance. One of the fortresses had been overwhelmed without a fight, the other – commanded by a better officer and staffed by better men – had managed to bar its gates, although Reginald's archers were keeping the fortress's archers from getting off more than a handful of shots. A grim-faced Isabella joined him as they walked down the gangplank, his bodyguards already waiting at the bottom. The stone felt odd, under his feet. He felt another pang of guilt as he saw a body lying by the side of the road, where it had fallen. A defender? Or someone who'd been in the wrong place at the wrong time? Either way, it was a tragedy.

"Your Highness," Sergeant Ruthven said. "They have captured the harbourmaster."

Reginald nodded as a fat man in fancy clothes – too fancy,

for a harbourmaster – was pushed into view by a pair of grim-faced soldiers. The man was pasty-white, trembling like a leaf. His eyes flickered from side to side, as if he expected the soldiers to tire of pushing him around and gut him like a trout. Reginald didn't blame him, not really. They'd all heard what happened when a city was stormed, these days. Humber had had no reason to expect attack, but ... it had been attacked. The harbourmaster was probably praying that his wife and daughters would have the wit to flee before it was too late.

"Bow before your king," one of the soldiers snapped, as he shoved the harbourmaster to his knees. "You piece of ..."

"That will do," Reginald said. He peered at the harbourmaster, who stared back at him in disbelief. "You. Who are you?"

The harbourmaster looked torn between stammering an answer and fainting. "Lord Tallish, Your ... ah, Your Majesty."

"Your Highness," Reginald corrected, absently. Lord Tallish? He'd never heard of the man. "Do you know who I am?"

"Yes ..." The harbourmaster seemed to grow even paler. "They said you were dead."

"I see," Reginald said. "I want you to go to the city fathers and order them to surrender the city to me. If they do so, they may keep their positions. If not" – he drew his finger across his throat – "you can imagine."

The harbourmaster grovelled. "Your Highness ..."

"Go." Reginald felt a twinge of disgust, mingled with the grim awareness the harbourmaster had no alternative. What else could he do? "Hurry."

The man turned and stumbled off. Reginald watched him for a second, then snapped orders as his senior officers assembled. The remainder of the ships were summoned, their troops primed for dispatch into the city; the advance elements were reformed, bellowing orders for civilians to go home and stay off the streets. Reginald shuddered as the lead elements crashed into a marketplace, knowing that most of the traders wouldn't have had time to pack up and run before it was too late. More dead bodies lay where they'd fallen, mostly middle-aged men. Only a couple of them were women.

"More destroyed temples," Isabella commented, as they passed the street of the gods. The temples were nothing more than piles of rubble, the statues Reginald had seen on his last visit to the city gone … presumably melted down for scrap. He wasn't much of a believer, but it still made him uncomfortable. He'd seen too much to *completely* dismiss the idea of the old gods. "They've been busy."

Reginald nodded, listening to a stream of messengers as they reported back. A handful of defenders had made a stand, but there weren't enough of them to make any real difference to the final outcome. They had been isolated, then left to wither on the vine. Others had broken, throwing away their weapons, tearing off their uniforms and trying to blend into the surrounding crowds. They'd be in deep trouble, when – if – their units were reformed. And yet … Reginald wasn't too surprised. Humber had never been a particularly seditious city. Indeed, it had been quite loyal to the king. Reginald's father had invested heavily in Humber and the city-folk had repaid him handsomely. He'd certainly never needed to position his elite troops in the local garrison.

And I stripped them bare to help my invasion, Reginald thought. *The ones who remained behind were the dregs of the service.*

He put the thought aside as he heard trumpets blowing, begging for a truce. Reginald considered it, quickly. The city fathers should know better than to move men around under cover of a truce – it wasn't a smart thing to do, when it would discourage others from offering and accepting truces – but there was no way to be sure. And yet … he frowned as he saw smoke starting to rise in the distance. Humber itself was built of solid stone, but the slums outside the walls were not. A fire could burn down most of the city before it was stopped, particularly if the defenders were busy fighting the invaders instead of the inferno. And if that happened, Sofia wouldn't *need* the entities to raise the country against him. They'd call him the Mad Prince and they'd be right.

"Blow the truce countersign," he ordered, calmly. "And tell the city fathers to come forward."

He set up his forward post in a merchant's shop and waited. It was nearly thirty minutes before the city fathers, wearing purple robes and chains of office, stumbled down the street and into the shop. They looked like peas in a pod, the nasty part of his mind noted; they were all overweight, ugly and generally unpleasant. Reginald rather suspected they were about as popular as a dose of the clap. City fathers tended to be either good for the city or deeply corrupt and he feared these were the latter. In some ways, it was a good thing. A corrupt man would do as he was told as long as a blade was pressed against his chest. But he still hated having to rely on them.

"Your Highness," the leader stammered. His chain was slightly more ornate than the others. Reginald guessed he was the mayor. "I ... I welcome you to Humber."

"Thank you," Reginald said, dryly. "You have two options. You can order your remaining forces to surrender, whereupon you can keep your positions under me, or you can try to continue the fight. If so, you will be treated as declared enemies and traitors when – not if – you fall into my hands."

He made a show of glancing at the clock someone had fixed to the wall. "You have one minute to decide."

The city fathers stared at him in horror. Reginald tried – not too hard – to conceal his disgust. They were fat and useless, probably more inclined to skim the cream from the city's merchants than invest in their future. They'd never had to make any *hard* decisions, certainly nothing harder than deciding what they should eat for lunch. They looked to have long since lost whatever nerve and skill they'd once possessed. Reginald was *sure* they had the city thoroughly sewn up to ensure their power was never challenged. If they hadn't, someone would have given them the boot well before he'd landed with an army at his back.

"We surrender, ah ... Your Highness," the Lord Mayor said, finally. The others nodded in unison. "I'll have the orders issued at once."

"Very good." Reginald resisted the urge to gloat. He needed their cooperation, for now. Afterwards ... it would be interesting to see if they kept their positions now they'd been exposed as cowards and fools. Strong men in their positions could have accomplished much, even if they had been caught by surprise. They could certainly have made the invasion a great deal harder. "Send one of your fellows. *You* can explain to me" – his eyes bored into the Lord Mayor's –

"precisely *what's* been happening since I left."

The Lord Mayor twitched uncomfortably. Reginald recognised the signs of a man who wanted to talk in private, but he wasn't inclined to care. It would be better, in the long run, if *all* the city fathers knew and understood what had been said. Besides, he really didn't care for the man. He wasn't going to let him claim an influence he didn't possess.

"Your father was taken ill, several months ago," the Lord Mayor said, slowly. "The heralds proclaimed his daughter as Regent, in your absence. We didn't dare to disagree."

"Quite," Reginald said. Sofia was a princess, even if she was ... well, a *princess*. The Lord Mayor was a jumped-up commoner. "And then?"

"Then the orders started to arrive," the Lord Mayor said. "We were told to smash temples and ... well, there was some resistance, but the Regent's army was too powerful. The garrison commander had no qualms about smashing anyone who got in his way. He was ... he was odd."

Reginald's eyes narrowed. Beside him, he felt Isabella tense. "In what way?"

"He ... I can't put my finger on it," the Lord Mayor said. "But he had a way of talking that made you want to go along with him."

"I see," Reginald said, slowly. An overshadowed man? Or simply an ass? They'd have to find out, quickly. "And then ...?"

The Lord Mayor hesitated. "I don't know for sure, Your Highness. There were a lot of stories, a lot of rumours ... nothing ever really confirmed. People were seeing strange creatures in the countryside. Others were reporting entire towns and villages emptied of people. The northern barons are supposed to be revolting ... in more ways than one, Your Highness. I don't know *what's* happened in Havelock, but *something* clearly has."

Reginald nodded. The northern barons really *were* revolting, in all senses of the word. He'd battered them into submission years ago, as his father's envoy, but he'd never really expected them to stay loyal. They'd probably been waiting for a chance to rise again, hoping to either secure their independence or extort better terms from their king. Reginald had a feeling they were going to be disappointed.

They simply lacked the kind of long-term thinking that would let them maintain their independence, even if the entities weren't involved. Sofia would crush them like bugs.

They may come in handy, as a diversion, he thought. He had no intention of allying himself with them, if it could be avoided. They would demand far too high a price. *If Sofia has already dispatched troops north, they might not be able to make it back in time.*

He dismissed the thought. "I'm going to deal with it," he said. "You and yours will assist me in preparing the city for the coming war. Do you understand me?"

The Lord Mayor nodded, quickly. Reginald wondered just how much he *really* understood. Reginald had the best army on the mainland, as far as he was concerned, but he was cut off from all sources of supply. A long drawn-out campaign would work in Sofia's favour, not his. And the entities were a wild card. Sofia would find *something* for them to do, but what? He was sure they'd think of something.

He dismissed the city fathers with a wave of his hand, then turned his attention to the map. Resistance had been very light, thankfully, although that might change when word reached the garrison. The defenders were outside the city walls, which meant they might not be able to keep his men from taking up position until it was far too late. His lips twitched, grimly. It was standard procedure – it wouldn't do for the garrison to be tempted into allying with the city, rather than its king – but this time it had bitten them hard. They wouldn't be able to prevent him from bringing in the rest of his fleet.

But if the commander has been overshadowed, he might try anyway, Reginald thought. A smart CO might pull back and harass him as he marched on Havelock, or simply take his men to the capital to strengthen the defences, but what would an overshadowed man do? Attack at once? Or the smart thing? *We have to get rid of him before he can cause problems.*

He looked at Isabella. "What do you make of it?"

"The next battle will be a great deal harder," Isabella said. "They'll have learnt from the past."

Reginald nodded, slowly. "Sofia won't be able to keep control of the country if she loses Havelock," he said, although he wasn't sure that was true. *Sofia* would have problems, sure, but the entities were a whole other story. "They'll have to stop me before I reach the city walls."

He gritted his teeth. Storming Humber had been a gamble … and the locals hadn't had any reason to suspect he'd attack. Storming Havelock would be a great deal harder, with or without the entities. He could win, only to be so weakened that he couldn't keep the barons from declaring independence or his aristocrats from dethroning him. The bastards would turn on him in a heartbeat, he was sure. There was no trusting men who'd kill their father and pimp their daughters for a tiny scrap of power.

And yet, the entities have to be stopped, he thought. *Whatever happens, they have to be stopped.*

He met Isabella's eyes, evenly. "Can I ask you to do something for me?"

His heart clenched. She wasn't someone he could send into danger … no, he just didn't want to do it. He liked her. Sending her into danger, perhaps to death – or worse – was more than he cared to do. It felt wrong, particularly when he knew he had to keep *himself* out of danger. But too much was at stake. He couldn't afford to feel doubts now.

"Of course," Isabella said. She gave him a half-smile. "What do you want?"

She's a trained sorceress, Reginald reminded himself. It didn't help. He felt like the worst of cowards. His enemies would mock him relentlessly if they knew what he intended to do. And yet … he pushed his doubts aside. *She knows what she's doing.*

"I need you to kill someone for me," he said. "And you'll have to take a blade of cold iron."

Chapter Nineteen

Silverdale had anticipated everything from a beating to a curse as she lay in her bed, waiting for Sofia or Emetine or one of their servants to punish her for trying to fiddle with Ruby's curse. She'd tensed every time the door had opened, only to relax as Greta stepped into the room with new trays of food. By the time she'd finally drifted off to sleep, proper sleep, she'd been half-convinced her sister was biding her time. Surely, if she'd known that Silverdale had been spying on her, she wouldn't be *calm* about it.

The following morning, Greta didn't show. Instead, the governess stepped into the room.

"Get dressed," she snapped. "Now."

Silverdale jumped, then practically *threw* herself out of bed as she hurried to obey. The governess wasn't angry, as far as she could tell. The governess was *scared*. Silverdale studied the older woman out of the corner of her eye as she plucked undergarments and dresses from the wardrobe and shoved them at her. She probably wasn't going to court, Silverdale decided as she scrambled to get dressed. Her clothes were fancy, but not *that* fancy.

The governess caught her hand and pulled her out of the room as if she were a child of five, not a young woman of twelve. Silverdale gritted her teeth against the pain, but refused to beg the governess to let her go. She was too stubborn to give the older woman the satisfaction of knowing she'd hurt her charge. Besides, the governess really *was* scared. It was a deeply personal fear, fear more for herself than Silverdale. Silverdale wasn't sure what to make of it. The governess could hardly be blamed for Silverdale's exploits, could she? It wasn't *her* who'd poisoned Silverdale's food.

Silverdale forced herself to remain calm as the governess shoved her into the throne room. Sofia sat on the throne, her expression dark and yet – somehow – inscrutable. Ruby stood next to her, her hands clasped behind her back. Silverdale felt her vision blur – just for a second, she saw her older sister bound and gagged – and blinked, hard, until the impressions went away. She had no idea what they were, but she didn't have time to worry about them.

"Stand next to your sister," Sofia ordered. Her voice was cold, angry. But it didn't seem to be directed at Silverdale. "And wait."

Silverdale dropped a curtsy and stepped onto the dais. Ruby didn't move. Her eyes were dull and flat, as if she wasn't there any longer. Silverdale shivered, remembering the vision she'd seen. Ruby had been cursed again, perhaps more than once. She couldn't do anything to help, not now. Silverdale wanted to shout and scream in frustration, but she didn't dare. She might wind up cursed too. Instead, she turned to face the empty room. The doors were already opening.

She blinked in surprise as three people walked into the chamber. The horde of noblemen, merchants and hangers-on she'd expected was nowhere in evidence. Instead … she felt her eyes narrow as she surveyed the group. Emetine, unfortunately. A man she didn't recognise, clad in a long red robe that covered him from head to toe. She thought she saw glinting eyes behind the eye-slit, but it was hard to be sure. It crossed her mind that the figure could be female instead … there was no way to know. The robe was completely shapeless. And behind him …

She sucked in her breath. Sir Oswald had been one of Sofia's more hopeless suitors, back when the world had made sense. He was handsome enough, Silverdale supposed, but there was nothing between his ears apart from sawdust and … well, she didn't know. She had the feeling he couldn't have counted past ten without taking off his boots. And even if he'd been the smartest man on the planet, he wasn't anything like high-ranking enough to marry the king's oldest daughter. Sofia had rejected him without a second thought.

And now he's here, Silverdale thought, glumly. *Why?*

She met Sir Oswald's eyes. He looked grimly determined to do … *something*. She wondered what it might be. Sofia had no *need* to summon him. He was so low-ranking that no one would have batted an eyelid if he was told to leave court and never come back. And yet, he was here. Why? Silverdale shivered. She had no idea, but she had a feeling it boded ill. The faint smile on Emetine's face was the icing on the cake.

Her vision blurred, again. Emetine was glowing with a brilliant light. A *lunar* light, Silverdale thought, although she had no idea why. Sofia was almost as bright, but dimmed somehow. Ruby was in chains, still. And Sir Oswald looked reassuringly normal. Silverdale would have run to him if she'd thought they'd make it out before Sofia reacted. The guards would have chopped Sir Oswald to pieces and probably thrown her back into her room, if they'd tried. He was too slow on the uptake to even get that far …

Silverdale blinked, hard. The vision faded.

"Humber has been attacked," Sofia said. Her voice was cold, but steady. "The city is falling, even now."

Silverdale blinked. She was no soldier, but she'd read the books on military theory and tactics Reginald had left behind. Humber wasn't that far from Havelock, yet … it was unlikely that word could possibly have reached Havelock before the battle had been decided, one way or the other. How could Sofia know what had happened? Silverdale shivered as she remembered her visions. If Sofia had been having them too, she might have been keeping an eye on Humber. But who could have attacked the city …?

Her mind raced. She knew how to read a map. The northern barons couldn't have reached Humber without going through Havelock. And the castle hadn't been attacked. She hadn't even seen any sign of an army passing by the city, outside the walls. The barons *couldn't* have attacked Humber? And that meant … her heart skipped a beat. Reginald?

"The city must be recovered," Sofia said. Her eyes alighted on Sir Oswald. "Will you serve me, as faithfully as you served my father?"

Sir Oswald looked surprised – and then overjoyed – that Sofia had spoken to him. "It will be my pleasure, Your Highness," he said. His pompous manner would have been laughable if Silverdale hadn't had a crushing, overwhelming, sense of doom. "I will do anything you wish."

Sofia rose. "Will you do *anything* for me?"

"Yes, Your Highness." Sir Oswald seemed to grow even *more* pompous. "It will be my pleasure."

"Then kneel," Sofia ordered. "You will carry my standard into battle."

"Anything," Sir Oswald said.

Silverdale frowned. The sense of overwhelming doom was growing stronger. And yet ... she found herself glancing around, trying to see ... she wasn't sure *what* she was trying to see. Sir Oswald was kneeling slowly, half-bowing his head as though he knew he should be downcast, but didn't want to take his eyes off Sofia. Silverdale cursed him under his breath. She was sure Sir Oswald should have run, even though she wasn't sure *why*. He was in danger. They were *all* in danger.

Emetine stepped forward. She held a golden goblet in one hand, which she held out to Sir Oswald. "Drink this."

Silverdale opened her mouth to shout a warning, but Emetine silenced her with a glare. Translucent shapes moved around her, threatening to become a gag ... she stumbled backwards, trying desperately to bat them away. The High Priestess paid no attention as she watched Sir Oswald put the goblet to his lips and drink. There was a coldly predatory look in her eyes. Silverdale shivered, once again, as the last of the translucent shapes faded back into nothingness. If she'd seen someone coming at her with *that* look in her eyes, she would have turned on her heels and run for her life.

Sofia stepped forward, resting one hand on her heart.

"I am the Lady Regent, rightful ruler of Andalusia." Sofia's voice held nothing, but utter conviction. "And I call upon thee, Lord of Might, to send me a general to command my forces and lead them to victory."

The chamber shifted. Silverdale felt reality itself spinning around her as the shadows grew and lengthened until she found herself staring into utter darkness. The shadows seemed to have teeth and claws ... she was sure unseen eyes, hidden in the darkness, were watching her with cold malice. The doors banged open as one, but ... beyond them, she could see passageways stretching in directions she couldn't grasp. She heard a low rumble echo through the air as she cringed back, suddenly utterly terrified beyond words. Her feet were rooted to the floor. She couldn't move. She couldn't run ...

She found herself staring down the passageways as another rumble echoed on the air, followed by another and another ... giant footsteps, she realised numbly. Something was approaching, something huge and old and very powerful ... she looked at Sir Oswald and shivered at the dazed look in his eyes. He didn't know what he'd agreed to, she guessed. He didn't realise what he'd done. Or what Sofia was going to do to him ...

Something moved, right at the end of the passageway. It was humanoid, but ... her eyes slid over it, as if they couldn't quite see it clearly. She could tell where it was by the absence of anything else ... her head spun, forcing her to look away. The sound of footsteps grew louder as the being approached, casually stepping into the throne room as if it were welcome. It *was* welcome, Silverdale realised in horror. Sofia had welcomed it into the throne room, into the kingdom, into the world ...

Sir Oswald whimpered, but remained on his knees as the creature strode towards him. There was a weird moment when Silverdale saw *both* the creature and the knight, as if they were somehow occupying the same space, then Sir Oswald stood. A low shiver ran through the room, followed by a flash of ... *something* ... that made her squeeze her eyes tightly closed. And, when she opened them, the room was back to normal. The man in the red robe was gone.

No, she realised, numbly. *It's not remotely normal.*

She heard Ruby gasp beside her. Sir Oswald had changed. He stood in front of the dais, tall, charming and devastatingly handsome. He hadn't said a word, but he somehow dominated the room. Silverdale felt a surge of overpowering trust and respect and ... and something she couldn't quite identify, something just a little sour. Sir Oswald stretched, taking a deep breath as he lifted his hands to the heavens. Silverdale forced herself to look closer. His face hadn't changed, yet it had. It had become a mask. She bit her lip, hard, as she realised what Sofia had done. She'd thrown Sir Oswald to the wolves. Literally. Whatever was wearing his face – now – wasn't human.

"My Lady." Sir Oswald's voice *had* changed. It was calm

and confident and it made Silverdale want to follow him into hell itself. "It will be my pleasure to take command of your armies."

Sofia smiled. "And it will be mine that you take command," she said. There was an edge to her voice that Silverdale *really* didn't like. "Bring me the head of the false prince."

That's your brother, Silverdale wanted to shout. *That's* our *brother*.

But the words refused to come. Sir Oswald bowed deeply, then turned and strode through the door. The guards on the far side, men who knew *precisely* how much respect to show courtiers at all times, snapped to attention, saluting so hard that Silverdale was sure they would do themselves an injury. The guards seemed so stunned by Sir Oswald's mere presence that they almost forgot to close the door. It took them several minutes to do it. It would have been funny if it hadn't been so terrifying …

Sofia let out a long breath. "And let that be an end to it."

Silverdale found her voice. "That's our brother …"

"He's no brother of mine," Sofia said. She sounded amused, rather than angry. "Is he not magnificent?"

"What did you do to him?" Silverdale knew it was unwise to question, but she couldn't stop herself. She'd never liked Sir Oswald – he'd certainly never had time for her – yet … did he deserve to be possessed? Or … or what? She forced herself to ask again. "What did you do to him?"

Sofia gave her a lazy smile. "Oswald wanted to be used," she said. "And I was happy to use him."

She sat down, resting her hands in her lap. "He will bring us victory," she said. "And then he will get his reward."

Reginald will beat him, Silverdale thought, desperately. She wanted – she needed – to believe it. And yet, it was hard *to* believe. Sir Oswald – or whatever he'd become – had had an air of being able to smash through everything that might try to bar his way. *Reginald will beat him.*

She swallowed, hard. "What are you going to give him?"

"What he wants," Sofia said. "He'll get it."

Silverdale shuddered. She couldn't mean she was going to *marry* him, right? Sir Oswald was too lowborn to marry a princess, right? And yet … it struck her, suddenly, that whatever wore Sir Oswald's body like a mask might want something very different. Her insides churned as she tried to decide what that something might be. It could be anything. Power, perhaps. Or … she saw the threads surrounding her older sister and gritted her teeth against the horror. Maybe the entity wanted something only Sofia could provide.

Her legs buckled. "With your pardon, I will return to my rooms," she said. It was suddenly very hard to speak. "I have studying to do."

"The High Priestess will escort you." Sofia's smile was cruel, a smile a cat might wear while playing with a mouse. "We don't want you getting lost along the way."

Emetine placed a hand on Silverdale's arm. "Come, Your Highness."

Silverdale felt ice brushing against her skin. She wanted to pull away, but she didn't quite dare. She couldn't force herself to *look* at Emetine. The High Priestess was maintaining her distance, save for the single unwanted contact, but it felt as if she were forcing her way into Silverdale's personal space anyway. She allowed the older woman to guide her to the door and down the corridor, trying not to wince as her cold hand got colder. Outside, the corridors seemed to be in chaos. Guards were staring, their faces astonished; maids were kneeling on the ground, as if the king himself had walked past. A couple had even fainted … she was amused to note that a particularly irritating highborn lady had *also* fainted. Silverdale would have laughed, if she hadn't been so scared. The woman had been too irritating for words – she was probably the most disliked person in the castle – but too highborn to banish from the court.

And everyone will make fun of her, if they didn't faint themselves, Silverdale thought, grimly. If she hadn't seen the new Sir Oswald herself, she wouldn't have believed it. *How many people are going to think that's truly him?*

"The world is changing," Emetine said, as they reached Silverdale's rooms. A guard stood outside, his face a blank mask. "And we must be ready."

Silverdale took the plunge as soon as they were inside. "What did you put in my food?"

Emetine didn't bother to deny it. "Something that opened your mind, just a little. You've got quite a talent, you know."

"Poisoning a member of the royal family is punishable by death," Silverdale said, trying to sound threatening. She didn't think it had worked, "And you ..."

"And *you* are not going to tell anyone, are you?" Emetine smiled. "Or do I have to take steps to ensure your silence?"

Silverdale shook her head, hastily. Emetine laughed. There was nothing *human* in the sound.

"I won't have to," Emetine said. She spoke with absolute confidence. "I won't have to because you want more. Don't you?"

"... No," Silverdale lied. She didn't sound convincing even to herself. "I ..."

Emetine cocked her head. "You're trying to lie to me?"

Silverdale glared. "What did you *do* to me?"

"I told you," Emetine said. "I opened your mind. Just a little ..."

She smiled, then reached into her pocket and produced a tiny glass bottle. "Just add a drop or two to a drink and swallow in one gulp," she said. "Try not to use more. You're not ready for it."

Silverdale took the bottle, numbly. "What's to stop me pouring it into the chamberpot?"

"Nothing." Emetine's smile grew wider. There was something so *knowing* about her smile that Silverdale wanted to punch her. "But you won't, will you?"

She turned and walked away, closing the door behind her. Silverdale barely heard the bolt slipping into place as she stared at the bottle. She knew, on a level she could never have put into words, that Emetine had told her the truth. The contents of the bottle would open her mind, allow her to become a ghost ... perhaps even save her sisters from slavery. And yet, she didn't trust the older woman. Why would she give Silverdale such a powerful tool, a weapon that could be used against her? There had to be a catch.

I won't drink it, Silverdale told herself. She wanted to open the bottle and pour it out the window, but somehow ... she couldn't. She couldn't bring herself to throw the liquid away. Her fingers started fumbling with the lid before she caught herself. *I won't ...*

But she knew, as she placed the bottle to one side for safekeeping, that she was lying to herself.

Chapter Twenty

The city walls were in absolute chaos.

Isabella pulled her cloak around her as she hurried towards the gatehouse. Hundreds of men and women – aristocrats, merchants, commoners – were fleeing, trying to jam themselves through the gates as if they feared the army was after them personally. Shouts rent the air as rich men tried to barter for freedom, for passage into the hinterland. Isabella tried not to feel guilty as she saw an elderly woman in fancy clothes trading jewels for transport west, giving away everything she could carry in exchange for safety. She wanted to tell the older woman there was nothing to fear, but she knew it wasn't true. Reginald could easily lose control of his army if all hell broke loose.

The guards on the gate looked as terrified as the fleeing civilians. They were trained for crowd control and customs inspections, not standing off an invading army that had practically appeared out of nowhere. Isabella doubted they'd heard anything from the city fathers yet. She wasn't even sure they'd *obey* when they were told to surrender. They belonged to the garrison outside the city, not the city itself. Humber wasn't their home. She was mildly surprised they were even allowed to man the gates. No doubt they were disliked enough by the population that any visit to the city would be as short as possible.

She kept her thoughts to herself as she joined the crowd pressing through the gates. The guards were opening them wide, rather than trying to barricade the civilians within the city. She wasn't sure if that was a good thing or not. The guards had every reason to want to clear the area as quickly as possible, but – at the same time – thousands of refugees flowing into the countryside would cause chaos. The local farmers would be eaten out of house and home within days, perhaps hours. But she didn't blame the locals for fleeing.

They had no way to know that Reginald's troops had strict orders to avoid atrocities.

Isabella felt a pang of guilt at the thought. Humber had been lucky. They'd had a strong king who'd kept his kingdom together with a minimum of violence, unlike some other kingdoms and free cities to the east. Isabella had walked through the rubble of once-great cities, trying to ignore the piles of bodies and the screams of women as their homes were ruthlessly sacked and burnt to the ground. Humber had been civilised, only a few short hours ago. The locals had been preparing for another routine day. And then the fleet had arrived and threw their entire world into chaos. Reginald had had no choice, but the locals wouldn't see it that way. The whole affair would be a terrifying blot on his record.

And they won't like it at all, she thought, as she passed through the gate. *And his enemies will use it against him.*

She put the thought aside as she cast a small glamour around herself and headed onwards, walking up the road towards the garrison. A handful of soldiers were directing the crowd away from the garrison, no doubt sweating buckets while the remainder of their comrades donned armour and grabbed weapons in preparation for a valiant last stand. Isabella felt a stab of pity, mingled with contempt. Humber might be a reasonably peaceful billet, but so what? They should have kept up with their drills. They'd no way of knowing for *sure* that Humber would remain peaceful forever.

A soldier caught her eye and started to amble after her, a big grin on his face. Isabella allowed him to follow her off the road and into the undergrowth, providing more than enough cover for whatever he had in mind. She smiled as he started to run, his face twisting into a leer. Isabella shaped a spell in her mind and unleashed it, as soon as he reached for her. He dropped like a stone, his body going limp as he hit the ground. Isabella was tempted to kill him, while he was asleep, but refrained. He'd have a great deal of trouble explaining himself to his superiors afterwards, anyway. Instead, she removed his armour and pulled it over her shirt and trousers. A little magic would ensure that no one looked past the armour, let alone thought to question her.

She smiled grimly and resumed her walk to the garrison. Dozens of infantrymen were milling around, hectored by sergeants as they formed into lines. They paid no attention to her as she reached the guardpost and walked right into the camp, more concerned – it seemed – with the prospect of putting their lives on the line for the first time in years. Garrison troops had a bad reputation, Isabella knew, but it was the first time she'd seen it. Reginald's troops could have crushed the entire garrison in less than an hour.

A pair of panicking officers ran past her, one of them holding a sword in a manner that suggested he'd forgotten how to use it. She glanced at them, then reached out with her senses. It was hard to be sure, but there *was* a slight distortion inside the headquarters building. The garrison CO had to be overshadowed. She'd been sure of it the minute the city fathers had started talking about him, but she'd hoped … she put the thought aside as she walked to the building. There were no guards on duty outside. She wasn't too surprised. The poor bastard would be practically unstoppable unless someone thought to stab him with cold iron.

She tapped the amulet she'd wrapped around her wrist as she stepped into the building. The overshadowed man's presence struck her like a physical blow, like a stench that pervaded the entire building and invaded her nostrils despite her best efforts. It was hard, so hard, to press forward, even though she *knew* nothing was stopping her. She wanted to set fire to the building, she wanted to do something – anything – that meant she wouldn't have to face the man in combat. She clenched her fist, digging her nails into her palm. The pain helped her to focus as she inched down the corridor, ready for anything. And yet, the entire building seemed empty.

A locked door barred her way. Isabella cast an unlocking spell, frowning as the spell came apart – the magic fading back into nothingness – before it could take effect. She'd seen it before, but … it still bothered her. She'd grown too used to using her magic in combat. She pulled a lockpick from her belt, opened the lock effortlessly and stepped into the room. A lone man stood, his back to her. She didn't have to see his face to know he was overshadowed. His mere presence, poisoning the air, was proof of *that*.

He turned, slowly. Isabella felt her skin crawl as he looked at her. His face was an indistinct mass, as if he'd never quite settled on an appearance. Or if he intended for people to see what they expected to see. His staff expected to see a general, so they saw a general. It struck her, suddenly, that the trick wasn't *that* different from her glamour. She found it oddly reassuring. The rules might be different, but the outcome was the same.

"Well." The overshadowed man's voice dripped poison. "And who might you be?"

Isabella gritted her teeth as his words rattled through her skull. They hurt, as if they were made of burning coals. Being so close to him was dangerous ... she could practically *feel* reality trembling around her, as if it was on the brink of shattering and dragging them both into the Godly Realm. She felt her body grow heavy ... she clutched her sword, drawing it from the scabbard. Her body felt better the moment the sword was in her hand. She grinned, readying herself. The overshadowed man looked back at her, evenly. He didn't seem worried.

"Leave this place," Isabella said. She didn't expect the banishment to work – they weren't in an ironhold – but it was worth a try. "Leave this place and ..."

The overshadowed man lunged forward, his body shifting into a shadowy mass that grew teeth and claws as he reached for her. Isabella realised, as she lashed out with the sword, that he must have been taken through the Godly Realm. She shuddered, feeling a twinge of pity for whoever the man had once been. He'd entered the realm as a human and ... something else had emerged, something wearing his face. She heard the entity howl in agony as her blade sliced through the shadows, parting them long enough for her to get closer. It would have been wiser to draw its sword, she thought, but ... it didn't have the time. She lunged forward, allowing her instincts to guide her. The sword stabbed into the creature's heart ...

Isabella stumbled back as the shadows vanished, flowing out of existence as quickly as they'd come. The entity's presence faded, until it was just a memory of a memory. She drew back the sword, careful not to return it to her belt until she was *sure* the creature was gone for good. She wasn't certain if she'd killed it or merely chased it back to its own realm. And yet ... the creature's *presence* was gone. It was suddenly very hard to remember what being so close to it had actually been *like*.

She heard running footsteps behind her and cursed under her breath. She'd hoped to make it out of the garrison without being detected. Reginald could take the garrison's surrender, if whoever assumed command was smart enough to realise that something was rotten in the kingdom. Or ... she put the thought aside as the door bust open, revealing an officer and two guards. The officer – she thought he was a colonel, although it was hard to be sure – gaped at her. Isabella almost laughed. She *had* to look like a visitor from another realm.

The man found his voice. "Who are you?"

"Isabella," Isabella said. The name would mean nothing to him. It was far from unique. "I serve Prince Reginald."

"Oh." The colonel sounded astonished. It took Isabella a moment to realise he hadn't known she was a woman until she opened her mouth. The armour concealed practically everything. "I ... it is the prince?"

"Yes, it's the prince." Isabella was tempted to say they were engaged, but she knew the colonel wouldn't believe her. "And he's come home."

"Thank the gods," one of the guards said. "I ..."

The colonel silenced him with a glare. "If he's here, I ..."

"Have no choice, but to surrender." Isabella cut him off, effortlessly. "Your former leader, the monster, is dead. Your king is a prisoner. You owe your loyalty to your prince."

She waited, readying a spell in case the colonel thought better of surrendering to the prince. It was never *easy* to decide where one's loyalties should go, particularly when there was no clear line of succession. It might have been easier if King Romulus had been declared dead ... that, Isabella was sure, was the only reason he was still alive. Men who would have gone to Reginald the moment he became the legal monarch would hesitate, fearful of being branded traitors if they jumped too early. As long as they thought the king was alive ...

The colonel looked stubborn. "I have orders from my king," he said. "I ..."

Isabella braced herself, but the guard acted first. He brought his mailed fist down on the colonel's head, knocking him out with a single punch. The man crumpled to the floor, blood streaming from a head wound. Isabella felt a flicker of pity, mingled with irritation. Surely, the man had realised that *something* was wrong. His former commander hadn't been human, not any longer. But then, officers like him weren't encouraged to be imaginative. That was how coup plots started.

"Thank you," she said, dryly. She looked the two men over. They looked solid enough, although that would change when they realised what they'd done. The colonel wouldn't be pleased, when he recovered. Reginald might not be pleased either. "Go tell the garrison to stand down, then dispatch a horseman to inform the city. The prince will take command when he arrives."

The guards nodded, then hurried away. Isabella made a silent bet with herself that they'd hesitate before carrying out their orders, then dismissed the thought and searched the office as quickly as she could. There were no written orders anywhere in evidence, nothing at all dated after Reginald had killed Havant and won the Summer Isle. She frowned as she picked through a list of requisitions. The entities had evidently taken control very quickly. Normal bureaucracy seemed to have stopped dead.

And that probably made them hundreds of friends and allies, she thought, as she worked her way through the rest of the papers. *Too many people hate bureaucrats ...*

She snorted, then put the rest of the papers aside. She'd hoped to find something Reginald could use, but there was nothing. No orders, no requisitions, no nothing. She found it hard to believe that *anyone* could run something larger than a platoon without paperwork – Lord Robin had bitched and moaned about paperwork, even though he'd never commanded more than a handful of men – but the entities didn't seem to care. The garrison had been lucky it hadn't had to go to war, at least until now. *Someone* had to do the staff work to keep the soldiers fed, watered and armed.

One of the guards returned, looking nervous. "I passed on your message," he said. "The prince *is* on his way?"

"Yes, he is." Isabella stood, brushing down her trousers.

"And when he's here, he'll take command."

She allowed the guard to lead her outside. The soldiers were forming up in rows and being directed to their barracks, where they would wait for the prince to take command. They wouldn't be in any real danger, she thought. They'd be allowed to switch sides without trouble. The aristocrats and officers might be in more trouble. Technically, they should be paroled and sent home, but ... the entities would probably refuse to honour the paroles. The conventions of war meant nothing to them.

And they'll probably just march the poor bastards through the Godly Realm, she thought, coldly. *And then they'll point them right back at us.*

The guards stood next to her as she waited, keeping a wary eye on the officers as they prepared for Reginald's arrival. If they had plans ... She relaxed, slightly, as Reginald and his bodyguard rode into view. The garrison commanders went to their knees, offering their surrender. Reginald gracefully accepted it, then dismounted. Isabella let out a breath. The first part of the plan had been completed. They had a solid lodgement on the mainland.

"My father is held prisoner," Reginald said. His voice echoed through the encampment. "Will you help me free him?"

The officers shouted their assent. Isabella wondered, cynically, just how many of them truly *meant* it. There had to be some unease about just who was sending them orders, but ... they could hardly defy direct orders from their king. Or orders that *seemed* to be from their king. And yet, Reginald would remember anyone who failed to join him. When he became king in truth, he'd take his revenge. The foot-draggers would be lucky if they were *merely* sent into exile.

"My troops will secure the roads leading to Havelock," Reginald said. Behind him, Isabella saw the lead elements moving into the garrison. "We'll be on the move as quickly as possible."

He nodded to Isabella, who fell into step beside him as Reginald reviewed the officers and men. The garrison was larger than she'd realised, although half the buildings seemed to be empty. Reginald had probably used the garrison as a forward base, when he'd been readying his troops for the invasion of the Summer Isle. A handful of shrines to various gods lay in ruins ... she wondered, sourly, just what the entities had been thinking. Soldiers were often very religious. She had a feeling that tearing down the shrines had probably resulted in a lot of bad feeling, although probably no real resistance. The overshadowed man had kept the troops in line until it was too late.

"We have to assume they know we're here," Reginald said, once the inspection was complete. "I want the garrison ready to move on my command, ideally tomorrow."

Colonel Thaddeus – the senior surviving officer – paled. "Your Highness, the troops aren't ready to march ..."

"It isn't a long march to Havelock," Reginald said, firmly. He sounded as if he wouldn't take *no* for an answer. "And we really *don't* have much time on our hands."

His voice hardened. "If you feel you can't do it in time ..."

"It will be done," Thaddeus said, hastily. "Your Highness, the troops will be ready."

"Good." Reginald looked around. "And I want the men to be battle-ready. Full armour and everything. No drinking, not now. We'll celebrate when we liberate my family from bondage."

"Yes, Your Highness." Thaddeus frowned. "What about your sister?"

Isabella shot Reginald a glance. They hadn't discussed it, not in great detail. What *was* he going to do about his sister?

"It depends on what we find, when we get there," Reginald said. He sounded calm. Only a person who knew him well could detect the anger and concern underlying his words. "But I am sure she was overshadowed, just like your former commander."

And that might not be true, Isabella thought, remembering Emetine. The Queen of the Summer Isle had been desperate, trapped in a loveless marriage and torn between her brother and her husband. *What will you do if Sofia served the entities willingly?*

Chapter Twenty-One

"I did as you asked," Greta said, as she put Silverdale's tray on the table. "The boss said I could stay as long as you liked."

"Good." Silverdale allowed herself a tight smile, trying to ignore the butterflies in her stomach. She'd tried to resist the temptation to drink the potion, but – as she'd known would happen from the start – she'd eventually given in. "You understand what I want you to do?"

"Stay with you." Greta sounded concerned. "Your Highness …"

Silverdale sat back on her bed. "I know what I'm doing," she lied. She understood Greta's concerns – and her understandable fear that she'd be blamed for anything that went wrong – but … she had no choice. *Reginald* would draw his sword and plunge into the maelstrom for the good of the kingdom. Silverdale could do no less. "Just stay with me and keep me company."

"Yes, Your Highness." Greta didn't sound any less concerned, but at least she was doing as she was told. "I'll be here."

"Thanks." Silverdale tried to push reassurance into her voice. It wasn't easy. "Just … don't go anywhere."

She picked up the tiny glass bottle and removed the cap. The liquid looked like water, but she knew – with a certainty that could not be denied – that it was something else, something different. She poured a tiny splash into a mug of water, then swallowed it in a single gulp. It tasted funny, watery and not watery. She lay back quickly, wondering just what would happen. Her body felt liquid. She heard a strange sound in her ear. Greta looked down at her, her face blurring … Silverdale almost cried out as she felt the world blur around her. It felt as if she was trapped at the bottom of the sea.

Things moved around her, strange currents and creatures that seemed to blur in and out of existence. A glowing ball of light – no, two balls of light – hung in the distance, visible even through layer after layer of solid stone. Silverdale found herself looking at one for a fraction of a second too long. It called to her, pulling her right out of her body. The world twisted again, then … she found herself in a tent, hovering above a line of men in fancy uniforms. They were so *real* she was sure they could see her, but they showed no reaction. And something was behind her …

She turned, slowly. Sir Oswald stood at parade rest, his hands clasped behind his back. His face seemed to blur, veering between the handsome – if bland – man she'd known and something that was utterly inhuman. Her skin crawled as she tried to grasp what she was seeing, a faint spidery image overlaying his human form. The more she looked at it, the more uneasy she felt. Threads of light spun around him, some leading back to the castle, others leading in a direction she couldn't follow. She had the feeling that, if she tried, it would be the last thing she ever did.

"There will be no mercy," Sir Oswald said. His voice echoed oddly, as if whatever was puppeting his body didn't quite know how to speak. And yet, it shivered with raw power and potential. "The rebels will be wiped from existence, as long as you fight in *my* name."

Silverdale shivered as the officers fell on their knees. No one was so craven, not even when facing her father, but … she recoiled in disgust as their faces hit the dirt. They were mad, completely mad. Sir Oswald was the lowest amongst the nobility, yet they were prostrating themselves in front of him, practically grovelling in the dirt. Silverdale drifted backwards, half-convinced that she'd be sucked in too if she went too close. Sir Oswald's presence seemed to be reaching out for her.

"You will chant my name," Sir Oswald said. "*Everyone* will chant my name."

He paused. "And my name is Mali."

Silverdale frowned. The name meant nothing to her. And yet, the men reacted as if Sir Oswald had just mentioned the king himself. She listened, puzzled, as they started to chant the name, over and over again. The word echoed on the air, reaching far beyond the tent. She could hear men outside picking it up and echoing it … she let herself drift further back as Sir Oswald drank in their words, the spider-image growing stronger. Silverdale had a sudden impression of the spider pressing against reality itself. It was on the verge of breaking through …

But it's already there, she thought. *It's anchored to Sir Oswald himself.*

She listened as Sir Oswald barked orders. She knew little of military affairs, but it sounded as if Sir Oswald's army was simply going to march to Humber and lay waste to the town – and anyone who got in their way. Reginald *had* to be there, Silverdale told herself. Her brother was going to kill Sir Oswald … or would he? Silverdale shivered. Sir Oswald was a fool, but the creature possessing him was dangerously powerful. She could *feel* the power pressing against her, threatening everything from her sanity to her life. It seemed to be growing stronger and stronger with every breath it took.

Silverdale forced herself to think as the presence drove her out of the tent. She couldn't escape the castle. She couldn't find her way to Reginald. Even as a ghost … there was no one on Reginald's side who could see her. She felt a strange sense of *discomfort* as she passed through the tent, emerging in the middle of the army camp. The soldiers were chanting the creature's name, over and over again. Beyond them, she could see piles of rubble. She knew, without knowing *how* she knew, that they'd once been temples. There was a strange sense of *something*, quickly fading, around them. She wasn't sure she liked it.

Her awareness drifted over the gathering soldiers. She tasted their hopes and fears, their loves and hates … she swallowed, hard, as she realised that some of the young men were no older than herself. And they were going to war … the chant grew louder, threads of power flowing from the men to the creature in the tent. She understood, suddenly, that the creature was *feeding* on them, drawing on their life energies to power itself. They were diminishing, their light fading even as the creature itself grew stronger …

She rose higher, staring down at the camp. There were hundreds – no, *thousands* – of men joining the chant. The creature was growing ever brighter, its presence raging through the air … she cursed Sofia, using words she wasn't supposed to know, for whatever she'd done to Sir Oswald. The man himself was gone, now. Something was using his body … she looked away, unwilling to risk drifting back inside the tent. The entity was too bright, now, for her to look upon it. It hurt to stay too close.

A trio of men hurried across the camp, wearing long red robes. They looked human, but … Silverdale winced as she saw two images, one transposed on top of the other. Her head swam as she tried to grasp what she was seeing. The men were human, but more than human. They were growing in directions she couldn't understand, let alone follow. Others appeared, shoeing soldiers into the chanting mass. They were tied to Sir Oswald and …

One of them looked up. Silverdale knew, without a shadow of a doubt, that he saw her. She was invisible, completely insubstantial … and yet he saw her. The creature – she couldn't think of it as human any longer – reached up and removed his hood, revealing a mass of *things* that Silverdale's mind refused to grasp. And then he drifted off the ground, coming after her. She realised, as she forced herself to run, that he had sent his mind into the ghostly realm too. She hadn't known the creatures could do that.

I should have known, she thought. It was hard, so hard, to run. The air felt as if it was turning into treacle. Her body was being pulled down by an invisible force. She sensed, more than saw, teeth snapping at her heels. *I should have known …*

Panic yammered at her mind as she felt *something* clutching her bare feet. She kicked out automatically, willing the blow to connect. A grunt of pain echoed through the air, heartening her. She didn't dare look down as she kicked out again, hoping she'd hit something solid. The creature felt as if it had turned to mist, as if it was reaching up and consuming the air around her. She sensed a gaping maw below her. Her panic rose … and then she realised her mistake. She didn't *have* a body, not here. She didn't *have* to be bound by its limits. She visualised herself back in the castle and snapped back, following her thread back to her body. The creature was left far behind.

A wave of impressions assaulted her as she crashed back

into the castle, passing through stone walls that felt as solid as water. There were more nobles than ever before, paying court to Sofia; there were more servants, even though Greta had told her that half the servants had been told to go home. She frowned as she found herself, just for a moment, peering out through a servant's eyes. The man was in pain, his agony leaking into the ghostly realm. She gritted her teeth as it tore at her, trying to overwhelm her. It was all she could do to untangle herself and slip back into her body. The world crashed down on her.

"Your Highness?" A voice. Greta's voice. "Your Highness?"

Silverdale opened her eyes, unsure when she'd closed them. Her mouth tasted … odd, as if she'd thrown up water. She swallowed hard as she forced herself to sit up, her body feeling strange after she'd drifted out of it. She felt as if she'd dressed herself in ill-fitting clothes, as if she'd picked an outfit intended for someone younger and smaller than herself. It felt … limiting, as if she was suddenly bound by rules she'd thought she'd escape. She looked down at her hands, wondering when her fingers had become so *strange*. They weren't part of her.

She shook her head slowly, fighting down an absurd urge to cry. She'd been *free* as a ghost, even though the only person who'd seen her had been one of the red-robed monsters. She could go anywhere, do anything … it crossed her mind, suddenly, that Emetine could presumably do the same. She could spy on anyone, Silverdale included. Silverdale looked around, but saw nothing. Emetine probably had other concerns. She didn't need to worry about a young princess. And yet, the thought wouldn't go away.

"I can't stay there," she muttered. Being a ghost was fun, when it wasn't dangerous, but she didn't want to be a ghost for eternity. "It isn't real."

Greta coughed. "Your Highness?"

"I saw too much," Silverdale said. "What did *you* see?"

"Nothing." Greta sounded worried. "You lay back on the bed and went still. Very still. I had to keep checking your heartbeat to make sure you were still alive. And then … you just woke up. You looked as if you'd had a nightmare."

"I had." Silverdale wasn't sure how much she dared say.

"Do you know how to get out of the castle?"

"No." Greta said. "There are guards on all the exits."

Unless there really is a way out through the secret passageways, Silverdale thought. If Ruby knew about them, *Sofia* knew about them. Reginald or their father would have told them about the passageways. And then … Sofia might have told Emetine. Might. She shouldn't have – the passageways were only useful if no one outside the royal family knew about them, but … Sofia seemed overshadowed by Emetine. *If they're blocked, there'll be no way out.*

She frowned. "Can you think of a way out?"

"Not unless we bribe the guards," Greta said. "And I thought that was impossible."

"Probably." Silverdale had been told, more than once, that her father paid the best wages in the kingdom. The guards wouldn't betray him, not even if they were offered a small fortune and a title of their own. She looked around the room, noting how many expensive toys and clothes were within eyeshot. She could try to bribe them, but … it would probably end badly for everyone. "Could we not get over the walls?"

Greta looked as if she wanted to say something cutting, but didn't quite dare. "Not without being caught, no," she said. "Do *you* know how to climb down a rope?"

"No," Silverdale said, shortly. She knew how to ride a horse … perhaps *that* was the answer. If she could get down to the stable, she could take a horse and tell the guards she had permission to go for a gallop. They'd never dare stop her, unless they had specific orders … they probably *did* have specific orders. Damn it. She bit down a word she *really* wasn't supposed to know. "Do you know what orders the guards have?"

"I imagine they've been told not to let anyone in or out," Greta said. "They didn't let Kitty leave, Your Highness, and *she's* got a sick mother. They put her in the cells for complaining."

Silverdale bit down another word. The guards *had* to have specific orders, then. Normally, they were quite understanding to the servants. The servants could make their lives easier – or harder – at whim. But if they'd stopped one of the cooks from visiting her mother … no, they had specific orders, orders that had to have come from Sofia. Silverdale cursed under her breath. There was no way *she* could override the Regent. Only her father could do that and *he* was in a coma.

Unless I find a way to wake him up, she thought. *But how?*

She looked at the glass bottle in her hand, unsure what she could do. If the king was being drugged … she cursed under her breath, again. How *could* she get him out? He was a big man, bigger than just about everyone else she knew. Even *Reginald* was smaller. Silverdale couldn't carry him, even with Greta's help. And she couldn't hide him from Emetine either … a dozen ideas ran through her mind, each one more impractical than the last. There was no way she could get him out of the castle without getting caught.

Her eyes slipped to her chest of drawers – and the knife she'd buried, under layer after layer of clothes. Reginald had given it to her, for reasons he'd never bothered to explain. Women were rarely allowed to carry weapons, even if they were *princesses*. They were even discouraged from hunting in the king's forest. And yet … she wondered, suddenly, what would happen if she stabbed Emetine. Would she die? Would Sofia return to normal? Or … or what? She remembered the creature wearing Sir Oswald's face and shuddered. Things would never return to normal.

"I have to head back to the kitchen," Greta said. "Do you need me for anything else?"

Silverdale glanced at the clock. Four *hours*? Really? She hadn't been a ghost *that* long, had she? Her stomach growled, convincing her that it had been a *long* time since she'd eaten. She stood on wobbly legs and stumbled over to the table. Her food was cold – another sign she'd been a ghost for longer than she'd thought – but edible. She ignored Greta's squawk of protest and ate quickly. The cold didn't matter. It wasn't Greta's fault.

"See if you can find a way out of the castle," Silverdale ordered. "And tell your boss I may need you again tomorrow."

"Yes, Your Highness." Greta looked resigned. "My boss was asking if I was to be assigned to you permanently."

Silverdale shrugged. It would be convenient, but … technically, she wasn't allowed a staff of her own until she was thirteen. Her governess was in charge until then, with ultimate authority over lesser servants. Silverdale made a mental note to wait until she could pick and choose her own staff. There would be objections if she took Greta, instead of girls from the lower-ranking noble families, but nothing she couldn't ignore. It wasn't as if she was Sofia. Or Reginald. He'd been surrounded by friends and sycophants from birth until he'd set sail for the Summer Isle.

"I'll see what I can do," she said, realising that Greta was still waiting for an answer. "But I don't know."

She finished her meal and sat back, allowing the maid to take the tray. "And if you hear anything …"

"I hear a lot of things, Your Highness," Greta said. "I just don't know how many of them are true."

Silverdale nodded. The servants talked, sharing everything from confidences to rumours that might – or might not – have some truth within them. She hadn't realised just how prevalent it was until Sofia had become Regent, until Silverdale had found herself talking to Greta. It was an odd insight into life below stairs that … she shuddered. She wouldn't want to be a maid. Greta had left out a few details, perhaps the ones she thought would worry or outrage the younger girl, but Silverdale's imagination had filled in the blanks. Greta's life was very insecure …

So is mine, Silverdale thought. Greta didn't have to worry about her father – or her elder siblings – arranging her marriage. Silverdale loved her family, but she had no illusions about them. *And if things don't change soon, I don't know what I'm going to do.*

Chapter Twenty-Two

"You don't have to be here," Gars muttered.

"Yes, I do," Reginald muttered back. "I passed sentence."

He scowled as he watched the three hooded men being marched to the gallows, their hands bound tightly behind their backs. Idiots. Stupid fucking idiots. The city was full of brothels, and women who loved men in uniforms, and the morons just *had* to snatch a pair of girls off the streets and rape them. They'd set his cause back *years*, damn them to hell. The townspeople would watch him warily now, even though the gathering crowd would witness justice. He'd passed sentence himself. And they'd still fear him …

The Master-At-Arms barked orders. The hangmen pulled levers. Two of the rapists died instantly, their necks snapping like twigs as the hatches opened and they plunged to their doom. The third struggled, dangling like a cork on a string as he tried – desperately – to remain alive for a few moments longer. Reginald watched, dispassionately, as the hangman gave him a shove. The poor bastard didn't fall fast enough to break his neck. Instead, he was strangled by the noose. Reginald would have felt sorry for him if he hadn't listened to his victims.

"It's done," Gars said.

Reginald stood. "The bodies can hang there for a day or two," he said. By then, the army would be well on its way to Havelock. "And then they can be cut down and buried outside the city."

"Yes, Your Highness," Gars said. "It will be done."

"Yes." Reginald took one last look at the bodies. "And if those fools had listened, perhaps they wouldn't be dead."

Isabella fell into step beside him as the crowds started to disperse, clearing the way for Reginald and his small entourage. The bodyguards kept their eyes open, watching for assassins lurking amidst the people. Sergeant Ruthven had warned him that there had been plenty of discontentment, even before the wretched rapists had been reported, arrested and unceremoniously hanged. Reginald had no doubt of it, but he refused to hide from the crowds. An appearance of weakness could easily *become* weakness, if it gave heart to one's enemies. He preferred to remind people that he wasn't afraid of anything.

Which isn't exactly true, he admitted. Fearless men — completely fearless men — were liabilities. *I'm just not scared of human foes*.

He put the thought aside as they walked through the streets towards City Hall. He'd taken it over as soon as the city had surrendered, ignoring polite suggestions from the political leadership that he should move himself and his staff to the garrison as soon as possible. He would have been tempted, if it hadn't been so important to make it clear that he couldn't be pushed around by the city fathers. He was his father's heir — technically, he might already be monarch — and he couldn't take the risk of setting precedents. It was just unfortunate that he didn't *know* what had happened to his father.

His teeth clenched at the thought. He'd interrogated everyone who'd visited Havelock in the last few weeks, but none of them had *really* been able to answer his questions. The city was changing, falling into darkness, yet … none of them had seen the king. A handful had seen Sofia, but … they hadn't been able to say much. It was worrying just how quickly they'd accepted her authority. She shouldn't have been able to do that, not *her*. It suggested the entities were involved.

As if we didn't know it, he thought, as he led the way into the meeting room. *We were never in any doubt*.

He took his seat and waved for the others to sit too. "Stuart?"

The Master of Horse smiled, humourlessly. "I've sent cavalry up the road to Havelock and established pickets on all the approaches," he said. "It's fairly clear they're dispatching an army westwards, probably intending to drive us back into the sea. I don't have a solid count, Your Highness, but it looks as if they're throwing at least ten thousand men at us."

Reginald heard the hiss of dismay running around the table,

but kept his face carefully blank. Ten thousand enemy soldiers weren't bad odds, on the face of it, yet … he shuddered, remembering how the entities had manipulated humans like putty. Who knew *what* they were facing? Ten thousand men … most of them would be poorly trained, unless Sofia had been massing the army around Havelock since well before she'd known Reginald was on his way. Unless she'd known he was coming well before *he'd* known … he rubbed his forehead in frustration. He was scared of the unknown. Not knowing what the entities could do – let alone what they *would* do – was worrying.

"Most of them will not be particularly well trained," he said, reassuringly. His father had kept a sizable number of trained soldiers on reserve, but they'd been parcelled out to guard the borders or watch the rebellious barons. "We can handle them."

"They're advancing on us," Gars pointed out. "They're not staying in Havelock."

Reginald nodded, curtly. It was worrying. Either whoever was in charge on the other side was a complete idiot, which he didn't dare believe, or he had a nasty surprise up his sleeve, just waiting for the right moment. If half the army was untrained, the *smart* thing to do was dig into Havelock and force Reginald to bleed his troops white getting them out. That they were looking for a pitched battle … he didn't like it. The enemy commander seemed to be playing into his hands.

He looked at Stuart. "Was there any report of … *strangeness*?"

"Nothing they saw," Stuart said. "But they couldn't get *that* close. The enemy archers were on alert."

"Naturally," Reginald said, tightly.

He looked at the map, although he already knew what he'd see. Their supply lines weren't just weak, they were practically non-existent. He'd brought as much as he could from the Summer Isle, but there would be no resupply missions … they'd have to take what they could get from Humber, then march on Havelock and put an end to the affair before they ran out of supplies. He wondered, sourly, if Sofia and her advisors understood the problem. He'd left a small army of experienced personnel behind. One of them would look at the map and understand his problems all too well.

And we have to win quickly, he reminded himself. The city fathers had made it clear that the northern barons really *were* revolting. *If we don't end the war quickly, whoever wins will be too weak to assert their authority over the kingdom.*

He glanced at Isabella. *She'd* pointed out that it would be better, in the long term, to expend the entire army if it meant defeating the entities. And, from one point of view, he agreed with her. The entities were a threat to the entire world. But, from another point of view, he'd be throwing away his patrimony – and his family's position – along with the army. He'd be dead, his sisters would be forced into marriage, his cousins would probably be killed too ...

"We march at once," he said. He jabbed a finger at the map. "We should be able to get here, to Frigg, before they do. We'll take up position and wait for them. If they want to pit themselves against experienced defenders, we'll let them."

Gars cleared his throat. "And what if they refuse to take the bait?"

Reginald felt a hot flash of annoyance. He forced it down. Gars was *meant* to point out problems with the plan – and, afterwards, remind Reginald that no battle plan ever survived contact with the enemy. If whoever was in charge declined to give battle ...

"They have to destroy us as quickly as possible," Reginald said. It was perfect military logic, whatever that meant when the entities were concerned. "They cannot allow us to maintain an army so close to Havelock."

He shook his head. "If they dig in themselves, we'll go around them," he added. "And if they start retreating, we'll run them down."

His lips curved into a cold smile. It wasn't *easy* to retreat, at the best of times. Even the most experienced army could come apart at the seams, if the enemy gave chase. He'd be *delighted* if he had a chance to run the enemy army down, destroying it piece by piece. He doubted he'd have the chance – very few commanders would risk a retreat under such circumstances – but it was worth bearing in mind. Who knew? Perhaps he *was* facing an idiot.

Don't take that for granted, he told himself, sharply. *Or you'll wind up an idiot if you don't get killed first.*

He looked at Gars. "When can we march?"

"The forward elements are already in place," Gars said. "They can be underway in minutes. The remainder of the troops can be assembled and dispatched in three hours, perhaps less."

"The reserve horses and their riders are also being brought forward," Stuart put in. "We should have flankers in place for the march."

"Good." Reginald had pulled off a few ambushes himself, during his early battles. A handful of flankers watching his flanks would make it much harder for someone to do the same to him. "Deploy extra patrols to the north and south. Tell them to be polite, if dealing with civilians, but find out if there are any surprises waiting for us."

"Yes, Your Highness." Stuart smiled, brightly. "We can handle it."

"They won't like aristocrats," Isabella said. She sounded as if she was worrying about something else and only barely paying attention to the discussion. "Your men will have to be very polite, very unthreatening."

"They can try." Stuart didn't look impressed. "But when have soldiers ever been *loved*?"

Reginald nodded, curtly. Stuart was right. The most well-behaved army in the world would be feared, hated and resented by the civilians whose lives it would disrupt, simply by being there. A farmer could lose everything if the army trampled across his fields, even if the soldiers were careful to leave the father, his wife and children strictly alone. It didn't matter to the commoners *who* sat on the throne, or the legal rights and wrongs of the whole affair, or … well, anything. They only cared about seeing the next summer. They'd sell him out in a heartbeat if they thought it would prolong their lives.

"Try," he ordered, stiffly. "Earl Oxley, your men will accompany the vanguard. You will lead them."

Earl Oxley didn't look pleased. "Yes, Your Highness."

"Remind your men not to loot," Reginald added. He'd overheard quite a number of islanders wondering why Reginald had bothered to invade the Summer Isle, when Andalusia was so rich. They'd been blown away by Humber. Even the poor of the city were richer than the middle-class islanders. "We don't want angry people chasing us."

Or selling us out to the entities, he thought, grimly. *If the stories are true, the entities are spreading ...*

He stood. "You know what to do," he said. "We leave in an hour. Prepare yourself for the march. Dismissed."

The men left, talking quietly amongst themselves. Isabella remained, her mind clearly still elsewhere. Reginald poured himself a cup of wine and waited for her to speak, knowing it wouldn't help to interrupt. Isabella didn't seem to be able to do more than one thing at a time, unlike most of the other women he'd known. Or perhaps she was simply brooding. She'd given up something that meant a great deal to her so that Reginald could lead his army across the water.

"You did well to hang them," Isabella said. "Thank you."

Reginald nodded, gravely. His father had once compared commoners to farm animals, pointing out that one had to feed and tend farm animals – and keep them safe from predators – if one hoped to harvest them in time. It wasn't a comparison he liked – and he had a feeling Isabella would detest it, if he ever told her – but he saw his father's point. One had to protect commoners if one wanted to build an empire – or even a stable, prosperous and ultimately wealthy kingdom. The Summer Isle would have been a great deal richer if the local aristocracy hadn't snatched everything they could ...

"I don't understand what they're doing," he said, instead. "They should be defending Havelock, not trying to attack Humber."

"You'll be pushed into the water," Isabella pointed out. "Right?"

Reginald frowned. "Yes and no. The map lies" – he smiled, remembering just how many problems had been caused by bad maps – "and there's more than enough ground for me to manoeuvre if they come right at me. This isn't a conventional war. I'd be quite happy to swap Humber for Havelock if I thought they'd take the bargain."

"You said they have to win quickly," Isabella said. "And their commanders might have decided to risk a pitched battle."

"Perhaps." Reginald had his doubts. Sofia wasn't *stupid*. If she was calling the shots, surely she would have put someone in charge who actually knew what he was doing.

But was there such a person? Any of their relatives who knew how to command an army would be a potential threat to her power. And there were the entities ... what would *they* do? He'd seen them do things no human magician could match. "I just don't like it."

Isabella met his eyes. "Do you have any alternatives?"

"None." Reginald laughed, more at himself than her. "We can't wait. We can't go around them and ... ideally, we can't risk prolonging the war."

"Then you have to move," Isabella said. She leaned back in her chair. "What do you want me to do?"

"Whatever you have to," Reginald said. Isabella was the only person who might be able to improvise a counterattack, when – if – the entities showed their hand. He'd armed his soldiers with cold iron, but he knew it had limits. "If they hit us, do something back."

He shuddered, remembering the battles on the Summer Isle. The entities had come very close to killing him, winning the war outright. And who knew what would have happened then? If they'd turned the island into an invulnerable fortress ...

Isabella stood. It struck him, as she ran her hands through her hair, that she was striking. Not beautiful – her face was a little *too* hard for beauty – but striking. Her muscled arms were realer, somehow, than the painted ladies he'd known at court, or the commoners who'd warmed his bed during his first campaigns. He'd always known he'd marry out of duty, not love, but ... he found himself smiling at her, like a boy having his first crush. It would be nice to have someone he liked as a wife. His father had refused to remarry after his wife had died, choosing to remain faithful to her memory. Reginald knew it had been love. A king could not – normally – put his heart ahead of his kingdom. That his father had ...

"I'll do what I can," Isabella promised. She met his eyes. "And I ..."

Reginald reached for her, half-unsure how she'd react. She was a sorceress. If she wanted to express her disapproval, she could. In truth, he found it a little exciting. He'd known girls who wanted to sleep with him because they thought he'd make them queen, or girls who wanted to brag of sleeping with the prince, or girls who wanted favours for their families, or girls who simply wanted money. Isabella was different. She didn't have to do anything for him. Or her family. She could make up her mind without interference.

They kissed, lightly. She settled onto his knees as if she belonged there. Reginald ran his hand up and down her back as their kisses grew more passionate, feeling traces of scars that had been inflicted long ago. It was strange, to feel scars on a woman. A high-born woman would never be *scarred* ...

She shifted, pressing against him. Reginald felt his excitement start to build as he slipped his hand under her shirt, half-convinced she'd draw back or hex him if he pushed too far. She leaned against him, her fingers pressing against the back of his neck. Reginald shivered as they explored each other, her touches exciting him in a manner he'd never experienced in his entire life. She didn't *have* to do anything for him. He touched her breast, feeling her quiver as he ran his fingers over her nipple. It hardened at his touch.

Isabella drew back, just slightly, as he slipped his hand into her pants. "We can't go any further, not now."

Reginald hesitated, torn between lust and a sense of danger. He wanted her. By all the gods, he wanted her. And yet, he knew he couldn't go any further. He didn't want to force her. He couldn't force her. He ...

He had to concentrate to calm himself. "I ... why?"

Isabella looked embarrassed, as if she'd wanted to go further too. "Instinct," she said. "We shouldn't. Not yet."

She stood, drawing away from him. Her face was flushed. Reginald knew he couldn't look any better. He watched as she adjusted her clothes, carefully putting everything back where it belonged. No one was going to believe they'd been kissing passionately only a few short seconds ago. His lips tingled at the thought. He wanted to pull her back to him. He wanted ... he told himself, firmly, to wait. She was worth waiting for.

"I'll get the troops underway," he said. His voice sounded harsh, even in his ears. He wasn't used to frustration. "You'll be at my back?"

"As long as you'll have me," Isabella said. It meant more to him than a histrionic declaration of love. "I'll be there."

Chapter Twenty-Three

Isabella felt … uneasy as she rode behind Reginald, feeling a gust of *something* in the air.

She honestly wasn't sure why she'd stopped, why she'd told him to stop before they actually went all the way. She was no teenage ingénue, no naive and sheltered girl who hadn't been undressed in front of anyone since she'd learnt to dress herself. It had been a long time since she'd had someone beside her, inside her. She'd wanted him. She'd wanted to feel him inside her. The yearning had been almost overwhelming. She hadn't felt any guilt at the thought of sleeping with him.

And yet, some instinct had warned her not to go too far.

She mulled it over, keeping her face a tight mask. It wasn't as if she was a virgin. It wasn't as if she was scared of him, or sex in general. It wasn't even the simple fact that they couldn't take the time to *really* get to know each other, not when the army was already starting to move. It was … she didn't know *what* it was, but she knew better than to ignore it. Mother Lembu had told her, time and time again, to *listen* to her instincts.

The horse shifted uncomfortably under her, as if it wasn't used to carrying people. Isabella sighed, silently grateful her father had forced her to learn to ride during summer vacations. She'd never been fond of horses – she'd certainly never cared for riding around the countryside, hunting foxes and other defenceless creatures – yet she had to admit that the lessons had finally come in handy. Reginald wouldn't say anything, not to *her*, if she made a fool of herself on horseback, but she knew his courtiers would be a different story. Highborn women were about the only women who knew how to ride. They'd make snide comments when they believed she couldn't hear them if they thought she didn't know how to ride …

She sat upright, looking around with interest as they rode east. Andalusia had been incredibly lucky. The civil wars that had blighted the last five years had barely touched the western side of the kingdom. The farms, towns and villages the army was marching through looked incredibly wealthy, compared to the Summer Isle. The only signs of trouble were the destroyed temples and the near-complete absence of people. Isabella frowned as they rode past an empty town, then told herself she was over-thinking it. No farmer in his right mind would show himself to an advancing army. The risk of being robbed – or worse – was simply too high.

And not everyone is going to believe that Reginald hanged a number of rapists, Isabella thought, sourly. It wasn't *easy* to discipline an army, particularly when one's power *rested* on that army. She was morbidly certain there would be some angry grumbling in the rank and file, particularly amongst the men who'd signed up to loot, rape and generally make life unpleasant for everyone around them. *The civilians won't see us as any better than the rest.*

She frowned as she took a long breath. A feeling *hung* on the air, a faint sense that something was wrong. She peered around, taking in the handful of empty farmhouses in the distance. There was no one in view, save for a trio of horsemen on a distant hill. Her eyes narrowed. The enemy commander probably had pickets out himself, watching Reginald's army as it advanced towards Frigg. And yet ... Isabella reached out with her senses, hoping she'd be able to make out what was wrong. But there was nothing, beyond a vague sense of disquiet. The army seemed utterly unopposed as it made its way eastwards.

The horse quivered underneath her, again. Isabella glanced down at the beast, wondering if the horse sensed anything wrong. Animals were sometimes better at picking up danger signs than humans, although there was no way the creature could *tell* her what was wrong. She wasn't a beast-talker, bonded to her steed ... she frowned, looking at Reginald's back as he spoke quietly to Gars. She wanted to tell him that something was wrong, but he'd want details. And she had none, beyond the vague feeling in the air. It wouldn't be enough to change his mind.

And it isn't like we have many other options anyway,

Isabella reminded herself. The road network was good, but … it made their march predictable. The enemy commander wouldn't need his pickets to know where they were going. She thought it might be better if they stayed off the road, but … they couldn't. Marching over the fields and through the thickets would slow them down, as well as doing a great deal of damage to the local economy. *We have to go this way and they know it.*

She glanced towards the enemy horsemen. One of them had vanished. She assumed he'd gone to carry the message back to his commander. The other two kept watching, from a safe distance. Reginald could send horsemen of his own after them, but they'd see the men coming and scuttle off before it was too late. Isabella shook her head, reminding herself – again – that they really didn't have any other options. Their route was predictable. And the enemy commander wouldn't have too much difficulty guessing just how long it would take for Reginald to reach Frigg.

Isabella put the thought aside and concentrated on the reports they'd received from Humber and the surrounding area. The rumours – and they really were nothing more than rumours – were odd. Strange creatures had been sighted, wandering along the edge of unsettled territory or forbidden zones. No two rumours agreed, but … they painted a disturbing picture. Others claimed that *miracles* had taken place, including people being raised from the dead, noble estates falling to ruin and entire armies turned to stone. Isabella knew that rumours grew in the telling – the rumours about *her* had been exaggerated to the point where even her father had refused to believe them – but she was sure there was a hard core of truth somewhere within the stories. She just didn't know what it was.

The dead cannot come back to life, she thought. *Can they?*

She shivered. There was no shortage of stories about sorcerers who'd tried to raise the dead, but they all ended badly. The lucky ones wound up with pitiful copies of their loved ones, animated by magic alone; the unlucky ones unleashed undead plagues onto the world or caused tainted magic to explode in all directions, warping and twisting beyond recognition everyone caught in the storm. No sorcerer in his right mind would try so much as to reanimate a dead animal, let alone a human being. It was better to let the dead rest in peace than break the barrier between the living world and the lands of the dead. And yet …

The faint chill refused to go away, no matter how much she might wish it. She'd sensed the sheer raw power of the entities. Could they resurrect the dead? Could they do something that no sorcerer had ever done? And if they could, what did it make them? She knew there were sorcerers who thought they should rule, purely because they had power. There were people who'd sell their souls if they thought it would give them what they wanted. And the entities could reward their followers in ways no human could match.

She shivered, again. The world was going to change. No, it *had* changed. She wished, suddenly, that she'd had time to write another letter to her brother. Alden had to know, although … he probably *already* knew. He'd once been at the centre of a giant web of informants. She found it impossible to believe that network was *completely* gone. But … maybe he wouldn't believe the stories. If they spoke of impossible magics …

I'll just have to tell him, she thought. She'd write a letter when they reached Frigg, then give it to a horseman to deliver. The poor bastard would have a long journey ahead of him. *And hope Alden listens to me.*

***

Reginald was careful not to show any trace of his discomfort, and unease, as the lead elements of his army moved into Frigg. The vanguard had secured the town an hour ago – an easy task, as the entire population seemed to have vanished – and there was no reason to fear immediate attack, but … he would have been happier if the population had been within eyeshot. Their absence meant they expected fighting to start at any moment.

A messenger hurried up to him as he dismounted, his muscles complaining loudly as his feet hit the ground. He was used to riding, but … that was the longest he'd spent in a saddle for several weeks. He hadn't even stopped to answer the call of nature. Behind him, he heard men hurriedly dismounting and running to the shitholes. They'd made the mistake of drinking during the march. His lips quirked, despite the aches and pains reminding him that he wasn't a teenager any longer. It had been too long since they'd made a forced march.

And it will be harder for the poor bastards on foot, he thought, as he glanced at the sky. The sun was already dropping behind the mountains, long shadows reaching out over the land. *They'll be in no state to fight if we get attacked tonight.*

The messenger went on one knee. "Your Highness. The town is apparently empty."

"Good," Reginald said, biting down the urge to point out that he had eyes. Most of the visible buildings were closed and shuttered. "And the enemy army?"

"The pickets claim that it is still several hours away," the messenger said. "Lord Greely thinks it won't be here until tomorrow morning."

"I see," Reginald said. He didn't have much faith in Greely – he'd had to give the man something important to do, damn it all – but he'd made sure to attach a handful of reliable sergeants to the aristocratic fop. *Their* reports would be as reliable as reports ever were. "Tell Lord Anders to report to me when he's sure the trenches are well underway."

"Yes, Your Highness."

The messenger banged his fist to his chest in salute, then hurried off. Reginald looked around, watching grimly as the first regiments marched into the deserted town. They'd have a few hours to rest, hopefully, before the enemy army hove into view. They'd won the race to Frigg, so … he frowned, wondering why he felt he'd stuck his neck into a noose. Frigg had been carefully chosen. If the enemy attacked, he'd have the edge; if the enemy declined to offer battle, he could still choose when and where he'd mount his own offensive. And yet, he felt uneasy.

Isabella stepped up beside him. "More destroyed temples," she said, pointing towards a pile of rubble. "I haven't seen a single intact temple since we left the island."

"Yeah." Reginald shot her a sidelong glance, wonderingly. She was like no woman he'd ever met. Highborn ladies pretended to be chaste; commoners, particularly camp followers, rarely bothered. Isabella was neither a simpering fool nor a calculating plotter. "And no one offered resistance."

She smiled at him, humourlessly. "What do you think

happened to anyone who tried?"

Reginald nodded, curtly, then turned to Gars and started to bark orders. The remaining men moved into the town, save for a handful of pickets who haunted the roads and fields outside the walls. He felt a pang of bitter regret. They had strict orders to be careful, when they broke open homes and billeted themselves in empty buildings, but the locals wouldn't like it anyway. Why should they? They'd curse his name and pray for his defeat ... he wondered, suddenly, just who or what would be listening. The gods? Or the entities? He put the thought to one side as they walked through the darkening town, the shadows growing longer as the last traces of sunlight faded away. It was suddenly very easy to understand why so few commoners walked out at night. The shadows felt almost alive.

The town hall itself was a solid stone building, positioned in the centre of the settlement. He led the way inside and frowned as he surveyed the hall. A portrait of a young woman in regal robes hung on the wall, illuminated by a pair of flickering lanterns. It took him several seconds to realise that it was meant to be Sofia, although whoever had painted the picture had never laid eyes on her. Reginald couldn't help a snicker. It looked, very much, as though one of his sister's ladies in waiting had dressed up in her clothes and posed for the painter.

If they even took that much care, he thought. Someone could easily have given the painter a third or fourth-hand description of the princess. The hair was the right colour, but everything else was *off*. *It isn't as if anyone is going to come and check.*

Gars unfurled a map as servants handed out tasteless rations. "The last reports placed the enemy here," he said. "They'll be on us in the morning."

"We'll be ready." Reginald washed the food down with wine, studying the map carefully. It was a shame it couldn't be trusted completely. "Have the guard remain on watch, but make sure everyone else gets some rest. They're going to be needed."

"Yes, Your Highness." Gars saluted. "You get some rest too."

"I will," Reginald promised. He rubbed his forehead. His

muscles were aching. He was gloomily aware that he stank of horse. He needed a bath, not … he shook his head. There were no bathtubs in the hall. "And you too."

Gars nodded, then turned and left the chamber. Reginald glanced at Isabella.

"You're being very quiet," he said. "Are you alright?"

Isabella shrugged. "I just feel naked."

Reginald made a show of looking at her. "You're not naked."

"Yeah." Isabella didn't sound amused. "That's what bothers me."

"I feel naked too," Reginald admitted. He unfurled his blanket from his saddlebags and laid it out on the stone floor. It wasn't going to be a comfortable night, but … he'd slept in worse places. Besides, he wasn't going to sleep in comfort when his men were sleeping on stone or cold earth. And as long as *he* didn't sleep in comfort, his officers couldn't either. "Do you have any reason to be worried."

"No," Isabella said. She lay down beside him, without bothering to do more than loosen her shirt. "And that's what bothers me."

Reginald was tempted to reach for her, to finish what they'd started hours ago, but he knew it would be a bad idea. He *had* to be alert, when the enemy army finally showed itself. He had to be as fresh as possible. Besides, he'd banned camp followers from the baggage train. His soldiers wouldn't be amused if they discovered he'd done *that* and then had sex himself. He snorted at the thought as he closed his eyes. There'd be rumours anyway. There always were.

He'd learnt to catch sleep when he could, on campaign, but it still felt like hours before he finally fell asleep. Isabella lay next to him, her breathing so regular that he was sure she was still awake herself. He forced himself to concentrate, calling on sleep … and yet, it felt like he hadn't slept at all by the time a guard woke him. Reginald straightened upright, one hand reaching for his sword. Bright sunlight was streaming through the window …

"The pickets reported," the guard said. "The enemy army will be here within an hour."

Reginald glanced at the sun. It was surprisingly early. The bastards mustn't have stopped for long, if at all. Had they force-marched through the night? That was a good sign, perhaps. They'd be tired and cranky and unable to fight properly if they were hurled into his lines ... whoever was in command wasn't very experienced. Or ... he had a trick up his sleeve.

Isabella stood. There was an edge to her voice he didn't like. "They're coming."

Reginald frowned. "What do you mean?"

"I can feel the army," Isabella said. "And something's with them."

"... Shit," Reginald said. "Can you do anything about it?"

"I don't know," Isabella said. "But I can try."

"Try, then." Reginald crammed a piece of hardtack into his mouth, took a swig of water and hurried to the door. "I'll see you afterwards."

Isabella blew him a kiss. "For luck."

"Thanks." Reginald had to smile. "But I make my own luck."

Isabella laughed. For an instant, her face lit up. "They all say that."

Reginald grinned, then hurried onto the streets. The town had come alive, hundreds of soldiers running in all directions as they manned the improvised defences. They looked ready to fight, although ... there was a faint sense of brewing trouble in the air that worried him. He reminded himself, again, that his men had faced the entities before. They knew what to expect. They wouldn't panic. And besides, they carried swords of cold iron.

He clambered onto the walls and peered into the distance. A faint sound echoed through the air, coming from the east. A chant ... he couldn't make out the word, but it was more than a marching cadence. It echoed, growing stronger and stronger as the enemy army came into view. He found it unnerving, even though he'd seen war. The enemy was trying to intimidate him ...

"Mali, Mali, Mali ..."

Gars appeared beside him. "That's all they're saying," he said. He was a seasoned campaigner, but he sounded a little unnerved. "What does it mean?"

"I don't know," Reginald said. The sound was getting louder. "But I think we're about to find out."

Chapter Twenty-Four

"Mali, Mali, Mali …"

Silverdale swayed as she stood on the dais, watching the City Fathers of Havelock bow and scrape in front of Sofia. The men were old enough to be her grandfathers, yet they were practically grovelling at her feet. One of them was actually giving her the keys to the city, even though – technically – Havelock wasn't part of the king's patrimony. Silverdale didn't pretend to understand the politics, but she understood her sister. She was enjoying lording over men who, a few short months ago, would have regarded her as nothing more than a brainless beauty.

And words were echoing in her head. "Mali, Mali, Mali …"

The world seemed to shift around her, becoming translucent. She was vaguely aware that her body was falling, that it was going to hit the floor at any second, but it was hard – so hard – to care as her awareness was yanked out of her body and dragged through the air. The insubstantial walls provided no barrier as she flew onwards and upwards, peering down at the landscape from a great height. The army was below her, steadily marching towards a mid-sized town. And the men were chanting …

"Mali, Mali, Mali …"

She shivered helplessly as her awareness expanded. A brilliant light stood at the rear of the army, marching behind the men. Threads of light linked it to the men, drawing on them … they pulsed in time with the chant. She understood, suddenly, that the creature wearing Sir Oswald's face had bound itself to the men, drawing …*something* … from them as they chanted its name. She felt sick, just looking at it. The men looked terrifying, their faces consumed with something worse than mere *hatred* as they picked up speed. She could barely look at them. She'd never felt so scared in her life.

And yet, she had no choice. The men were blooded, droplets of red blood dripping down their faces and pooling on the ground ... it took her long seconds to realise that they'd cut themselves. She felt her stomach churn. If she'd had physical form, she thought she would have thrown up. Some of the men were no older than herself ... she knew it, although she wasn't sure *how* she knew it. Reginald had been training for war from the moment he could pick up a wooden sword and wave it in the air, but ... it still felt wrong. The young men, chanting the name of their inhuman master, were about to die. She could practically *see* the shadow of death looming over them.

A wave of memories – *their* memories – blurred through her mind as she drifted up and out of the mob. They tasted ... odd, as if everything *human* had been blanked out by the chant. The men were no longer thinking of things she understood, but something inhuman. They'd given themselves completely to their master. She wanted to run, but her ghostly body refused to cooperate. All she could do was drift over the battlefield and watch. She couldn't even feel her body any longer.

Her head started to pound as she drifted *over* the creature. It was so bright, in her mind's eye, that she couldn't *look* at it directly. The threads of light were growing brighter too. She tried to twist away, but – no matter how she moved – she couldn't get clear. It was a pulsing presence, burning at her mind. She couldn't escape ...

"Mali, Mali, Mali ..." The chant grew louder, pounding against her insubstantial ears. She tried to cover them, but it was useless. "Mali, Mali, Mali ..."

***

"Mali, Mali, Mali ..."

Reginald blinked in astonishment as the enemy army came into view. He'd expected everything from a professional force to a disorganised rabble – the pickets hadn't been able to get *that* close to the enemy – but the bastards had still managed to surprise him. The enemy was odd, their behaviour a strange mixture of professional and laughably amateurish. They moved in solid rows, swinging swords as if they expected to face helpless peasants rather than armed and experienced soldiers. Reginald had seen people make similar mistakes through inexperience – hardly anyone had fought a real war before the Empire had collapsed – but that had been five years ago. No military officer worthy of the name should have made the mistake now.

Gars snorted. "What are they thinking?"

"Good question." Reginald rubbed his forehead. He'd seen some right idiots in the army, mainly aristocrats who couldn't be forced to climb the ladder, but most of them had been sent to places where they couldn't do any damage. His father had never tolerated fools. "I don't know ..."

He lifted his spyglass and placed it to his eyes. The enemy soldiers looked ghastly, blood smeared over their faces and their uniforms covered with strange sigils. It puzzled and alarmed him as he took in their faces, their utterly fanatical faces. A handful at the back were indistinct, his eyes slipping over them as if his mind refused to believe they were real. He felt his blood run cold. Red monks? If they were here ...

The enemy soldiers picked up speed, the chant rising in volume as they practically flew towards the trenches. Reginald shivered, feeling a hint of terror yammering at the back of his mind. One couldn't reason with a fanatic, or even beat him into submission. Fanatics ... it was kill or be killed. He could sense fear wafting through his ranks, the men shifting uneasily as they realised they might be facing men who were ready to die as long as they took someone with them. Reginald gritted his teeth. It had to be stopped. Now.

He raised his voice. "Archers, ready."

The archers snapped into position, lifting and drawing back their bows. They wouldn't have any difficulty hitting their targets, not when the oncoming soldiers weren't making any attempt to protect themselves. And the arrows themselves were tipped with cold iron. If the enemy had a trick up their sleeve, they'd find it harder to use. He hoped.

"Loose," he barked.

He winced, feeling a twinge of sympathy as the archers loosed their bolts. They hadn't had time to aim properly, but it hardly mattered. There were so many men coming at them that the archers were bound to hit *something*. He smiled, coldly, as the shafts plunged into the enemy troops, knocking over dozens of men. They fell to the ground, where they were trampled by their fellows. Reginald sucked in his breath as the enemy force kept advancing. A smarter army would have wavered, maybe even broken, under the impact, but fanatics … they kept moving. The onrushing horde didn't seem even remotely deterred.

The archers fired again, without orders. More men died, but the remainder just kept coming. Reginald gritted his teeth, barking orders as he felt his men starting to waver themselves. Even experienced men were scared of fanatics … a third wave of arrows crashed down, then a fourth … hundreds of men died, yet … the remainder just kept coming. Their chant was growing louder and louder. He couldn't block it out.

"Mali, Mali, Mali …"

He cursed under his breath as the oncoming men hit the trenches. They died – in dozens and then hundreds – but there were always more, ready to take the place of men who'd been killed and left to rot. He thought he saw a handful of bodies crumble into dust as they died, yet … he wasn't sure. The men his archers had killed were buried under their own people, their bodies smashed to bloody chunks by the advancing horde. He feared he might be seeing things.

"The outer trenches are starting to break," Gars said. "Should we send in the cavalry?"

"No," Reginald said, grimly. The cavalry would have been effective, if the enemy troops hadn't been fanatics. They could have broken a regular army that had already taken crippling losses … he shook his head. The cavalry would be worse than useless, if he threw them into the maelstrom. They'd be slaughtered for nothing. "Order the archers to fire one final volley and then retreat to the walls."

"Yes, Your Highness," Gars said.

Reginald glanced over the battlefield as Gars dispatched messengers to the defence lines. The enemy were pressing in harder, clambering over their own bodies to get into his trenches and tear his men limb from limb. He cursed as he saw a handful of his men panicking, turning and fleeing for their lives; others, perhaps more determined to live, picked up the chant and echoed it. They seemed to be absorbed into the mass, becoming part of the enemy army. He stared, unsure if he believed his eyes. It wasn't uncommon for soldiers to change sides, but not during a battle! There'd certainly been no time for anyone to make arrangements for a defection.

He felt a sense of ... *something* towards the rear of the enemy lines and frowned. A handful of officers were standing there, their faces oddly blurred. Behind them ... his vision skipped over whatever was there. He cursed again, some instinct cautioning him to lower his gaze before the entity looked back at him. The enemy commander was literally inhuman, drawing on his troops to power himself ... Reginald shuddered. Some of the dead men – his men as well as the enemy – were stumbling to their feet. But not all of them.

"Impossible," Gars breathed.

"Not impossible, not now." There was a pattern, Reginald was sure of it. It came to him in a moment of insight. "They weren't killed with cold iron."

"Your Highness?"

"The men who were killed with cold iron are staying dead," Reginald said. It made sense. He could see a bunch of corpses that were nearly intact yet unmoving, while others – seemingly badly wounded – were staggering to their feet. "Pass the word. Every corpse is to be struck with cold iron."

He swore under his breath as the trench lines shattered, the survivors turning and running to the walls. Thankfully, the enemy commander – the entity – didn't seem to realise it was the perfect moment to send in the cavalry. Horsemen could do a *lot* of damage to his retreating men, although they couldn't take the walls. And yet, it looked as if they were barely needed. The onrushing men were *still* coming. He couldn't believe it. A regular army would have broken under the weight of such losses. But the fanatics were unfazed.

"Tell the battlements to stand at the ready," he ordered. He couldn't see any siege engines, nothing that might be used to take the walls, but ... he had a feeling it didn't matter. The enemy would climb over their own corpses to get at him, piling them under the walls until they could scramble up and over the battlements. "And ..."

There was a brilliant flash of light. The ground shook, violently. Reginald stumbled, falling to his knees. He silently thanked all the gods, particularly the ones that had had the decency to remain imaginary, that he hadn't donned full armour. Getting up wearing heavy armour was difficult, almost impossible. He stumbled to his feet as the ground shook again, just in time to see a section of the wall collapse into rubble. A handful of men fell to their deaths, screaming in terror. There was no time to mourn. The enemy troops cheered and rushed to the sudden gap in the walls.

"Order the reserves to block the hole," he snapped, knowing it might already be too late. Once the enemy gained a foothold, the end could not be long delayed. Technically, he should ask for terms if further resistance was pointless, but he had a feeling the entity wouldn't give a damn. It wanted blood. He could *feel* it. "Hurry!"

The chant grew louder. "Mali, Mali, Mali …"

***

A wave of *something* crashed into Silverdale, picking up her ghostly form and tossing it through the air as easily as she might have thrown her doll across the room. She spun in the air, feeling as if she'd been hit and yet she hadn't been … her head swam as she tried to work out what had happened. It felt as if she'd been swimming in the sea and caught in a wave … a wave of something. She honestly wasn't sure.

She tumbled over and over, the world far below starting to curve into a ball before she finally stopped herself. Or was stopped … she felt something tugging at her, as if she were on the end of a string. She felt a stab of panic as she was yanked back down, her astral self at the beck and call of something completely alien. The battlefield seemed to have changed, half the threads of light seemed to have vanished … she shuddered as she saw the bodies, feeling sick. She knew people died – her mother had died giving birth to her – but she'd never been allowed to see a dead body, not until now. A young man lay below her, so young he couldn't be more than a year or two older than her. His body was cold and grey, the life stripped from it and …

The body jerked, manipulated by a malevolent force. Silverdale could *see* it, something dark and ugly and deadly, sinking into his body as if it were just another tool. The body rolled over and stood, moving with a jerkiness that suggested its new owner didn't quite know what to do. But he – it – was learning fast. Silverdale recoiled in horror as it stood, one hand reaching out to snatch her astral form. She was sure that, on some level, the undead monster could *see* her. She felt herself rising as the creature resumed its march on the town. The walls had fallen and the army was advancing through the gap.

Her awareness drifted away as more and more troops advanced, running *through* her to get to the town. Sir Oswald was behind her, but she could feel his presence as he directed his men to join the attack. He wasn't even *pretending* to be human now. She could feel his influence spreading into the town, touching minds too weak to resist him. His mere presence poisoned the land for miles around. She was relieved she was trapped in her astral form. She had the feeling she wouldn't have been able to resist him, now, if he demanded her submission. He was surrounded by men, men who'd been strong and solid ... and were now his puppets. She swallowed, hard. Did Sofia *know* what she'd summoned and bound to her service?

A nasty thought struck her mind. *Is it truly bound to Sofia's service?*

She was young, but she wasn't naive. Not *that* naive. Her governess hadn't sheltered her *that* much. She'd watched her father, balancing noblemen and setting them up against each other to ensure that he remained in control. An overmighty subordinate was a danger, in fact if not in name. And the creature Sofia had summoned was growing stronger with every man who joined the chant ...

"Mali, Mali, Mali ..."

She caught a glimpse of someone standing on the battlements, barking orders. Reginald. It had to be Reginald. She drifted towards her brother, but he didn't seem to notice her. How could he? And yet ... he was issuing orders, but they didn't seem to be enough. The army was steadily breaking into the city. She could see the entity's power pressing against the stone walls, breaking them ...

Tears prickled at her eyes. Was she about to watch her brother die?

***

Reginald drew his sword, silently grateful he'd taken the time to practise with the new blade before he took it into battle. The cold iron felt heavy, uncomfortable in his hand. He wasn't sure why, but there was no time to think about it. He cut through the head of a fanatic, then sliced a rotting corpse in half. His eyes narrowed as he saw the body hit the ground for the second time. He'd seen enough battles to know that corpses decayed, but not *that* quickly.

Gars fought next to him, his sword flashing in the light. "Just like Northing, Your Highness!"

"Only worse," Reginald said. A low rumble echoed through the air, barely audible over the chant. Whatever the entity had done to the wall was spreading. The gap was growing wider, chunks of debris falling into the streets and crippling his defences as the enemy army pushed its advantage. He was starting to wonder if he'd been deliberately lured into a trap. The enemy commander, the damned entity, had been smarter than he'd thought. "We're in a killing ground."

He forced himself to think as another fanatic charged at him, screaming the chant as loudly as he could. The fool impaled himself on Reginald's blade, but kept coming – somehow – until Gars beheaded him with a stroke. Reginald cursed the dead man as he pulled the blade out of the corpse, trying not to notice how close he'd come to death. The light went out of the bastard's eyes, a second later. He thought he saw ...*something* ...flickering over the corpse, but it vanished before he could pin it down. The cold iron might have banished it ...

"Hold the line," he barked. The enemy army wasn't *that* strong, was it? It felt as if the entity commanded more troops than he'd known existed. He supposed recruitment wouldn't be a problem, not when the conscripts could be pushed through the Godly Realm and warped into monsters. "Don't let them get through."

But he knew, as the chant grew ever-louder, that he might be fighting his last battle.

"Mali, Mali, Mali ..."

Chapter Twenty-Five

"Mali, Mali, Mali …"

Isabella felt a chill at the back of her neck as she knelt in the room she'd carefully cleaned and washed while the enemy army made its approach. She was in the heart of the town hall, with solid stone walls between her and the chanters, but she could still hear their chant … somehow. It felt as if she were imagining it, even though she knew it was real. The word seemed to appear in her mind without ever going through her ears. She couldn't banish it.

But you don't want to banish it, she thought, as she braced herself. She'd given some thought to the ritual, but she knew half of it was guesswork. *You need a key to his mind.*

She took a long breath as she drew out the summoning circle. There had been no time to craft a proper ironhold – and she had the feeling that, if she'd tried, it would have failed. The ironhold would be a two-edged sword. She added a handful of words, laying down commands of protection as well as summoning and binding. Mother Lembu had taught her some, but she'd deduced others. She told herself, firmly, that they would work. Belief in oneself was half of ritual magic. It made a certain amount of sense. If one believed that one would fail, one *would* fail. She'd learnt that as a little girl.

It was hard to shape her mind, but – somehow – she managed, focusing on a single word. It hung in her mind, a dull presence that grew stronger the longer she thought about it. It was an aching tooth, a shadow of an headache unsure whether it was going to breed poisonous fruit or fade back into her mind. She nudged it, shaping the word until it felt like burning coals inside her mind …

"Mali," she whispered. "Mali …"

She was suddenly aware, very aware, of the entity. It wasn't far away, in one sense, and yet – in others – it was impossibly distant. Its will pervaded the town, poisoning the air and brushing against vulnerable minds. She could sense a handful of people breaking, surrendering to the entity's control. And, beyond them, she could sense the enemy army. They'd been broken long ago.

A hot flash of anger burned through her. "Mali," she said, louder this time. "Come to me."

The air seemed to darken, as if reality itself was about to sneeze. She felt the entity resisting her, somehow. It was anchored to the human world, held in place by bonds that were both intangible and unbreakable. She felt the pressure growing stronger, as if the entity were trying to push her away. But every time it tried, it only made things worse for itself. She allowed herself a tight smile, reminding herself she hadn't won *yet*. But it felt good to be turning their rules against them. She'd summoned the entity, calling it by name and offering a sacrifice … and it had to come. It couldn't evade the rules that bound it.

Something *broke*. Isabella could feel it. She refused to believe, even at the back of her mind, that she might have failed. A dark shadow materialised in the circle, held in place by a chalk outline that wouldn't have slowed her down for a second. She couldn't see any eyes, but she sensed that it was looking at her … that it was consumed with a malevolence that chilled her to the bone. It was a deeply *personal* feeling, although they'd never met. She'd known hundreds of people who'd disliked her, who'd hated her, but … the entity was worse. Far worse. She knew she could never allow herself to fall into its clutches. It would be the last mistake she'd ever make.

"Mali," she said. The chant outside stopped, abruptly. "I bind you, with this circle and my will. I command you, speak honestly to me. I command you …"

The entity's hatred seemed to grow, as impossible as it seemed, as she worked her way through the commands. She didn't really want to issue orders – she didn't want to give the entity an excuse to leave – but she wanted, she *needed*, to bind it in place, to render it as close to harmless as possible. She shivered as she finished speaking, reminding herself that the entity was still very far from *harmless*. A single mistake, a single opening, would be enough to give it a clear shot at her. And she might not survive its retaliation.

On impulse, she cast a detection spell. Magic coiled around her, but not around the entity ... around Mali. Her magic thought the entity didn't exist. And yet, she could feel it pulsing against her mind. The circle was holding it in place, but ... she told herself, firmly, that it couldn't hurt her. It could weaken her resistance, it could probe for chinks in her armour, yet ... it could do nothing she didn't allow it to do. The thought gave her strength. She pulled herself upright and stared at the shadow. It seemed to be staring back at her.

It spoke, the words pounding against her head. "What do you want?"

"I want you to stay there," Isabella said. She felt a flash of triumph. "And you are not to even *try* to escape."

***

It happened very quickly.

Silverdale heard the voice, calling to Mali. The creature possessing Sir Oswald seemed to struggle, power crackling through the air as it tried to resist, before it found itself unceremoniously yanked out of its host and pulled through the air. Silverdale had a glimpse of something half-seen, something unbearably alien, before it was gone. Its influence snapped at the same moment, leaving Sir Oswald standing in the middle of a group of officers. A moment later, his body crumbled to dust. The officers collapsed into a heap of sobbing men.

She looked away ... and found herself following the call. Mali – now a twisted knot of power, confined within a circle – was standing in front of an older woman, with short black hair and a faintly twisted smile. She was real, as far as Silverdale could tell, but she was sparkling with ... *something*. Magic? It felt different, almost human. She was speaking to Mali, her words shimmering in the astral realm. Her words were binding the entity in place. Silverdale could almost *see* the chains snapping into existence. The threads that had tied Mali to his thralls were gone.

The woman looked up, sharply. For a moment, they stared at each other. Silverdale knew, beyond a shadow of a doubt, that the woman could see her. She hesitated, then threw herself back through the walls as fast as she could. Her link back to her body was growing stronger, now that Mali was a prisoner. She allowed it to drag her back to the castle, back home … she caught a hint of someone calling to her, but the name wasn't *hers*. It had no effect …

The battle is lost, she thought, numbly. The world was starting to blur as she plunged into her body. *What now?*

***

Isabella frowned. A young girl – a ghostly young girl – had been right in front of her, just for a second. She wasn't sure quite how she'd known the girl was there, but … she had been there. Isabella sucked in her breath, convinced she'd been watched … she glanced back at Mali, watching her with evil intent. An ally? An enemy? Or … merely an interested party? She tried a ritual to call back the girl, but it didn't work. She didn't have anything she could use to focus the rite.

"Stay there," she said, as she headed for the door. "You have no permission to leave."

She felt a wave of anger, as if a human was shouting curses, as she closed the door behind her. The entity couldn't leave, as long as the circle remained unbroken. But … she locked the door, putting up a pair of wards to deter anyone who ignored the warning signs. The circle couldn't be broken from the inside, according to Mother Lembu, but Mali would keep looking for weaknesses. The wretched creature wasn't bound by human limits. Sooner or later, it would find a loophole and return to the Godly Realm.

Outside, the streets were chaos. She could see a giant hole in the wards, as if it had been hit with a dozen blasting spells simultaneously. Hundreds of soldiers lay on the ground, some sobbing like babies. She felt a wave of disgust – grown men shouldn't cry – mingled with pity. The crying men were the lucky ones. Others, sitting on the ground and staring at nothing, had clearly been broken by their experiences. Their minds had been snapped beyond repair.

She took a long breath as she walked towards the walls. The air felt clear, the sense of foreboding gone. Mali was a prisoner now. It felt as if dawn was breaking, even though the battle had lasted for hours. She felt her heart sink as she saw the bodies, dozens of men wearing Reginald's livery. They'd died for their prince, fighting for a cause few of them had truly believed in. They'd fought for Reginald instead.

Reginald was standing by the gash in the wall, peering towards the enemy camp. The muddy field – it was hard to believe that it had been green, only yesterday – was strewn with even more bodies. She shuddered as she saw, beyond them, more crying men. They were badly shaken, completely helpless. Dust drifted through the air, brushing uncomfortably against her skin. Her instincts warned her to be careful. The dust had once been human.

"We won," Reginald said, quietly. "What happened?"

"I summoned the entity in command of the enemy force," Isabella said. She didn't question how he knew she'd done *something*. "And that won the battle."

Reginald glanced at her. "Is he trapped, now?"

"Yes." Isabella spoke flatly, hoping he trusted her enough to accept her word. His doubts might not weaken the circle, but she wasn't *certain*. "He can't hurt anyone any longer."

She followed Reginald and his bodyguards as they advanced across the field, picking their way through the bodies. The slaughter had been terrifying, worse than anything she'd seen since her early days as a mercenary. She tried to count how many people had been killed, but gave up very quickly. Too many bodies had been hacked apart, as if they'd kept walking after they'd been killed. It wasn't impossible. Mali was certainly powerful enough to animate the dead and keep them moving.

A circle of officers sat at the rear of the battlefield, all but one of them either crying or staring at nothing. Reginald muttered a word under his breath – it dawned on Isabella that he *knew* the men – as he drew his sword and pressed it against the only officer who seemed unaffected. The man looked up, his eyes full of tears. He'd been stronger than the others, but not strong enough to escape *everything*. Isabella felt sick. They might have been on the other side, but she didn't think the officers had deserved to be broken. They'd never be the same again.

"Lord Wynn, isn't it?" Reginald sounded annoyed. "You appear to be the sole survivor."

Lord Wynn giggled. It was a deeply disconcerting sound.

"Your Highness."

"You have a choice," Reginald said. "You can surrender, on behalf of your army, or you can die right now. I'm not interested in anything else."

"Hah." Lord Wynn snorted. "Do you think it matters now?"

"Yes." Reginald seemed unmoved. "Surrender?"

"Sure. Why not?" Lord Wynn bowed his head. "I'd grovel, except I can barely move."

Isabella frowned. Lord Wynn was at Reginald's mercy, but ... she realised, numbly, that Lord Wynn had seen terrible things. Reginald could hardly treat him worse than his former master. The man giggled, even as he surrendered. His sanity rested on a knife edge.

"What happened?" Isabella knelt down beside Lord Wynn, despite Reginald's sound of protest. "What happened to you?"

Lord Wynn looked at her. "Who are you?"

"Answer the question," Reginald snapped. "Now."

"She ... ah, your sister ... put Sir Oswald in command of the army," Lord Wynn said. "It was a total shock. Naturally, we weren't going to stand for it. We were ready to protest until he arrived, at which point we ... we ... we ..."

His voice trailed off. He swallowed hard, then restarted. "We did as he wanted," he said. "It just felt *right*. We slaved for him. We worshipped him. We ..."

"Sir Oswald must have been the host," Isabella muttered. It made sense. Sir Oswald must have been the anchor holding Mali in place. "And he dominated his subordinates."

"Probably." Reginald snorted. "Sir Oswald couldn't count to eleven without taking off his boots or his pants – and he was dumb enough to expose himself to do it, too."

"We did as we were told," Lord Wynn said. "And then ... he's gone. He's gone and ..."

"It doesn't matter," Reginald said. He reached down and yanked Lord Wynn to his feet. "Get your people organised, the ones who can still obey orders. Start digging graves for the dead. I'll deal with the rest of you afterwards."

He nodded to his guards, detailing two of them to remain with Lord Wynn. The man looked too shaken for treachery, but ... Isabella was sure, if he tried, that it would be the last thing he ever did. Reginald seemed shaken too as he looked at the other officers, his face oddly unguarded. There had clearly been little love between him and the officers, or he would have taken them to the Summer Isle, but ... they didn't deserve to be warped and twisted until they could no longer think straight. She wondered, morbidly, if they'd ever recover.

"He was one of my father's lickspittles," Reginald said, nodding to one of the crying men. "He didn't have an imaginative bone in his body, but ... he could be relied upon to do as my father said. And now, look at him. He's a mess."

"He might recover," Isabella said. "They might *all* recover."

"I hope you're right," Reginald said. "I really do."

Isabella nodded. "I have to make very certain that no one can disturb our guest," she said. "I'll speak to you later?"

"Yeah." Reginald smiled at her, tiredly. "We'll resume the march tomorrow."

"Yes, Your Highness." Isabella kissed his cheek. "I'll see you later."

***

Reginald was no stranger to death. Men had died under his command from the very first day he'd fought for his father, men he knew and men he didn't know ... more of the latter, if he were honest with himself. He'd made an effort to learn the names of his sergeants, the men who really made the army work, but ... he didn't know everyone. It was easier not to know the men who died for him. And yet ...

He forced himself to keep working as the hours ticked away, trying not to think about the shattered remains of the enemy army. The crying men seemed ... *broken*, so fragile that he knew there was no point in trying to incorporate them into his army. The others seemed worse, unable to feed themselves or wipe their bottoms without help. They'd starve to death fairly soon, he was sure. There was no way he could spare the manpower to take care of them. He didn't even have time to send them back to Humber.

Gars marched up to him, Earl Oxley on his tail. "We lost nine hundred and seventeen men," Gars said. He held a notebook in one hand, where someone had tallied up the dead and wounded. "Four hundred or so more are injured. A handful of those are mad."

"They joined in the chant," Earl Oxley put in, grimly. *That* was a surprise. The man had more steel than Reginald had realised. "And then … whatever infected their minds just vanished."

"Yeah." Reginald had a feeling it would be better not to mention the captive entity. "How many of the wounded can return to duty?"

"Not many." Gars looked grim. "Their wounds were pretty bad, Your Highness."

"They can stay here, for the moment," Reginald said. He didn't like it, but he couldn't see any other option. "Detail a reserve company to remain behind for their protection until we secure Havelock. We don't want the locals returning and cutting their throats."

Earl Oxley looked astonished. "They would dare?"

"Probably." Reginald shrugged, heavily. The locals had no reason to love the army … either army. They had plenty of grudges to repay. He knew from bitter experience that wounded stragglers rarely made it back to camp. "We'll do our best to keep them from doing something we can't ignore."

He looked at the bodies, now being dragged into the mass grave. "How many did we kill?"

"Around two to three thousand," Gars said. "We think. There's no way to be sure."

Reginald wiped his forehead. Two to three thousand … he was used to gross exaggerations, and claims he'd killed millions or billions of enemy soldiers, but still … two to three *thousand*? A sizeable chunk of the army he'd helped build was now dead or effectively out of combat. The barons would not hesitate to take action now. And what would Sofia – and the entities – do when they learnt they'd been defeated? If this went on, there might not be a kingdom left by the time it finished.

"Ready the army to continue the march tomorrow," he ordered. "Send out pickets to sweep the roads to Havelock. If there are any other surprises before the city walls, I want to know about them."

"Yes, Your Highness," Earl Oxley said.

Chapter Twenty-Six

Her body felt heavy.

Silverdale fought her way back to wakefulness, through a haze of pain that felt like hot needles being stabbed into her eyes. Her stomach roiled, threatening to throw up everything she'd eaten for the last decade. She swallowed hard, tasting … *something* unpleasant in her mouth. It was hard, so hard, to recall what she'd seen. There'd been a battle, there'd been a woman … she'd captured Sir Oswald. No, she'd captured the creature that had possessed Sir Oswald. And then …

"Welcome back to the world," a familiar – and unwelcome – voice said. "Would you like something to drink?"

Silverdale's eyes snapped open. She was lying in her bed, in her room. Emetine was sitting beside the bed, holding a glass of water in one hand. Silverdale felt an instinctive urge to get away, to crawl out of bed and run for her life. Emetine looked … *wrong*. Something much greater than a mere human, even a *royal* human, was overshadowing her frail human form. Silverdale blinked. The impression was gone. But Emetine still looked inhuman.

"I …" Silverdale coughed and started again. "What are you doing in my room?"

Emetine looked oddly amused by the question. "Your sister told me to look after you."

Silverdale winced. Her rooms were *hers*. Her sisters – and her brother, and her father – were not supposed to enter her chambers without permission. It was bad enough that the governess was allowed to come and go as she pleased, no doubt reporting everything Silverdale did to her father and now her sister. Sofia shouldn't have allowed Emetine into Silverdale's rooms, even if she *was* – for the moment – the mistress of the castle. It was a breach of the unwritten rules governing their lives. Even their father wouldn't have allowed someone into Silverdale's rooms without making a show of asking her first.

"Here." Emetine held out the glass. "Have a drink. You need it."

"Thanks." Silverdale felt parched. And yet, she wasn't sure she should drink *anything* from Emetine's hands. "What is it?"

"Pure water, given freely and without obligation," Emetine said. She managed a smile that tried to be reassuring. It wasn't particularly successful. "It's safe to drink."

Silverdale hesitated, then put the glass to her lips and drank. There was no point in trying to resist, not when Emetine could simply hold her down and *force* her to drink. The gods knew the druids had forced her to drink their potions, back when she'd had an awful fever as a little girl. The water tasted bland, as if it had been boiled repeatedly. She told herself, firmly, that boiling the water made it safer to drink. She'd had that drilled into her as a child.

"You're starting to see the world as it really is," Emetine said. She took back the glass and refilled it. "Have you been *enjoying* expanding your mind?"

Silverdale sucked in her breath. "I ... I didn't take anything earlier, not when I was in the throne room."

"No." Emetine returned the glass. "Your mind has already expanded well beyond the need for potion. The barriers that kept you from seeing the *real* world are steadily breaking down."

Her lips curved into a cold smile. "You really *do* have a great deal of potential."

"Reginald beat you," Silverdale said. She knew it was foolish, but she said it anyway. "I saw everything. He beat your troops and your ... your ..."

"God." Emetine sounded very certain. "He beat a god."

Her form shifted, just slightly. Silverdale felt her skin crawl. Something was hiding behind her smile, something utterly inhuman. Emetine hadn't moved closer – she was still sitting beside the bed – but the room suddenly felt a great deal smaller, as if Emetine were invading her personal space. She fought the urge to cringe back against the wall as the shadows grew longer and darker. The room was no longer entirely *hers*.

Emetine's smile grew wider. "You need a teacher," she

said. "Or else you will lose your mind in the Godly Realm."

Silverdale swallowed, suddenly understanding – all too well – why she'd been allowed to experiment with her new talents. Emetine had *wanted* Silverdale to experiment, to open her mind ... just so Emetine could offer to teach her, to shape Silverdale in her own image. The shape behind Emetine seemed to grow stronger, darker ... she shivered, almost dropping the empty glass. Her father had told her of noblemen who offered protection in exchange for submission. Emetine was no better than those predatory monsters.

"I don't know," she hedged. "You tricked me!"

"Did I?" Emetine shrugged. "Or did you trick yourself?"

"You put the potion in my food," Silverdale charged. "Didn't you?"

Emetine shrugged. "Did I?"

Silverdale stared at her. "Are you telling me ...?"

"I'm telling you nothing, save this," Emetine said, cutting her off. "You have a talent. That talent has now come to life. Either you let me teach you how to use it properly, and safely, or eventually you will go mad. Or something will come out of the Godly Realm with you. In you. And it will wear your face for a while, but it won't *be* you and ..."

The world shifted. Silverdale scrambled backwards as a wave of cold anger radiated through the room. She'd never felt anything like it, not even when her father had discovered that two of his courtiers were plotting to murder him and his family. She found herself pressing against the stone wall, fingers feeling desperately for a catch she knew wasn't there. The anger was growing stronger, as if someone was screaming their rage right into her face. She cowered in fear ...

Emetine screamed. She practically threw herself off the chair, landing on the floor in an undignified heap. Her entire body convulsed so violently that Silverdale was *sure* she was going to snap her own spine. Emetine rolled over, jerking as if she was being beaten by invisible sticks. Silverdale hesitated, then closed her eyes and reached out with her mind. Tendrils of light and power were reaching out to Emetine, tearing at her very soul. The woman seemed weaker by the second, each flicker of light diminishing her still further. And a voice, pounding through the air …

"WHAT HAVE YOU DONE? WHAT HAVE YOU LOST?"

Silverdale flinched. She'd seen her father in a rage, although his anger had never been directed at her. But it felt like her father … no, like something fatherly. Something – someone – who meant so much to her that his rage was worse than a physical blow. She fought the urge to beg forgiveness, even though the rage wasn't aimed at her. The power was so great that she felt utterly helpless in its wake.

The tendrils of power grew stronger. She saw – or thought she saw – a shadowy figure whipping Emetine to death. She tried to look closer, but her inner eye started to hurt and she closed it frantically. Emetine screamed – she'd always been screaming – and rolled over and over, as if she were trying to escape an invisible attacker. The voice grew louder, each word a burning coal of pain pressing into Silverdale's very soul, then faded back into the Godly Realm. It dawned on Silverdale, as the shadowy figure receded, that Emetine was being punished. But punished for what?

She gathered herself as the world returned to normal. She could hear someone whimpering, a pitiful sound that was somehow worse than screams of pain. She pulled herself together and peered over the edge of the bed. Emetine lay on the floor, curled into a ball. She looked … *diminished*, as if her inner light had been drained by the torment. Silverdale stared in horror and disbelief. Her governess had whipped her and her older sisters for misbehaviour, but the wretched woman had never done anything like *that*. There'd always been limits. The governess had known better than to go beyond them.

"No …" Emetine sounded as if she hadn't realised the torment was over. "No …"

Silverdale swallowed, hard. She'd never seen *anyone* so beaten down, never. Emetine looked utterly broken, as if she could no longer muster the will to say no to anyone. Her face was pale and wan, her dress stained with sweat … she almost looked human. Silverdale nearly pitied her, despite everything. The woman had traded her soul for power and now … it struck Silverdale, suddenly, that Emetine's master had been furious with her. She'd summoned a god – or whatever the creatures really were – only to lose it. Silverdale giggled, helplessly. Emetine had *really* angered her master.

"Be quiet!" Emetine stumbled to her feet, arms flailing around as if she were lashing out at unseen enemies. "Be quiet or I will …"

"He was *really* mad at you," Silverdale said. She knew she shouldn't be tormenting Emetine, not now, but she couldn't stop herself. "What did you do to deserve it?"

Emetine loomed over her, but the impression was weaker now. She definitely looked *human*, not … something greater. Silverdale couldn't help herself. She laughed in Emetine's face. The older woman looked shocked, then drew back her arm and slapped Silverdale across the face. Silverdale cried out in pain, watching helplessly as Emetine turned and strode towards the door. Her face hurt, yet … she tried to keep from giggling again. There was no way Emetine could hurt her anything like as badly as Emetine herself had been hurt. Her master had *tortured* her. She grabbed a blanket, pressing it against her mouth to keep from laughing as the door slammed closed. Emetine would have to be *very* lucky to avoid being seen as she made her way back to her rooms. She didn't look all-powerful any longer.

She's not all-powerful, Silverdale thought. She removed the blanket, swung her legs over the side of the bed and stood. Her legs felt wobbly, but she managed to stay upright. Her head hurt, but – perversely – the throbbing pain in her cheek helped her to focus. *She's not all-powerful and nor are the creatures she serves*.

She stumbled over to the window and peered outside. There were more soldiers on the battlements, more soldiers – and hooded figures – patrolling the streets beyond. The sky was darkening rapidly, but she thought she could see movement on the roads outside the city walls. Hundreds of men were streaming towards the city, running from a threat only they could see. Silverdale wondered, numbly, if they'd be allowed to pass through the gates and into the city. Traditionally, they were shut at nightfall. Who knew what might try to enter the city under cover of darkness?

Silverdale shivered. Reginald was out there, somewhere to the west. She peered into the gloom, but saw nothing. Her brother had won a battle he should have lost and he'd captured one of the creatures … no wonder Emetine's master had been angry. She'd summoned the creature into the mortal realm, only to lose it. Silverdale had no idea what that meant – she had no idea who'd actually captured the creature either – but she had a feeling it boded ill for the future. Emetine would be more desperate than ever before.

They're not all-powerful, she reminded herself, again. *They can be beaten.*

There was a knock at the door. Silverdale turned, wondering who it could be. Emetine, coming to hit her some more? Or to apologise, for daring to slap someone of the blood royal? That was a hanging offence, unless one had special permission. Somehow, Silverdale doubted that Emetine would either apologise or be hanged. Sofia was dependent on the High Priestess. She wouldn't throw away her one advantage when she knew there was no shortage of people who wanted to overthrow her and take the kingdom for themselves.

"Come," Silverdale called.

Greta stepped into the room, carrying a tray of food. "Your Highness? Have you recovered?"

"Barely." Silverdale felt odd. She had a headache, but … she felt as if she was *imagining* the headache. "What happened?"

"The stable boy claimed the army was defeated and Sir Oswald was killed," Greta said. If she'd noticed the mark on Silverdale's face, she said nothing. "The guards took him away before he could give details. If he had them."

Silverdale nodded. "It wasn't Sir Oswald," she said. She felt a flicker of pity for the pompous youth. Fool though he'd been, he hadn't deserved to be possessed and then killed. "It was something wearing his body."

"I figured." Greta's voice was very tight. "I heard the rumours."

She put the tray on the table. "They said he wasn't the same person," she added, as Silverdale sat down. "They kept saying …"

Her voice trailed off. Silverdale looked up. "They kept saying *what*?"

Greta coloured. "Something I probably shouldn't be

discussing with you, Your Highness."

Silverdale winced. It would be nice to have a friend, just one. But she knew the gulf between Greta and herself was completely insurmountable. She was tempted to press, to demand that Greta told her, but ... she knew she'd be putting Greta in an impossible position, one where she'd wind up in trouble whatever she did. Silverdale sighed, wishing she could tell the maid that everything would be alright. But she knew she'd be lying. Greta would know it too.

"He was charming and personable and everyone followed him," Greta said. It was impossible to escape the sense that she was choosing her words very carefully. "He wasn't the same person."

"No." Silverdale took a bite of her food. "What else have you heard?"

"Very little," Greta said. "People are too scared to talk. They're even scared to ... to do anything, beyond their duties. The castle feels *wrong* now. They'd leave if they could."

"So would I," Silverdale said. She wondered, suddenly, if she should flee to Greta's family. But where did they live? How could she find them? And would they take her in? Sofia would tear the city apart looking for her. And ... she smiled, tiredly. "I'd have to get out of the castle first."

"No one gets in or out, without permission from the Regent," Greta said. "I haven't had any letters from my family since ... since *she* arrived."

Emetine, Silverdale thought. *Why has she isolated the castle?*

Her mind raced. She could try to bribe a guard to take a letter to Reginald, but ... she didn't know which guards could be bribed and which guards would betray her without a second thought. There were plenty of pieces of gold and silver within reach, yet ... she frowned as she realised she didn't have anything that wouldn't pass unnoticed. She could give a guard her golden figurines, but if he was caught with them ... he'd be accused of theft. Or worse. And even if he did take her gold, what then? Would he even be able to get out of the castle?

I need to get back into the secret passages, she thought. *And see if one of them leads to the outside world.*

Silverdale listened to Greta's chatter as she finished her dinner, the food resting uneasily in her stomach. She felt as if she'd been sick, although – as far as she could tell – she hadn't thrown up. She'd simply collapsed on the dais ... she wondered, suddenly, who'd carried her back to her rooms. Emetine? She touched her cheek lightly. The pain was almost gone. The High Priestess wasn't *that* strong, not physically. Or maybe she'd been weakened by her torment.

"Let me know if you hear anything," she said, slowly. "Have you seen my sister? Either of my sisters?"

"No, Your Highness." Greta sounded worried. "I've been assigned to you – and you alone. I haven't so much as laid eyes on either of your sisters. There was a brief rumour that Princess Ruby was going to marry Lord Oscar, but ..."

"Poor guy." Silverdale giggled, even though she knew she shouldn't. "What horrible crime did he commit to deserve *her*?"

Greta looked as though she wanted to giggle too. "It's just a rumour, Your Highness. I don't know if there's any truth to it."

"No." Silverdale felt cold. Lord Oscar was old enough to be her grandfather. He'd buried two wives already. And yet ... she shivered, helplessly. Ruby's marriage would be arranged for political expediency, not something so trite as romance. Who cared if the man was nearly fifty years older than his bride, as long as the match served a greater purpose? She felt her stomach churn at the thought. Surely Sofia wouldn't go so far for power. "I ..."

Her blood ran cold. Sofia might be feeling desperate. No, she *was* feeling desperate. If Reginald had beaten her army, he could take the city. And if he took the city, *someone* inside the castle would throw open the gates and invite him to put an end to the regency. Sofia had everything to lose. She had ample reason to offer her sister as a human sacrifice to secure her grip on power. She'd be lucky if Reginald didn't throw her into prison and toss away the key. Or strip her of her title and marry her off to someone who owned a part-interest in a pig farm.

But it won't be enough, Silverdale thought. Her father had made her memorise everything she could about the aristocracy – and the balance of power. Lord Oscar was powerful, but he wasn't *that* powerful. Yes, he'd want to marry a princess, yet … it wouldn't be enough to tip the balance in Sofia's favour. Or Lord Oscar's, for that matter. His rivals would close ranks against him. *She might throw the entire country into civil war.*

"Tomorrow, I have to see Ruby," Silverdale decided. "And you have to help me."

Greta nodded. "Yes, Your Highness."

Chapter Twenty-Seven

Havelock *was* a beautiful city.

Reginald felt a twinge of guilt as the rising sun cast its light over the city. Havelock had escaped much of the chaos of the last five years and it showed – the city walls were strong, the buildings on both sides looked largely undamaged and, even now, hundreds of ships moved up and down the river. A number were still heading down to Humber, taking for granted that he wouldn't try to impede their passage. It was unfortunate, he considered, that the dockyards were on the wrong side of the city walls. He would have happily used ships to transport his troops if he hadn't known it would make them sitting ducks. Instead, he'd had to move his troops up to the walls and occupy the outer city under cover of darkness.

And the civilians within the outer city had already fled, he reminded himself. There had been no point in trying to hide the army's march. The civilians had seen the remains of the defeated army trickling back to Havelock. Of *course* they'd tried to hide. *They're either inside the walls or hiding in the countryside.*

He glanced at Isabella, who looked as if she hadn't slept a wink. "Can you sense anything?"

Isabella scowled. "There's a *presence* within the city," she said, looking towards the giant castle. "It feels different to the others, as if it hasn't quite *arrived.*"

"Or it doesn't own the city," Reginald said. His father had left the city in the capable hands of the city fathers, although both sides had known that it was a technicality. The king could take the city at any point, if he was willing to sacrifice his long-term interests for short-term gains. "Sofia hasn't tried to overrule the city's ancient liberties. She'd have had a riot on her hands."

"Perhaps." Isabella rubbed her forehead. "Does it matter?"

Reginald laughed, humourlessly, as he swept his spyglass over the walls. He could see hundreds of men in position, waiting for his troops to begin the attack. There would be hundreds – perhaps thousands – more held in reserve, ready to seal off any breaches and counterattack before he managed to get his reinforcements into position to exploit any local breakthroughs. Taking the city quickly was going to be bloody. He would have preferred to lay siege to the city, to starve the defenders into submission, but that would just guarantee a civil war. He *had* to win quickly, if he wanted to win at all. His scouts had caught spies watching his troops from a distance. The nobility were watching, weighing the odds. If he bled his army white, they'd rebel.

Gars hurried up. "Your Highness," he said. "The first units are in position."

"Good." Reginald winced. He was going to take horrific losses, whatever happened. "Order the archers to start sweeping the walls. Send in the first assault force as soon as the arrows start to land."

"Yes, Your Highness," Gars said.

Reginald glanced at Isabella. "Can you use magic?"

"The walls are charmed to resist magic," Isabella said. Her voice was taut, so taut that Reginald almost ordered her back to bed. "And the presence is interfering with my senses."

And that means your magic might be useless, Reginald thought. He had no idea why the entities interfered with magic, but there was no denying that they *did*. Isabella's spells had grown increasingly unreliable on the Summer Isle, her magic simply breaking up when it came into contact with the entities and their victims. *We're going to be pitting sword against sword ...*

He shook his head as the trumpets blared. The archers loosed their bolts a second later, unleashing a swarm of arrows into the city. Reginald hoped – prayed – the civilians would have the sense to remain in their homes, well out of the way. There'd be hundreds of thousands of deaths if they got caught up in the fighting. He'd picked his assault route carefully, intending to avoid as much of the city as possible, but there was no way he could keep from going through the wealthier suburbs. Too many people had bought houses around the castle for him to avoid them entirely. In hindsight, perhaps his great-great-grandfather should have been more careful about who he allowed to build near his castle.

"It was a golden age," he muttered, more to himself than to anyone else. "And no one thought it would come to an end."

Isabella glanced at him. "Reginald?"

"Just woolgathering," Reginald said. Down below, the first rank of troops was hurrying towards the walls. "We made so many mistakes over the last few years because we didn't know what we were doing."

Isabella smiled, rather tiredly. "Everyone makes mistakes," she said. There was a hint of bitterness in her voice. "Except my father. He never made a mistake in his life. He'd tell you as much himself, if you asked."

"I know the type," Reginald said.

He felt his expression darken as his men started putting ladders against the walls and scrambling up them. He should be down there, sharing the risks even though he knew very few first-line troops survived long enough to collect their bounties and early discharges. He couldn't afford to put his life at risk ... he scowled, watching as the enemy archers started to take a toll. They weren't aiming very well, but they were firing so many arrows that it hardly mattered. Dozens of his men were hit, even as their fellows pressed the offensive. The wounded probably wouldn't last long enough to reach the healers.

"They're on the walls," Isabella said. "And pushing towards the gates."

Reginald nodded. They *had* to take a gatehouse – quickly – if they wanted to win. The city fathers would probably surrender, the moment they realised their city had become impossible to defend. They'd have no choice, unless they wanted to risk Reginald's troops rampaging through their city. And yet ... his eyes narrowed as he saw a man falling from the battlements, almost certainly to his death. The defenders were fighting savagely, trying their hardest to hold the gatehouse while they brought up reinforcements. He was starting to suspect he wouldn't be able to get his men up and onto the walls in time.

And we don't have time to undermine the walls and bring them crashing down, he thought, numbly. He was used to blood and suffering – and death – but this was different. *We have to take the city in a single blow.*

He shuddered, helplessly, as enemy reinforcements charged down the battlements, shouting something as they ran. He couldn't make their words out over the din of battle. Surely ... there was another entity, pushing them forward. Sofia might be beautiful, but she'd never led troops in battle. How could she fire them up? He scowled as the two forces collided, knowing all too well that the defenders had men to spare. Sofia might be a more effective commander than he'd thought.

Or she has help, he reminded himself. *She could easily have summoned another entity.*

He glanced at Isabella. "Can you capture another one?"

"I don't think so." Isabella looked pale. "I can't make out the name."

Reginald winced. "Then we have to take the city by force," he said. "Damn it."

He spat, then waved to Gars. "Send in the secondary units."

"Yes, Your Highness," Gars said.

***

"You shouldn't be at the window," Greta said. "Your Highness ..."

"It's perfectly safe," Silverdale said, although she wasn't sure that was true. Reginald had often bragged of his skill with bow and arrow. "I have to see ..."

She rubbed her eyes as she peered into the distance. Her brother's army had materialised out of nowhere – or so it seemed. She'd been woken at dawn and informed that the enemy army was massing outside the city gates. The governess had wanted her to go downstairs, into the throne room, but Silverdale had refused. Oddly, the older woman had let her stay, rather than try to drag her downstairs. Silverdale couldn't help finding that a little ominous. The governess rarely tolerated defiance in her charge.

The sound of battle echoed in the distance. Arrows hissed through the air, a handful coming alarmingly close to the castle itself. Swords clashed, men screamed ... she watched a tiny man fall from the battlements, his arms waving frantically as he plunged to his death. She was suddenly grateful she couldn't see him hit the ground. She knew she didn't want to see men die, not for real …

It *was* for real. The realisation struck her like a hammer blow. The tiny men on the battlements weren't *tiny*, they were just so far away they *looked* tiny. She swallowed hard, remembering some of the friendlier guards. Were they out there, fighting and dying for Sofia and the High Priestess? Or were they being held in reserve as the militia struggled to hold the city walls. She wasn't sure. The men were so far away that she couldn't make out their livery. For all she knew, they could have been Lord Oscar's household troops. The wedding might have already taken place.

Sofia would have insisted I attend, she told herself. Her sister hadn't been married off, not yet. *They didn't even have time to make a formal announcement.*

She put the thought out of her head as she saw more men swarming the walls. They were pressing onwards, charging at the gatehouse … she shuddered as a handful slipped and fell to their deaths. Shouts and screams echoed through the air, growing louder as more and more men threw themselves into the fray. She felt her stomach churn as she saw a man getting his head chopped off, the head flying into the distance even as the body crumpled to the battlements and lay still. It wasn't the first time she'd seen a man die, but … she cursed out loud as an arrow smashed into the stone wall beside the window. An inch to the left and it would have punched through her body.

"Your Highness." Greta sounded as if she were panicking. "Come away from the window!"

Silverdale shook her head. "I have to see …"

"Not like this!" Greta caught hold of Silverdale's arm and dragged her out of the room. "You could be hit at any moment!"

"Let go of me," Silverdale protested. She tried to struggle, but Greta was too strong. "I …"

She caught herself before she could remind Greta that touching her without permission was a serious offence. Greta was a friend … well, the closest thing she *had* to a friend. Greta meant well … Silverdale relaxed and allowed Greta to close the door on the battle. She promised herself, silently, that she'd never tell anyone what had happened. Sofia would probably reward Greta for saving her sister's life, then hang her for touching Silverdale without permission. And then …

"That's my brother out there," she said, numbly. "He's coming for us."

"Yes, Your Highness," Greta said. "And what will happen when he reaches the walls?"

"He'll put everything back to rights," Silverdale said, although she knew it wasn't completely true. There was no way Reginald could fix *everything*. Sofia and Emetine wouldn't go down easily and there were … *things* … behind them. "Father will be back on the throne and everything will be sane again."

Greta didn't look convinced. "You'd better stay in your room, Your Highness," she said. "If your brother has to storm the castle, you could get caught in the midst of the fighting and killed."

"Reginald wouldn't kill me," Silverdale said. "I'm his sister!"

"And how many of his troops know you by sight?" Greta met her eyes, evenly. "Stay out of sight, Your Highness. You do *not* want to be seen."

Silverdale swallowed. She'd heard whispers, whispers she wasn't supposed to have heard. "I understand …"

***

"Your Highness," Earl Oxley said. "This isn't working."

Isabella barely heard him. Something was interfering with her senses, interfering so subtly that she hadn't realised what it was doing for far too long. It wasn't magic, as she understood it; it wasn't the ritualistic tricks she'd learnt over the last six months. She wasn't sure what it was, but it worked. It was hard, so hard, to concentrate. She wasn't sure she could shape a spell, let alone cast it. The pressure against her mind was too strong.

"We have to take that gatehouse," Reginald insisted. He spoke calmly, but with an edge Isabella didn't like. "If we fail to break into the city, we may as well pull back and surrender."

Isabella tried to focus her mind. The looming presence

overshadowing the city didn't *feel* any clearer, even though she was well aware of it now. It was twanging at her mind, constantly derailing her train of thought ... she didn't think it was doing it on purpose. It seemed to be focused on something greater, something she couldn't comprehend ... she wanted to send her astral form gliding to the castle and yet she knew, at some level, that it would be the last thing she ever did. She'd be a moth, drifting to the flame.

"And the gatehouse is being held too strongly for us to break in," Earl Oxley snapped, angrily. "Can't your pet sorceress do *something*?"

"Right now, I don't want to risk any magic," Isabella said. She was too distracted to be angry at being called a *pet*. "There's something in the city interfering with me."

"Hah," Earl Oxley said. He sounded as if he were pleading. "Your Highness, how many of my men are you going to send to their deaths before you realise this is futile?"

Isabella blinked, rubbing her forehead as she stared at the gatehouse. She had no spyglass, but she didn't need one to see that the defenders were still holding the structure. She wondered, sourly, why the Golden City had *let* Reginald's ancestors turn Havelock into a hellishly effective fortress. Surely, they'd thought twice about it ... or maybe not. They'd always assumed they'd have magic, enough magic to take down an entire city if it defied the Grand Sorcerer. The walls could have been turned into paper, if the Grand Sorcerer wished it. They'd never imagined they could lose power, that most of the sorcerers would die ...

She sucked in her breath. She wasn't Reginald – or Lord Robin, may he rest in peace – but she'd seen enough campaigns to know the fighting wasn't going well. Reginald simply didn't have the men to take the gatehouse, not if he wanted to take the castle afterwards. The brooding structure was simply too large to fall quickly ... she glanced at Reginald, knowing all too well that the prince wouldn't want to concede defeat and pull back. His pride would be against it, but so too would common sense. If he lost a battle, his enemies – and his family's enemies – would start gathering like vultures.

Earl Oxley nudged her, not gently. "You tell him!"

Isabella felt a hot flash of anger. How *dare* he? How dare

he touch her? How dare he put her in a position where she had to either openly disagree with her fiancé or let him throw away hundreds of lives fighting an unwinnable battle. She wanted to kill him. Her blood boiled. It would be so easy to draw her sword and cut him down like the dog he was. Or simply hit him with a killing spell. He wouldn't be expecting it. Women on the Summer Isle weren't trained to fight. He wouldn't even realise she was *serious* when she drew her sword until she buried it in his gut.

She put rigid controls on her temper, even as her magic yearned for release. The presence was wearing away at her mental defences, pushing her to do something stupid ... she took a long breath, focusing as best she could. She was used to combat, magical and mundane, but this was different. She felt as if she'd been hexed. Her head was ringing ...

Reginald met her eyes, just for a second. They shared a moment of pure understanding.

"Gars, sound the trumpets," he ordered, curtly. "Recall the troops. Have the archers cover the retreat."

Gars looked relieved. "Yes, Your Highness."

Isabella glanced at Reginald as Gars and Earl Oxley hurried off. "I'm sorry."

"Not your fault," Reginald said. He sounded more annoyed with himself than anyone else. "But we lost this battle. It's going to cost us."

"I know." Isabella wished she could say something reassuring, but ... there was nothing she could say. One way or the other, the campaign had just hit a major snag. "Is there no way into the castle? No secret passages?"

Reginald smiled, as if she'd said something funny. "Yes, *inside* the walls. We'd have to take the city first."

"Of course." Isabella let out a sigh. "It couldn't be that easy, could it?"

"No," Reginald said.

Isabella said nothing as the men fell back, the archers covering their retreat with practised ease. There was no panic, no rout, but ... it was clear they'd lost the battle. A handful snatched up bodies, trying to ensure their dead comrades received a proper burial; the others, more practical if less sentimental, made sure they weren't burdened as they ran away. She silently counted the dead within eyeshot, then gave up in dismay. Hundreds of men had died, for nothing. It was going to do a *lot* of damage to morale.

She frowned. "What now?"

"I'll think of something," Reginald said. His voice was bitter, vindictive. She wanted to reach for him, decorum be damned. "If nothing else, we can starve them into submission."

But Isabella knew, as the last of the men hurried away from the unbroken walls, that they might just have lost the war.

Chapter Twenty-Eight

"Your Highness." Lord Oscar's representative was almost as obnoxious as his master, a remarkable feat Reginald would have believed impossible. "Princess Sofia, Regent of Andalusia, has offered my master Princess Ruby's hand in marriage. What will *you* offer him, if you want his support?"

Reginald felt a flash of pure hatred. Lord Oscar was lucky he hadn't come in person, although … Reginald supposed he was lucky too. Putting his hands around Oscar's neck and squeezing the life from him would have been very satisfactory, but it would only have sparked a civil war. There would be no way to avoid it. Oscar wasn't *that* important – and there were quite a few noblemen who'd want to see him taken down a peg or two – but the aristocracy could hardly allow the Crown Prince to start strangling them at will. Who knew who'd be the *next* nobleman to be brutally murdered by his future king?

He composed himself with an effort. The representative was only doing his job, representing his master's interests. No doubt he was expendable, if he went too far. Lord Oscar wouldn't hesitate to throw his subordinate to the wolves if he provoked a showdown with the king or his heir. Reginald wondered, idly, if he could get away with strangling the asshole, then decided it would be pointless. The poor man was only following orders.

"My sister's hand cannot be offered without my father's consent, as well as mine," he said. It wasn't easy to keep his voice calm. "And my father has not pronounced on the issue."

"His Regent has," the representative pointed out. "And she has already signed the papers."

Reginald felt his temper begin to fray. "So … why are you here?"

The representative looked surprised. "My master wishes to …"

"See who offers him the best terms?" Reginald finished. He allowed his anger to leak into his voice. "I am the legitimate heir to the throne. My sister, for all her talents, does not stand in the line of succession. I don't know if her claim to the regency is legal or not, but I do know it came to an end when I stepped back onto my native soil. She is no longer the Regent and cannot, legally, sign away my sister's hand in marriage."

His voice hardened. "I can, if I wish" he added. "But what could your master offer me to make it worthwhile?"

The representative looked stunned. "Your Highness, Lord Oscar will put his troops at your disposal ..."

Reginald snorted. "And how much are they worth?"

He smiled, humourlessly. Lord Oscar had raised a sizeable army, but it wasn't anything like as effective as he might have hoped. Its commanders were all from Lord Oscar's extended family, his soldiers were practically conscripts, with neither training nor experience. It wasn't clear if they'd fight outside their homelands, if they'd fight at all. Reginald wasn't one to shun numbers, but numbers weren't enough to win a war. Lord Oscar's troops wouldn't be decisive, not unless they'd improved markedly over the last few months. Reginald wouldn't have bet a single copper, let alone the kingdom, on it.

"Go tell your master to rethink his choices," he ordered. "And to send you back with a more reasonable demand for his ... services."

The representative reddened, but had the sense to rise, bow and leave the tent, rather than continue the argument. Reginald watched him go, feeling sick. Lord Oscar was old enough to be *his* grandfather. The idea of him sharing a bed with Ruby ... his stomach churned at the thought. Reginald wouldn't have wanted Lord Oscar as a brother-in-law even if his troops were actually useful. *And* it would trigger a civil war as Lord Oscar's rivals lined up against him ...

He rubbed his forehead in irritation. Two days. Two days of camping near the city, trying to keep it isolated from the rest of the kingdom ... knowing, all too well, that every day they held the lines ensured more and more noblemen rethinking their positions and considering a bid for independence. He'd already had a dozen messengers from the nobility, each one demanding vast concessions in exchange for doing as little as possible for the cause. He wasn't blind to the simple fact that the nobility would prefer the royal family to tear itself apart … or, in some ways, that the most *dangerous* noblemen hadn't bothered to send messengers. He knew that boded ill. He'd have to reunite the kingdom by force after liberating his father and chasing the entities out of the castle. It wasn't going to be easy.

The day wore on. Three more messengers arrived, bringing the same message from their masters. Reginald listened politely, even though he had no patience left. They might say something different, something useful. But there was nothing. He looked weak, so they were demanding concessions he'd find difficult – if not impossible – to walk back after winning the war. He had no doubt that they'd sent messengers to Sofia too. The older families hadn't lasted so long without learning how to hedge their bets. They wouldn't declare openly for one or the other until a clear victor emerged.

And then they'll have to be put back in their place, he mused, tiredly. The war had stalemated – and that worked in the enemy's favour. *We could lose this …*

He looked down at his hands. It went against the grain to admit defeat, but … no matter how he worked the problem, he couldn't see any way of getting into Havelock and storming the castle without bleeding his army white. And there was no way to strengthen his forces before it was too late. His recruiting sergeants had reported only a trickle of recruits from Humber and the smaller towns and cities he controlled, while there were no recruits at all from outside his territory. There was nothing to be gained, he thought, by conscripting troops. They wouldn't be worth the effort, if they didn't run for the hills the moment his back was turned. Conscripts were simply unreliable.

The tent flap opened. He looked up. Isabella stepped into the tent, her eyes wary. Reginald frowned, suddenly worried. He'd seen that look on men who were on the verge of storming castles, knowing they might be dead in the next couple of hours. Isabella … there was no reason for Isabella to be wary, not here. Reginald looked around, just to be sure. There was no threat in the tent, nothing that could hurt either of them. The shadows were just … shadows.

Isabella met his eyes. "Another set of messengers has arrived."

"Oh, joy," Reginald said. "And how much of my time are *they* going to waste?"

"They're from the city," Isabella said. "They claim to be councillors."

Reginald blinked. "City Fathers?"

"Apparently so." Isabella looked oddly amused. "They seem to think you'd know them."

"I had to recognise their independence from the crown last year," Reginald said. He stood, wondering just how and why the councillors had passed through Sofia's lines. Their independence wouldn't last if Sofia decided to take it away. "It was a deeply humiliating ritual."

He shrugged. "Let them in. If I recognise them … we can talk."

"As you command," Isabella said.

Reginald rested one hand on his sword as the councillors were shown into the tent. They looked … *human.* They didn't put his teeth on edge, like men who'd been overshadowed by the entities. They were all old enough to be his father, wearing clothes that pushed the limits as far as they would go without actually breaking any of the Sumptuary Laws. They would all be independently wealthy, he reminded himself grimly, if they'd won election to the city council. It was a shame, in some ways, that they couldn't be raised to the nobility. They were smarter and harder than most of the aristocrats who looked down on them.

"Your Highness," Councillor Phelps said. He bowed, formally, then straightened. His eyes lingered on Isabella, who was standing beside Reginald. "Thank you for receiving us."

"You're welcome," Reginald said. He studied the three men briefly. Phelps himself was a banker, if Reginald recalled correctly; his companions, Bunche and Harkness, were merchants and middlemen, buying low and selling dear. They'd all earned the ire of the nobility, if only because the aristocrats could never admit they'd been outwitted by commoners. "I'm surprised you were allowed to cross the lines."

"The Regent understands the value of our contributions to the kingdom," Phelps said. He seemed to be the spokesman. "She raised no objection to us upholding our traditional liberties."

"And yet, she's destroyed your temples and forced you to pray to her ... gods," Reginald said, stiffly. He doubted Sofia cared one whit about the city's ancient liberties. "You know as well as I do that it's only a matter of time before things get harder for you."

"Your Highness, we are practical men." Phelps smiled, as if he were inviting Reginald to share a joke. "We do not believe in the gods. Nor do we disbelieve. If the people wish to worship, so what? They will still require our services, when all is said and done."

"Perhaps," Reginald said. Beside him, he felt Isabella tense. "I think you're in for a surprise."

"Worse than a surprise," Harkness said. He had a gravelly voice that got on Reginald's nerves. "We do not want you to storm the city."

Reginald bit down the urge to point out that *he* didn't want to storm the city either – or starve it out, for that matter. He didn't blame the city fathers for being concerned about their fates, if the city fell to his troops, but ... there was little they could do about it. They could beg and plead all they liked, yet ... neither Sofia nor himself could give up and go away. The entities had to be removed before they turned the entire kingdom into a living nightmare. Reginald had no doubt that, sooner or later, they'd *make* the city fathers believe.

"I am aware of the dangers," he said. He was tempted to dwell, at length, on the treatment the city could expect if it tried to hold out once the walls were breached. "I am also aware that I don't have much choice. What do you suggest?"

Phelps leaned forward. "A discussion, Your Highness. A meeting, between your representatives and hers. She has already agreed to have a representative meet you on neutral ground, inside the city itself. We have agreed, in turn, to host the meeting."

Reginald barked a laugh. "You expect me to walk into an obvious trap?"

His mind raced. There were no grounds for a meeting of minds, none at all. This was no border dispute, no discussion between parties who could afford to compromise without weakening themselves fatally. Sofia couldn't give up her power and position without losing everything, assuming – of course – that the entities would *let* her. She'd live – Reginald had no intention of killing her, if it could be avoided – but she'd never see power again. She would spend the rest of her life in an isolated castle, a prisoner in all but name. And Reginald couldn't afford to surrender either. What was he supposed to do? Go back to the Summer Isle and watch, helplessly, as the mainland fell into anarchy?

"Her Highness has given her word." Phelps sounded vaguely offended. "And she is prepared to make whatever pledges you like to allow the meeting to go ahead."

"Really," Reginald said, drawing out the word. "In that case, I want my troops to take possession of the Western Gatehouse *first*, so they can intervene if something should happen to go wrong."

"That would be acceptable," Phelps said. "They would even be welcome to search the area beforehand."

Reginald blinked. He'd thought he was naming an unacceptable condition. And Phelps had orders to agree ... he forced himself to think, hard. Did the city fathers have more power than he'd realised? It *was* their city, something that might have given the entities pause. Or ... was it a trap? Did Sofia think she could trap and kill him? It was possible, but ... it was hard to see how she could pull it off. She'd have to get troops into position without being detected ahead of time.

He glanced at Isabella, who looked impassive. He knew her well enough to guess she was as suspicious as himself. Sofia was giving up a lot, just for talks. Hell, *Reginald* could stage an ambush himself. She had to realise that ... didn't she? And yet ... she didn't have any *real* experience in ruling. She might have a childish faith that everyone would keep their word, even when they had a strong incentive to break it. Reginald wasn't so naive. People would break sworn oaths in a heartbeat if they thought they'd get away with it.

And the entities might be messing with her mind, he reminded himself, numbly. *She might not even be able to think straight any longer.*

He frowned. "I will discuss the matter with my advisers," he said. "But we will want a number of concessions and securities before we consent to a meeting inside the city."

Isabella spoke, suddenly. "Why doesn't she come *here*?"

Phelps gaped at her. Reginald concealed his amusement with an effort. Isabella ... technically, Isabella shouldn't have spoken at all. She wasn't a powerful aristocrat or the city fathers would have recognised her at once. Hell, the city fathers might not even have realised she was *female*. She could pass for a slightly effeminate man as long as she kept her mouth shut. But they probably would have heard her speak outside ... Reginald felt a flicker of sardonic amusement. Phelps was probably shocked that Isabella had spoken out of turn. He'd be outraged that *he* wasn't allowed such freedom of speech.

"Good question," he said. "Why *doesn't* she come here?"

"She refuses to meet you as anything, but an equal," Phelps said. He looked down, as if he didn't want to meet Reginald's eyes. "She wants to meet you on neutral ground."

"I see," Reginald said. It was a good answer, he supposed. Part of the reason everyone sent representatives everywhere, rather than going themselves, was to avoid petty and pointless scrabbles over precedence. If he went to her ... it would be an admission of her supremacy. Or vice versa, if she came to him. "We'll discuss it, then give you a final decision."

He called an attendant and ordered him to escort the city fathers to a separate tent, then sat back in his chair and looked at Isabella. "What do you think?"

"It's a trap," Isabella said. Her voice was low, angry. "It couldn't be a more obvious trap if they wrote T-R-A-P on the doors."

"Perhaps," Reginald said. He could hardly disagree. *Something* was off about the whole deal. "It's hard to see how they intend to spring it, though. They seem to be going out of their way to make us comfortable."

Isabella gave him a sharp look. "And that should worry you. You know as well as I do that the rules are different, now."

"Yes," Reginald agreed. "But Sofia doesn't *own* the city. There are limits to what the entities can do, right?"

"So I've been told." Isabella didn't sound particularly confident. "But there are always loopholes."

"We'll have troops garrisoning the gatehouse and patrolling the streets," Reginald pointed out. "The meeting point will be searched from top to bottom before we even set foot in the building. How would *you* carry out an ambush under such conditions?"

"Transfigure a small army into something harmless, something that can be left in plain sight, then break the spell when the victim walks into the trap," Isabella said, bluntly. "It's been done before. Someone can do it again."

Reginald cocked an eyebrow. "Can the *entities*?"

"I don't know," Isabella admitted. She shook her head, slowly. "For all we know, they have a *real* sorcerer on their side too."

"There were never many living in Havelock, even *before* the Golden City fell," Reginald said. It was true. Havelock had never been a particularly magical town. "And you'd spot a transformed soldier, wouldn't you?"

"Perhaps." Isabella frowned. She didn't sound as though she believed herself. "My senses aren't reliable here. I could easily miss something."

Reginald looked down at his hands. Cold logic and common sense told him to ignore the request for a meeting. The situation was bad, but it wasn't desperate. And yet ... the chance to secure a gatehouse and a chunk of the city without a fight wasn't one he could afford to ignore. If Sofia had treachery in mind, he might be able to fight his way out of the trap and then take the entire city. There weren't any strong defences between the walls and the castle itself. He could smash any improvised barricades well before they could become a real threat.

Sure, his thoughts mocked him. *That could be just what they* want *you to think.*

"We'll take every precaution," he said. If nothing else, it would be interesting to see just how many concessions Sofia was prepared to make. "And if we detect even a hint of a trap, we'll ram the entire army through the gatehouse and into the city."

And burn the entire city to the ground, his thoughts added. *I can't let them get away with luring us into a trap.*

"I hope you're right," Isabella said. "And if you're wrong?"

"Time isn't on our side," Reginald pointed out. He took her hand and squeezed it lightly. "If we can't take the city quickly, we might lose everything."

"Yeah," Isabella said. She looked down at him, her dark eyes shadowed. "And if we lose our lives, we lose everything too."

Chapter Twenty-Nine

There were times, Isabella had been taught during her training, when one had to knowingly walk *into* a trap, deliberately springing it to ensure that one gathered the evidence one needed to put a dark wizard in jail. She had never found the argument particularly convincing. Dark wizards, all too aware that jail was the *least* they could expect, tended to make their traps as lethal as possible, hoping to make their escape while whoever sprang the trap tried to get *out* of it. She was quite willing to take one for the team, if necessary, but ... she would prefer for it *not* to be necessary.

She felt uncomfortably naked, despite being fully dressed, as she strode through the gatehouse and into the city. Her leathers itched. Her tunic felt odd, weighed down by a collection of weapons, tools and even a pair of wands. She'd crammed everything she could into her pockets, even risking a handful of charms to lighten the load. She was sure they were walking into a trap, yet ... she had no idea how the enemy intended to spring it. Reginald and his officers had worked hard, steadily closing off each and every avenue for treachery. Hell, they'd done their level best to ensure that *they* could indulge in treachery themselves. And the city fathers had just gone along with it. Isabella didn't like it. There *had* to be a nasty sting in the tail.

The bodyguards fanned out around them, cold iron in their hands. Isabella reached out with her senses, again, but felt nothing beyond the looming presence in the dark castle. She couldn't even sense background magic, the faint haze of power that had been a part of her life ever since she'd come into her magic. It was so slight that it was easy to miss, until it was gone. She wondered, as she glanced at Reginald's cold face, if the entities were draining the magic from the world. It was possible, she supposed. Her spells had never been remotely effective against them and their creatures. She wouldn't have believed it, if she hadn't seen it. Alden might not have believed it either ...

If he got my letter, Isabella thought. She had no way to *know*. The ship could have gone down in the channel, lost with all hands. Or the horseman might have been killed on his way to the Golden City. Or ... she shook her head. There was no point in brooding, particularly not now. She had to keep her senses alert. *The trap could be sprung at any moment.*

The sense of being naked grew stronger as they made their way down the street. She glanced from side to side, noting how the homes had been emptied and the shops had been shuttered well before Reginald's troops had secured the gatehouse. They'd spent the last hour searching the district, tearing houses, apartment blocks and shops apart for hidden traps and tricks. And yet, they'd found nothing. Isabella would almost have been happier if they'd uncovered thousands of troops hidden in the looming buildings. Instead, the only real problems had been caused by Reginald's troops stopping to loot.

She let out a long breath, wondering just what was going to happen. It defied belief that the meeting was anything more than a formality, if it wasn't a trap. Reginald himself had admitted as much, when they'd discussed the issue in council. Sofia could hardly surrender, not now. The entities wouldn't let her. And yet ... she wondered, sourly, if *they* had their own reasons for wanting to open talks. They might hope to convince *Reginald* to let them proselytise openly. *That* wasn't going to happen. If there was any ruler who understood the danger the entities represented, it was Reginald. *He* wouldn't let them into his kingdom.

Unless we really can come to terms with them, Isabella thought. *Perhaps ...*

She shook her head. She'd never been particularly religious. The Golden City had enforced religious tolerance, insisting that citizens had a right to worship who and what they liked, from a god of fire and thunder to a giant sheep. Who cared? But she knew, all too well, what happened when tolerance began to slip. A religion that produced *real* miracles might start trying to expand, perhaps even imposing itself on everyone else. The city fathers were playing with fire. They should have declared for Reginald while they had a chance.

Her eyes hardened as she looked at Phelps. The city father probably hadn't realised what was happening until it was too late, if he understood at all. He'd said it himself. He didn't care *what* people chose to believe, or to worship. But ... she felt a flicker of sympathy, mingled with grim understanding. Phelps was no nobleman, with rank and status and a private army. He was no sorcerer, with the power to destroy his enemies with a wave of his hand. He was a commoner, a man who couldn't stand up to the great and the good. He had to bend the knee to anyone with the power to destroy him ...

He owns a bank, Isabella reminded herself. *And that makes him the target of envy as well as hatred and spite.*

"Your Highness," Phelps said. He indicated a dark stone building. "The meeting will be held in there."

Reginald nodded and came to a halt, waiting for his bodyguards to search the building for the second time. Isabella glanced at him, then followed them into the building. The interior felt oddly cold, even though it was spring. It took her a moment to realise that it was designed to maintain a steady temperature, without magic. She glanced into the first set of rooms and frowned, trying to understand what they were for. They looked like a shop, but a very odd shop ... it took her a moment to realise that she was looking into a bank. There were banks in the Golden City – or there had been, five years ago – but her family had never waited in line to be served. The bank manager had normally welcomed them into his office the moment they stepped through the door.

She reached out with her senses as she entered the meeting room itself. It was surprisingly austere, the table made of bare stone rather than marble or elegantly-carved wood. The chairs were wooden, but – again – remarkably crude. She looked up, noting how the lanterns had been placed to illuminate the entire room. The light reflected off the walls, driving away the darkness. There were no shadows, not even under the table. Her skin crawled, even though she couldn't put her finger on why. There was something about the room that bothered her.

Shaking her head, she produced a flask of water from her belt and splashed cool liquid on her eyes. Mother Lembu had taught her the trick, explaining that it would illuminate any traces of ritual magic. Isabella's eyes itched uncomfortably as she swept the room, making sure to look everywhere. But there was nothing. The flickers of light she'd expected to see were missing. The room was creepy, but safe. She frowned, torn between the urge to suggest they went somewhere – anywhere – else and the sense she was imagining it. Perhaps she was just a little *too* paranoid.

There's no such thing, she told herself, severely. *We have to be careful.*

She felt her fears grow as she walked through the rest of the bank. It was utterly untouched by the entities. Someone had empted the vaults, leaving the heavy metal doors hanging open so she could peer inside. She smiled at the sight, wondering what had happened to the gold bars and expensive treasures the bank's customers had buried in the vaults. Banks rarely lasted long, these days. Too many kings and princes tried to seize their vaults to pay their debts.

The world seemed to grow brighter as she stepped back outside. She could *feel* the castle, even without looking at it directly. She rubbed her eyes, then nodded grimly to Reginald as she outlined what she'd seen. The sense of unease was still there, but she couldn't put her finger on it. And they had cold iron ... she told herself, firmly, that it would be enough. She hoped she was right.

"We'll wait for Sofia," Reginald said, once they were in the meeting room. "I'm sure she won't mind entering after us."

Phelps looked unconvinced, but hurried away anyway. Isabella watched him go, her gaze moving to the troops assembled by the walls. She'd seen the plans. Reginald had brought a small army to the meeting, while the rest of his troops were waiting just outside the city. It was hard to say how Sofia intended to spring the trap. Perhaps it really *was* what it said on the tin. Sofia might have more free will than Isabella had assumed.

Emetine had a certain degree of free will, she recalled. *She wasn't completely overshadowed by her master.*

She sucked in her breath as Sofia's representative stepped into the chamber. Emetine ... Isabella wondered, suddenly, if merely thinking of her name had been enough to summon her. It worked for the entities, sometimes. Emetine hadn't changed much, as far as Isabella could tell, but ... there was something about her that was utterly inhuman. There was something about her dress that suggested it was concealing more than her bare skin. She radiated a naked sexuality that both called to Isabella and repulsed her. And yet ...

"Your Highness." Emetine's voice was soft and sultry. "Thank you for answering our call."

Reginald cleared his throat. "You can turn it off," he said, harshly. "I haven't forgotten how you tried to kill me."

Isabella reached for his hand and held it as Emetine sank into a chair. If *she* found it hard to resist the allure, she hated to think how hard *Reginald* must find it. Behind them, even the professional bodyguards were staring. Reginald squeezed her hand, hard enough to hurt. She dug her nails into his flesh, hoping it would help. He shot her a thankful look, then kept his eyes firmly on the table. Isabella hoped it would be enough.

"I did what I had to do," Emetine said. "I did what you would have done, if you were in my place."

"A common excuse." Reginald's voice was still harsh. "Why are you here?"

"I'm here as both the representative of Sofia, the Lady Regent, and as the High Priestess of Ethane," Emetine said. She favoured them both with a sweet smile. "It was felt that it would be unwise for the Regent to attend in person."

"Really?" Reginald sounded amused. "Is Sofia pulling your strings or are you pulling hers?"

Emetine looked as if he'd kicked her puppy. "Do you really think so little of your sister?"

Reginald ignored the question. "Where is my father?"

"Ill," Emetine said. Her voice remained cold and calm. "He appointed his daughter as Regent before his condition worsened."

"Ah," Reginald said. The word hung on the air for a long chilling moment. "But now I'm back, so her regency is legally over. I'm in charge until my father recovers."

"Legally, that isn't actually true." Emetine smiled, coldly. "As Crown Prince, you will – of course – succeed your father when he dies. The king is dead, long live the king. But as long as your father lives, he can appoint whoever he likes to rule in his stead. Your father is still alive."

Isabella felt Reginald's grip tighten. "And will you prove that for me?"

Emetine looked displeased. "And will you risk declaring yourself the monarch without being *sure* your father is dead?"

Which would be treason, if he isn't dead, Isabella thought, coldly. She wondered, suddenly, if that *was* the point. If Reginald was branded a traitor, he'd be kicked out of the line of succession. And that would lead to … what? If nothing else, he wouldn't be able to bar the entities from his kingdom if he wasn't the legitimate monarch. *Is the whole point of this meeting to goad Reginald into doing something stupid?*

Reginald, perhaps, was having similar thoughts. He leaned forward, resting one hand on the stone table. "Enough games," he snarled. "What do you want?"

Emetine shrugged. "What makes you think we want anything?"

"Nothing may be known until it is spoken," Isabella said.

The High Priestess flinched. "I … I speak for the Regent, but I also speak for the gods. They wish to bargain for your captive. They want him back."

Reginald smiled, coldly. "Does *Sofia* know about this?"

"She is aware," Emetine said. "The gods wish you to know that they will punish you in ways beyond your imagination if you refuse to release your captive."

"We're not totally ignorant," Isabella said, tartly. "We know there are limits to their powers."

"And if the punishment is beyond our imagination," Reginald added with a wry smile, "how are we supposed to imagine it?"

Emetine glared. "Do you believe them *powerless*?"

"We know their power," Isabella said, quietly. "You know we do. We've faced their power on the Summer Isle. You were there."

She tried to sound confident. "But we also know its limits."

Isabella frowned, wishing she could trust her instincts. Emetine was hard to read. Her body didn't seem to be changing, yet … it was. She was wrapped in a sensuality that made it hard, almost impossible, to look at her without feeling a tingle between her legs. And yet … Isabella bit her lip, relying on the pain to keep her mind focused. She was bluffing, yet … did Emetine – or the power behind her – *know* she was bluffing? She had no way to be sure.

Emetine gave her a sharp look, then turned her attention back to Reginald. "If you return the captive, we will allow you to return to the Summer Isle without further ado."

"Unacceptable." Reginald kept his voice steady, somehow. "I want you and yours out of my kingdom."

"We made promises to your sister," Emetine said. "Those promises cannot be broken."

"They can," Reginald said. "Take your … people, all of them, and leave my kingdom."

Isabella frowned as they haggled back and forth. She didn't know if the entities *could* break their word, not once they'd given it. They weren't human. She wasn't sure *what* they were, but they did have limits. Their rules were part of them. They couldn't break them. They weren't *human*.

"Your terms are unacceptable," Emetine grated. Her face turned harsh and cold, yet – somehow – still sensual. "You are in no position to bargain."

"You wouldn't have invited us here unless you thought we *were* in a position to bargain," Reginald countered. He smiled an irritating smile, a smile that would have made Isabella want to hit him if it had been directed at her. "And you wouldn't have bent over backwards to accommodate us if you had a choice."

"You misunderstand." Emetine's voice was suddenly very earnest. "Our people are already across your kingdom. Your people already believe in us. Your little army is badly outnumbered. You are pinned against the city, while we can simply go around you. Humber will be in our hands once again, soon enough. And then you will be crushed if you refuse to submit. We can defeat you and *then* liberate your captive."

You never refer to the entity by name, Isabella mused. It made no sense to her. Surely, the entities knew their fellow's name. And they had to know she knew it too. There was nothing to be gained by keeping it out of the conversation. *Why not?*

Reginald stood. "You have our terms," he said, firmly. "Leave our kingdom and we will release our captive. You have my word, sworn upon my name, that I will treat my sister with respect and consideration ..."

Emetine's face twisted. "*Men!*"

Isabella braced herself. Something was happening ...

"You thought you were safe," Emetine hissed. The ground shook. Isabella jumped to her feet as she felt the stone start to give way underneath her. "But you didn't think. The city fathers surrendered the city to the Lady Regent. This is *her* territory. It has been all along. And you are in our power."

Reginald drew his sword. Isabella followed him. Emetine smirked, her body changing ... twisting into something utterly inhuman. Reginald lashed out at her, the cold iron glowing with an eerie blue light as the Godly Realm manifested around them, but it was too late. Emetine was gone. Isabella felt the floor collapse, pieces of stone falling into an ever-widening pit. The lanterns exploded, plunging the room into darkness. She could sense *things* moving within the shadows. She had the feeling that looking at them would break her mind.

Tricked, she thought, as she felt *something* strike her arm. The sword clattered away, landing ... *somewhere*. The dark was so complete that she couldn't see anything. Someone cried out – one of the bodyguards, she thought – but there was nothing she could do. Her magic refused to come at her call. *We were thinking too small ...*

She fell. The darkness reached up and caressed her. It felt like a violation, an unwelcome touch on so many levels ... it was invading her body, her mind, her very soul. She gritted her teeth, reminding herself that the entities had no power over her ... but was that true, in the Godly Realm? She'd protected them as best she could, yet ... she couldn't be sure. Her body twisted, her bones threatening to break as it bent in impossible directions. She could sense giant *thoughts* all around her, flickering images of an entity that existed outside the laws of reality itself. She felt utterly alone, utterly isolated ...

... And then she fell into darkness.

Chapter Thirty

Reginald fought his way back to wakefulness, slowly.

His head felt fuzzy, as if he couldn't think clearly. It felt as if he'd been knocked out by one of his tutors, when he was on the training field, or suffering the after-effects of an evening spent drinking, dancing and generally raising hell in the certain knowledge that he might not live to see another evening. He was used to waking up with a hangover, but this was different. It took him several minutes to remember just what had happened – and to realise that he was a prisoner. Emetine had tricked them and won handsomely.

Bitch, he thought, feeling a shiver running down his spine. He knew how dangerous Emetine could be and yet … he'd stayed in the room, even when it became clear he wouldn't be meeting his sister. *What did she do to me?*

A splash of ice-cold liquid struck his face. Reginald jerked, his eyes snapping open. A jailor was standing in front of him, holding an empty bucket in his hand. Water – he *hoped* it was water – dribbled down his face and trickled down his shirt. He cursed the man in four different languages as he struggled to move, finding it almost impossible. Chains had been wrapped around his hands and feet, so heavily wrapped that he couldn't hope to move. The strongest man he knew couldn't have hoped to move. He wondered, sourly, what his jailors feared. Did they think he could break the chains by force of will?

Probably, he reminded himself. The entities were ruled by symbolic magic, not *human* magic. *Maybe they think I can turn myself to mist and fly away.*

"Welcome back to the world, Little Prince," the jailor said. The mocking politeness in his voice *stung*. "I trust you'll enjoy your stay."

Reginald ignored him, silently taking the measure of his jail cell. It was a small room, illuminated by a single lantern hanging from the ceiling ... well out of reach, even if he'd been able to move freely. The door was wooden, rather than metal ... it took him a moment to realise that someone had torn out the iron door and replaced it with something more friendly to the entities. Oddly, the sight gave him hope, although he wasn't sure why. The entities had definitely made themselves at home. He could see signs of their influence everywhere, when he turned to look.

The jailor caught Reginald's chin and moved his head until Reginald was looking directly at him. "Cat got your tongue, Little Prince?"

Reginald met his eyes, evenly. "I intend to survive this, *little man*. I am your Crown Prince and I will be your King. And, on that day, you will be sentenced to spend the rest of your life in a cell just like this one."

The jailor flinched. Reginald felt a flicker of cold amusement, even though he knew he was merely provoking the man to do something dangerous and stupid. Reginald couldn't carry out his threats if he suffered a little accident while he was in the cell. But the jailor was responsible for his captive's health. He'd be brutally executed if anything happened to Reginald, even if – perhaps especially – Sofia ordered it. She'd want to make sure that no living witnesses survived, just in case a future challenger accused her of murdering the rightful heir ...

Reginald made a dismissive sound. "You can go now."

The jailor scurried away, his tail between his legs. Reginald watched, trying not to laugh as the man practically ran through the wooden door and banged it shut. He listened carefully, silently counting the number of bolts the man drove home ... seven, at least. The door was ridiculously secure. He rolled his eyes, then remembered the entities. They might have good reason to order their servants to literally cover the wooden door in bolts. He'd be surprised if they hadn't sealed the entire dungeon block too.

He sat back, testing the chains even though he knew it was futile. He'd had some experience wriggling out of chains and ropes, but they'd all tended to depend on the enemy making a mistake or two. Here ... he didn't even have a lockpick within reach. Someone had searched him thoroughly once he'd blacked out, removing his armoured undershirt, his sword and his collection of hidden weapons and tools. And he could barely move his hands ... despair rippled at the back of his mind, mocking him. He couldn't even kill himself. They'd practically turned him into an eunuch.

At least they didn't overshadow me, he thought, as he forced himself to relax.

Are you sure? He scowled as the thought struck him. *How would you know?*

He gritted his teeth as he heard a rat scratching its way through the cell. Rats and insects and ... he cursed as he realised he was probably going to be sitting in his own filth, sooner or later. There was a chamberpot in the corner, but he couldn't move. He directed his attention towards the links and frowned, realising that someone had literally ruined the locks after chaining him in place. There was no hope of unpicking himself. They'd thought of everything.

The rat jumped over his legs and vanished into the shadows. It showed no fear of humanity, no awareness that Reginald could end its life at any moment. He wasn't really surprised. The prisoners were almost always chained up, if they were placed in the lowermost cells in the dungeon block. They couldn't kill the rats ... maybe they even made *friends* with the rats. They'd been prisoners who'd been put in the cells and left to die ... Reginald wondered, suddenly, if *he* was intended to starve to death. Sofia wouldn't have killed him directly, but she'd have made damn sure he'd be dead.

He concentrated, silently counting the seconds in his head. He'd always been an active person. He'd never liked sitting still and listening to the academics boring him to death ... being forced to sit in chains and wait was torture, real torture. And yet, what else could he do? He tried to imagine Gars leading a second assault on the city, breaking through the lines to get to him ... he shuddered. The army's leader was a prisoner. There was no one else who could hold the army together, not even ...

Isabella, he thought. *Where is she?*

He looked around again, although he knew it was useless. The cell was empty, save for himself. He knew he should be grateful she hadn't been crammed into the cell with him, but ... he wondered, feeling true fear for the first time since he'd regained awareness, just what had happened to her. If they knew she was a sorceress, and someone who knew the entities better than almost anyone else, they'd kill her. Or do worse to her. Reginald knew it wasn't uncommon for female prisoners to be raped, or sold to pimps and slave dealers … the thought was sickening. And yet, he knew he'd played a role in encouraging it. He promised himself that it would stop, when he became king. The civilised world didn't need slaves …

The door rattled. Reginald looked up, wondering who was on the far side. The jailor, having regained his nerve? Or, perhaps, having made the decision to ensure his unwilling guest suffered a little accident? Or someone else? His father had kept a stable of torturers, men gifted in the art of extracting confessions through pain. That was something else that would have to change, Reginald promised himself as the door opened. The king shouldn't have to resort to torture to keep his kingdom in line.

Sofia stood outside the door, looking at him. Reginald stared, wondering when the girl he'd left behind only a few short months ago had grown into a cold-faced woman. Sofia had always been beautiful – kings and princes from across the entire continent had vied for her hand – but now she looked to be carved from ice, her face a picture of eerie inhuman beauty. Reginald had been raised to protect his sisters, but … the woman in front of him didn't need protecting. She wore a long white dress, like a virgin walking to her wedding, yet there was nothing *vulnerable* about her. Reginald felt his heart sink. Sofia had given herself to the entities. She'd practically been overshadowed.

"Reginald," Sofia said. Her voice was cool. "Welcome to *my* castle."

Reginald felt his heart sink. His sisters had always called him *Reggie*. Not *Reginald*. But the woman in front of him was a stranger. He wanted to turn back time, to tell his younger self not to leave the country, yet … it was impossible. He'd invaded and occupied the Summer Isle, only to see his homeland taken from him and …

He forced himself to meet Sofia's blue eyes. They'd always been cool and striking, to the point where hundreds of poets had written praise-poems to them, but now they were cold and heartless. She'd given up more than just her worship, he realised numbly. She'd given her very *soul* to the entities. He tried to think of something – anything – to say, but drew a blank. The girl he'd known was long gone. A stranger stood in her place.

"Sofia," he managed. "Where's Father?"

"In bed, dangerously ill." Sofia's voice was … *strong*. It was hard to doubt anything she said. "I am his appointed Regent."

"And now I'm back," Reginald said, with scant hope she'd listen. "I am the legal successor …"

"If Father dies," Sofia agreed. "But, for the moment, *I* am the legal Regent."

"Emetine made the same argument," Reginald said, dryly. He doubted it would stand up in a court of law – there were hundreds of precedents that told against it – but the entities wouldn't care. "Did she come up with it herself or did you help her?"

"I studied the legalities carefully, when you sailed away," Sofia said. "The argument will stand in the only court that matters."

"Probably." Reginald changed the subject. "Is Father alive?"

Sofia's cold eyes flashed murder. "Father is alive, yes. I told you he was alive."

Reginald cocked his head. "Can I see him?"

"No." Sofia shook her head. "You will stand trial for making war against your father and usurping his authority. You brought fire and sword into the kingdom and for that you will pay."

"You'd better make damn sure father doesn't die, if you manage to take my head." Reginald knew he shouldn't taunt her, but he didn't care. "Your authority will die with him."

"By then, things will be different," Sofia said. "It will be a whole new world."

"I fear you will be right," Reginald said. He took a breath. "Sofia … what happened to you?"

Sofia met his eyes, evenly. "You never thought of me as a *person*, did you?"

Reginald blinked. "You're my *sister*!"

"Yes, but I was also a *princess*." Sofia clenched her fists. There were faint scars on her pale skin. "Father planned to sell me to whoever paid the most, even before the Golden City died and the world went mad. You got to go out and fight. I had to stay behind and look beautiful, pretending to allow hundreds of men to court me while Father haggled over the price. And … whatever I did, it would never be enough. You would have married me off yourself, if you'd been king. You'd have told yourself that it would be for the good of the kingdom. I'm just a tool to you."

"I wouldn't have married you off without your consent," Reginald said, although he wasn't sure it was true. What did the happiness of a princess – or a prince – matter, when the whole kingdom was at stake? He'd been raised to know *he* might be pushed into an unwelcome marriage too. Sofia … might have been told to do her duty or else. "Sofia …"

"I turned to the gods because they were the only ones who might listen to me," Sofia said, her voice rising. "And they answered! They came to me! They promised me everything I ever wanted, if I served them. And they kept their word. The kingdom is mine!"

"The northern barons are revolting, in all senses of the word," Reginald snapped. "It won't be long before the other noble bastards revolt too."

"They'll lose," Sofia said. "*My* armies will be fired with faith, faith driven by miracles that have powered a religious awakening across the entire continent. Have you not heard the rumours? The noblemen in their castles haven't listened to stories from people who grub in the dirt, but … oh, the commoners are listening. Word is spreading from village to town, from town to city … the people know. The world is going to be theirs, soon enough. And those who stand in the way will be crushed like bugs."

Her voice rose. "Those castles they think are so strong? They'll come tumbling down. The petty sorcerers they hire? Their powers will fail them and they will be plunged into utter darkness. The men who wanted me, who treated me as an object, will be turned to slaves; the women who laughed and mocked to hide their fears will be turned to stone. They will all fall before me. And then my troops will march out, bringing fire and sword to everyone who dares stand in my way. The entire continent will be mine!"

"Theirs," Reginald corrected. "You'll be serving them …"

"But that's the point!" Sofia's eyes shone with an unholy light. "They are the *gods*. We exist to serve and worship them. And they reward us for our service."

"They'll use you and then they'll throw you aside," Reginald said. "They discarded Emetine ..."

"They sent her to me," Sofia corrected. "*She* was the one who showed me how to call on the gods, so they would answer. She is the one who ..."

"She killed her husband," Reginald said. "She's a monster."

Sofia slapped him, hard. "Do you think *I* would *not* have killed my husband, if I found life with him unbearable?"

Reginald stared up at her. "Sofia ..."

"You never think, do you?" Sofia stepped back, her hands clenching and unclenching. "You have the freedom to do whatever you like, whenever you like. You lead troops in battle in the morning, then drink yourself senseless at night. You dance chastely with the ladies of the court in the evening, before taking a whore to your bed ..."

"Sofia," Reginald began. "I ..."

Sofia cut him off. "Me? I was trapped, right from the very start. Wear these pretty dresses – gods help me if I dirty or tear the cloth! Be watched at all times by wretched governesses. Master all the arts of being a pretty, mindless princess, get put on the marriage market as soon as I have my first blood ... *know* that, sooner or later, my luck will run out and I'll be married off to some ageing wreck who'll keep me prisoner in his tower and ...

"You have more freedom than Father ever allowed me. Or Ruby. Or Silverdale ... do you know it broke my heart when I realised that they'd have the same experience as me, only worse? They're not *firstborn* daughters, are they? You were going to be king! We would never be so lucky."

"I'm sorry," Reginald said. "But ..."

"It's too late for *sorry*," Sofia said. "Tell me ... why *should* I treat you any better than you treated me?"

"I didn't think," Reginald said. "And ..."

"That's your problem," Sofia told him. "You don't think. You never *had* to think. It never occurred to *you* to convince the city fathers to give you the keys to the city, did it?"

"It never crossed my mind," Reginald admitted. In

hindsight, like all great ideas, it was blindingly obvious. It made perfect sense, yet – by all previous standards – it was unthinkable. And it meant the city could never be taken. It would always be Sofia's unless she handed over the keys to the city. "You thought of it?"

"You always underestimated me," Sofia said. The bitterness in her voice was almost palpable. "And now it's cost you everything."

"It doesn't have to be this way," Reginald said. "Sofia ..."

Sofia laughed. There was no humour in the sound.

"Tell me ... what are you going to offer? A nice little prison cell in a nice big castle? Or a place I can live the rest of my life, powerless and alone? Or ... are you simply going to beat me until I fall back into submission? You can't offer me anything I'd want – and even if you did, I wouldn't trust you to keep your word."

"My word is good," Reginald insisted. "I ..."

"Maybe you'd mean to keep it. Now." Sofia didn't sound convinced. "But, sooner or later, you'd find a way to break your word. You'd tell yourself that you had no choice. Someone would demand my hand in marriage or ... or something. You'd regret it. I'm sure you'd regret it. But you'd do it. Now, I have power. *Real* power. Why would I give that up?"

"Because the creatures you serve will destroy the world," Reginald said. "If you give them the chance ..."

"The *gods* are the ones who gave me what I want," Sofia said. "Why would I turn on them? And what could you possibly offer me to make me *want* to abandon them?"

"The kingdom would be saved," Reginald said. "Doesn't that mean anything to you?"

Sofia snorted. "Tell me, what has the kingdom done for me?"

"It made you a princess," Reginald said. "If you'd been born a commoner ..."

"Perhaps I wouldn't have been constantly threatened with marriage," Sofia finished. "The kingdom did nothing for me, but I will do everything for it!"

She turned and headed to the door. "Wait," Reginald called. "Where are my sisters?"

"They're growing into a whole new world," Sofia said.

She stepped through the door. "I'm afraid you and your whore won't live to see it."

And she slammed the door closed.

Chapter Thirty-One

"Well," a cold voice said. "Let's have a look at you."

Isabella reluctantly opened her eyes. She was sitting in a prison cell, her arms chained behind her back and her legs shackled to a wooden board. Someone had searched her thoroughly, removing all of her weapons, her tools and her wands. The cold iron she'd relied on to defend them had failed, she realised numbly. They'd fallen through the Godly Realm and landed ... where?

A man knelt in front of her, leering like a pig. His companion stood behind him, his arms folded over his chest. Isabella tried not to shudder as she reached for her magic, but felt nothing. Her magic refused to come at her call. She reached out with her senses, only to feel a suffocating presence all around her. The entity wasn't with her, as far as she could tell, but it was blocking her magic anyway. She could practically *feel* it hovering behind her. It had her trapped.

"Pretty little thing," the standing guard said. He smirked at her. "Are you going to be nice to us?"

Isabella ignored him. She'd been warned, back when she'd started training, that she could expect to suffer horribly if she were taken captive. They'd put her through all kinds of drills, although none of them came close to *really* being taken captive. She tested her bonds as quietly as she could, hoping to find a weakness. But even if she did ... she felt weak and frail, too weak to muster the energy to raise an arm. She doubted she could fight both guards and win.

Bide your time, she told herself. *There will be a chance to escape.*

The kneeling guard leaned forward. "Give us a kiss."

He pressed his lips against hers. Isabella started to recoil, then felt a hot flash of anger that overrode common sense. She opened her mouth, just wide enough for him to insert his tongue, and then bit him as hard as she could. He jumped backwards, blood dripping from his mouth. Isabella spat out his blood, watching calmly as he raised his mailed fist to hit her. Perhaps he'd beat her to death, angering his masters ...

"Leave her," the second guard said, sharply. "She'll be more cooperative soon."

Isabella forced herself to show her teeth. "You want to put your manhood in here?"

The first guard started forward, his face darkening with rage. The second grabbed his arm and pulled him to the door. They fell through, slamming it behind them. Isabella laughed at their retreating backs, then sobered. She was in deep trouble. The guards might not kill her, but – unless she missed her guess – they could do whatever else they liked to her. She was no noblewoman, not yet. And ... degrading her might mean something to the entities. They might want her hurting so badly that she'd *welcome* them into her soul.

Damn it, she thought, once she'd glanced around the cell. *How do I get out of* this *one?*

She gritted her teeth. Her chains were unbreakable. She couldn't hope to pick the locks. She wondered, briefly, about snapping her own wrists to free her arms, but that would just render her completely helpless when the guards came back. Ice washed down her spine as she realised she was going to be helpless anyway. They'd weigh her down with chains or simply beat her into a pulp before having their fun. Hell, they could simply knock out her teeth. She'd seen that, back when she'd been a mercenary ...

The entity pulsed behind her, around her. She opened her mind gingerly, feeling the world start to teeter on its axis as she touched the Godly Realm. Reality itself suddenly seemed fragile, as if she was starting to untether herself from her body. The entity grew stronger, yet ... she had the strangest feeling it was sleeping. She'd assumed it was a guard dog, watching to make sure she didn't escape, but ... it wasn't. It wasn't doing anything deliberate to her, as far as she could tell. It was its mere presence that was blocking her magic.

She forced herself to think. Reginald was gone ... where was he? She didn't know, but she doubted he'd remain alive for long ... he might already be dead. Alive and free, he was a rallying point for the kingdom and its nobility. Sofia wouldn't let him live for long ... she couldn't. Reginald couldn't be crowned king without shattering his sister's claim to power.

I need help, Isabella thought, grimly. She had no friends in the castle, no one who'd come to rescue her. The army might have scattered already ... it dawned on her that she had no idea just how long she'd spent in the darkness. Captain-General Gars might not be able to keep the army together if Reginald was dead. *And there's only one person who might be able to help me.*

She touched the Godly Realm again, then closed her eyes and focused her mind. A single name danced through her mind, drawing her attention and shaping it into a call. She squeezed her eyes tighter, trying to convince herself that it would work. It *had* to work. It *really* had to work. She'd been warned that *believing* it would work *made* it work. She braced herself, then opened her eyes. Mother Lembu – the Mother – was standing in front of her.

"My," she said. She looked frailer, somehow. This wasn't *her* land. "You *have* gotten yourself into a mess."

"Yes," Isabella said. She rattled her chains, mournfully. "Thank you for coming."

"You called me," Mother Lembu said. She paced the cell, lips thinning in disapproval. "I had to come, even here."

"I thank you, anyway," Isabella said.

"Not a good place to be," Mother Lembu commented. She paused, studying Isabella so intently that Isabella found herself blushing. "And quite a tricky place, symbolically speaking."

Isabella rattled her chains. "I know."

"They tied you up well," Mother Lembu agreed. "And here ... this isn't my place, you know."

"But you came, when I called," Isabella said. "Can you ... *will* you ... help me?"

"I can," Mother Lembu said. "But this time there *will* be a price."

Isabella felt her heart sink. Yes, there would be a price. Of *course* there would be a price. But this time, she might have to pay it. She couldn't stay imprisoned for long. Sofia had absolutely no reason to keep her alive and *plenty* of reasons to want her dead.

"I know," she said, numbly. "Name your price."

Mother Lembu's shadowed eyes seemed to grow brighter. "I want you."

Isabella blinked. "What?"

"I want you to give yourself to me," Mother Lembu said. "To worship me, as your ancestors did in days of old. To serve me, as I see fit. To obey me, to follow my laws and my commandants and submit utterly to me. I want you to be *mine*."

"I ..." Isabella swallowed, hard. "You want my *worship*?"

"I want your *submission*," Mother Lembu said. Her face was suddenly utterly inhuman, mercifully cloaked in shadow. "You are to be mine. You will serve me, completely. You will spread my word to everyone ..."

Isabella stared at her, shocked to the core. She'd never submitted herself to anyone. Not her father, not her tutors and trainers, not her commanding officers ... not even *Reginald*. She'd always maintained a hard core of independence, of free thinking, even when it had cost her beatings and punishments and – sometimes – being told to find herself somewhere else to go. She wouldn't – she couldn't – give that up, not even for Reginald. It was so much a part of her that she would almost sooner die.

And yet, she could feel a strange *yearning* to open her heart and let the entity into her soul. It was odd and creepy – and growing steadily creepier, every time she let herself dwell on it – but it was there, calling her onwards. It felt like some of her more unsuitable boyfriends, the ones she'd dated to spite her father, yet ... worse. She knew, deep inside, that she would never be able to change her mind. There was no way she could escape, once she'd been overshadowed. She'd be little more than a puppet, dancing on her strings,

She looked up. Mother Lembu was no longer maintaining even the *pretence* of being human. Her form drifted on the air, power pulsing against Isabella's soul like a giant heartbeat. Isabella sensed, for the first time, threads of light linking the entity to ... her awareness followed the threads, catching glimpses of women, other women, who'd pledged themselves to Mother Lembu. She felt a hot flash of jealousy, mingled with a grim awareness that Mother Lembu had never suggested otherwise. She'd had other students, well before Isabella had ever known she existed. And some of those students had pledged themselves to her.

Like Emetine, Isabella thought. *And how many others ...?*

She allowed her gaze to linger on the threads ... and saw, suddenly, what they truly *were*. Mother Lembu drew her power from her worshippers, taking what they gave her and using it to power herself. She had vast power, yet ... it was bound by rules and laws laid down by the Godly Realm itself. Isabella couldn't tell if the entities themselves had set the rules or if they were simply laws of nature ... it was possible, she realised dimly, that both were true. They embodied the true nature of the entities themselves. They weren't gods. They were parasites.

"Parasites," she said, out loud.

Mother Lembu's presence seemed to grow stronger. "I beg your pardon?"

"Parasites," Isabella hissed. "That's what you are. That's *all* you are."

"You dare?" Mother Lembu reared up. The shadows darkened as her anger washed through the Godly Realm. "Bow your head! Demand forgiveness! Forsake all ..."

"Or what?" Isabella remained calm, despite the terrifying waves of anger. They washed around her, never touching her. "What can you do to me?"

A series of impressions assailed her. Men turned to mindless deer, goats, pigs ... women turned to drooling morons or slaves or worse. Dead bodies returning to life, animals twisted into monsters and sent out to wreak havoc. Fire and lightning and storms tearing apart entire villages and towns and cities ... ships sinking in the sea, armies being crushed by avalanches in the mountains ... magic and miracles, on a scale beyond belief. She wanted to cower, but she held her head up high. She knew the rules, now. She knew Mother Lembu couldn't hurt her, not directly.

"You can't do any of that, not to me," she said. "I choose *not* to submit to you."

Mother Lembu seemed to calm herself. "You think you can call me without paying a price?"

"I think you came willingly, when I called," Isabella said. She understood, now. Mother Lembu had *known* there would come a time when Isabella, at her lowest ebb, would contemplate complete surrender. "I offered you nothing."

"And next time, you will offer me something of great price," Mother Lembu said. Her voice was almost a hiss. "And be warned. What you do next may cost you more than you can pay."

The lantern shattered. Pieces of glass rained down from above. Isabella closed her eyes, feeling Mother Lembu's presence recede. When she opened her eyes, the entity was gone. The cell was completely dark. There wasn't even a hint of light from under the door. She wondered, morbidly, if she was supposed to stay in the cell until she starved to death. That would explain how willing the guards had been to molest her, she supposed. Dead women told no tales.

Except they might now, she thought, as she mustered all the concentration she could. The darkness, ironically, made it easier. *The entities can bring the dead back to life.*

She braced herself, then carefully reached out to the Godly Realm. This time, there was no sense of reality breaking down. Instead, she drifted out into the maelstrom. The sleeping entity was still sleeping, its snores pulsing through the realm ... she wondered, as she reached further into the alien universe, if it really *was* snoring or if her mind was simply trying to interpret what it was sensing in a manner she could understand. She honestly had no idea. A wave of images and thoughts struck her as she pressed further, glinting flickers of emotions and threads leading back out of the Godly Realm. One of them was linked to Sofia, she guessed. The others ... Emetine? Or had Sofia created a whole coven within the castle?

She can't surrender, not now, Isabella realised, numbly. She'd let the entities into her soul, submitting herself to them. There was no way for Reginald to save her, as far as Isabella knew. Sofia would have to want to free herself ... and then be willing to pay the price. Isabella refused to consider that there might be *no* way for someone to free themselves. Even the strongest of compulsion spells could be broken, if one had the will. *But does Sofia even want to be free.*

Isabella put the thought aside and looked down at herself. Her body looked oddly translucent when she peered from the Godly Realm. A handful of threads reached out in all directions … she felt a flicker of panic before realising they linked her to other humans, not to the entities themselves. One of them – she knew which one, although she wasn't sure *how* she knew – linked to Reginald. She followed it, finding herself floating in his cell. He was practically *covered* in chains, as if they expected him to start snapping wrought metal with his bare hands. Her lips twitched. Reginald was strong, one of the strongest men she'd met, but he wasn't *that* strong. No one was.

And they didn't think to chain him with cold iron, she mused. *They're going to regret it.*

She allowed her mind to reach out, slowly imposing her will on the Godly Realm. It responded to her touch, drawing her onwards. It *wanted* to be used, yet … it was snapping away at her thoughts, threatening to pull them apart. It was almost like being drunk, something she'd learnt to avoid when she was a great deal younger. She forced herself to remain calm, to stay focused. The Godly Realm was both connected and *not* connected to the human world. The slightest mistake could dump them both hundreds of years into the future – or the past. She recalled all the stories about people spending a day in the forbidden zones and coming out to discover that years had passed. The thought nearly spoilt her concentration. She knew, now, what had happened to them. They'd had no way of knowing that they'd stumbled into an alien universe, let alone that they had to make sure they didn't lose contact with their world. And it had spat them out too late.

"Reginald," she said. She wasn't sure if she was actually *speaking*, but it hardly mattered. "I'm coming."

She wrapped her arms around him and *pulled*. The Godly Realm twisted, the entities suddenly reaching out for them as they fell out of their chains, their bodies falling through the alien universe. She kept a tight grip on both of them, all too aware that if she let go too early they might lose themselves … or leave their bodies behind. Even the mere *thought* was poisonous. She heard voices whispering promises of everything she might want, from ultimate power to eternal life, if only she gave herself to them. She saw … she thought she saw homes and palaces and temples, the realms of the individual entities … glimpses of heavens so paradisiacal that her heart yearned to run to them and hells so vile that she would do anything, anything at all, to escape them. She felt Reginald's very soul pressing against hers, an intimacy that stunned her even as it nearly distracted her, a moment before the real world snapped back into focus. The light was suddenly so bright she could barely see. She heard someone cry out …

"Your Highness!"

Isabella rubbed her eyes, frantically. They were kneeling on the floor. If she'd made the slightest mistake, if she'd dumped them into the wrong place or time or …

"Gars," Reginald said. He helped Isabella to her feet. "Report."

"We still hold the gatehouse," Gars said. "I … Your Highness, I thought they'd killed you!"

"Lies, as you can see." Reginald grinned at Isabella. "I'd better see to the troops, and then …"

"You can't hit the city, not now," Isabella said. Her eyes were still sore. Strange colours drifted across her vision. She kept rubbing them, trying to produce tears. "They *own* it."

"We kept half the City Fathers hostage," Reginald reminded her. His voice was calm, but she could tell he was shaken. She wondered what had happened to him while she was being threatened with a fate worse than death. "They can give *me* the keys to the city too."

Isabella frowned. She wasn't sure that would work. She'd owned a key to her family mansion, but she hadn't owned the mansion itself. But symbolically … it *might* work, particularly if the City Fathers realised they'd been thrown to the wolves. Hostages could be legally executed. Sofia had probably counted on the merchants becoming martyrs after she captured and killed her brother. City-folk wouldn't fight for the crown, not with any great enthusiasm, but they'd definitely fight for their ancient liberties.

"We'll see," she said. It was worth trying, at least. Perhaps – symbolically – only one person could hold the keys to the city at any time. "And afterwards, we have to talk."

"Yes." Reginald sounded pained, as if she'd said something wrong. "We do."

Chapter Thirty-Two

Something had happened.

Silverdale sat in her room, feeling cold and antsy. *Something* had happened, after the attack on the city had been beaten off, but what? She'd been locked in her rooms, with a new pair of guards – creepy red-robed guards – manning the doors. Greta had slipped in to deliver her food, as always, but she hadn't been allowed to stay for any longer than it took to put the tray on the table and walk away. The guards had ignored Silverdale's requests, then her orders and finally her threats. One of them had practically *dragged* Greta out of the room when it looked as if she'd try to stay.

She felt uneasy, even though she wasn't sure why. Something was *looming*, as if something *bad* was going to happen. She paced her room, trying to think of a way out that didn't involve walking past the inhuman guards. But there was nothing. The bars on her window were solid. She could peer out and see the army, camped beyond the walls, but there was no way she could force her way out. And even if she did, what then? She'd heard stories of princesses who'd turned their bedclothes into makeshift ropes and descended to the ground – and weirder stories of princesses who'd used their *hair* to escape – but none of the stories seemed particularly realistic to her. The blankets and duvets didn't seem strong enough to carry her weight, no matter how tightly she tied them together. She'd plunge to her death if she tried.

The door remained resolutely solid, no matter how much she glared at it. She could almost *see* the guards on the far side, like a mouse might sense a silent cat lurking outside the mouse hole. Whatever the guards were, they weren't human. Or normal. A *human* guard wouldn't push her around, no matter who gave him his orders. Silverdale *was* a princess, after all. A guard who pushed her around might find himself in jail – or worse – if she complained. But she would almost have preferred one of her father's nastier guards. They, at least, were *human*.

She sat back on the bed, feeling a wash of … *something* moving through the air. A cold breeze seemed to drift across the back of her neck. She spun around, expecting to see someone – or something – standing behind her, but the room was empty. Her hair tried to stand on end as she looked around, feeling the world starting to go off-kilter. The walls started to look translucent, as if they weren't there. She shivered, helplessly, as she sensed *things* lurking at the corner of her eye. She hadn't taken the potion – there was only a single dose left – but it didn't seem to matter. She was drifting out of her body …

Something caught her and *pulled*. She found herself being dragged through fading walls, falling downwards … down and down until she reached parts of the castle she'd been told never to go. Her governess had made it clear, time and time again, that she was not to go *anywhere* near the lowest levels. Her father had driven the lesson home, when she'd gone to him for justice. But now … she found herself floating in front of the walls, the call pulling her onwards. The walls and floors seemed solid, until they weren't. She plunged down and into a prison cell. A young man was sitting on the stone floor, in chains. It took her longer than it should have done to recognise her brother.

"Reggie," she said.

He didn't show any reaction. Silverdale shouted again and again, but she was a ghost. *Less* than a ghost, really. She couldn't touch the mortal plane. Her brother stayed still, utterly unmoving. She would have thought he was dead if she hadn't been able to sense the life pulsing through his body. She could practically see his heartbeat, pounding like the beat of a drum. She wanted to run to him, but … how could she get out of her room? She was a prisoner, trapped behind a locked door. They didn't have to weigh her down with chains to keep her in her room.

The world spun around them. The force of the impact knocked Silverdale back, a tidal wave of power slamming into her chest and sending her spinning through the ghostly world. It felt as if she'd been hit, but as if she was *imagining* being hit. She managed to steady herself, somehow. The pain was a dull ghostly sensation that punched through her body, but refused to linger. She turned and saw a whirlpool of light surrounding her brother. It was bright, so bright that she knew she should look away ... but she didn't. She couldn't really be hurt, could she? She wasn't *really* here.

A woman stood in the light. No, she *was* the light. Power roared around her, pulling at Reginald and yanking him out of his chains. Metal clattered to the ground as his body went translucent, then vanished altogether. The woman vanished in the same moment, the bright light flickering and dying a second later. Silverdale saw shadowy *things* running towards her, huge spiders that drank the last flickers of light before they were gone. She sensed, more than saw, eyes turning towards her. They could *see* her. Unpleasant sensations crawled over her scalp, as if the spiders were inside her skull. They were coming for her.

She fled, falling back towards her body. The spiders didn't give chase. She breathed a sigh of relief, unsure what they were or what they could do to her. Her governess had assured her that giant spiders didn't exist, outside high-magic regions, but ... in the ghostly realm, they seemed to be larger than her, larger than life itself. She caught herself, hovering in the corridors and watching as a bunch of guards ran past her ... no, *through* her. A couple seemed to shiver, as if they'd sensed her on some level. But they paid no heed as they clattered down to the dungeons below.

Reginald escaped, Silverdale thought. She gave a little crow of triumph, even though she had no idea who might be listening. Her brother had been captured and he'd escaped! Sofia was *not* going to be pleased. *She captured him and he escaped.*

She found herself drifting upwards, up to Sofia's private chambers. She'd never been allowed inside her sister's rooms before, not since Sofia had grown too old and too grand to play with her little sister. Silverdale had thought it was terribly unfair – Sofia had entered *Silverdale's* rooms whenever she felt like it – but, at the same time, Silverdale was sure Sofia's chambers were boring. The older girl hadn't had any *time* to play. She'd been too occupied with learning to be a good little wife and helpmeet to whoever she married.

Silverdale almost felt sorry for him. She didn't know anyone who *deserved* to marry her priggish older sister.

The walls seemed oddly firm, as if they were protruding into the ghostly realm. They felt ... solid and yet *not* solid, although – when she tried to push through the walls – she found them an impassable barrier. She stared at them, trying to see a way through – or around – the barricade. They didn't seem to have any cracks, but ...she drifted up and *around* the rooms, passing through the floors and walls as if they weren't there, then went down. The walls – the ceiling, she corrected herself – didn't seem so solid here. She found herself peering down into the room from high overhead.

Sofia sat cross-legged on a cushion, looking oddly agitated. Silverdale had *never* seen her looking so agitated, not since she'd misplaced her garter at a formal dance four years ago. The governess had not been amused. Silverdale started to smile at the thought, then froze as she saw Emetine entering the chamber. She didn't dare breathe. The High Priestess could see her ... if she thought to look *up*. Silverdale concentrated on staying as still as possible. Her sister might be able to see her too, if *she* looked. And then ... Ruby hadn't been amused a year ago, when she'd caught Silverdale listening to her conversation. Silverdale was sure Sofia would be even *less* amused.

"They escaped," Sofia said, without preamble. "How?"

"Isabella had help," Emetine said. "She called on one of the gods."

Sofia looked stunned. "How?"

"Our master has rivals," Emetine said. "And he couldn't prevent one of them from manifesting within the cell."

Silverdale kept as still as possible, even though she was reeling inside. Reginald had been helped by another creature? What had happened? And who was *Isabella*? Emetine spoke as if she knew her, but ... that answered nothing. Who *was* she? What was she doing with Reginald? Silverdale couldn't help wondering if Isabella had lured Reginald into pledging himself to one of the creatures, just like Emetine and Sofia. Or ... she swallowed, hard. She refused to believe *Reginald* could make such a mistake. He'd been trained to serve as prince, then king. He would know better than to accept any deals, with *anything,* that weren't clearly laid out ahead of time.

"And now he's escaped." Sofia stood and started to pace the room. "What will he do now?"

Emetine kept her voice steady. "If he realises what he has, he can destroy this castle. And us."

"He wouldn't kill his *family*," Sofia protested. She sounded as if she didn't believe herself. "He *wouldn't*."

"He's pledged himself to a very different god," Emetine said. "She could wear him down with promises of whatever he wants, until he can no longer tell right from wrong."

Really, Silverdale thought. *Is that what you did to Sofia?*

"And he has another god at his disposal," Emetine added. "If he realises what he can do, what he can demand in exchange for the god's freedom, he can get almost *anything*."

"The dream will die." Sofia spoke as though she'd already made up her mind to do something terrible. "I cannot let that happen."

She turned to Emetine. "Can we perform the ritual?"

Emetine smiled. "You do realise you'll be making a huge sacrifice?"

"Father will understand," Sofia said. Her eyes shone with an inhuman light. "He always told us that a king had to be ready to sacrifice for his people. I'm sure he'll understand giving his life so the new order might survive. Our master will honour his sacrifice and accept him into his realm."

Silverdale felt her blood run cold. Sofia was talking about *sacrificing* their father? About *killing* their father? It was unthinkable. Sofia's claim to power wouldn't survive their father's death. And yet ... she found herself staring at her elder sister in disbelief. Sofia was coldly talking herself into doing something *truly* awful. She looked at Emetine and *knew* that she wanted the king sacrificed for power. She'd been pushing Sofia into murdering her father for weeks, perhaps months. Sofia had mentioned a ritual. Who knew what it would *really* do?

"Then I will start making the preparations," Emetine said. "It cannot be done here."

"I know," Sofia said. "We'll leave the city as soon as possible."

Emetine nodded. "Of course ..."

Her presence started to grow stronger. "Let us pray

together," she said. She knelt on the stone floor. Sofia joined her. "We will beg *his* blessing for what we have to do."

Silverdale shuddered as she saw an eerie flickering light dancing between Emetine and Sofia. It illuminated bright threads of power, reaching up and away in directions she could barely grasp. She looked up, trying to follow them. Something was sitting at the far end, something sleeping ... something *waiting*. Her eyes started to hurt, even though they weren't truly *there*. She had a flash of something truly *monstrous* waiting to be born, something so alien that her mind couldn't comprehend it. And then she saw Emetine starting to raise her eyes to the heavens.

She felt a flash of panic and fled, pushing through the ceiling and up through a dozen floors until she was floating over the castle. There appeared to be walls hanging in the empty air, preventing her from going further ... it struck her, suddenly, that *Isabella* – whoever she was – might be able to project herself into the astral realm. Emetine was trying to bar the ways into the castle, to keep Isabella from spying on them. Silverdale remembered the woman who'd snatched the creature wearing Sir Oswald's body. Isabella? She wondered if she could find a way out of the castle, to go looking ...

Instead, she found herself falling back towards her body. It jerked as she plunged back inside, as if she'd suddenly woken from a sound sleep. Her eyes snapped open – she wasn't sure when she'd closed them – and looked around. The room was empty, but she had the feeling she was being watched. Emetine? She looked around again, trying to peer into the ghostly realm. The shadows grew and lengthened, the walls of reality itself threatening to shatter, but she saw nothing. And yet, *things* were moving within the shadows.

She blinked, hard. The room returned to normal. She took a deep breath, trying to steady herself as panic yammered at the back of her mind. They were going to sacrifice her father. They were going to *kill* her father. Sofia had gone mad. Emetine ... Silverdale felt her heartbeat start to race as she tried, desperately, to think of a plan. She *had* to save her father. But how?

She glanced at the wooden door. The guards were on the

far side, but she could still *feel* their presence. They were *definitely* not human. A dozen plans ran through her mind, each one more impractical than the last. She couldn't get through the door, she couldn't get through the window, she couldn't get through the floor or ceiling or ... she shook her head. She couldn't think of *anything*.

Her eyes alighted on the last drops of potion, sitting in the vial. She was tempted to drink it, but then ... what? She couldn't transport herself out of the room, not physically. Sooner or later, she'd either be dragged back to her body or die when it died. Or ... perhaps she'd become a ghost permanently. She knew better than to try. The only people she knew could see her were the bad guys. Isabella *might* be able to see her, but ... she was an unknown factor. Silverdale had met enough people who wanted to be her friend to know that very few people lacked ulterior motives. Isabella might just be another Emetine.

The name isn't common either, Silverdale thought. She couldn't think of any noblewomen called *Isabella*. Not in Andalusia, not anywhere. *A commoner? Or ... or what?*

She looked up as the door rattled, then opened. Greta stepped into the room, a nasty bruise clearly visible on her pale face. Silverdale felt a hot flash of anger, mingled with the grim realisation that she probably couldn't do anything about it. Whoever had hit Greta didn't care about *Silverdale's* opinions. And that meant ... Sofia? Ruby? Or simply someone below stairs without the wit to know that he was going to get himself into trouble?

"Your Highness," Greta said. She put the tray of food on the table. "I can't stay for long."

"I'll eat quickly," Silverdale promised. These days, she was no longer sure Greta would be safe from harm ... even if she was merely following orders. "What happened?"

Greta touched the bruise with a pale finger. "The guards were wild. Something happened and ... they were mad at everyone."

Reginald escaped, Silverdale thought. *And the guards were angry.*

She ate quickly, without taking the time to savour the taste. The food had grown blander over the past few days, although she had no idea why. Her father had assured her that the castle was provisioned to survive a major siege. There'd be a shortage of fresh fruit and vegetables, naturally, but they wouldn't starve. *That* wasn't a bad thing. She liked raw carrots and celery and other vegetables, but the cooks only seemed to be capable of turning them into a bland mess that tasted like compost. Or so she thought. She'd never actually *tasted* compost.

Greta spoke quietly, filling Silverdale in on what had happened while she'd been locked in her room. The rumours had grown in the telling, but ... something had clearly happened, something bad. And yet, no two rumours agreed. An army was moving to raise the siege and drive Reginald back to the Summer Isle; no, an army was moving to destroy Reginald and then take the city and castle for its master ... whoever that happened to be. The northern barons had declared independence, or fealty ... no one seemed to know which. And the neighbouring kingdoms were apparently invading ...

"But you don't actually *know* what's happening," Silverdale said. The rumours couldn't *all* be true. Could they? "Does anyone?"

"The Regent, perhaps," Greta said. "I don't know about anyone else."

Silverdale finished her tray and pushed it to one side. "I need to get out of here," she said, as a thought struck her. She pocketed her royal seal, then reached for the vial before she could think better of it. "Will you help me?"

"If I can," Greta said. "But I can't fight the guards."

"I know." Silverdale thought she was immune – the guards couldn't actually kill her – but *Greta* was a different story. "All you have to do is drag me out of the room and down the corridor to the green room."

Greta frowned. "Your Highness ..."

"Open the door," Silverdale ordered. She pushed as much command into her voice as she could. "Now."

Bracing herself, she put the vial to her mouth and drank.

Chapter Thirty-Three

The effect was immediate.

Silverdale felt her legs buckle, even as her astral form drifted out of her body. Greta let out a gasp, then caught Silverdale's body with one hand even as she yanked open the door with the other. The maid was strong, stronger than Silverdale had realised. She kept the thought to herself for later consideration as she drifted out of the door, her astral form flinching as she came face-to-face with the red robed guards. They looked creepy to her physical eyes, but worse – far worse – to her astral form. Their robes concealed something very far from human, something with eerie greenish-yellow eyes and a sense of decaying foulness. She fought the urge to retch – she had no idea what would happen if she threw up while in her astral form – and reached for their hoods, yanking them down. The guards started to tumble forward, deeply confused. They couldn't see her …

Greta threw Silverdale's body over her shoulder and ran down the corridor, her eyes opening wide in panic as a clawed hand reached for her. Silverdale caught the hand, her ghostly touch somehow hurting the robed creature. She *felt* it howl in pain as it stumbled, falling towards the ground. Its partner seemed dazed, confused. Silverdale thrust a ghostly hand right *through* its head. It collapsed, screaming in agony. She was tempted to stay long enough to *really* hurt it, but she didn't have time. The sound was echoing through the ghostly realm. Emetine would hear it …

She threw herself back into her body as Greta reached the green room. Silverdale felt oddly helpless, even as she kicked to signal that she should be put down. Her head spun, as if she weren't quite balanced. Greta helped her to stay upright as she hurried to the draperies, pulling them away to reveal the secret tunnel. She heard Greta gasp behind her as she picked up a lantern, yanked open the door and plunged inside. Hopefully, it would be a while before Sofia realised how she'd made her escape. She wasn't supposed to know about the tunnels.

"Keep your voice down," she hissed, as they hurried up the stairs. They were too narrow for her peace of mind. The lantern kept flickering warningly. "I don't know if they can hear us."

"I never even knew these tunnels existed," Greta said. "Where do they go?"

"One leads to my father's bedchamber," Silverdale muttered. She paused, trying to decide which way to go. "The other is supposed to lead out of the castle."

She shivered as she climbed onwards, hoping and praying they'd be in time. Greta was strong. She could carry the king back into the tunnels and drag him out of the castle ... Silverdale wasn't sure what they'd do then, but ...they'd have to go to Reginald. There was nowhere else they *could* go. She didn't know the city, she didn't know where she could hide ... it wouldn't take long for them to realise that Greta had helped her escape. And then they'd find her family and put them to the question. A pang of guilt struck her, mingled with the grim awareness she hadn't had a choice. She'd just have to find a way to make it up to them afterwards.

The doorway opened, just as she remembered. She braced herself as she slipped into her father's antechamber, her nose twitching as she smelt something unfamiliar – and unpleasant – in the air. It brushed against her nostrils, mocking her. She paused, listening carefully, but heard nothing. She couldn't even hear her father's snores. She glanced at Greta, then stepped into the bedchamber. The bed was empty. Even the *sheets* had been removed.

She muttered a word that would have got her in real trouble, if her governess had heard. Her father was gone. He'd already been taken ... she looked around, more out of desperation than any real hope of seeing her father. The room had been stripped of his regalia, amongst other things. The oak chest that held his crowns – he had three, one of which was held in trust for Reginald – was open. The crowns themselves had been removed. She wondered, sourly, who'd taken them. It was death for any non-royal to even *touch* the crowns. Sofia, probably. Perhaps she was wearing it …

Greta stepped up beside her. "Where *is* he?"

"I don't know." Silverdale took a long breath. "Wait here."

She walked forward and peered into her father's private meeting room. She'd never been allowed to enter before, not even when she'd been a toddler calling desperately for her daddy. The room was empty, but a handful of documents lay on the table, weighed down by a single golden key dangling on the end of a chain. Silverdale frowned, then remembered where she'd seen it before. The City Fathers had presented it to Sofia, calling it the key to the city … to Havelock. She rolled her eyes, then stopped herself as she realised the key had a presence in the ghostly realm. She didn't know what it meant, but her instincts told her to take it. She picked it up, placed it around her neck and turned as she heard someone coming up behind her. Ruby stood there, her eyes cold and hard.

"Ruby," Silverdale managed. "I …"

Her awareness seemed to split in two. Her physical eyes saw her older sister as she'd always been, an older girl wearing a surprisingly simple dress. Her astral eyes saw Ruby wearing chains around her arms and feet, a metal gag covering her mouth … Silverdale shuddered, then tried to reach for the locks. But … she couldn't pull them free. Ruby caught her arm a second later – Silverdale's head spun as she tried to work out if she'd been caught physically or mentally – and yanked her forward. Her hand felt like a vice, crushing Silverdale's wrist. She whimpered in pain, but Ruby ignored her. Her older sister's face was so unreadable that she might as well have been a machine.

Ruby stumbled, then fell. Silverdale pulled her hand free as Ruby hit the floor. Greta stood behind her, holding one of the king's sceptres in her right hand. It took Silverdale a moment to realise that Greta had struck Ruby's head … she'd committed several different crimes in the space of a few seconds. The sceptre clattered to the floor a second later, Greta swaying as she realised what she'd done. She'd be put to death for daring to wield the sceptre, let alone striking a princess …

"I won't tell anyone if you don't," Silverdale said. Ruby

wasn't in her right mind. She wouldn't complain, when – if – she returned to normal. "We have to go."

The key felt heavy around her neck as they hurried back to the tunnel. Ruby was under enemy control. Emetine *knew* where she'd been ... she'd guess what had happened, even if she didn't know everything. And then ... who knew? Gritting her teeth, she led the way back into the secret passageway and headed down. She had to find the way out before it was too late.

"I hit her." Greta sounded stunned. "I ..."

"Blame it on me," Silverdale told her. "I won't tell them the truth."

She wondered, as the tunnel sloped downwards, just what would happen when Ruby recovered. Would she remember that Silverdale had been in *front* of her? Or would her memories have been scrambled by the blow? Head injuries were nothing to laugh at ... Silverdale felt sick as she remembered a young man who'd been injured during a joust, a few years ago. He'd seemed normal until he'd keeled over and died, a few days later. The healers had insisted there was nothing they could do.

"Thanks, Your Highness," Greta said. "I appreciate it."

Silverdale smiled, then frowned as the tunnel started to level out. How deep *were* they? She couldn't tell. The roof seemed to be lowering ... she looked up, wondering how her father and Reginald had used the tunnel. They were both tall men. She found it hard to imagine them walking down the tunnel without banging their heads every few metres. The walls were rough stone now, not smoothly-carved passageways. It struck her, suddenly, that they were under hundreds of tons of rock. They'd be crushed in an instant if the roof fell on them.

"We must have left the castle by now," Greta said. "It isn't *that* big."

"We have to keep walking," Silverdale said. She couldn't hear anything, apart from themselves, but ... it didn't matter. They had to keep moving. Ruby might have recovered by now. And Ruby was the only one who was aware that *Silverdale* knew about the secret tunnels. Would Emetine think to ask her? Would she volunteer the information? Or ... or what? Did she have any free will left? "I ..."

She broke off as the tunnel started to slope upwards again. The lantern flickered, nearly making her panic as she ducked past a piece of rock that would have dented her head if she hadn't seen it. If they lost the light ... she thought she could see with her astral eyes, but she had no idea how she could keep her body moving while she was in her astral form. She glanced back at Greta, seeing the older girl's eyes wide with fear, then forced herself to keep moving. The tunnel kept rising until it reached a single iron hatch. Silverdale wasn't sure why, but she found it a little reassuring. The latch looked tough, but it was actually easy to open.

"Well," she said. "Here we are."

She stepped through the hatch, into what looked like a small house. The air was cool and tasted of dust. She walked down the corridor, peering into each of the rooms as she passed. It looked as if the house belonged to a wealthy merchant or, perhaps, one of her father's agents. Probably the latter, she decided. A merchant would be expected to host dinner parties and other events that might lead to the tunnel being exposed. Unless ... she frowned, wondering just what sort of cover her father might have used. Maybe he'd found a way to keep the house untouched for decades.

Greta followed her into the living room. "It's getting dark out there," she said, grimly. "Your Highness, you have to change your clothes."

Silverdale blinked. "Why? What's wrong with my clothes?"

"You look like a princess," Greta pointed out, dryly. "You'll stand out a mile."

"Fine." Silverdale didn't *think* she was dressed like a princess, but she'd never walked the city streets. "What should I wear?"

Greta searched the house rapidly, eventually returning with a pair of trousers, a shirt and a small cloth cap. "Put these on, then tie your hair under the cap," she ordered. "You'll look like a boy."

"Yes, Your Highness," Silverdale muttered, sardonically. She'd never worn trousers in her life. They itched uncomfortably as she changed into them, then concealed her hair as best she could. The key to the city went into a small knapsack that barely seemed large enough to hold it. "How do I look?"

"Try not to talk." Greta had changed into a dark skirt that looked more suited to a housewife than a maid, then stuffed a pair of socks into her shirt. "As far as anyone's concerned, you're my younger brother. Don't let anyone hear you speak or we'll both be for the high jump."

Silverdale bit down the urge to remind Greta that *Silverdale* was the princess. Greta was only trying to help. And besides, she *needed* Greta. If the maid walked away and lost herself in the streets, Silverdale was doomed. She peered out at the darkening streets as Greta tied her hair into a bun, then opened the door. She'd do whatever she could for the maid and her family, if the world returned to normal. And she'd make sure that no one ever realised who hit Ruby, even if it meant taking the punishment herself.

She felt an odd thrill of freedom as she walked through the door and onto the streets. The air was cold – the shirt didn't provide much protection – and the streets felt creepy, but she was free. She turned and looked at the castle, feeling her eyes itch as they threatened to see both the real castle and the monstrosity it had become. She could sense something pervading the castle now, a sense of something so prevalent she honestly hadn't realised it was there until it was gone. Greta caught her arm and pushed her down the street, heading away from the castle. The sense of lingering doom started to fade as they walked.

The streets seemed largely empty, even as they moved away from the castle. A handful of buildings lay in ruins, smashed beyond repair. She saw a person lying against a wall, a bottle of liquid clasped in one hand. A number of others were slipping up and down the streets, wrapped in long cloaks that covered their faces. She saw a pair of women standing by the side of the road, waving to everyone who crossed their path. Greta let out a sniff of disapproval, took Silverdale's arm and led her past. Silverdale had no idea who the women were, or what they were doing, but it didn't look good.

She waited as Greta stopped a passing man and asked him a handful of questions. The man had a sly look in his eye Silverdale didn't like at all, but he took the coin Greta offered him and answered as best he could. His gaze lingered on

Silverdale long enough to make her feel uncomfortable, although she couldn't tell if he'd seen through her disguise. If there were people looking for them, she couldn't *see* them. And yet ... she tried not to meet his gaze as he took one final look at her. She really *didn't* like him.

"He said your brother is in control of the western gatehouse," Greta said, once they were on their way again. "We have to get there, quickly."

The streets grew quieter as they kept moving. A handful of night watchmen strode past them, their faces tired and worn. They made no attempt to speak to either of them, much to Silverdale's relief. She knew she should keep her head up high – *Reginald* would have kept his head up high – but she was too scared. She'd felt vulnerable in the castle, yet – perversely – she'd also felt safe. Here ... she had the feeling she *really* wasn't safe. The commoners could do anything to her, or Greta, if they caught them. They might not even realise who they were.

"There." Greta pointed into the distance. A barricade blocked the road, manned by soldiers who gazed towards the castle. "Are you ready?"

The soldiers watched them carefully as they walked up to the barricade. Silverdale hesitated, then relaxed – slightly – as she realised they were wearing Reginald's livery. They wouldn't do anything to *her* ... she thought. She reached into her pocket and produced her seal as Greta spoke to the leader. It was impossible to fake, she'd been told. They'd know it was her.

"That's not a princess," one of the soldiers said. "It's a little boy."

Silverdale pulled off her cap. Her blonde hair spilled over her face. The soldiers laughed – the one who'd challenged her seemed to redden, although it was hard to be sure in the twilight – and then motioned for them to wait. A pair of horsemen cantered up, the leader a man Silverdale vaguely recognised. Sir ... something or other. One of Reginald's friends. She couldn't remember his name. She kicked herself for forgetting, knowing that it might have cost her everything. Junior noblemen got so irked when their seniors forgot who they were.

"Your Highness," the nobleman said. He jumped off his

horse and knelt. "It is my very great honour to meet you."

"I thank you," Silverdale said, every inch a princess. "Escort us to my brother."

She grinned at Greta as she scrambled onto the horse, then allowed herself to be led down the streets, through the gatehouse and stopped outside a large tent. A grim-faced woman stood outside, arms crossed over her breasts. Silverdale stared, recognising her at once. It was strange – the woman appeared to have two faces, like so many others in the castle – but, at the same time, it was a little reassuring. The woman felt nothing like Emetine. She wasn't corrupted by the creatures.

Silverdale found her voice. "Isabella?"

Isabella's eyes opened wide. "I saw you …"

She shook her head. "Come inside," she said, helping Silverdale and Greta clamber off the horse. "Your brother is keen to see you."

Silverdale glanced at her. "Did you see us coming?"

"The guards sent a message," Isabella said. She sounded friendly, although a little reserved. It was odd to see a woman in her post … Silverdale studied her back, wondering just who and what she really was. "Coming?"

She put the thought aside as Isabella led them into the tent. Reginald sat on a wooden chair, smiling. Silverdale threw decorum to the winds and ran to him, wrapping her arms around her elder brother. She'd missed him, more than she could say. Behind her, she heard Greta falling to her knees. Silverdale silently willed Reginald to realise that Greta didn't *have* to kneel. Her brother picked up on the silent message and motioned for Greta to rise. He'd reward her, even if Silverdale had to spend the rest of the night nagging him.

"It's good to see you again," Reginald said, as she released him. "I …"

His eyes went wide as Silverdale gave him the key to the city. "I … what happened to you?"

"It's a long story," Silverdale said. "But I'll tell you everything."

She took a long breath, then began.

Chapter Thirty-Four

"We have the key to the city," Reginald said quietly, as the first assault units moved into position. "And we hold a gatehouse. We should be able to take the castle quickly."

He couldn't keep the urgency out of his voice. There was no way to be *sure* that his possession of the city – his *symbolic* possession of the city – would be enough to keep the entities from interfering. And yet, he *had* to move fast. Silverdale hadn't been very clear on just what Sofia and Emetine intended to accomplish by sacrificing King Romulus to their master, but it was clear that they intended to do *something*. Reginald didn't care to wait and see what it was.

"Yeah." Isabella didn't sound convinced. She'd spent the last few hours interrogating Silverdale and Greta, trying to figure out what they knew … and what they didn't know they knew. "And we have no idea what might be waiting for us."

Reginald nodded, stiffly. They were already inside the city walls, thanks to the surrendered gatehouse. He had no doubt that the civilians would try to stay out of the fight as much as possible, if they had a choice. He'd already dispatched influencers to try to keep the locals quiet, promising everything from a civilised occupation to the resumption of the city's ancient liberties. The key to the city felt oddly heavy, hanging around his neck. He had the feeling he shouldn't hold on to it any longer than was strictly necessary.

He turned to Gars as the first glimmers of sunlight washed over the city. "Signal the attack."

The trumpets blared. The first assault units started forward, heading straight for the improvised enemy defences. Havelock had never had to fight a *real* battle for survival and it showed. The barricades looked tough – the defenders hadn't lacked for manpower – but Reginald had fought his way through tougher. They wouldn't stand up to his troops for more than a few seconds. The real danger lay in enemy archers and rooftop warriors, men who'd force him to waste time clearing the houses instead of marching on the castle. He hoped – prayed – that the enemy hadn't thought to prepare traps for his men. Their blood would be fired up by the time they punched through the defences and pushed onwards.

And then it would be difficult to keep them from committing atrocities, he thought, coldly. *And then the entire city might turn on me.*

Isabella caught his eye as the enemy barricades crumbled. "They're not bothering to mount a real defence."

Reginald's eyes narrowed. She was right. Only a handful of enemy soldiers manned the barricades, not even *trying* to maintain a pretence that the structures were fully manned. He leaned forward, watching as the enemy soldiers fled. They were hurrying straight back to the castle ... he cursed under his breath. Sofia wasn't even *trying* to hold the city. She'd pulled most of her men back to the castle walls.

"Smart move, if she's trying to stall us," he muttered, darkly. Storming a castle was always costly, even for the winner. Reginald might take the castle, only to be knifed in the back by the nobility. They'd see him bleed his army white and strike before he could rebuild his strength. "And I bet she's cleared the homes around the walls."

"Looks that way," Isabella agreed. She shot him a sharp glance. "Are you *sure* you want to accompany the assault force?"

"Yes." Reginald knew she meant well, but there was no way he could stay back. Not now. Not when his sisters and father were in danger. "I have to go too."

He shook his head slowly as his bodyguard formed up around him, escorting him into the city. The tunnel had been a secret, until now. It was quite possible – almost certain, really – that Sofia had now had it blocked off. Did *she* know about the tunnel? If she'd realised Silverdale had fled, she'd have to guess at its existence even if their father hadn't told her about it already. And if she'd searched the castle from top to bottom, she might uncover a whole host of little secrets passed down from king to king. Who knew where *that* would end?

I'll have to have the tunnel blocked off myself, he thought.

Too many people know about it now.

He touched his iron sword as they made their way through the streets. The civilians were staying inside, hiding behind wooden and metal doors that wouldn't stand up to his troops – or anyone, really – if they wanted to break them down. He hoped the civilians would have the sense to *stay* inside, at least until the city was secured. The townsfolk were known for being riotous, if they thought their liberties and economic rights were under threat ... he spotted a destroyed temple and knew, deep inside, that the civilians would be unsure of which side they should take. Hopefully, they'd stay quiet until a clear victor emerged.

A rider cantered up to him. "Your Highness, we have surrounded the castle," he said, as he jumped to the cobblestones. "The gates are closed, but there has been no resistance."

Reginald shared a glance with Isabella. The castle's defenders could hardly *keep* him from securing the area, and preparing an assault, but they could certainly make it a great deal harder. A handful of archers in good positions could take a heavy toll on his men. And yet, they were doing nothing. He puzzled over it for a moment, then dismissed it. He wouldn't be sending in a major assault unless the tunnel was blocked. There was no point in wasting men if he had an alternative.

"Tell Gars to set up the lines, as planned," he ordered. "But he's to wait for my order before attacking."

He watched the rider gallop off, then turned his attention to the house. It was just another wealthy merchant's house, as far as the neighbours were concerned. The nominal owner was rich enough to afford the house, but not rich enough to live there permanently. It wasn't an uncommon pattern, Reginald had been told. The locals wouldn't expect to see the owner daily. He rather doubted the impression would last, if anyone was paying attention. They'd see a small assault force go into the building and not come out again.

"Let me go first," Isabella said. "If there's a trap ..."

Reginald reminded himself, sharply, that Isabella was a trained soldier as well as a sorceress. It still felt *wrong* to let her take the lead. People would comment, if they ever found out about it ... he put the thought aside as she picked the lock and led the way into the darkened house. Inside, it was surprisingly bare. Reginald wondered, idly, if that was a mistake. It didn't *look* as if anyone lived in it, even briefly.

"Odd place to have a tunnel," Isabella commented. Silverdale and Greta had left the hatch open. "Why doesn't it open in the basement?"

"There isn't one," Reginald said. "This part of the city was built on solid rock."

He watched her slip into the tunnel, Sergeant Ruthven and his men following her. Reginald brought up the rear. The tunnel started to descend sharply, reminding him of the handful of times he'd used it as a younger man. His father had forbidden him to use the tunnel except on princely business, pointing out that it would be disastrous if the secret came out. There was no way they could dig another tunnel without making it obvious.

"You could have used magic to conceal the tunnel," Isabella said, as the passageway started to level out. "Why didn't you?"

"I imagine my ancestors didn't want to ask their wizardly superior," Reginald said. His father had been bitter beyond words at having to take orders from a magician. No wonder he'd moved so quickly to secure his power when the Golden City fell. "And it would have been very noticeable to *another* magician."

Isabella snorted, but said nothing. Reginald was almost relieved, even though the stone walls were pressing in. They looked as if they'd been hacked out of solid stone by dwarves – or children, he supposed. He heard several men curse as they bumped their metal helmets against the ceiling or knocked into stalagmites hanging down from overhead. Silverdale had tensed when he'd mentioned the tunnels, as if she'd expected him to order her back to the castle. Reginald felt his heart clench at the thought. His sweet little sister would be protected, he swore. The entities would get to her over his dead body.

The tunnel started to head upwards. Reginald muttered directions as they reached a crossroads, directing the assault force towards the lower regal levels. There was nothing to be gained by using the hatch in the servant quarters, not unless he wanted to alert the entire castle. He wondered, morbidly, why his ancestors had built an entrance there, in the first place. It wasn't as if they'd had any reason to visit the kitchens when they could simply call for food at all hours of the day.

"I can't sense anything," Isabella muttered. The hatch was firmly closed. "Shall I …?"

"Yes," Reginald said. He had the odd feeling they'd made a mistake. "Now."

Isabella kicked open the hatch, pushed the draperies away and jumped into the corridor. The remainder of the guards followed her, swords at the ready. But there was no one there. Reginald felt a shiver creep down his spine as he stepped out of the tunnel, telling himself that he was ready for anything. The castle was home – he'd been born and raised within the stone walls – but it no longer *felt* like home. His eyes darted along the corridor, noting how many paintings and portraits had been removed. Years ago, he'd been forced to memorise every long-dead king and queen his homeland had ever had. Now, their portraits were gone. He found himself caught between horror and grim amusement. He'd wanted to destroy them too …

Sergeant Ruthven looked worried. "Where's the welcoming committee?"

"The throne room is just through those doors," Reginald said. They weren't being *quiet*. They should have attracted a small army of guards by now. "Quickly."

He shivered, feeling as if he were committing a mortal sin, as he led the assault force through the doors, the antechamber and into the throne room itself. It was a capital crime for someone to bear arms within the regal chambers, unless one happened to have the king's permission … Reginald was the only person who'd *had* that permission, once upon a time. He rather suspected that it had already been revoked. But …

"Shit," Sergeant Ruthven muttered.

Reginald followed his gaze. The throne stood on the dais, as it had since days of old. And, on the throne … he could barely grasp what he was seeing. His father sat there, his eyes so dull and depleted that – for a horrific moment – Reginald thought he was dead. He looked more like a rag doll than anything *living*. He found himself running forward, sword in hand. He wanted – he needed – his father to come back to him. But the king didn't react as he jumped onto the dais.

"Father," Reginald breathed.

King Romulus had always been a strong man. Reginald had known it from childhood, even though there had been little real prospect of the king wielding *real* power. His father had trained hard as a young man, then tutored Reginald himself as he'd grown into adulthood. Reginald knew there were princes who yearned for their fathers to die, but *he'd* never been one of them. How could he? His father had been the most important person in his life since his mother's death. But now he was … what?

Isabella stepped up beside him. "His mind has been damaged," she said. "I don't know how to fix it."

Reginald wanted to scream at her as he saw a trickle of drool fall from the king's mouth. He wanted to shout and rage and do whatever it took to bring Sofia to justice … he stopped, kicking himself for getting distracted. Where *was* Sofia? Where *was* she? And where were her guards? The entire *castle* should have been on them by now. Where *was* she?

He glanced around, realising – slowly – that the building was too quiet. The castle had always buzzed with life, even during winter. There should be a small army of servants and guards lurking nearby, ready to attend upon the king's every whim. The royal mistress had her own rooms, only a few short metres from the throne. Where was *she*? Reginald wondered, suddenly, if the castle was *empty*. Had Sofia fled into the night?

"Sergeant, take four men and check the gatehouse," he ordered, tersely. "If there's no one there, open the gates and let the army in."

"Yes, Your Highness." Sergeant Ruthven banged his chest in salute. He didn't try to argue, mercifully. "Watch yourself."

Reginald nodded, watching as the men hurried out of the room. Isabella was kneeling beside the king, muttering a handful of spells. Reginald felt an odd little pang, fearing – suddenly – that his father would never know his daughter-in-law. Would he approve of Isabella? Or would he insist his son married someone more suitable? Reginald sighed, inwardly. He would sooner have the argument over his future bride than watch his father sink into madness. And …

He swallowed, hard. Sofia had left their father behind … why? He was the source of her power … or was he? Had she thrown the regency aside? Or had she concluded that her father was in no state to revoke her power, let alone pass the throne to his son? Reginald wondered, morbidly, what he'd do if his father *didn't* recover. The days when he could have appealed to the Golden City for his father to be removed from power were long gone. He couldn't kill his father, yet – as long as his father was still alive – he couldn't succeed him either.

"Where are they?" He glanced at Isabella. "And why didn't they fight for the castle?"

"I don't know," Isabella said. "I …"

She swore, viciously. "I'm a fucking idiot!"

Reginald had no time for self-blame. "How so?"

"They got out the same way *we* did," Isabella said. "They went through the Godly Realm. They could be *anywhere* by now."

"… Shit," Reginald said. He tried to consider the implications. Teleporting was supposed to be impossible, but if one took a shortcut through the Godly Realm … *anywhere* could be … well, *anywhere*. They might be back on the Summer Isle, or in the Golden City, or somewhere on the other side of the world. A thought struck him and he frowned. "Why didn't they take father with them?"

"I … they broke his mind," Isabella said. "They might not have wanted to risk taking him through the Godly Realm. Who knows what might climb into his mind?"

Reginald frowned. It was a sensible explanation, he supposed, but it didn't *feel* right. If Sofia had wanted to sacrifice their father, why would she leave him behind? Or … a chill ran down his spine as he turned to look at his father's body. Was his father still in there, somewhere? Or was his body being controlled by something utterly inhuman?

"Keep a sharp eye on him," he ordered. The king didn't *feel* overshadowed, but Reginald didn't dare take that for granted. "And … I want him chained up. In cold iron."

Isabella didn't argue. He supposed that made her unique. Everyone else, even his chosen officers, would have raised objections to binding the king. Symbolically …

Sergeant Ruthven clattered back into the room, followed by a small army of guards. "Your Highness, the gatehouse was empty," he said. "The entire castle appears to be empty."

"Then search every level," Reginald ordered. He already knew what they'd find, but he had to be sure. Sofia was missing. Emetine was missing. Ruby was missing … his heart clenched again in bitter pain. He'd had a few fights with Ruby when they'd been younger – she'd always taken more after their father – but she didn't deserve to be enslaved. Silverdale had seen the invisible bonds around their sister's mind. "Check everywhere."

He forced himself to calm down as the soldiers hurried to obey. If the entire castle was empty … where had they gone? His mind raced, desperately. How far could they go? If Emetine had jumped from the Summer Isle to Havelock, why couldn't she have jumped back? Or … Sofia wouldn't leave the country, would she? She wouldn't be Regent if she deserted her post. Legally, she could be stripped of her post …

Which is silly, Reginald told himself. *Power comes from swords and sorcery, not legal rights and wrongs.*

Captain-General Gars appeared. "Your Highness," he said. "The castle appears to be empty."

"I noticed." Reginald spoke with heavy sarcasm. "Have the men interrogate the locals who live nearby, find out what they saw … if anything. And then order the city fathers to present themselves to me."

He rubbed his forehead. Sofia had placed him in a very nasty spot. His father was unfit to rule, yet … Sofia was still – technically – his regent. The nobility would hesitate to accept Reginald as their monarch, as long as his father was still alive. He doubted they gave much of a damn about legality, but they could make use of the confusion over who was actually in charge to reclaim some of the power they'd been forced to surrender over the last few decades. Or demand a high price for their submission. He wondered, sourly, just what the representatives in his camp were doing. They were probably already sending messengers to their masters, updating them on events.

And as long as my father lives, they'll have room to

manoeuvre, he thought. Cold logic told him he should kill his father. Compassion insisted that his father might prefer to be dead, rather than live as a drooling imbecile. But he couldn't bring himself to cut his father's throat. He couldn't. *It isn't over yet.*

Chapter Thirty-Five

"This building feels creepy," Silverdale commented, as Isabella brushed aside the wards and led her into the antechamber. "What happened here?"

Isabella kept her face impassive with an effort. Silverdale was nice, she supposed, but ... there was something about her that rubbed Isabella the wrong way. Maybe it was that they were both younger siblings, born to power and place ... Silverdale's father had been nicer than Isabella's, but he'd wanted much from his daughter too. Isabella told herself, firmly, that she'd been in a far better position. Silverdale wouldn't have been able to fight back when her father – or brother – told her who she was going to marry.

Or maybe she would have been able to resist, Isabella thought, coldly. It was clear that Silverdale had a talent for symbolic magic, maybe even *real* magic. The young girl seemed to have taken to it like a duck to water. She had less to unlearn. *If Emetine had managed to turn her into a student ...*

She pushed the thought aside. "I captured one of the entities," she said. "And I trapped him here."

Silverdale chuckled. "The one that possessed Sir Oswald?"

"Yeah." Isabella remembered catching sight of someone – Silverdale, she knew now – when she captured the entity. "That's him."

She led the way down the stairs, feeling conflicted. Reginald had insisted she keep Silverdale with her, despite the dangers. Silverdale needed a chaperone. Isabella wondered, sourly, if they *both* needed a chaperone. Reginald had spent the last two days fielding questions about his engagement as well as potential partners for his three sisters. He would be embarrassed – or worse – if Isabella accidentally caused a scandal. He was probably lucky, she decided, that he didn't know why her family had disowned her.

The door at the bottom of the stairs was firmly shut, held in place by a dozen bolts and charms. She reached for the first charm, then turned to look at the younger girl. Children grew up quickly these days, even the ones raised in royal castles, but ... Silverdale was still a child. She shouldn't be taken into danger. Isabella had seen countless children killed during the wars, but that didn't make it *right*. She wanted to tell Silverdale to wait outside. But she already knew the younger girl had nerve. Silverdale wouldn't listen to her.

"It could be dangerous," she said, as she started to open the door. "You can stay outside, if you like. I won't tell Reginald."

Silverdale favoured Isabella with a brilliant smile. "Reggie said I was to stay with you."

Isabella snorted as she finished opening the door. The sense of *presence* struck her like a mighty gust of wind. It didn't seem to have diminished in any way, as far as she could tell. She peered into the darkness, then took a lantern from the wall and held it out in front of her. The binding circle remained intact, even though it was just a chalk line on the floor. She smiled, coldly, at the flickering shadow within the circle. If the line had failed, the entity would be gone by now.

Behind her, Silverdale muttered an oath. Isabella kept her face straight with an effort. The entity had no eyes – it was just a shadow, not even humanoid – but she could tell it was watching them. The slightest mistake, the slightest hint of weakness, could give it an opening. Isabella wondered, suddenly, what Silverdale was seeing. She'd seemed much more in tune with the cracks in reality, and the Godly Realm, than Isabella herself. In hindsight, it was clear that Emetine had been trying to lure her into committing herself ...

Just like a dark wizard might seduce an apprentice, Isabella thought. She knew the dangers. It was easy to fall into madness, to become addicted to dark magic well before one realised that one had gone too far ... oddly, she found it a little reassuring. The threat was still terrifying, but it was starting to take on shape and form. *Emetine has a lot of practice in seducing people.*

She walked up to the circle, careful to keep her distance. The entity hovered in front of her, pressing up against an invisible wall. It seemed to be calling to her, trying to lure her onwards ... Isabella snorted, rudely. Did it think it could trick her into breaking the circle? Or even stepping on the line? There was no way to be sure that that *would* break the circle ...

"Well," she said, coolly. "Here we are again."

The entity didn't change, but she had the impression that it was angry. It hadn't been in the circle *that* long. And it was timeless, effectively immortal ... she wondered, suddenly, if it was just biding its time. Or if she was effectively torturing it by trapping the creature within the human realm. Isabella hadn't enjoyed being chained up, back when she'd been captured by Emetine. Perhaps it was worse for the entity.

She scowled, glancing at Silverdale to make sure the younger girl wasn't on the verge of breaking the circle. There hadn't been any sign of Sofia and Emetine since Silverdale had fled the castle, there hadn't been any sign of their captives or servants. Reginald was sure Sofia hadn't left the country, but that was meaningless. Andalusia was a *big* country, over two hundred thousand square miles ... a relative handful of people could pass unnoticed for years, if they were careful. Someone would notice eventually, but when? And how much trouble could Sofia and Emetine cause before they were caught?

A lot, Isabella thought. She'd read the reports, heard the stories. Miracles were happening everywhere. It was just like the Summer Isle, only worse. The commoners were starting to fall for the entities, to offer them worship, while the nobles scrabbled for power ... never noticing that their houses were starting to burn down around them. *Sofia and Emetine could take advantage of this if they're not caught quickly.*

She allowed her expression to darken as she stared at the entity. It *might* be able to answer her questions, if she was careful. Mother Lembu had said as much. And she had something it wanted, desperately. She was the only one who could free it from imprisonment. Maybe it *could* wait for centuries for the building to collapse or something else to happen that would break the circle and let it go. It didn't mean that it would *want* to wait. And yet ... Isabella gritted her teeth. The need for information was warring with a lifetime of warnings that some things came with too high a price.

"You are our prisoner," she said, keeping her voice calm. "We want information."

The entity's voice seemed to beat against her head. "Release me."

Isabella felt her head start to pound. "Not until you cooperate with us," she said. "Answer our questions, truthfully, and we will let you go."

"Release me," the entity repeated. "You know not what you do."

"I know I'm holding you here," Isabella pointed out. "And I know I can keep you here for a very long time."

The entity laughed. "I can wait. We waited for longer than you could comprehend to return to this world. I can wait forever."

Isabella stared at the shadow. "Do you want to test that? Really?"

"I am nothing *but* want," the shadow said. Laughter hissed through the air. "I can't *not*."

Isabella shrugged. "Answer my questions," she ordered. "Where did Princess Sofia and Queen Emetine go?"

The laughter grew stronger. "You already know the answer," the entity said. It seemed to *sneer* at her. "You just don't want to think about it."

Isabella gritted her teeth. She was being mocked. She *knew* she was being mocked. The entity wasn't going to give her an answer now, perhaps ever. It didn't want to be trapped, but … it probably didn't want to incur the anger of its fellows either. Mother Lembu had hinted that the entities weren't all of one mind. The entity in front of her had served a greater entity. Perhaps it still did. She had no way to know.

Silverdale stepped forward. "If we already know the answer, what is it?"

"Obvious," the entity said. "*That's* what it is."

Isabella glanced at Silverdale, motioning for the younger girl to step back. The entity was playing with them. The answer was obvious … most answers were, in hindsight. It took an uncommon mind to make the first breakthrough, but once it was made …

She forced herself to think. The answer was obvious, was

it? The Summer Isle? No. Reginald was right. Sofia couldn't leave the kingdom without giving up the regency, something that – ironically – would impede the entities far more than their human enemies. And yet, what did Sofia intend to do? She'd taken her younger sister with her. Another sacrifice? There were hundreds of rituals involving virgins, ranging from the relatively harmless to terrifyingly dangerous. Isabella hated to think what Sofia might do if she sacrificed her sister. She'd be sacrificing something that meant a great deal to her ...

And she can't have gone very far, Isabella mused. *She couldn't leave the kingdom.*

A thought struck her. There were places people weren't allowed to go. They were tainted with ancient combat, marked by dark magic and darker intentions. The Inquisition had enforced the forbidden zones, preventing anyone from entering and executing people who came out. Now ... the Inquisition was gone. And she'd bet half her remaining fortune, such as it was, that there was a forbidden zone in Andalusia. There might even be more than one.

And if there's one close to the city, she thought, *Sofia might have gone there.*

"Your time is running out," the entity mocked. "The cycle will soon end. The endless cycle will begin again. And you don't know where to go."

"Yes, I do." Isabella said. She turned and led the way to the door. "Enjoy the remainder of eternity."

She walked through the door, making sure to seal the chamber again. Perhaps something would happen, sooner or later, to free the creature. It was going to be alone for a very long time. If she understood the rules properly, it would almost *have* to happen by accident. The other entities couldn't free it. They couldn't even send a human slave to free it. They'd have to wait for time and tide or simply accident to let the entity go.

And that will be a very long time in the future, she thought, as they clambered up the stairs. *I'll see to it personally.*

Silverdale caught her arm. "Where ... how do you know where they went?"

"I have a hunch," Isabella said. She waved to the garrison commander as he emerged from his office. She'd met him briefly, when they'd returned to the small town. He'd made it clear that he wanted to be somewhere else, rather than tied down guarding the army's supply lines. "Do you have any *good* maps of the country, maps dating back ten years or so?"

"Sure." The garrison commander barked orders. Two of his subordinates hurried away and returned with a handful of maps. "What are you looking for?"

"A clue." Isabella unfolded the first map, allowing herself a moment of relief that it had been produced by the Empire's cartographers. Local map-makers tended to leave important details off their maps, for all sorts of reasons. "What areas are forbidden here? Near Havelock?"

"There's a forbidden zone fifty miles to the east, within the mountains," the commander said, slowly. "We were told never to go there, even when we were practising forced marches."

Isabella frowned as she studied the map. Fifty miles away … barely a moment's travel, if one went through the Godly Realm. She contemplated the problem for a long moment. She could take hundreds of soldiers through the Godly Realm with her, if she was prepared to accept the risk. She knew better. The odds of losing some of them to the entities were too high. Sofia might already be there, waiting for … waiting for what? The only sign that Sofia hadn't already pushed ahead with the ritual was … what? Isabella was sure she would have sensed *something*. But was that true?

"That's one possibility," she said. A thought was nagging at her mind. "Are there others?"

"There's another one in the northern reaches," the commander said. "I think there's a third over the border, but that's outside the kingdom."

And might be useless to Sofia, Isabella thought. *And …*

She gritted her teeth as she realised what the entity had been telling her, clearly under the belief it wouldn't make any sense to her. Cycles … cycles and moonrises … she remembered how her womanly cycles had synchronised with the rise and fall of the moon when she'd started practising ritual and symbolic magic. They had two days, she thought, until the moon was at its peak. Two days … it was going to be a hard march.

"Get the horses ready," she ordered, sharply. They were

going to have to gallop back to Havelock, then follow the road eastwards until they reached the forbidden zone. She cursed under her breath. She'd sworn oaths never to allow anyone through the barriers. Now ... Sofia and her servants would probably have no trouble walking through the wards. "And hurry!"

The garrison commander looked at her. "Ah ... Lady Sorceress, can my men and I accompany you?"

"Leave a small unit here," Isabella said. Reginald might not be happy, but they'd need troops if they were to stop the sacrifice. "And the remainder of your men can come."

She forced herself to think, hard. She'd have to send a messenger ahead, warning Reginald to be ready to leave. He kept a troop of horsemen on alert, unless he'd stood his men down since she'd left Havelock, but it was going to take time to assemble the remainder of his army. He'd been having problems keeping the city under control. The locals wanted their freedoms back, but Reginald wanted the city fathers penalised for their role in giving Sofia the keys to the city. They'd nearly gotten him killed.

Which wasn't their fault, Isabella thought. *They didn't know what she could do with them.*

Silverdale glanced at her. "Can we get there in time?"

"I don't know," Isabella said. She ran through her calculations again and again, grimly aware that weather and road conditions could make her best estimates little more than guesswork. "And you really should stay behind."

She sighed. Reginald wouldn't leave Silverdale behind. She had talents he could use ... and, even if she didn't, he could hardly risk her falling into unfriendly hands. Silverdale was the youngest of his sisters, too young to marry for several years, but if she wound up the only survivor of the Royal Family ... whoever married her might have a claim to the throne. Perhaps someone would betroth Silverdale to his son, then rule in their joint names ... it would certainly be harder to challenge than anything else. And besides, Reginald wouldn't have left her behind anyway. He loved his sisters. Isabella was almost jealous. Her siblings had never really liked her.

"I have to come with you," Silverdale said. "I know it."

Isabella eyed her. "*How* do you know it?"

She shrugged. Silverdale wouldn't have an answer. She was merely following her instincts. It was what she was supposed to do, when symbolic magic was involved. Isabella felt her eyes narrow as she remembered the younger girl's stories, wondering just who – or what – was nudging her in a particular direction. Emetine hadn't tried to force Silverdale into submission … perhaps she'd been waiting, biding her time until Silverdale was ready to pledge herself. Isabella's thoughts ran in circles. The entities were too powerful, too dangerous, too … *alien*. It was impossible to predict what they might do.

And yet, we risk calling on them, she mused. She'd heard Emetine's rant – and Reginald's account of *Sofia's* rant. Sofia had had a point, *several* points. She'd had nowhere to go, no one she could *rely* on … it sounded strange, to someone who'd grown up in the Golden City, but Isabella understood. Sofia had been powerless. She'd been ready to sell her soul for a hint of power. *And now she's paying the price gladly.*

Silverdale nudged her. "Do you know how to make more potion?" she asked, holding up a small vial. "I used the last of it to escape."

"Perhaps," Isabella said. She took the vial and sniffed. It smelt like water. She hesitated, then cast an analysis spell. It *was* water. "Did you wash the vial afterwards?"

"No," Silverdale said. "Why …?"

Emetine gave her water, knowing she'd believe it was potion, Isabella thought. *And in doing so, she unlocked Silverdale's mind.*

"I'll get you some more," she said, slowly. Placebos didn't work, except when they did. They certainly never worked with the potions *she'd* been taught to make as a child. She shook her head, slowly. "Once we get back to the castle, I'll get you some."

Silverdale smiled. "Thank you."

"You're welcome," Isabella said.

She let out a long breath. She'd have to discuss it with Reginald first. If she told Silverdale the truth … would Silverdale lose her talents? Or would she be able to use them without tricking herself? Isabella wasn't sure what to make of it. She could tell herself that she was the strongest and richest magician in the world, with magic coming out of her ears and enough gold in her vaults to hire a private army, but that wouldn't make it true. Except it did, where symbolic magic was concerned. If one believed, one *was*.

"We'd better get on our way," she said. "We don't have much time."

Chapter Thirty-Six

Silverdale felt … *alive*.

She sat on the horse's back, feeling the wind blowing through her hair. A small army of bodyguards surrounded her – and Greta was somewhere behind her, riding behind an army officer – but she felt alone. And alive. She'd learnt to ride horses as a young girl, of course, but she'd rarely been allowed to canter along the roads. Princesses were supposed to ride with dignity … she threw back her head and laughed, even though she had a sense they were riding towards terrible danger. It was worth it, just to be free for a few short hours. She'd never have the chance to ride freely again.

The bodyguards smiled at her, rather weakly. Silverdale smiled back at them, then peered towards the distant hills. There hadn't been much time to study the maps, during the hasty preparations for the march, but she'd discovered that the area was almost completely abandoned. The handful of towns and villages they'd ridden through had been populated, but … the people had watched them with baleful eyes, as if they were ready to turn on the riders at any moment. Silverdale had been told that her family was loved, but she was starting to suspect that wasn't true. The handful of destroyed temples they'd passed bore mute testament to the changes sweeping over the land.

Her eyes narrowed as she studied the hills. They looked desolate, scarred by hints of a conflict on a scale she couldn't imagine. The distant trees looked cracked and broken, an impression she couldn't escape even though she knew they were too far away to see details. She wished she'd thought to bring a spyglass, something that would let her see. She had the awful feeling they were riding into a trap.

She gritted her teeth as they cantered through a darkening forest. The road seemed undamaged, but … she thought she saw *things* within the shadows. Eyes – unfriendly eyes –

were watching them. Her hand dropped to the vial of potion Isabella had given her, before she thought better of it. There were ancient secrets within the forest. She might send her mind roaming, only to find she couldn't get back. She wanted to pull back into herself, in hope it would save her from darkness. The land was no longer entirely human.

Another village rose up in front of them, completely abandoned. Silverdale was no judge, but it looked as if the population had simply downed tools and walked away. The hovels and shacks were intact, but empty. A pair of bodyguards stopped long enough to peer into the buildings, then jumped back on their horses and hurried away. Silverdale shivered as she caught sight of a scarecrow marking the edge of the village. It seemed immobile, but she was sure she saw glinting red eyes looking back at her. She shivered, helplessly. She didn't want to turn her back on the sight. She had the feeling it would be the last thing she'd do.

She felt the horse shudder underneath her as they picked up speed, fleeing a threat none of them could have put into words. The bodyguards fell quiet, no longer chattering amongst themselves. They clutched their weapons, eyes flickering from side to side as they watched for threats they knew they might not be able to perceive until it was too late. Silverdale felt uncomfortably naked, even though Reginald had insisted she wore leathers under her riding clothes. There were powers lurking within the shadows now ...

The riders slowed as they passed a large pile of rubble. Silverdale thought, at first, that it might be a temple, but the rubble suggested a far larger building. The outline was clear: a large manor, a handful of smaller homes, a stable ... she sucked in her breath as she realised it had belonged to the local lord. It had been stormed, burned to the ground. She wanted to look away, but she couldn't. Her eyes swept the rubble, looking for ... something. She wasn't sure what.

"No bodies," Isabella called. She rode next to Reginald, as if she had a perfect right to ride beside him. "What happened to them?"

Reginald shrugged, raising his voice. "Ride on!"

Silverdale felt a hot surge of jealousy as the horses picked up speed, once again. *She* should be riding beside her brother, damn it. Isabella ... she scowled, utterly unsure what to make of the older woman. She wasn't nobility. She wasn't anywhere *close* to Reginald's level. And yet she was a sorceress, a sorceress who'd drawn her brother's attention. Silverdale wasn't sure what to make of that either. On one hand, she liked Isabella. On the other, she was holding Reginald's attention. And ... she was a woman, sharing counsels with the men. Silverdale envied her. Her life would have been so much easier if *she'd* enjoyed that kind of respect.

So would Sofia's, Silverdale thought. It was growing harder to remember the person Sofia had been, before Reginald sailed away and everything changed. Reginald had told her about Sofia's rant, when he'd been her prisoner. *She would have had a happier life*.

She looked back towards the hills, then up towards the horizon. The sun was starting to sink in the distance, casting long shadows over the land. She could see darkness edging towards them, all manner of bad concealed within its shroud. A shudder ran down her spine as she finally understood, at a level she couldn't deny, why the commoners shut their doors so firmly at night. The entities were governed by rules. A closed door kept them out as surely as iron bars and bolts kept her *in*. They couldn't enter unless they were invited. It made her wonder just what had happened, so long ago. Recorded history said nothing about the entities, but ... they'd left scars on the land. And on the souls of the human race.

Reginald raised his hand as the road started to narrow, the cobblestones cracking under their feet. "Company, halt!"

Silverdale pulled on the reins, slowing her horse as they cantered up to a single stone placed by the side of the road. It looked harmless, yet ... she felt an urge to turn and flee that was so strong it simply *couldn't* be natural. The horse shifted uncomfortably, picking up on the discontent spreading through the small force. Hardened men clutched their weapons, looking ready to turn and flee at any moment. Silverdale bit her lip to keep from looking scared. She had the feeling that things would go very badly if she gave in to fear.

"Wait," Isabella said. "I'll deal with it."

***

Isabella dropped to the ground, passing her reins to Reginald as she reached into her saddlebags and removed a handful of tools. She was mildly surprised the wards were still intact, given how easily the entities brushed human magic aside, but ... she guessed that Sofia and her crowd had bypassed the wardline completely. They'd probably materialised *inside* the forbidden zone. She wondered, sourly, how they'd done that without crossing a line, then shrugged. If she was right, the forbidden zone already belonged to the entities. They had permission to be there dating back over thousands of years.

She felt sweat trickling down her spine as she walked towards the runestone, fighting the urge to turn and run. The stone was ancient, a menhir that an ancient sorcerer had covered with runes ... she shivered, remembering all the stories about devices that had been steeped in power for generations. She wondered, suddenly, if she'd feel more comfortable if she'd stayed in the Inquisition, but ... she shook her head. She would be dead, along with the rest of them. The Last Emperor had made sure of it.

The stone felt oddly unwelcoming as she rested her hand against the runes. She had the odd sense that *something* was looking at her, judging her. It was a rare person who could walk up to the runestone without turning tail and running, rarer still who could pass through the outer wardline without being pushed away. And anyone who did would find there were stronger defences further in. She wondered, as she pushed magic into the stone, just how much her ancestors had known. They'd sealed off hundreds of places, declaring them utterly forbidden, without telling anyone *why*. Even their servants hadn't known the truth.

Because they might try to summon the entities, she guessed, as she pushed the runestone a little harder. She wanted – she needed – it to recognise her as a friend. *And who knows what might happen if they did?*

The wardline collapsed. The menhir shuddered, then crumbled into dust. Isabella plunged forward, throwing her hands out in front of her to break her fall. She hit the ground hard enough to hurt, the force of the impact jarring her to the bone. The air suddenly seemed much darker, the world pregnant with menace. She pushed herself upwards, glancing towards the hills. *Something* lurked there, waiting to be born.

She *knew* it.

And now the wards are gone, she thought, as she dusted herself off. The Inquisition no longer existed. There was no one left who could rebuild the menhir network and seal off the forbidden zone. *Anyone could come here ...*

She felt the call as she turned and walked back to her horse. It was growing darker now, as if time itself had sped up. She saw a handful of pale faces looking at her, their fears clearly visible. She didn't blame them. The runestone had kept them from feeling the full force of the call, but now ... they could feel it, at a very primal level. It called to them, yet ... it also repelled them. She scrambled onto her horse and took the reins, silently grateful that the beasts were so well trained. She could tell the horse wanted to turn and flee too.

"Company, onwards," Reginald barked.

The horses started to move, galloping past the remains of the menhir and up into the darkness. Isabella braced herself, silently praying they'd get there in time. The sense of imminent doom was growing stronger and stronger, as if their time were steadily running out. She sucked in her breath, feeling ice stabbing into her heart. Sofia and Emetine were up to something. She knew it.

But what?

***

Silverdale nearly fell off the horse, the moment the menhir crumbled into dust. The distant presence, so faint she'd never really been aware of it, was suddenly so strong that it stunned her. She found herself clutching the reins for dear life, gasping for breath as if she'd been hit in the stomach. The sensation was so strong that she couldn't quite understand why there was no pain. She could sense *something* in the distance, the beat of a mighty heart echoing across the land. Each thud set her head to ringing, as if she was being slapped time and time again. It was all she could do to keep from dropping the reins and covering her ears. The astral plane was *raging ...*

She felt herself being yanked forward, out of her body. She wanted to resist, but the pull was too strong. She barely had a moment to secure herself before she was dragged onwards and upwards, moving through a sea of questioning shadows and lurking dangers. There was great power in the forbidden zone, she realised numbly. It looked harmless to the naked eye, but she could sense immense strata of power running in directions she couldn't comprehend. She remembered what Isabella had said and shuddered. The forbidden zone was intimately linked to the Godly Realm.

Towering buildings – ghostly structures – rose up in front of her. They were blurred shapes, strangely built … ziggurats and pyramids that looked as if they'd been designed for something other than humans. They looked *wrong* to her, as if there was something about them her mind couldn't grasp. She thought she saw *things* moving through the corridors, but she couldn't look at them directly. They just seemed to slip away from her gaze.

The call pulled her onwards, through the translucent buildings and into a wide open place. A stone altar sat at the very centre of the courtyard, surrounded by a small army of men and women. They wore long white robes that made them look as if they were going to their wedding … she shivered as her presence was drawn towards and through them. Beyond the white-robes, she could see the red-robed creatures standing guard. She thought they could see her, but … they ignored her. They knew she couldn't hurt them.

I hurt you before, Silverdale thought. *I got away from you …*

But this time was different. This time, she had no control. She drifted over the crowd, trying to absorb as much detail as possible. Ruby lay on the altar, her hands and feet chained to the stone. She was screaming – the invisible gag was gone – but no one seemed to care. Sofia stood beside her, one hand resting on her sister's forehead. Emetine stood in front of the crowd, addressing them. Silverdale couldn't make out the words – the growing heartbeat seemed to drown out everything else – but the crowd ate it up with spoons. They chanted, stamping their feet in unison. Silverdale felt her vision widen, catching sight of the threads linking the worshippers to Emetine … and beyond. They'd given themselves to their god.

Sofia looked up. Silverdale stared at her. Sofia was no longer entirely human, not on the astral plane. She was beautiful, yet it was an icy painted beauty … as if it were the smile on the face of the tiger. There was nothing remotely vulnerable about her, not any longer. She said nothing, but she dominated the scene. Threads glowed around her, one reaching out and *through* Silverdale. She looked down, alarmed, but it didn't seem to be linked to *her*. And yet, it felt weirdly familiar. It called to Silverdale in a way that felt almost like ... *home*.

"The moon has risen," Sofia said. It was hard to tell if she was actually *speaking* – the words echoed in Silverdale's head without seeming to pass through her ears – but she had no trouble hearing. "We begin."

Silverdale turned, just in time to see a pair of worshippers walk out of the crowd, pulling silver knives out of their robes. She heard a squeak from Ruby as the worshippers brandished their weapons – for a horrible moment, Silverdale thought they were going to *stab* Ruby – and then they stabbed themselves. Blood splattered to the stone, droplets falling on the altar. A wave of dark energy, pregnant with menace, flared through the air as the bodies fell to the ground and lay still. Silverdale recoiled in horror as the energy brushed against her, before it went elsewhere. Sofia and Emetine were channelling it into the Godly Realm.

She tried to pull back as another pair of worshippers killed themselves, then another and another ... a small pile of bodies was starting to appear beside the altar. Ruby looked to have fainted, unable to bear the sight any longer. Silverdale tried desperately to pull away, to look away from the growing horror. But whatever force was binding her in place wouldn't *let* her look away. It wanted her to bear witness. She tried to look at her sister, her form glowing ever brighter as more and more worshippers threw their lives away, but ... she was held captive, unable to escape.

A low chant echoed through the air. Silverdale tried to catch the name, but ... it was muffled, obscured by the growing surge of energy. The entity behind Sofia and Emetine was emerging into the light, growing stronger and stronger with each dead worshipper. Blood pooled on the stone, dripping into the ancient temple ... Silverdale knew, with a certainty that could not be denied, that it *was* a temple. She could sense dark *things* lurking on the edge of reality, waiting to be born. She shuddered, trying to look away. But they refused to let her go …

Sofia caught her eye. "Bear witness," she said. "Watch and remember."

Silverdale wanted to argue, but she couldn't move. Her ghostly self was frozen, unable to do anything but watch. Sofia *knew* she was there. Terror roared through her head, mocking her … she knew, all too well, that when the entity emerged she'd be brushed aside … they'd *all* be brushed aside. The entity was slipping back into the world …

And then she fell back into her body. It hurt. Her body was hurting so badly … she looked up into Isabella's eyes. She was holding Silverdale gently, but firmly. Silverdale's throat was dry. She could barely speak. Her face hurt … Isabella had slapped her, perhaps more than once. Silverdale found it hard to care. Isabella might just have saved her life.

She tried to stumble to her feet, but her legs refused to cooperate. Her entire body felt black and blue … had she fallen off the horse? Or … or what? She'd never been in such agony. And yet, she could think …

"They've started," she said. Silver light ghosted across the valley. The moon was rising. Silverdale could feel it calling to her, on a level she couldn't deny. "They're killing themselves. And they're …"

She felt her stomach heave. "I …"

"Keep her here," Reginald ordered. His voice was very firm. "The rest of us will go on."

"Hurry," Silverdale urged. She wanted to argue, to insist that she came with them, but she was in too much pain. Had she been drugged? Or … or enchanted? She didn't know. It didn't matter. Her thoughts were already starting to break up. "They've already started."

Chapter Thirty-Seven

Reginald tried not to worry about Silverdale as he spurred his horse up the darkening road, hoping and praying that they didn't encounter any traps. A skilled force of cavalrymen would have no trouble at all delaying them, simply by scattering caltrops or placing a handful of archers in the trees to snipe at the horsemen as they rode towards the ancient structure. But nothing materialised out of the darkness ... he allowed himself a moment of relief, mingled with a flicker of amusement. Neither Sofia nor Emetine had led troops in battle. They might not have realised just how easy it would be to slow him down.

A faint light – a flickering light that was somehow wrong – shone in the distance, illuminating the ruined structure. Ghostly shapes hung in the air, as if they were riding through an entire ghostly city. Reginald blinked hard. The images vanished, but the light remained. It felt somehow *wrong*, as if it was burning into his very soul. He tried to look away, even as a lone shaft of moonlight stabbed down the valley and into the structure. It felt ... as if the entire world was holding its breath, waiting to see what would happen.

Sergeant Ruthven pulled up beside him. "The ground's getting rough, Your Highness."

Reginald nodded, stiffly. He'd hoped to get closer before they had to abandon the horses, but ... Sergeant Ruthven was right. The ground, what little he could see in the semi-darkness, was torn and broken, as if some angry god had ripped the city apart with his bare hands. He shuddered at the thought as he dismounted, drawing his iron blade in one smooth motion. That wasn't impossible, not now. The entire structure might have been smashed by one of the entities ...

He hissed orders as his men formed up, readying themselves for the fight. They'd probably be irked at fighting on foot, rather than riding their beloved mounts, but they had no choice. Reginald would have preferred to bring infantry, yet … they simply hadn't had time. A small force of cavalry was their only hope. He wished, as he braced himself for the fight, that they'd had time to listen to Silverdale. She'd seen what was happening, up ahead. She could have told them what to expect.

The thought didn't please him. It was hard enough to take Isabella into combat, even though he knew she'd been fighting for almost as long as himself. Silverdale … he shuddered to think what could happen to her in the middle of a pitched battle, particularly if she didn't have the sense to turn and run. She wasn't weak, but she wasn't very strong either. She could barely carry a sword. A knight in armour, in the dead of night, might cut her down without ever realising who he'd killed. Her body might never be found.

He glanced at Isabella, then motioned for his men to start walking towards the structure. A faint sound echoed through the air, a chant that blurred into a single ominous dirge. He hefted his sword as the buildings grew closer, trying not to look at them directly. They seemed normal until he looked at them, whereupon they started to shift into something else. He'd never seen anything like it, not even on the Summer Isle. It made him wonder why his father had never been told why the forbidden zone was forbidden. People tended to act smarter when they genuinely understood the threat.

Or they start plotting to take advantage of it, Reginald thought, coldly. He knew the dangers, but he'd seen the entities. Others might not realise how deadly the entities could become until it was far too late. *What wouldn't a man do for power?*

He shivered at the thought as the sound grew louder. There had to be hundreds of men crammed into the structure, hundreds … he frowned, remembering the empty towns and villages they'd ridden through. Had they been called to the ritual? Or … had they simply fled to the hills? He didn't blame them, but … he shuddered, feeling as if the world was shifting underneath him. He'd been so focused on Sofia and Emetine – and revolting noblemen – that he might have missed the real threat. If *he'd* been born a commoner, and found himself forced to watch noblemen riding through the fields and abusing everyone below them, would he not want to trade places? Would he not sell his soul for a shot at revenge?

We passed one manor that was burned to the ground, he thought. *How many others are there?*

Something *flickered* at the corner of his eye. He snapped into a defensive position as a red monk appeared out of nowhere, rushing towards him with inhuman speed. Reginald stabbed out with his sword, throwing good technique to the winds. There was no need for elegance, not with an iron blade. The creature *yowled* – the sound hammered against his very soul – and collapsed in a heap. Its body flickered, then snapped out of existence. Another one appeared, reaching for him with giant clawed hands. Reginald beheaded it with a stroke, watching dispassionately as it hit the ground. The robes crumbled to dust, revealing a monstrous parody of the human form. Reginald retched, knowing the poor bastard had once been human. The entities had warped and twisted him into a monster.

Isabella stepped up to cover his back as more and more red monks appeared out of nowhere, slicing through two of them with effortless ease. A third struck out at Reginald, hitting his chest plate hard enough to leave a dent. He grunted in pain, then killed the creature with a sidelong blow. His old duelling master would have thrown a fit – the old bastard would have swatted his hands, just to make it clear there was no room for showboating in swordsmanship – but it worked. A single cut from a cold iron blade was enough to kill the overshadowed men.

"We have to get closer," Isabella called. "We're running out of time."

Reginald nodded, sensing more than seeing another trio of monks appearing out of nowhere. They were coming out of the Godly Realm itself, channelled from their base and thrown into the battle ... he shuddered, realising – again – that the old world was gone. There was no way to keep someone from massing an army on the other side of the continent and then teleporting it into the fray. He wondered, morbidly, just how long it would be before kings and princes started making deals with the entities. They'd be desperate to ensure their rivals didn't make deals first. And now, there was no unified power that could tell them no.

We have to rebuild the Empire, Reginald told himself, as he cut down another monk. The monks were losing badly, but they were slowing him down. And they were expendable. Their master could replace them, easily. He … he saw one of his men die and shuddered, knowing there'd be no replacement. They were being worn down. *And yet, how are we going to rebuild it?*

He put the thought aside as the ground heaved, a yawning pit opening up behind him. He glanced at Isabella, then ran forward, cutting through a pair of monks. The pit kept growing, threatening to bring the remainder of the structure crashing down. He could *feel* things pressing against his mind, mocking him. It felt as if the entire world was on the verge of falling into the void … or, perhaps, the void was coming to him. Isabella let out a low moan, pressing one hand to her head as she stumbled. Reginald caught her and dragged her onwards, ducking a stone flying through the air. The red monks – or their master – had come up with a new plan.

"He's coming," Isabella said. She sounded, just for a moment, like a frightened little girl. "I can *feel* him."

"Shit," Reginald muttered.

He decapitated another monk, then risked a glance behind him. Seven of his men were missing, presumed dead. Five more were barely holding their own. He saw one of them torn to pieces by a monk, blood and gore flying everywhere. The remainder … he cursed under his breath as he realised they were not only outnumbered, but bogged down. They were running out of time. They might not be able to make it to the ritual and stop it before they ran out of time completely.

She's gone mad, he thought, desperately. *Sofia doesn't care what she's unleashing as long as she comes out on top.*

He felt a wave of *something* shimmering through the air and shuddered. "I'll cover you," he shouted, kicking one of the monks in the chest. It felt as if he'd kicked a stone wall. He stabbed the creature a second later and watched it die. "You get up there and stop the ritual!"

Isabella nodded. "Yes, Your Highness."

***

It was hard, so hard, to *think*. Isabella felt trapped, caught between two worlds ... three, perhaps. Something was looming at the back of her mind, pressing against her thoughts as if it truly *was* in her mind. Her vision was blurred, utterly confused. She thought she saw two structures – a ruined building and an intact temple – existing in the same space and time. The laws she knew, the laws of reality itself, were steadily breaking down. And an entity was imposing itself on the world.

She hated to leave Reginald, but she knew the ritual *had* to be stopped. She gritted her teeth, muttering a charm she'd learnt from Mother Lembu as she ran forwards. It seemed to work. The red monks ignored her as they walked out of the Godly Realm, their mere presence polluting the world until they were cut down by Reginald and his remaining soldiers. Isabella knew, all too well, that the good guys were being ground down. She wondered, as she scrambled over a half-translucent piece of stone, where the red monks were *coming* from. They couldn't have been created from nothing ...

If the entities have enough power, they could do anything. Her tutors had told her, more than once, that one could do *anything* with enough power. It was an article of faith for them, although they'd never been able to gather the power to do something *really* special. Isabella wondered, sourly, what they'd make of the entities. Would they envy them? Or would they try to *use* them? *Maybe they can create life from nothingness.*

She scrambled up a half-ruined stairwell and peered into the courtyard. An eerie light pervaded the structure, illuminating a scene of pure horror. Hundreds of bodies surrounded an altar, with a girl lying in bloodstained robes. She looked like an older version of Silverdale, right down to the long blonde hair. Ruby, Isabella guessed. Sofia and Emetine stood behind the altar, watching coldly as pairs of worshippers walked up to the altar and killed themselves. Isabella sensed great waves of sacrifice surging into the Godly Realm, giving the entity the power it needed to manifest in the human world. It was already coming, pressing against the boundaries of reality. In a way, she realised numbly, it was already *here*. She could sense it, drifting behind Sofia. The older woman was tied to the god.

Not a god, she thought, savagely. She didn't dare start thinking of the entities as *gods,* particularly not here. *It's not all-powerful.*

A hand caught her shoulder and yanked her back. She rolled, dodging a blow that would have taken her head off if she'd stayed still. The worshipper was a woman – a farmwoman, by her dress – her eyes alight with fanaticism. She was chanting loudly, the words blurring into a single grumbling sound. Isabella gritted her teeth, brought her legs up and kicked the woman as hard as she could. The woman buckled, but didn't drop. Farmwomen were always strong. Anyone who thought they were weak had never worked on a farm.

Isabella ducked another blow, then drew her knife from her sleeve and threw it at the farmwoman. She staggered as the blade entered her throat, then stumbled and fell to the ground. Isabella yanked back her knife and watched, grimly, as the woman bled to death. She had to be more than *just* a worshipper, if she'd been able to *see* Isabella despite the concealment spell. A priestess? Or someone smart enough to *bargain* with the entities, rather than merely submitting herself unconditionally? She looked human enough, despite everything. Her body wasn't crumbling into dust.

The chanting grew louder. Isabella stood and peered towards the altar. The last handful of worshippers were killing themselves now, their bodies dripping blood over the stone. Their life energies were bleeding away, touching something buried deep *below* the stone ... Isabella had a sudden vision of the temple being built to *contain* something, to keep it buried under layer upon layer of solid stone. Whoever had built it had been trying to keep something underground ... her head span as wave after wave of energy brushed against her soul. It was growing harder to think ...

Sofia stepped forward as the last of the worshippers died. She held a single golden sword in her hand, glowing with an eerie light of its own. Isabella guessed that it was a relic, probably something from the very early days. The king would have had a sword to symbolise his authority ... she cursed, realising that the blade *was*, in some sense, the king's authority. They hadn't thought to look for the king's crown, let alone his sword. She cursed her mistake as she lifted her knife. Sofia would have to die. There was no way around it.

A hand caught hers, yanking her back. Isabella struggled, but the grip was unbreakable. She looked up and saw Emetine, smiling at her. There was nothing human about her now, either. Her face crawled with … *things*, lurking under her flesh. Strange shapes moved around her, faint hints of something greater hidden under her skin. Isabella felt her skin *creep* as she looked at the older woman. Emetine had always been beautiful, but now she looked … diseased. Just looking at her made Isabella feel sick.

"Let me go," Isabella said. She scrambled for the other iron blade in her belt, but Emetine caught her hands and wrenched them behind her back before she could draw it. "Don't you know what …"

Emetine pressed her against the stone wall, giggling like a schoolgirl. Isabella struggled, but it was futile. She'd met men who were stronger than her – she'd learnt to fight dirty because she *knew* men were stronger – but Emetine was the strongest person she'd ever met. The woman seemed to manhandle her effortlessly, laughing at Isabella's attempts to free herself. She even ignored a kick that would have put a grown man on the ground, probably with a broken knee. Isabella tried not to wince. Her foot felt as if she'd slammed it into a stone wall.

"Your time is up," Emetine hissed. Her voice was as inhuman as the rest of her. She was no longer the seductive woman Isabella had met, a lifetime ago. "Our lord will soon be born. And then the world will plunge into fire and ice."

Isabella twisted her head, trying to look at her. Emetine was shifting, translucent tentacles flickering around her. She tried to peer at her through the Godly Realm and shivered, repulsed by a flaring mass of tentacles that seemed to co-exist with the older woman. It was hard to believe that *anyone* could mistake her for human, not now. One didn't need to look through other planes to know that something was deeply wrong.

"Listen to me," she said. In the distance, she could hear Sofia chanting. The world seemed to fall silent, leaving her words the only sound hanging on the air. "You can't do this."

"We can. We will." Emetine hefted Isabella up so she

could see Sofia undoing Ruby's chains and raising the blade. "This world will become ours."

"You'll destroy everything," Isabella protested. She'd never been so helpless. Never. She could see the blade glinting in the light, preparing for the final sacrifice. Threads of light ran around the altar, feeding power into the Godly Realm. She could practically *see* something materialising above the altar, as if the sacrifice had become inevitable. "Listen to me …"

Emetine's grip tightened. "I have power now," she hissed. She twisted Isabella's arm until she cried out in pain. "Do you think I would give it up? For you? For *anyone*?"

"No." Isabella forced herself to think. Emetine was holding her too firmly. She didn't have a hope of breaking free, yet … she gritted her teeth, reaching out to the Godly Realm. There were options, symbolic options. If she could call on them … Silverdale had touched things in the Godly Realm, if she'd told the truth. Isabella should be able to do it too. "I think you've become a maddened animal who needs to be put down."

She cursed under her breath. Emetine was holding her too tightly, in both realms. She couldn't slip away. Her magic failed when she tried to call on it. She kicked out again, but this time she couldn't even *touch* the older woman. Emetine was in complete control. The sword was starting to descend. Ruby was doomed. The world was doomed with her …

"Let go of her," a voice snapped. Reginald was standing behind them, sword in hand. "Now!"

Emetine's grip weakened, just for a second, as she dodged Reginald's sword. Isabella didn't hesitate. There was no time. She reached out through the Godly Realm, calling on all of her remaining power …

… And found herself staring up at Sofia as the blade came down.

Chapter Thirty-Eight

Sofia hesitated, just for a second.

Isabella didn't. She drew back her legs and kicked up as hard as she could. Sofia recoiled, too late. Isabella's feet struck her arm and sent the blade clattering to the ground. Sofia bit out a word Isabella didn't recognise and hit out with her other arm. Isabella twisted, grunting in pain as Sofia struck her chest. The blow hurt, but not enough to slow her down. She rolled over and threw herself at Sofia as hard as she could, slamming into her with all the force she could muster. The princess was stronger than she looked, but she wasn't as inhumanly strong as Emetine. She fell backwards and cracked her skull into the ground. Isabella could have sworn she saw cracks underneath the younger woman's head.

"Damn you," Sofia growled. She sounded more animal than man. Her arms twisted, as if they were forming claws. "What have you done?"

"Stopped you," Isabella said, drawing back. Sofia should be out cold, yet … she was talking normally. "This is madness …"

The world twisted around her. She heard someone cry out – she wasn't sure who – as the sense of power grew stronger. Ruby hadn't been sacrificed, but … Isabella could still feel the presence looming over the scene, waiting to be born. She braced herself, then slammed Sofia's head into the stone as hard as she could. If she could knock the princess out, she could buy time … time to deal with Emetine, time to safeguard the kingdom. But the blow didn't seem to do more than daze Sofia. Her hand lashed out and caught the sword, lifting it effortlessly as she swept out towards Isabella. Isabella drew her dagger from her belt and blocked the sword, a move she would never have risked if she hadn't been desperate. The impact nearly broke her wrist. The pain almost made her drop the dagger.

"I am the rightful ruler of this kingdom," Sofia shouted. Her words pounded on the air, drumming into Isabella's very soul. The sword was glowing with an unearthly light. "And I will never give it up."

Isabella stumbled backwards, bumping against the altar. She saw Sofia's eyes light up as she lunged forward, clearly intending to sacrifice Isabella in Ruby's place. Isabella had no idea if that would work, but she didn't want to find out the hard way. She dodged a thrust that would have skewered her, then forced herself forward again and slammed into Sofia. The princess had no formal training, according to Reginald, but she fought like a possessed wildcat. Isabella had to fight desperately to hold Sofia down and force her to let go of the sword. The light faded as soon as Sofia let go. Isabella caught the blade, only to discover that she couldn't budge it. The blade felt impossibly heavy.

Sofia laughed, madly. "Only the rightful ruler can wield the blade!"

"Shut up." Isabella pounded Sofia's head into the stone, again and again. It should have smashed her skull to a pulp, but ... the blows seemed to have no impact. It felt like a bad dream, a nightmare from which she would never escape. "Shut up!"

She heard Reginald cry out and looked up, just in time to see Emetine leap right across the courtyard and land neatly on top of the altar. She was smiling, even as blood dripped from her hands and splashed on the stone. Isabella sensed a sudden surge of power and cursed, out loud, as Emetine's form grew and twisted in directions she couldn't follow. The world span around them as the presence started to manifest, overwriting Emetine and replacing her with itself. She cringed back, feeling as if she was a tiny creature in a world of giants. Something was scrabbling on the walls of reality, the sound tearing at her thoughts. It wanted in. It wanted ...

"We win." Emetine's voice thundered on the air. "We win!"

Sofia thrust upwards, shoving Isabella back. "We win!"

Isabella ducked a blow that threatened to take her head off and forced herself to concentrate. The pressure was almost overwhelming, as if the entire Godly Realm was pressing down on her ... as if it was pressing down on the entire human world. Vast slow thoughts hammered through her skull, each one promising death and destruction on a scale she couldn't even begin to imagine. She called out in desperation, but no one answered. None of the entities could come to her, not now. There was only *the* entity and it wanted her dead. She would merely be the first to die.

"Yes," Sofia shouted. She threw Isabella back, springing to her feet. "Come to me!"

Reginald appeared behind her, wrapping his arms around her. Sofia struggled, but couldn't break free. Isabella forced herself to stand, despite the pain, despite the omnipresent *din* that was making it impossible to *think*. Something in her recognised it, something in her wanted to throw herself to her knees and *submit* to it. She bit her lip as Emetine's form glowed white, brilliant light – sickly light – almost blinding her as it threw the entire scene into sharp relief. Emetine was so *real* that everyone else was nothing more than shadows. The entire world felt translucent, as if it was breaking down into madness. She felt as if she didn't dare move for fear of making things worse …

She clutched the other dagger from her belt and threw it, aiming at the High Priestess. The dagger turned to water as it reached her, droplets splashing in all directions. Emetine smiled at her, a mocking smile that burned at Isabella's soul. She could *feel* the presence growing stronger, imposing itself upon reality. Was there anything that could stop it now?

They never managed to complete the ritual, she thought. It gave her hope, even though she knew it wasn't enough. *And they're tying the entity to its servant …*

She dug her fingernails into her palm, hard enough to draw blood. Power – her power – bubbled around her, slowly flowing into the Godly Realm. She reached out, allowing the blood to lead her thoughts towards the entity. It was twisting the Godly Realm itself – she had an impression of the entire universe screaming in agony – but it wasn't in complete control. Not yet. She couldn't stop it from materialising, from turning Emetine into something that could play host to its power and glory, but … she could hamper it. She could cripple it.

Her thoughts threatened to shatter. Madness yammered at the back of her mind. She drew more blood, trying to focus

... no, *not* to focus. She had to let the power lead her, she had to let it blur into the maelstrom ...she heard someone scream in rage and frustration and anger as she guided the power into something else. The world twisted around Emetine and she vanished in a flash of light. Isabella heard a thunderclap, felt air rushing towards her ... and collapsed, falling to the ground like a puppet whose strings had been cut. The entity was gone. Emetine was gone. The power was gone ...

She swallowed, hard. The entity wasn't *gone*. It was merely ... *elsewhere*. She could feel it at the back of her mind, a sour taste at the back of her throat. It had been reborn, even though it had been crippled. Emetine had surrendered herself completely to her master. And it was loose. Isabella tried to reach out, to feel where it might be, but came up with nothing. The only upside was that she thought the entity was a *long* way away.

Reality rushed in as she slowly pushed herself to her feet. Her arms and feet and clothes were stained with blood, little of it hers. She felt ... she felt as if she'd been beaten black and blue, her body battered to within an inch of her life. Emetine hadn't been human, not any longer. Isabella had been in fights with bigger and stronger men that hadn't been anything like so one-sided. If Emetine had snapped her neck instead of toying with her ...

Emetine is gone, Isabella thought, numbly. She wondered, morbidly, if she should feel *sorry* for the older woman. It wasn't as if she hadn't had *reasons* to be disconcerted. Isabella could swear to that, if she wished. But none of her legitimate grievances justified destroying the entire world. It was treason against humanity, a crime on an unimaginable scale. *Emetine is gone and something is wearing her body.*

She shuddered, feeling an urge to throw up. The thought alone was enough to bring the *sense* of the entity into prominence. It was polluting the land itself, poisoning the air ... poisoning the mental plane and reaching out to touch everyone's nightmares. Isabella knew, now, how the entities had been banished so long ago. It was obvious. But she also knew it would never happen again. They'd chosen their time well, if such creatures could be said to choose anything. The world would be theirs, in time.

"We'll stop them," she muttered, as she brushed her hands down her shirt. Her eyes ached, as if they'd been permanently damaged. The moonlight wasn't bright enough to drive away the shadows. "We'll stop them."

But, in truth, she had no idea how they *could*. Not yet.

"Let me go," Sofia said. "Let me go!"

Isabella looked up. Reginald was still holding Sofia tightly, his arms pinning hers to her side. She couldn't break free, but it didn't keep her from struggling. Reginald was injured, blood dripping down his face and staining their clothes ... Isabella felt her stomach churn. Emetine had used *Reginald's* blood to complete the ritual, the modified ritual. She told herself, firmly, that Reginald wasn't dead. The ritual had been weakened. She just hoped it had been weakened enough to allow them a chance to banish the entities once again.

"Let me go," Sofia repeated. "I am the ruler ..."

"Not any longer." Reginald's voice was quiet, but there was an undertone of bitterness Isabella didn't like. "Sofia, calm down. It's over."

Isabella winced as it dawned on her that Reginald *couldn't* let his sister go free. Or even imprison her. Sofia would have to be hanged, just to make it clear that her string of crimes wouldn't go unpunished. And then ... she picked up her dagger, wondering if she should cut Sofia's throat herself and save Reginald passing judgement on his sister. But he'd never forgive her. She knew that all too well.

"It isn't over," Sofia insisted. "He will return! And I will ..."

Reginald looked at Sergeant Ruthven as he walked up and stood next to Isabella. "How bad was it?"

"Seventeen men are dead, three more badly injured," Sergeant Ruthven said. "The Red Monks have retreated, for the moment."

"Vanished back into the Godly Realm," Isabella said. She wondered, grimly, just where they'd come from. She had the uneasy sense that they'd been outplayed. "We haven't seen the last of them."

"He has risen!" Sofia stopped struggling and stood upwards, her eyes meeting Isabella's. "And you will die. You will *all* die. The kingdom will pay in fire and blood for defying me."

"No," Reginald said, quietly. "We'll stop him."

Sofia laughed. Her eyes remained fixed on Isabella's. "Your wedding night will be a sham," she said. "You'll give it up for nothing. Believe me."

Her eyes moved to Reginald's. "Your first child will break your heart."

Reginald tightened his grip. "Enough!"

"No." Sofia smirked at him. "It will *never* be enough."

Reginald ignored her. Instead, he looked at Sergeant Ruthven. "Have the entire area swept," he said, as he pulled Sofia away from the bloodstained altar. "If there are any of the cultists left alive, bind them and bring them back with us. And have Ruby taken back to Silverdale. They can look after each other."

"Ruby offered her life willingly," Sofia said. "She knew the price and she paid it gladly."

Isabella saw Reginald's face darken, but he refused to rise to the bait. "Isabella? Are you alright?"

"I've been better," Isabella said. She was still aching. Her magic felt raw, as if she'd pushed it to the limit even though she'd barely used it. She wanted a warm bath and a good night's sleep, perhaps not in that order. But she'd have to wait until they got back to Havelock. She doubted anywhere between the forbidden zone and the castle was *safe*. "Yourself?"

"My brother will not make a good husband," Sofia said, nastily. She spat, making Isabella wonder how Sofia knew Reginald had asked Isabella to marry him. "You'll regret marrying my brother. He'll treat you like an bauble on his arm, then work you to death bearing his children and beat you if you refuse to have any more …"

"Be quiet," Reginald snapped.

"You see?" Sofia smirked, again. "He's already telling women to shut up."

Isabella rolled her eyes, then glanced at Reginald. "What do you want to do with her?"

"Bind her, search her *thoroughly*, march her back home." Reginald still sounded bitter. "I'll pass formal judgement on her when we're back at the castle."

Sofia spat, again. "You're not the Regent," she said. "I

am. And this is treason."

"Yeah," Reginald said. He didn't sound as though he believed her. "Someday you'll have to explain to me how hexing one's father, who happens to be the *king*, isn't treason. I look forward to hearing the explanation immensely."

"I would have reshaped the world," Sofia said. "I would have brought forth a new world."

She glared at Isabella, then switched her gaze to Reginald. "And all you will do is plunge it into war."

She lowered her voice. "What would *you* have done, my brother, if you'd been in my place?"

"I wouldn't have betrayed my father," Reginald said, harshly. "I know, you didn't have an easy time of it. I know, you were doomed to wed for the good of the realm. I know, you thought you had no way out. I know … it doesn't matter. You turned into a monster. I know, you went through hell. It doesn't justify a single damned thing you did."

He looked at Isabella. "Deal with her."

Isabella stepped forward, inspecting Sofia. Her bloodstained gown clung to her skin, suggesting she didn't have anywhere to hide *anything*. Isabella knew that was meaningless. There were all kinds of places one could hide a weapon, if one was prepared to take the risk of awkwardness or accidental injury. She'd even concealed a folded dagger in her vagina, when she'd joined the mercenaries. *That* would have been a nasty surprise for any would-be rapist. She wondered, as she started to run her hands down Sofia's body, what Reginald would make of *that*.

Sofia jerked, then slammed her head back as hard as she could, smacking Reginald right in the nose. His grip loosened, just enough to allow Sofia to break free. She slapped Isabella with terrific force, sending her sprawling to the ground. Isabella rolled over, ready to fight, but Sofia didn't go to her. Instead, she tried to pick up the sword. It refused to budge.

"I think you've lost the regency," Reginald said. His nose looked broken, but he'd had worse. He picked up the sword effortlessly as Sofia backed away, holding it in one hand. "Give up. It's over."

Sofia howled something incoherent and threw herself to the ground. For a moment, Isabella honestly thought Sofia was throwing a tantrum, then realised – too late – that Sofia had thrown herself on the dagger. *Isabella's* dagger. She started forward as Sofia sat upright, holding the dagger in one hand. It wasn't a big blade, but if she knew how to throw it … Isabella started forward, raising a ward. In hindsight, it might have been a mistake to charm the blade to punch through protective wards.

"I'll make you pay." Sofia looked torn between anger and fear. And, perhaps, the kind of feeling one has when one wishes that something – anything – had never happened. "I'll make you pay!"

There was a surge of power. Isabella held up a hand as Sofia touched the Godly Realm, threads of light shimmering into existence around her. Isabella let out a curse as Sofia reversed the dagger, then stabbed it into her womb. Her entire body convulsed, one of the threads of light snapping out of existence. Isabella heard Silverdale scream, the sound echoing through the air, as Sofia cut her chest open. A torrent of blood cascaded from her body and spilled on the ground. Sofia smiled, brightly, and died.

"… Fuck," Reginald managed. He sounded absolutely stunned. "What did she do?"

Isabella swallowed, hard. She knew what had happened. She knew … she heard Silverdale scream again and realised the younger girl knew too. Sofia hadn't just killed herself. She'd taken someone with her. Isabella knew, beyond a shadow of a doubt, just who was dead.

"Isabella." Reginald's voice was very quiet, but firm. "What did she do?"

"I'm sorry," Isabella said. She felt tears prickling at her eyes, although she wasn't sure why. It wasn't as if *she* had reason to mourn … perhaps she was mourning what it would cost Reginald and his family, rather than her personally. "But I think your father is dead."

Chapter Thirty-Nine

"This isn't how I wanted to be king," Reginald said. "And while I imagine some of you thought you'd be on my council, none of you expected it to be quite so soon."

He stood in front of the Privy Council, silently assessing the blank faces looking back at him. A handful were his nominees, but the remainder were his father's legacies. He scowled, inwardly. Technically, the Privy Council was dissolved upon the previous king's death and reformed by his successor, but Reginald wasn't king *yet*. The formal coronation wouldn't be held for another week. Until then … he had authority, both through his position *and* through command of the army, but he wasn't quite *king*. If the councillors wanted to cause trouble, they'd never have a better chance.

"The kingdom is in disarray," he said, quietly. "My sister did a great deal of damage. The north is in open revolt. Many other regions" – *and noblemen, including some of you,* he added silently – "are restless. Our economy has taken a beating and our enemies are eyeing our weaknesses and sharpening their swords. And – somewhere out there – there's a monster that wants to destroy the world."

He paused, wondering if anyone would dare challenge him. They'd be putting their careers at risk, but … they wouldn't have been appointed to the council if they hadn't been powerful in all senses of the words. None of them, with the possible exception of Earl Oxley, could be ignored. Even Oxley could cause a considerable amount of trouble if he were discontented. He kept his face expressionless with an effort. He'd barely started his reign – in truth, it hadn't started at all – and he already understood why his father had called upon his councillors as little as possible. The meeting might not go his way.

"We will meet these challenges and overcome them," he

continued. "Does anyone doubt it?"

"No, Your Majesty," Lord Holliston said.

Your Majesty, Reginald thought. It didn't feel right, not yet. *Father is dead and ...*

He pushed the thought aside. "We'll hold a second formal meeting after the coronation," he said. "If any of you do not wish to *continue* to serve on the council, let me know before then so I can nominate replacements. Until then ... are there any matters that need to be discussed as a matter of urgency?"

Captain-General Gars leaned forward. "The question of your marriage, Your Highness."

Reginald sensed the shimmer of ... concern echoing around the room and smiled. The men in front of him were all practised politicians. They knew better than to believe that Gars was taking a stand against Reginald, or even defying him in any way. They'd suspect – rightly – that Reginald had discussed the matter with his old friend and comrade before the meeting had been convened. A handful of glances flickered to Isabella, who was sitting at the far end of the table. They knew Reginald had asked her to marry him. No doubt they were torn between relief that the prince hadn't chosen the daughter of one of their rivals and irritation he hadn't chosen *their* daughter. And wondering at the wisdom of the king marrying a sorceress ...

"The question is not up for discussion," Reginald said. "I do not believe that it would be appropriate – now – for me to have a big and expensive wedding. A simple gathering and hand-fasting will be more than sufficient."

Gars, as planned, looked dissatisfied. "Your Highness, the question of who you will marry ..."

"Will be decided by me, as is my right," Reginald said, pleasantly. "My father never completed a set of marriage negotiations for me. I am not contractually bound to anyone. And that will not change."

He allowed the words to hover in the air for a long moment. No one was fooled, unless some of them were bigger idiots than he dared assume, but ...they'd know the issue wasn't on the table, that it would *never* be on the table. They'd also assume that anyone *else* who raised the issue risked his displeasure. And they'd be right. Reginald had no intention of allowing anyone to dictate to him. They could state their opinions, if they wished, but nothing more.

"The coronation will be held as planned," he said. He stood, indicating that the meeting was definitely over. "Dismissed."

The councillors rose as one and headed for the door, leaving Reginald and Isabella alone. Reginald wondered, in a moment of droll amusement, if they had qualms about leaving them without a chaperone. They were hardly the type of people to care about such things – and most of them had mistresses or pretty boys of their own – but they'd see it as something they could use to weaken him. Reginald shrugged, snorting at the thought. It wasn't something that bothered him. He was well aware that the marriage would be controversial even if they were both inexperienced virgins who'd never even met before their wedding.

"I was expecting that to go worse," Isabella commented, once the door was firmly closed and locked. "How many of them do you think are planning to put a knife in your back?"

"At least half of them, " Reginald said. "A couple were pains in my father's backside, a couple more have ties to the revolting barons … and now, with the Golden City gone, I imagine most of them are wondering how they could increase their own power at my expense. And even the ones who aren't are thinking about how they can secure their own positions if I weaken."

"Ouch." Isabella stood and paced over to him. "It's just like home, then."

"I imagine so." Reginald smiled as she sat down beside him, then sobered. "Will you marry me?"

Isabella's lips twitched. "Do I have a choice?"

Reginald winced, remembering Sofia's final words. "Yes. If you don't want to marry me, then go. I'll deal with the consequences."

"I know you would," Isabella said. She gave him an odd little smile. "Will you marry me?"

"If you'll have me," Reginald said. It might not be the flowery romance the bards sang about, let alone the courtly love he'd practised as a young man, but it would do. He wanted someone he could rely on, not someone with more beauty than brains. "I hope you don't want a big wedding."

"I'll settle for something simple, like you said." Isabella shrugged. "I'll have to write to my brother, of course. I need to tell him I'm getting married."

"Of course." Reginald wondered, suddenly, if Isabella's brother would object. *Could* he object? Reginald wouldn't have cared to bet on it, either way. "What will he say?"

"He'll probably question your sanity," Isabella said. "And then he'll give us his blessing ... insofar as it counts for anything, these days."

Reginald nodded, slowly. "I think ..."

He looked down at his hands. "I wish ... I wish my father had met you."

"He might not have liked me," Isabella pointed out. "Or he might have wanted you to marry for political reasons."

"He'd have liked you," Reginald said. "If Sofia hadn't killed him ..."

He felt his heart twist. It could not be denied, as some of his councillors had pointed out when they'd returned to the castle, that Sofia's suicide had saved him from ordering her execution. There'd been no way to avoid it, even though she was a royal princess. Either her father or her brother would have had to issue the orders condemning her, then watch as they were carried out. But ... he'd wanted his father to live. He'd loved his father. He hadn't wanted the throne, certainly not so soon. He'd wanted ...

Isabella rested a hand on his shoulder. "He was a good father," she said. "Better than mine."

"So you say," Reginald said. Isabella hadn't said *much* about her father, but – reading between the lines – Reginald had the impression that Isabella's father hadn't been a very nice man. "And I hope to be as good as him myself."

He winced, inwardly. They hadn't discussed children yet. Or ... any of the multitude of duties and suchlike that might be expected of a woman who married the Crown Prince. The woman who would be Queen. There was so much they needed to discuss, but ... he shook his head, slowly. They'd have to spend much of the week discussing it, if only because Isabella would be Queen very quickly. She'd have no time to ease into the role.

And Emetine is still out there somewhere, Reginald thought. Isabella and Silverdale both swore blind they could sense the entity, somewhere within the world. *What is she doing?*

There was a knock on the door. Reginald stood and opened it. Silverdale and Ruby stood there, Greta standing watch behind them. Reginald smiled at the maid, who blushed and lowered her eyes. Greta had been promoted to Silverdale's personal maid, a position that brought prestige as well as a higher salary. Reginald intended to make sure she married well, to someone who would love her and care for her as well as support her. Greta had saved his sister's life and soul.

"Reggie," Silverdale said. "May we come in?"

"Of course," Reginald said. He'd have to make sure his sisters watched council meetings, even if they couldn't sit at the table. And, somehow, try to make sure they had an easier time of it than their elder sister. "Greta, wait outside."

He closed the door and turned to face them. "How are you?"

Ruby shook her head. "Not good."

Reginald nodded. Ruby had always been fiery, the most stubborn of his sisters, the one who had constantly incurred the governess's anger ... Reginald smiled, remembering how he'd sent for the governess, in order to dismiss her, only to discover that the elder woman hadn't returned to the castle. Had she been a cultist? Or had she feared punishment for her conduct and chosen to abandon her post? Or ... it didn't matter. She'd failed to keep her charges safe and *that* was all that mattered.

"I keep having nightmares about *her*," Ruby said. "And Sofia, what she became. I don't know how to cope."

"It will get better," Isabella said, quietly.

"Not until we get rid of the creatures once and for all," Silverdale said. Her voice was harsh, for someone who was still – in so many ways – a child. Royal children had to grow up fast, but ... Silverdale had had no time to prepare herself for adolescence. "They're still out there, waiting for us."

"I know." Reginald had read the reports. His father's intelligence network had been badly weakened, but most of the operatives and observers were still in place. There were hundreds, perhaps thousands, of people who were worshipping the entities, in a country that was steadily becoming infested with supernatural creatures ... he let out a breath. The reports made it clear that the country was shifting under his feet. "We have to find him."

"I can help," Silverdale said, in a manner that made it clear that she expected him to say no. "I can find him …"

"You'll get your chance," Reginald said. "But we need more than just *you*."

"I have an idea," Isabella said. "But it will be risky."

Reginald had to smile. "Is it ever *safe*?"

Isabella didn't smile. "And it will cost us," she said. "We'll discuss it later."

"We can help," Silverdale said. "Really."

"Not here." Isabella's voice was so flat that Reginald *knew* she was hiding something. "This is something I have to do."

Reginald kept his face expressionless. Their relationship was *definitely* going to be a bumpy ride. He was quite looking forward to it, even though … everything he knew about romance and marriage suggested he should keep his wife out of danger. But Isabella would refuse to even *listen* if he suggested it. She was no weak-willed aristocratic daughter. She was someone used to fighting her corner …

He put the thought aside. "We'll hold the ceremony two days before the coronation," he said, bluntly. People would talk, but … it hardly mattered. Isabella wouldn't get pregnant quickly, of that he was sure. The chatterboxes would chatter until it dawned on them, seven months after the wedding, that the bride hadn't even put on weight. "Will you two be ready?"

"Of course, Reggie." Ruby shot Isabella a sidelong glance. "We will, of course, have to warn Isabella about the terrible danger of marrying you …"

Isabella laughed. "Is he more dangerous than a madman with a wand in one hand and a sword in the other?"

"Well …" Ruby drew the word out as much as possible. "He *can* get quite cross when *someone* borrows his horse without asking."

"I wasn't angry at you for borrowing the horse," Reginald said. Truthfully, he'd nearly forgotten the incident. He'd loved the horse, but the poor creature had died while Reginald had been on campaign. "I was mad at you for not mucking the beast out afterwards."

"Whatever." Ruby winked at Isabella. "And he was also

very angry when I asked one of his friends to dance."

Reginald resisted the urge to roll his eyes. "Isabella has met worse people," he said. "You can shut up now."

"You see?" Ruby giggled. "I have an *awful* brother."

"Better than mine," Isabella said. "Believe me."

Reginald squeezed her hand. "I do."

Silverdale looked at them. "Do you want us to do a dance? Or make a speech? Or … marry you."

"I'll have to have one of the prelates perform the ceremony," Reginald said, slowly. A royal wedding would normally be performed by the king. His heart ached, remembering his father before his death. The old man would have approved of Isabella, he was sure. And now … was Reginald supposed to marry himself? "Or maybe ask someone from the aristocracy …"

He shook his head. *That* would be a nightmare. Whoever got the job could cause a great deal of trouble, while everyone who *didn't* get the post would complain. Loudly. Maybe it would be better if he performed the ceremony himself. It would be awkward – he might accidentally marry himself, in all senses of the word – but doable. Or maybe he should just ask one of the new City Fathers. The old ones had been kicked out of office after giving Sofia the keys to the city.

"It might be better if Ruby or Silverdale performed the ceremony," Isabella said. "No one could dispute it."

"Not easily," Reginald agreed. People would talk about that too, but … whatever. It was the best of a set of bad options. "Ruby, start practising."

"Yes, Reggie." Ruby grinned at him. "Am I allowed to make a speech about how horrible you are in front of the gaping masses?"

"That depends," Reginald said. "Am *I* allowed to whip you in front of the gaping masses?"

Ruby scowled. "You're no fun."

"I don't think I get to be fun any longer," Reginald said. He was king, in fact if not – yet – in name. "And you two can go off now. I'll see you at dinner."

Ruby curtseyed, then retreated. Silverdale followed her. For a moment, it was easy to believe that nothing had changed over the last year, that they were still the same carefree girls he'd left behind. But they both carried scars within their souls, scars that could have been a great deal worse. Reginald watched them closing the door and scowled. There was nothing he could do to make things better, not for them. They'd have to get over it, somehow. If they could …

"They're good children," Isabella said. "I'll be teaching Silverdale how to use her talents, of course."

"Of course," Reginald agreed. "I … I can't stop thinking about Sofia either. Why? Why did she do it?"

Isabella met his eyes. "Do you want a honest answer?"

"Yes." Reginald looked back at her, evenly. "Always."

"We'll see." Isabella pulled back her sleeve to reveal a muscled arm. "I'm pretty much the strongest girl – woman – I've ever met, except for Emetine and she wasn't really *human* any longer. I worked hard to build up muscle … I even cheated a little, with potions and spells to build my strength. And I know how to use it too. I have fists" – she clenched hers – "and I have magic.

"And yet, most experienced men are stronger than me. *You* should be stronger than me, physically. Magically … there are men and women who were stronger than me, before the Golden City fell, but Sofia didn't have magic. Not *my* magic … she was always vulnerable, no matter what she did. She knew her father would eventually marry her off to someone and she'd always be at that person's mercy … my father was a bit like that too, magic or no magic. He had no qualms about beating me if I did something wrong. And, no matter how I fought, I couldn't stop him."

Reginald wanted to meet Isabella's father, just once. He could wrap his hands around the man's neck and squeeze, hard. And then … he pushed the impulse out of his mind. The old bastard was dead, gone to meet the gods. Reginald's lips quirked at the thought. *Which* gods?

"It wears you down," Isabella said, quietly. "It curdles you. It would have curdled me, if I hadn't managed to get myself disowned. And I had far more options open to me than Sofia ever did. Sofia … had none. And Emetine took advantage of it."

"Ruby and Silverdale won't have that problem," Reginald said. "I'll see to it."

"And what will you do," Isabella asked him, "when the

only way to get an alliance is to marry your sisters to a stranger?"

"I won't," Reginald said. "And I won't do it to our daughters either."

Isabella smiled, wryly. "I knew there was a reason I fell in love with you."

"And there I was thinking it was my handsome body," Reginald said. "I am so disappointed."

"Hah." Isabella sobered. "You remember what Sofia said about our wedding night?"

Reginald shivered. "Yes …?"

"I had an idea," Isabella said. "I think we can take advantage of it."

Chapter Forty

Isabella had never really *thought* about being married, not really. As a little girl, it was a mummy and daddy thing; as a teenager and a young adult, it was a fate to be avoided at all costs. And as a mercenary ... she'd known, all too well, that the only way to keep her comrades from treating her as a woman was to avoid *acting* like a woman. It hadn't sat well with her, but there'd been no choice. Who knew what they would have done if they'd believed, emotionally, that she was a woman?

She felt an odd string of emotions as she walked down the stairwell and into the former dungeons. The ceremony had been simple, hardly the kind of grand ceremonies that she'd attended as a child, but – somehow – the very simplicity had made it all the more powerful. The ring on her finger, passed down from Reginald's mother, felt heavy, as if it was more than *just* a ring. And the wedding night ... she glanced up at the stone ceiling, feeling a pang of guilt. She and Reginald had kissed, but they hadn't consummated their marriage. And, even though she'd discussed it with him as much as she'd dared before the ceremony, she knew he was disappointed. She was disappointed too. She'd wanted him more than she could say.

Nothing may be known until it is spoken, she reminded herself. She'd been careful, very careful. She hadn't dared discuss the plan with anyone, for fear of who – or what – might be listening. *And if this works ...*

Her lips tingled as she entered the large room, closing the door behind her. The staff had done as they'd been told, emptying the room, washing the walls and mopping the floors before leaving the room as pristine as possible. A pair of lanterns hung from above, their flickering light illuminating walls stained with blood or worse. The maids hadn't been able to clean the room completely. But they'd tried. That was all that mattered.

She took a moment to compose herself. She was a wife now. She had a husband and sisters-in-law … she smiled, remembering the time Ruby had tried to talk to her about manly urges and demands. It was funny … no, it wasn't *really* funny. Whoever had given Ruby the talk had made it sound terrifying, suggesting that Ruby was expected to lie still and endure a monstrous assault. Had Sofia gotten the same lecture? Isabella had no idea, but … she made a mental note to find out who'd given Ruby the lecture and do something horrible to her. No wonder Sofia had been so desperate to avoid marriage …

Isabella took a breath, then started to draw out the patterns on the floor. A circle, a handful of summoning and binding sigils … she checked them carefully, time and time again. The slightest mistake could be disastrous. Silverdale had offered to accompany her – the younger girl seemed to have guessed what Isabella had in mind – but Isabella had refused. If something went wrong, only one person would be at risk. And then … she wondered, sourly, just what Reginald would do. There was no way his enemies *wouldn't* take advantage of Reginald's wife dying on their wedding night. The stories would be unstoppable. Some of them might even be true.

She stepped back, taking one last look. The air seemed pregnant with possibility, as if someone was just *waiting* for her to begin. She fought down the urge to get on with it, checking and rechecking until she was entirely sure. Confidence was an important part of symbolic magic. Silverdale had managed as much as she had because she'd *known* she could do it. She still didn't know the potion Emetine had given her had been nothing more than water.

"Now," Isabella said. "We begin."

She felt the power begin to build as she drew a silver dagger from her belt and carefully sliced her palm open. Blood welled up, dripping over her fingers and splashing to the floor. There was no pain, save for a dull sense of discomfort. Isabella felt the power flow out, into the circle. The sigils seemed to come alive under her gaze. They were ready for her.

"I offer the sacrifice of my wedding night," Isabella said. She focused her mind on the thought. She should be upstairs, in Reginald's bed. They were man and wife now. They *needed* to consummate the match. "And I summon Lembu to my circle."

The power built rapidly, the call echoing into the Godly Realm. Isabella sensed resistance, as if Lembu – all three aspects of Lembu – didn't want to answer the call, but they had no choice. She'd offered a sacrifice, a sacrifice that meant something to her ... they *had* to answer. She braced herself, feeling a wind starting to blow even though she was deep underground ... power exploded, a flash of light forcing her to cover her eyes. When she uncovered them, the Crone was standing in the circle. Her mere presence was enough to weaken Isabella's resolve.

"What have you done?"

"I called you," Isabella said. She'd hoped for the Maiden or the Mother, not the Crone. The circle held the entity firmly, but ... it was hard, so hard, not to let the entity intimidate her. "And you are my prisoner."

The Crone took a step forward. Her face was a monstrously ugly blur. "Release me. Now."

"You cannot leave unless I bid you go," Isabella said. She'd worked *that* into the circle, doing her best to ensure that no one *else* could free the entity. "It's time for answers."

She forced herself to meet the entity's stare. "You *will* answer my questions, freely and completely," she said. "Or you will remain here forever."

"You know not what you do," the Crone stated, coldly. "If you do not release me ..."

"I think I understand you and yours a little better now." Isabella forced herself to look and sound confident. "And I think I understand you have far less power – here – than you led me to suppose."

The Crone said nothing. Isabella could feel her presence beating the air, pressing against Isabella's mind despite the circle. It felt as if she'd committed a transgression so terrible that she couldn't hope to atone, no matter what she did. It felt as if she'd failed someone who truly loved her, as if she'd raised a hand against her own true mother. It was hard, so hard, not to drop to her knees and beg forgiveness. She bit her lip, using the pain to focus. The entity was trying to use emotional blackmail, to all intents and purposes. And she knew herself to be effectively immune.

Who would have thought it? Isabella almost smiled at the irony. *Daddy's lessons came in handy after all.*

"First question," she said. "What *are* you? Really?"

The Crone smiled, coldly. "I will show you."

Isabella had no time to object before a wave of visions blasted into her mind, almost carrying her into the darkness. She fought hard to centre herself, to try to see the visions in order, but ... it was hard to focus. She had to bite her lip, again, to keep herself calm. She had to watch the visions ...

She saw a world. No, a universe. It was odd, to her eyes; the inhabitants were so utterly inhuman that they had nothing in common with her. There were concepts being displayed that were beyond her. It struck her, as time ran backwards and reality was unreality, that the beings themselves were concepts. They were living ideas, thoughts given shape and form. And they lived in a universe where there could be nothing else.

Until there was. She couldn't see when or how the contact was made, but suddenly two worlds were in contact. The result was utter devastation, for both worlds. She saw the Godly Realm reeling in agony, its inhabitants suddenly forced to comprehend concepts like the steady flow of time and a fixed view of reality; she saw the human world, madness spreading like a plague as human minds touched the conceptual entities ... the entities. The mere touch was enough to drive humans insane. Their world was shattered beyond repair ... both worlds were shattered beyond repair. And it birthed a whole new generation.

She saw newer entities taking shape, somehow bonding with humans to trade power for worship. She saw the newcomers turning on the older entities, pushing them further into the Godly Realm ... agony, to creatures who'd had no concept of distance until it exploded into their world. And then she saw the humans double-crossing their allies, banishing them completely from the human world. Except ... the links were too deep for them to be cut completely. The entities couldn't be expelled completely. And ...

"The Empire banished you because the Emperor spoke for the entire world," she said, as reality slammed back into her mind. "And now the Empire is gone."

The Crone seemed oddly amused. "We were trying to help you adapt to the new world," she said. Her voice brought visions of hundreds of millions of lesser creatures swarming the world, taking on shapes and forms drawn from humanity's worst nightmares. "And instead, you turned on us."

"You're not gods," Isabella said.

"Are you sure?" The Crone's amusement grew stronger. "We *are* your gods. You made us. We made you."

"You have power," Isabella said. "But I have power too."

The Crone seemed to falter. "We were trying to help you."

"That's what my father said," Isabella snapped. "He was fond of telling me that everything he did was for my own good. He'd claim it hurt him more than me, but" – she shook her head – "maybe he was right, from his point of view. So what? It wasn't right from *mine*."

"Let us help you," the Crone said. "I can take that burden from you …"

"You're begging," Isabella said. The other aspects had talked about the Crone as if she was a monster, not … an entity begging for freedom. It was pitiful, yet … oddly reassuring. "And I don't *want* you."

She took a moment to compose herself. "Your brother. The one who possessed Emetine. Where is he?"

The Crone smirked. "Here. There. Everywhere."

"I want a truthful answer," Isabella told her. "You are ordered to speak the truth."

"I *am* speaking the truth," the Crone said, in a superior tone that made Isabella want to hit her. "You bound me to speak the truth, didn't you? You just don't understand it."

Isabella gritted her teeth. "What is he …?"

The Crone cut her off. "Going to do? He's going to take your little world, and your people, and everything. You will become ours. You'll feed us. And we will grow beyond the limits imposed on us. Your time is running out. It has already run out."

"We'll stop you," Isabella said. She fought to hold on to the thought. "We'll banish you again."

"No," the Crone said. There was nothing but certainty in her voice. "You won't."

Isabella turned away, feeling as if she was exposing her

back to the enemy. She'd have to sit and think, to sort out what she'd have to ask next and what she'd tell Alden … and to tell Reginald, finally, what she'd done. Who knew what he'd say? Her lips quirked at the thought. Her husband might object to how she'd squandered their wedding night …

Your wedding night will be a sham, Sofia had said.

And she was right, Isabella thought, grimly. *I spent the time discovering the truth instead …*

She felt her blood run cold. If the Crone was right, the entities couldn't be banished. Not again.

And if that was true, the entire human race might be doomed to a fate worse than death.

End of Book II

The Story Will Conclude In:

The Truthful Lie

Coming Soon

Elsewhen Press

delivering outstanding new talents in speculative fiction

Visit the Elsewhen Press website at elsewhen.press for the latest information on all of our titles, authors and events; to read our blog; find out where to buy our books and ebooks; or to place an order.

Sign up for the Elsewhen Press InFlight Newsletter at elsewhen.press/newsletter

Bookworm series by Christopher G. Nuttall

Bookworm

Elaine, an inexperienced witch in Golden City, has her life turned upside down when she triggers a magical trap to end up with all the knowledge in the Great Library stuffed inside her head. Avoiding the Inquisition she tries to understand what has happened to her. But she is a pawn in the dark plans of one who wants the Grand Sorcerer's power.

Bookworm won the Gold Award in the Adult Fiction category of the 2013 Wishing Shelf Independent Book Awards.

ISBN: 9781908168320 (epub, kindle) / 9781908168221 (368pp, paperback)

Visit bit.ly/Bookworm-Nuttall

Bookworm II – The Very Ugly Duckling

Not every ugly duckling becomes a swan ...

In the wake of the disastrous attack on the Golden City, Lady Light Spinner has become Grand Sorceress and Elaine, the Bookworm, has been settling into her positions as Head Librarian and Privy Councillor.   But any hope of vanishing into her books is negated when a new magician of staggering power appears in the city, one whose abilities seem to defy the known laws of magic.

ISBN: 9781908168382 (epub, kindle) / 9781908168283 (432pp, paperback)

Visit bit.ly/Bookworm2-Nuttall

Bookworm III – The Best Laid Plans

Elaine and Johan prepare to leave Golden City, with Daria and Cass, to search for the Witch-King. But Elaine is arrested on the orders of a new Emperor, puppet of the Witch-King. She must escape and destroy him. Privy Councillors and Heads of the Great Houses have bowed to the Emperor. Only Elaine and her friends can prevent an all-out war.

ISBN: 9781908168764 (epub, kindle) / 9781908168665 (400pp, paperback)

Visit bit.ly/Bookworm3

Bookworm IV – Full Circle

Until now the Witch-King had remained hidden as a lich. But Elaine was intent on his destruction. Bonded to the unknowingly powerful Johan, she was the only other magician who understood the deeper layers of magic. As they slowly made their way towards the catacombs in Ida where his lich was hiding, he had to rely on the new Emperor to stop them.

ISBN: 9781908168948 (epub, kindle) / 9781908168849 (416pp, paperback)

Visit bit.ly/Bookworm4

Now available as audiobooks from Tantor

Christopher G. Nuttall's Royal Sorceress series

Book I: The Royal Sorceress

In an alternate history, the principles of magic, discovered in the 1770s, saw Britain win the American War of Independence. Master Thomas, the King's aged Royal Sorcerer, needs a successor with mastery of all magical powers. The only candidate, untrained & unacknowledged, is perfect in every way but one: the Royal College of Sorcerers has never admitted a girl before.

But even before Lady Gwendolyn Crichton can begin her training, London is plunged into chaos by a campaign of terrorist attacks co-ordinated by Jack, a powerful and rebellious magician.

ISBN: 9781908168184 (epub, kindle) / 9781908168085 (400pp, paperback)

Book II: The Great Game

After the uprising in London, Lady Gwendolyn Crichton is settling into her new position as Royal Sorceress and fighting the prejudice against her gender and age that seeks to prevent her from fulfilling her responsibilities. But when a senior magician is murdered in a locked room and Gwen is charged with finding the culprit, her inquiries lead her into a web of intrigue that combines international politics, widespread aristocratic blackmail, gambling dens and personal vendettas... and some of her discoveries hit dangerously close to home.

ISBN: 9781908168375 (epub, kindle) / 9781908168276 (400pp, paperback)

Book III: Necropolis

The British Empire is teetering on the brink of a war with France that may, for the first time, see magicians in the ranks on both sides. As Royal Sorceress, Gwen will be responsible for the Empire's magical resources when the time comes. But her adopted daughter Olivia, the only known living necromancer, has been kidnapped. Intelligence soon establishes that it was Russian agents who took Olivia, so an incognito Gwen joins a British diplomatic mission to St Petersburg.

ISBN: 9781908168726 (epub, kindle) / 9781908168627 (416pp, paperback)

Book IV: Sons of Liberty

War! South East England has been invaded, and Gwen and the Royal Sorcerers Corps are helping to fight off French magicians and drive the invaders back into the Channel. When an inexperienced major disobeys orders, sending two hundred hussars to their deaths, Gwen compels him to sit down and shut up but, in doing so, permanently damages his mind. Afterwards Lord Mycroft suggests she needs to be less prominent for a while. The colonies are also under attack, so he sends her to New York to train the few locals with any magical talent. She sets off on HMS Duke of India, along with Irene Adler and Irene's new apprentice Raechel Slater-Standish, accompanying a naval squadron and a regiment being sent to reinforce colonial defences. But even before they reach New York they meet armed opposition.

ISBN: 9781908168986 (epub, kindle) / 9781908168887 (416pp, paperback)

Visit bit.ly/RoyalSorceress

Now available as audiobooks from Tantor

Existence is
Elsewhen
Twenty stories from twenty great authors
including
Christopher G. Nuttall
John Gribbin
Rhys Hughes
Douglas Thompson

The title *Existence is Elsewhen* paraphrases the last sentence of André Breton's 1924 *Manifesto of Surrealism*, perfectly summing up the intent behind this anthology of stories from a wonderful collection of authors. Different worlds... different times. It's what Elsewhen Press has been about since we launched our first title in 2011.

Here, we present twenty science fiction stories for you to enjoy. We are delighted that headlining this collection is the fantastic John Gribbin, with a worrying vision of medical research in the near future. Future global healthcare is the theme of J A Christy's story; while the ultimate in spare part surgery is where Dave Weaver takes us. Edwin Hayward's search for a renewable protein source turns out to be digital; and Tanya Reimer's story with characters we think we know gives us pause for thought about another food we take for granted. Evolution is examined too, with Andy McKell's chilling tale of what states could become if genetics are used to drive policy. Similarly, Robin Moran's story explores the societal impact of an undesirable evolutionary trend; while Douglas Thompson provides a truly surreal warning of an impending disaster that will reverse evolution, with dire consequences.

On a lighter note, we have satire from Steve Harrison discovering who really owns the Earth (and why); and Ira Nayman, who uses the surreal alternative realities of his *Transdimensional Authority* series as the setting for a detective story mash-up of Agatha Christie and Dashiel Hammett. Pursuing the crime-solving theme, Peter Wolfe explores life, and death, on a space station; while Stefan Jackson follows a police investigation into some bizarre cold-blooded murders in a cyberpunk future. **Going into the past, albeit an 1831 set in the alternate Britain of his *Royal Sorceress* series, Christopher G. Nuttall reports on an investigation into a girl with strange powers.**

Strange powers in the present-day is the theme for Tej Turner, who tells a poignant tale of how extra-sensory perception makes it easier for a husband to bear his dying wife's last few days. Difficult decisions are the theme of Chloe Skye's heart-rending story exploring personal sacrifice. Relationships aren't always so close, as Susan Oke's tale demonstrates, when sibling rivalry is taken to the limit. Relationships are the backdrop to Peter R. Ellis's story where a spectacular mid-winter event on a newly- colonised distant planet involves a Madonna and Child. Coming right back to Earth and in what feels like an almost imminent future, Siobhan McVeigh tells a cautionary tale for anyone thinking of using technology to deflect the blame for their actions. Building on the remarkable setting of Pera from her *LiGa* series, and developing Pera's legendary *Book of Shadow*, Sanem Ozdural spins the creation myth of the first light tree in a lyrical and poetic song. Also exploring language, the master of fantastika and absurdism, Rhys Hughes, extrapolates the way in which language changes over time, with an entertaining result.

ISBN: 9781908168955 (epub, kindle) / ISBN: 9781908168856 (320pp paperback)
Visit bit.ly/ExistenceIsElsewhen

THE MAREK SERIES BY JULIET KEMP

BOOK 1:

THE DEEP AND SHINING DARK
A Locus Recommended Read in 2018

"A rich and memorable tale of political ambition, family and magic, set in an imagined city that feels as vibrant as the characters inhabiting it."
Aliette de Bodard
Nebula-award winning author of *The Tea Master and the Detective*

You know something's wrong when the cityangel turns up at your door
Magic within the city-state of Marek works without the need for bloodletting, unlike elsewhere in Teren, thanks to an agreement three hundred years ago between an angel and the founding fathers. It also ensures that political stability is protected from magical influence. Now, though, most sophisticates no longer even believe in magic *or* the cityangel.

But magic has suddenly stopped working, discovers Reb, one of the two sorcerers who survived a plague that wiped out virtually all of the rest. Soon she is forced to acknowledge that someone has deposed the cityangel without being able to replace it. Marcia, Heir to House Fereno, and one of the few in high society who is well-aware that magic still exists, stumbles across that same truth. But it is just one part of a much more ambitious plan to seize control of Marek.

Meanwhile, city Council members connive and conspire, unaware that they are being manipulated in a dangerous political game. A game that threatens the peace and security not just of the city, but all the states around the Oval Sea, including the shipboard traders of Salina upon whom Marek relies.

To stop the impending disaster, Reb and Marcia, despite their difference in status, must work together alongside the deposed cityangel and Jonas, a messenger from Salina. But first they must discover who is behind the plot, and each of them must try to decide who they can really trust.

ISBN: 9781911409342 (epub, kindle) / ISBN: 9781911409243 (272pp paperback)
Visit bit.ly/DeepShiningDark

BOOK 2:

SHADOW AND STORM

Never trust a demon… or a Teren politician
The annual visit by the Teren Throne's representative, the Lord Lieutenant, is merely a symbolic gesture. But this year the Lieutenant has been unexpectedly replaced and Marcia, Heir to House Fereno, suspects a new agenda.

Teren magic is enabled by bloodletting. A Teren magician will invoke a demon and bind them with blood. But demons are devious and if unleashed are sure to create havoc. The Teren way to stop them involves the letting of more of the magician's blood – often terminally. But if a young magician is being sought by an unleashed demon, their only hope may be to escape to Marek where the cityangel can keep the demon at bay. Probably.

Once again Reb, Cato, Jonas and Beckett must deal with a magical problem, while Marcia must tackle a serious political challenge to Marek's future.

ISBN: 9781911409595 (epub, kindle) / ISBN: 9781911409496 (336pp paperback)
Visit bit.ly/ShadowAndStorm

Thorns of a Black Rose

David Craig

Revenge and responsibility, confrontation and consequences.

A hot desert land of diverse peoples dealing with demons, mages, natural disasters ... and the Black Rose assassins.

On a quest for vengeance, Shukara arrives in the city of Mask having already endured two years of hardship and loss. Her pouch is stolen by Tamira, a young street-smart thief, who throws away some of the rarer reagents that Shukara needs for her magick. Tracking down the thief, and being unfamiliar with Mask, Shukara shows mercy to Tamira in exchange for her help in replacing what has been lost. Together they brave the intrigues of Mask, and soon discover that they have a mutual enemy in the Black Rose, an almost legendary band of merciless assassins. But this is just the start of their journeys…

Although set in an imaginary land, the scenery and peoples of *Thorns of a Black Rose* were inspired by Egypt, Morocco and the Sahara. Mask is a living, breathing city, from the prosperous Merchant Quarter whose residents struggle for wealth and power, to the Poor Quarter whose residents struggle just to survive. It is a coming of age tale for the young thief, Tamira, as well as a tale of vengeance and discovery. There is also a moral ambiguity in the story, with both the protagonists and antagonists learning that whatever their intentions or justification, actions have consequences.

ISBN: 9781911409557 (epub, kindle) / 9781911409458 (256pp paperback)
Visit bit.ly/ThornsOfABlackRose

Resurrection Men
The first book of the Sooty Feathers
David Craig

Glasgow 1893.
Wilton Hunt, a student, and Tam Foley, a laudanum-addicted pharmacist, are pursuing extra-curricular careers as body snatchers, or 'resurrection men', under cover of darkness. They exhume a girl's corpse, only for it to disappear while their backs are turned. Confused and in need of the money the body would have earnt them, they investigate the corpse's disappearance. They discover that bodies have started to turn up in the area with ripped-out throats and severe loss of blood, although not the one they lost. The police are being encouraged by powerful people to look the other way, and the deaths are going unreported by the press. As Hunt and Foley delve beneath the veneer of respectable society, they find themselves entangled in a dangerous underworld that is protected from scrutiny by the rich and powerful members of the elite but secretive Sooty Feathers Club.

Meanwhile, a mysterious circus arrives in the middle of the night, summoned to help avenge a betrayal two centuries old…

ISBN: 9781911409366 (epub, kindle) / ISBN: 9781911409267 (400pp paperback)
Visit bit.ly/ResurrectionMen

QUAESTOR
DAVID M ALLAN

When you're searching, you don't always find what you expect
In Carrhen some people have a magic power – they may be telekinetic, clairvoyant, stealthy, or able to manipulate the elements. Anarya is a Sponger, she can absorb and use anyone else's magic without them even being aware, but she has to keep it a secret as it provokes jealousy and hostility especially among those with no magic powers at all.

When Anarya sees Yisyena, a Sitrelker refugee, being assaulted by three drunken men, she helps her to escape. Anarya is trying to establish herself as an investigator, a quaestor, in the city of Carregis. Yisyena is a clairvoyant, a skill that would be a useful asset for a quaestor, so Anarya offers her a place to stay and suggests they become business partners. Before long they are also lovers.

But business is still hard to find, so when an opportunity arises to work for Count Graumedel who rules over the city, they can't afford to turn it down, even though the outcome may not be to their liking.

Soon they are embroiled in state secrets and the personal vendettas of a murdered champion, a cabal, a puppet king, and a false god looking for one who has defied him.

ISBN: 9781911409571 (epub, kindle) / ISBN: 9781911409472 (304pp paperback)
Visit bit.ly/Quaestor-Allan

THE EMPTY THRONE
by DAVID M ALLAN

Three thrones, one of metal, one of wood and one of stone, stand in the Citadel. Between them shimmers a gateway to a new world, created four hundred years ago by the three magicians who made the thrones. When hostile incorporeal creatures came through the gateway, the magicians attempted to close it but failed. Since that time the creatures have tried to come through the gateway at irregular intervals, but the throne room is guarded by the Company of Tectors, established to defend against them. To try to stop the creatures, expeditions have been sent through the gateway, but none has ever returned.

On each throne appears an image of one of the Custoda, heroes who have led the expeditions through the gateway. While the Custoda occupy the thrones the gateway remains quiet and there are no incursions. Today, Dhanay, the newest knight admitted to the Company, is guarding the throne room. Like all the Tectors, Dhanay looks to the images of the Custoda for guidance.

But the Throne of Stone is empty. The latest incursion has started; a creature escaping into the world, a kulun capable of possessing and controlling humans.

The provincial rulers, the oldest and most powerful families, ignore the gateway and the Tectors, concentrating on playing politics and pursuing their own petty aims. Some even question the need for the Company, as incursions have been successfully contained within the Citadel for years. Family feuds, border disputes, deep-rooted rivalries and bigotry make for a potentially unstable world, and are a perfect environment for a kulun looking to create havoc…

ISBN: 9781911409359 (epub, kindle) / ISBN: 9781911409250 (304pp paperback)
Visit bit.ly/TheEmptyThrone

GENESIS

GEOFFREY CARR

A conjunction of AI, the Cloud, & interplanetary ambition…

Hidden somewhere, deep in the Cloud, something is collating information. It reads everything, it learns, it watches. And it plans.

Around the world, researchers, engineers and entrepreneurs are being killed in a string of apparently unrelated accidents. But when intelligence-agency analysts spot a pattern they struggle to find the culprit, blocked at every step – by reluctant allies and scheming enemies.

Meanwhile a multi-billionaire inventor and forward-thinker is working hard to realise his dream, and trying to keep it hidden from everyone – one government investigating him, and another helping him. But deep in the Cloud something is watching him, too.

And deep in the Cloud, it plans.

What could possibly go wrong?

Geoff is the Science and Technology Editor of *The Economist*. His professional interests include evolutionary biology, genetic engineering, the fight against AIDS and other widespread infectious diseases, the development of new energy technologies, and planetology. His personal interests include using total eclipses of the sun as an excuse to visit weird parts of the world (Antarctica, Easter Island, Amasya, the Nullarbor Plain), and watching swifts hunting insects over his garden of a summer's evening, preferably with a glass of Cynar in hand.

As someone who loathed English lessons at school, he says he is frequently astonished that he now earns his living by writing. "That I have written a novel, albeit a technothriller rather than anything with fancy literary pretensions, astonishes me even more, since what drew me into writing in the first place was describing reality, not figments of the imagination. On the other hand, perhaps describing reality is what fiction is actually for."

ISBN: 9781911409519 (epub, kindle) / 9781911409410 (288pp paperback)

Visit bit.ly/GC_Genesis

About the author

Christopher G. Nuttall has been planning fantasy and sci-fi books since he learnt to read. Born and raised in Edinburgh, Chris created an alternate history website and eventually graduated to writing full-sized novels. Studying history independently allowed him to develop worlds that hung together and provided a base for storytelling. After graduating from university, Chris started writing full-time. As an indie author he has self-published a number of novels, but this is his eleventh fantasy to be published by Elsewhen Press. *The Ancient Lie* continues the story of Isabella and Reginald in the next instalment of *The Unwritten Words*, set in the world of his bestselling *Bookworm* series. Chris is currently living in Edinburgh with his wife, muse, and critic Aisha and their two sons.